AT THE
VANISHING POINT

AT THE VANISHING POINT

A Critic Looks at Dance

M A R C I A   B .   S I E G E L

Saturday Review Press

New York

Many of the pieces in this book appeared in slightly altered form in *The Boston Herald Traveler*, *New York* Magazine, *Ballet Today*, *The Wall Street Journal*, *Dance Magazine*, *Juilliard News Bulletin*, *The Hartford Courant*, *Los Angeles Times*, and *Arts in Society*. They have been reprinted with permission.

"Dancing in the Trees and over the Roofs" reprinted by permission from *The Hudson Review*, Vol. XXIV, No. 3 (Autumn, 1971) Copyright © by The Hudson Review, Inc.

"The Real McCoy" is unpublished and printed with the permission of the New York State Council on the Arts and Charles Weidman.

Published simultaneously in Canada by Doubleday Canada Ltd., Toronto.

Library of Congress Catalog Card Number: 72-79040

ISBN 0-8415-0174-2

Saturday Review Press
230 Park Avenue
New York, New York 10017

PRINTED IN THE UNITED STATES OF AMERICA

Design by Tere LoPrete

CONTENTS

INTRODUCTION   I

I. BALLET: THE UNCERTAIN ESTABLISHMENT   7
    Troubles, Trifles, and the Return of a Prodigal
        Son   II
    New York City Ballet Opens   15
    Suite No. 3   17
    Kodaly Dances   19
    Home on the Back Burner   20
    The Goldberg Variations   24
    Square Dance   25
    PAMTGG   27
    Another Opening   28
    Dancers Upstage Repertory   30
    Makarova's Ballet Theatre Debut   33
    A Rose for Miss Emily   35
    ABT Ending Season   37
    A Great Opening Night   39
    Paquita   40
    La Sylphide   42
    Romeo and Juliet   43
    Romeo and Juliet (II)   45
    The Miraculous Mandarin   46
    Every Inch a King   48
    Bread and Circuses   50
    More Geese than Swans   53
    Petrouchka: A Modern Fairy Tale   57

v

Contents

The Green Table: Movement Masterpiece 61
Maximiliano Zomosa (1937–1969) 66
Dancing on a Precipice 67
Esprit de Joie 73
Eliot Feld and the Extinct Metaphor 76
They're Alive. That Counts. 79
Romance 81
The Gods Amused 83
Theatre 84
Noblesse Oblige 86
Ballet Patronage: How Not to Do It 98

II. POP DANCE: THE DISPOSABLE NOW 105
Creeping Orthodoxy 109
Moon Worship, circa 1968 111
Spare the Confetti 114
Trinity 117
Reflections 118
Valentine 120
Real Rock Ballet: Why? 121
Louis Falco 124
Lar Lubovitch 125
Béjart Opens 127
Poster Art 129
I Can't Hear the Music 131
Dance Muzak 134

III. BLACK DANCE: A NEW SEPARATISM 137
Starting with Dance 143
New York Goes Tap-Happy 148
Selling Soul 150
A-Changin' 153
Flowers 156
Choral Dances 158
Child of the Earth 159
Cry 160
Modern Dance—with Pizzazz 162
Dance Theatre of Harlem Debut 166

Contents

Home to Harlem 168

The Pattern-Breakers 171

IV. MODERN DANCE: THE PROCESS OF REDEFINITION 175

Are Graham's Gods Dead? 179

Graham in Brooklyn 183

Martha, or Mother 185

Mailing Her Letter to the World 187

Ex-Post-Graham 190

Early Floating and Twilight Turbulence 193

Zone of Safety 195

Something Beyond Steps 197

Spoils of Success 203

Food for the Eye 209

Big Bertha 212

The Theater of Vision 213

Deus ex Machina 218

Nikolais' Theater of Marvels 220

Scenario 223

The Reluctant Showoff 224

The Real McCoy 227

Reaction and Vanguard: Which Is Which? 230

Cunningham's Here and There 233

Come in, Earth. Are You There? 236

More than the Museum 244

V. EXPERIMENTAL DANCE: FIREBRANDS AND
      VISIONARIES 247

Televanilla: Theater in Two Flavors 253

Working Out 256

Marathon at Manhattan School 258

Smut and Other Diversions 261

Radicalizing the Dance Audience 264

Progress in a New Environment 267

Two Museum Pieces 269

Trip in a Time Machine 273

Dancing in the Trees and over the Roofs 276

Tasks and Games 289

Contents

Psyched Out   292
Mind's-Eye Theater   294
Virgin Vessel   297
Sensitivity Performing   300
Jazzing   302

ACKNOWLEDGMENTS   305

INDEX   309

LIST OF ILLUSTRATIONS
(following page 116)

Serenade (1935—George Balanchine): New York City Ballet

Theme and Variations (1947—George Balanchine): Cynthia Gregory and Bruce Marks of Ballet Theatre

Harbinger (1967—Eliot Feld): Christine Sarry and Larry Grenier of American Ballet Company

Lilac Garden (1936—Antony Tudor): Carla Fracci, Gayle Young, and group from Ballet Theatre

Afternoon of a Faun (1953—Jerome Robbins): Helgi Tomasson and Allegra Kent of New York City Ballet

Trinity (1970—Gerald Arpino): City Center Joffrey Ballet

Revelations (1960—Alvin Ailey): Alvin Ailey American Dance Theater

There Is a Time (1956—José Limón): José Limón Dance Company

Letter to the World (1940—Martha Graham): Pearl Lang

Deaths and Entrances (1943—Martha Graham): Mary Hinkson

Three Epitaphs (1956—Paul Taylor): Paul Taylor Dance Company

Winterbranch (1964—Merce Cunningham): Merce Cunningham Dance Company

Tent (1968—Alwin Nikolais): Nikolais Dance Theatre

Vessel (1971—Meredith Monk): The House

Express (1968—William Dunas): William Dunas

Bad (1971—William Dunas): William Dunas

Ajax (1969—William Dunas): William Dunas

Wail (1969—William Dunas): William Dunas

Walking on the Wall (1970—Trisha Brown)

Dancing in the Streets of Paris and London, Continued in Stockholm and Sometimes Madrid (1969—Twyla Tharp): Twyla Tharp

AT THE
VANISHING POINT

INTRODUCTION

DANCE EXISTS at a perpetual vanishing point. At the moment of its creation it is gone. All of a dancer's years of training in the studio, all the choreographer's planning, the rehearsals, the coordination of designers, composers, and technicians, the raising of money and the gathering together of an audience, all these are only a preparation for an event that disappears in the very act of materializing. No other art is so hard to catch, so impossible to hold.

Even in its earliest states as a theater form, dancers and audiences must have been aware of this ephemerality, and used it. Being such an insubstantial quantity itself, dance was well suited to invoke the supernatural and tell tales of mythical heroism. When virtuosity and spectacle took over, in the seventeenth-century French courts, dancers were trained to do prodigious feats of strength, balance, and agility; they could leap higher in the air, stretch their limbs farther and straighter, turn faster than ordinary human beings. Not only did dancers perform like gods, the actual virtuosity seemed to be an illusion. A thing was done; you saw it happen; but a moment later, who could be sure?

As ballet developed in Europe during the eighteenth and nineteenth centuries, its character was heavily influenced by this dual air, of magic and of the flesh. Dancers could be wor-

I

shiped and flattered as the splendid instruments they were and at the same time discounted from serious cultural contention because it was so hard to know exactly what they did. Except for a few innovative ballet masters, choreographers were not considered creative artists in their own right until the twentieth century. Even now there is a side of us that wants to settle for sheer physicality, that looks to choreography only as a vehicle for the timeless excellence of the dancer.

For reasons I don't fully understand, choreography in the United States has grown to impressive stature as a creative art. Choreographers had no ready-made armies of dancers to practice on, no trusted, approving audiences, no benevolent governments who would underwrite their careers out of national duty. Nor have they had enough rigorous, searching criticism or any of the badges of scholarly acceptance. Yet they have flourished, out of all proportion to their material resources and, aesthetically, far beyond their tradition-hobbled European counterparts. And as they have grown, dancers have grown up to meet their demands.

By the middle of the 1960s American dance had produced two ballet companies of national dimensions and some very good smaller ones; at least half a dozen important modern dance companies and an enormous quantity of less formal modern dance activity; and a vigorous countermovement that was to expand all dance horizons eventually. Our dancers and choreographers had attained world recognition. But dance had yet to take its place among the other performing arts in the American consciousness. Several events occurring around that time initiated a period of enormous change.

Most important of these developments was the entrance of government into the area of arts subsidies. In 1965 the National Foundation on the Arts and the Humanities was established to give direct assistance, and the Elementary and Secondary Education Act provided for aid to professional arts programs through the schools. The same year the New York State Council on the Arts, which had operated on an annual basis since 1961, became a permanent unit of the state government. These three agencies were only the most prominent of many programs aimed at taking responsibility for the arts, which government had ignored for so long. None of them has ever had enough money to give, but the artists' initial doubts about bureaucratic interference and control were quickly put aside, and government aid has come to figure substantially in dance's economic life. Together with the big foundation grants that were coming into the field at that time, it provided the first large-scale help dance had ever had apart from private donations.

In April, 1964, the New York City Ballet moved into its new home, the New York State Theater at Lincoln Center, with massive assistance from the Ford Foundation. Soon afterward the old Metropolitan Opera House was torn down and the new Met at Lincoln Center took its place as the city's alternative large theater for dance. In one stroke Lincoln Center drastically altered several facts of dance life. It propelled NYCB into the national limelight, along with American Ballet Theatre, which was determined to hold equal prominence with its rival although it lacked NYCB's political and economic advantages. The smaller, swingier Joffrey Ballet inherited NYCB's old home, the City Center Theater, and became New York's third major company.

Lincoln Center and the subsequent rash of little Lincoln Centers that broke out all over America turned dance—that is, ballet —into a full-fledged constituent of fashionable culture. But in making this leap to respectability, the big ballet companies found themselves catering to broader audiences with less informed taste—and these audiences had to be served. Their continuing patronage paid the bills, and the price tag was high in these newer, fancier theaters.

Modern dance at the same time was finding improved financing and sponsorship. The Hunter College dance series and the American Dance Theater at Lincoln Center during the 1964–65 season presented modern dance for the first time to a wide public and for multiple performances. Almost immediately, it seemed, modern dance was on Broadway, at City Center, and— under the enlightened direction of a former dancer, Harvey Lichtenstein—in the splendid opera house at Brooklyn Academy. The one-night stand in New York just about disappeared.

The work of black choreographers, and eventually other eth-

3

nic and community projects, got a big assist through the various government programs started in the post-Kennedy years to redress racial injustice and halt urban deterioration. The arts qualified as instruments for "job training," "cultural enrichment," "community action," and various other hopefully titled ghetto programs. Out of this period, in which art was often combined with some social purpose, came a new appreciation of something called "black dance," a very elastic name for any dance that especially wished to identify itself as by or for black people.

After this initial series of shocks and dislocations, there was no returning to the old, comfortable poverty. The period covered in this book, from about 1967 to 1971, has seen continuing growth and adjustment. As audiences got bigger and seasons longer, companies added personnel—both artistic and administrative—to cope with the increased activity. Everything from the advertising to the costumes was being done more professionally, and even dancers' salaries improved. New patterns of financing are badly needed; the old season-by-season routine of piecemeal subsidy from government agencies and foundations will never allow dance companies to plan sensibly for the future. The big ballet companies, in any case, are already dinosaurs, eating up too many local resources compared to their national influence; I think only permanent federal subsidy can save them now, as well it should.

Besides this expansion and the practical problems it has brought, the most important factor in dance at the turn of the decade was its popularization. With so many more people seeing dance, so much more dance to be seen, the distinction between good and bad dance got harder to make. Modern dancers for the first time had to choreograph to build their repertories, not out of creative necessity as had always been their pride. Black dance often carried political overtones that could not be discounted even if the choreography wasn't first rate. And ballet needed desperately to get rid of its stodgy, snooty reputation. Everywhere, Broadway-TV dance hung seductively in the wings, jingling the easy solutions of speed, clarity, and personality. Most people were discovering dance as a new form of entertainment —and dance managements were only too happy to sell it that way if they could.

4

Why did Americans suddenly turn to dance after all but ignoring it for more than three incredibly fruitful decades? For one thing, they weren't tired of it. Precisely because it doesn't lend itself to any form of reproduction, dance was the only one of the arts that had not been cut up into handy packages and distributed to a mass market. Dance was the last precision-tooled American product that wasn't ready for recycling.

I think even the people who didn't understand the technicalities of dance, or go very deeply into its aesthetic, responded to its immediacy. Live entertainment for grown-ups is rare. Symphonic music and the legitimate theater are calcified with repetition, but dance is different every night; the programs change, the performers aren't bored, and the pace and sensibility—even in a single company's repertory—are varied.

Having come so much more recently into popularity, and still being far from a commercial success, dance has eluded the stranglehold in which the unions and promoters have the other performing arts gasping, and it can still keep its ticket prices comparatively low.

The rise in dance is also closely related to the dissolving of Puritanism in our society. Gradually we are getting rid of sex hangups and fear of our bodies; we've increased our respect for the nonverbal; nearly everyone has opened up to some form of consciousness-raising or lib or sensitivity movement. All of this has broken down the tacit resistance that many people had to dance. We know now that we need authentic human contact, however much it may disturb us or demand of us. The plastic world that we tried to make do has failed us badly, and we're turning to what's left of the earth. Dance, even when dressed in its richest costumes and most sophisticated techniques, never loses its connection with gut reality.

As a critic looking at all of this, I don't know whether the concrete experience or the evanescent metaphor is harder to capture. We have no traditions, no techniques or guidelines that tell us how to be dance critics. But this pleases me, because I was never good at following rules, and I like it when I can devise my own ways of accounting for experience. These articles are in part a record of myself as well as of the progress of dance.

The articles appear as they were written, except that cuts

5

made by the original publishers have been restored. This book is not balanced or objective. It doesn't pretend to be history. It reflects not only my own consideration of what happened during a brief time span, but the judgments of editors as to what dance events people would or would not want to read about—and sometimes it's the result of accident: a choice among three things to see the same night, a sudden cancellation, a feeling I took into the theater with me from the world outside. Dance is constantly in process, and whatever we think is true about it may very well not apply a moment later. Almost all the articles that follow were written for the most perishable, least didactic of media—daily newspapers and weekly magazines—and I feel that's not altogether inappropriate. I know I'm trying to catch the wind, and I like the impermanence of knowing that almost before you've written the words they're being superseded. I hope that this collection will be read in that spirit.

I

BALLET:
THE UNCERTAIN
ESTABLISHMENT

CLASSICAL BALLET is the cornerstone on which all American theater dance rests. As a strong, durable technique and a highly specialized means of presenting dance performance, it has been the instrument for the choreographic pursuits of some incomparable artists. Its virtuosic possibilities have been exploited by pop forms. Its stage effectiveness has been used for politics and proselytizing. And the formality of its language has been the villain against which each new generation of modern dancers rebels, and to which many moderns are gradually returning.

Yet ballet itself undergoes redefinition and modification. It is the cryptic passions of *Serenade* and the slick, jazzed-up trivia of *PAMTGG*. It is tutus and toe shoes, and it's also the first section of *Suite No. 3*, in which the girls are barefooted, and *Ivesiana*, where they crawl around on their knees. It is style in the service of narrative—*Petrouchka* or Tudor's *Romeo and Juliet*—and it is style creating narrative—*Dances at a Gathering*. It is a land of never-never and a world of here-and-now, both at the same time.

I've always thought of *Swan Lake*, the all-time favorite classical ballet, as a metaphor for the whole ballet mystique. It is a symbol of earthbound man's aspirations for the pure and the beautiful, it transports us from our plodding everyday life to a world of spectacle, virtuosity, magic, and noble behavior, and it poses a clearcut, unqualified dramatization of good versus evil, of love, betrayal, and honor. I think, too, the circumstances in which *Swan Lake* is given—by big ballet companies with star dancers in showy opera houses and theaters, and under the choicest social and civic auspices—enhance its popularity. There is something that middle-class Americans love about the vestiges of aristocracy, something grand and melodramatic that they want to get close to. People bring to ballet the same greedy intimacy with which they worship the Kennedys.

Yet they don't understand it profoundly, and they don't want it to be profound. Balletomanes and to a lesser extent dance critics probably see a performance quite differently from the general audience. Most people agree that *Serenade* is beautiful, but its depth is something many don't see. What thrills me about this work is the way Balanchine has abstracted it from *Swan Lake*, the way he lets us recognize a theme or a tableau and then ingeniously turns it into something else; the way he introduces his soloists anonymously—having them emerge from the flock —and then presents not one star Swan Queen, but many mysterious individuals who each state something and fade back into the crowd, hinting that the other thirteen too have special secrets if they cared to tell them; the sudden flights and rushes of mass movement, the stillness and solemnity, all without apparent reasons but carrying the emotional weight of centuries.

I wish more people could appreciate more about good ballets, but I suspect they still prefer the lightweight theatricality of the old fairy tales. For many people, ballet is the ideal escapist entertainment; the fact that it is nonverbal, instead of opening new avenues for serious communication, guarantees that nothing serious will happen. In fact, many people avoid ballets that make them think or that dwell on unpleasant subjects. At the very least, the standard ballet audience insists that content hide its disturbing presence behind sufficient brocade and ruffles.

This leaves ballet companies in trouble. Since the establishment of the major American companies in the 1930s and '40s, ballet in this country has been both art and entertainment. The outstanding creative accomplishment of American ballet may have been spurred by the parallel progress of the modern dancers, who withdrew to make what they considered important dances in severe isolation from the ballet's frivolities. Certainly without governmental sponsors to appease and flatter, the unusual choreographic mind was freer to develop its own ideas here than under the conservative strictures of European companies. As long as their particular angels would support them, big ballets could keep on doing what inspired them. Audiences were fairly stable, and were exposed to the same works often enough to appreciate their subtleties. Sometimes the creative vitality ran out, the talent moved elsewhere, the audiences drifted away. Companies died. But they were allowed to die; their job was finished.

In the last five years or so, however, several factors have disrupted this pattern. The fortunes of ballet's private benefactors became insufficient to cover its growing needs. Government and quasi-public agencies have taken over more and more of its huge deficits, with a corresponding pressure for more egalitarian artistic policies. Companies became institutions, totems. Whether they do good ballets or not seems to have little more effect on their survival than the whims of fashion and habit, politics and civic virtue. Big ballet's role has quietly shifted from serving the artist to serving society.

As the dance public grew, the proportion of old-timers and balletomanes to newcomers decreased. And through a series of publishing disasters, New York (which is to say the nation, I suppose) was reduced to one powerful dance critic, Clive Barnes, who happened to be committed to the old European attitude that ballet was supposed to be undemanding intellectually and should produce an endless supply of flossy little numbers not expected to last longer than one season.

A good deal of the credit for the phenomenal rise of dance in recent years must be given to Clive Barnes. He is so clearly a regular fellow, not weird or faggy or intellectual the way ballet critics are supposed to be; he convinced ordinary people they could enjoy the ballet after all. He convinced them in droves. What I do indict him for is failing to educate these new fans to see real excellence and real innovation. Barnes, with his extraordinary power over the box office, is the single man most respon-

9

sible for the deluge of bad ballets that falls on us every season. In his enthusiastic pursuit of novelty he encourages mediocrity and neglects fine works that should be growing more precious with time.

Eliot Feld's American Ballet Company fell victim to these converging pressures. Feld is the only major choreographer to come out of ballet recently who doesn't deal with bastard forms and easy compromises. His company had no rich patron or any kind of economic backstop. As it struggled for life, Barnes was ambivalent. He begged people to go see the company, while questioning its right to exist. Feld should have continued to use his talents within the established mechanism of Ballet Theatre, Barnes thought, instead of setting himself up in competition. With one breath Barnes extolled Feld's depth and originality; with the next he demanded more, lighter-weight ballets to pad out the repertory.

American Ballet Company's only real asset was Feld himself, a tremendous young talent and also an obstinate, difficult, and not always realistic man. He wanted not only his own company, but his own terms, and there was not enough money or audience or patience in two brief years for it to happen. Perhaps without the company to worry about he will make even better ballets, but I am unreservedly grateful for ABC's momentary existence. There was something about that company, especially in the first couple of seasons, that was vulnerable and tender and not forever calculating effects. The way they did Feld's ballets was, to me, the way those ballets were meant to be done, and I doubt if we'll ever see them performed as sensitively again.

The truth is, there's damn little great ballet. No one can define great ballet or deliberately set out to make it. One thing I'm sure about, it won't look exactly like all the other ballets you've already seen. Feld's *Harbinger* was just such a ballet—I knew, watching its premiere, that it was special, though it wasn't until Feld's own company showed it two years later that I began to find out why. We must allow the artist to take us by surprise. And having found him, we must both be given a chance to taste his differentness. To me, that's the reason for ballet companies to exist. The rest is moments. A leg coming down slowly out of a high extension. An articulate back. A fugitive smile between two partners. A turn in midair. Just moments.

Troubles, Trifles, and the Return of a Prodigal Son

The New York City Ballet seems troubled, and the trouble has very little to do with the sudden departure last May of one of its principal ballerinas, Suzanne Farrell. Although press and public spent an excited few weeks speculating about the personal quarrels of Miss Farrell, her husband, dancer Paul Mejia, and NYCB artistic director George Balanchine, people in the dance world are not asking "What will happen to the company without Farrell?" but "What will Farrell do now without the company?" Suzanne Farrell is an outstanding product of the NYCB and in some ways a symbol of its most serious weaknesses: an ever-narrowing refinement of style and an excessive dependency on the artistic influence of George Balanchine.

The NYCB today is an incredibly accurate fulfillment of the visionary ideas and the single-minded determination of Lincoln Kirstein, who in the early 1930s wanted to build a dance institution modeled after the Imperial School in Saint Petersburg, and who has said that, after meeting Balanchine in 1933, "My mind jumped forward in time and I saw the completed school achieved and functioning, and even more, a great stage swarming with dancers the school had trained, situated somewhere in America."

But New York in 1969 is not Imperial Russia, and New Yorkers, who have their choice of every conceivable form and persuasion of dance, can hardly be blamed if they are beginning to find the NYCB rather precious and ingrown.

With only a rare exception, like the Danish guest artist Peter Martins, New York City Ballet dancers have been just that all their dancing lives. Suzanne Farrell came to study at the company's School of American Ballet when she was fifteen and has never been connected with another company. Through Ford

Foundation grants totaling over $4 million, the school has been able to spread a vast talent net across the country to catch promising young dancers and bring them to New York on scholarships. All over America there are soft-eyed little girls with beautiful bodies who are hoping Mr. B. will notice them and turn them into another Suzanne Farrell. Needless to say, no other company in America has a comparable apparatus for choosing and molding new material.

Technically, the School of American Ballet students receive superb training. There are mannerisms—the arching back, the broken wrist, the exaggerated angularity—but these are also components of Balanchine's choreography, for which the students are being groomed. What bothers me about many SAB dancers, both before and after they graduate into the company, is their impassivity. Emotionally their faces and their bodies seem to be in neutral most of the time. I am much less interested in a Suzanne Farrell nonchalantly touching her head to her knee while standing on pointe and doing a split in the air than I am in the joy and expectancy Edward Villella can convey while standing still. At the recent spring workshop performance of SAB students, one could almost see a transformation taking place, as lively twelve-year-olds matured into bland, sedate teenagers.

This reserved attitude is characteristic of Balanchine's choreography, which started as a reaction against the exhibitionistic hoo-ha of the classical ballet. Indeed, I am grateful for his no-nonsense reductions of works like *Swan Lake, Firebird,* and *Raymonda.* I admire the prolific inventiveness, the coolly virtuosic use of movement for its own and the music's sake, in a pure-dance piece like *Four Temperaments* or *Agon.* But as I look at the NYCB again and again, I begin to feel uncomfortable about this separation of the body's physical feats from the undercurrent of feeling that supports them. The antiromanticism that motivated Balanchine and many early modern dancers seems to have run its course, and today some of our most important theater and dance forms are looking for ways to reintegrate the performer's expressive potential with his technical know-how. The City Ballet, however, is really a one-choreographer company, and the company is so immersed in Balanchinian objectivity that it has difficulty transferring to the other styles that infrequently appear in the repertory, the elusive sentimentality of Antony Tudor's *Dim Lustre,* for instance.

Every company tries to develop an identity, and twenty years ago when the NYCB was getting started, Balanchine was a revolutionary choreographer. But now the company has attained semiofficial status, with control of its own theater in Lincoln Center, a school that is about to take over two-thirds of the facilities of the dance division at the new Juilliard, and foundation support that gives it precedence over all its competitors. Balanchine, the former tradition-smasher, today represents an academic style that is being propagated all over the country just as if America had not produced dozens of other choreographic styles and points of view.

Balanchine is now sixty-five. He choreographs less frequently and less daringly, and there has been considerable talk this year about who will succeed him. As if to guarantee that no choreographer *could* possibly succeed Balanchine, the NYCB was never interested in encouraging new choreographic talent. The few members of the company whose works have reached performance are distinctly minor choreographers working in the Balanchine style. Almost in desperation, it seems, the company has turned to the young John Clifford, a dancer barely out of his teens whose choreography so far—three pieces for the company and a few works for SAB students—indicates he has a great deal to learn. Clifford's work doesn't even carry the urgent conviction that sometimes saves a young choreographer from his inexperience.

For the spring student workshop Clifford made a neo-Balanchinian piece to the last two movements of Bartók's Concerto for Orchestra that not only ignored the emotional qualities of the music but omitted any focus of its own, and a murky "modern" piece to rock music, one of those ballets where the kids crawl around on the floor a lot, apparently being expressive. Clifford's *Prelude, Fugue and Riffs,* set to an early Leonard Bernstein jazz trifle, was enlivened at its NYCB premiere in May by an exuberant Allegra Kent, who was having such a good time I couldn't take my eyes off her. When I saw the piece later, without Kent, the choreography seemed unconscionably trashy.

13

Films and TV are saturated with facile jazz, and it takes a choreographer of special gifts to handle this medium with any originality.

I think it is a ludicrous mistake to place Clifford's present work in the repertory of a major company. In addition, the exaggerated publicity he has received may arrest the progress he must make before he can be called a mature artist.

After years of Balanchine and imitation-Balanchine—the last time an outside choreographer worked with the company was 1966, when Merce Cunningham adapted his *Summerspace* for a revival that lasted only one season, and it's hard to remember when any original choreography has been done for this company by anyone other than a NYCB disciple—everyone including the dancers seems doubly delighted with the new Jerome Robbins ballet, *Dances at a Gathering*. Robbins hasn't choreographed a ballet since his 1965 triumph, *Les Noces*, for Ballet Theatre. *Dances* is in a totally different style and mood, but it demonstrates once again what a genius Robbins is. Set to piano music by Chopin, *Dances* is a work of striking musicality and unflagging movement invention, but most of all, it communicates. Without the slightest pretentiousness, it is a work about people dancing, not just bodies doing movement or dancers impersonating characters.

Although at times breathlessly difficult, this choreography is open, simple, like a hand extended in friendship. And the ten dancers in the piece respond with a warmth and vitality one seldom sees at the City Ballet. It is lovely to behold. I hope that the great success of *Dances at a Gathering* will nudge the NYCB out of its institutional rut. It certainly proves that the company can be tremendously exciting without Suzanne Farrell, and—on occasion—even without George Balanchine.

July 14, 1969

New York City Ballet Opens

Opening night at the New York City Ballet is a very grand affair. The elderly audience is dressed in those expensive, archaic clothes you see only at private formal gatherings, and it chatters with blithe impartiality during pauses, overtures, and dancing alike. The New York State Theater, a monument to ostentation that has almost no decorative flair of its own, is one of the least intimate theaters in the city, and the NYCB's dancing can be equally showy and ungracious. The program notes get longer and less informative every year, as if someone is trying to persuade us that the experience is going to be ineffable.

It's easy to wonder, as I do at the beginning of every NYCB season, what all this has to do with me or anyone who loves dance. And the answer always comes by the end of the first performance. George Balanchine is a genius. If it takes a creaky, uninspired sociocultural organism known as the New York City Ballet to get his choreography off the ground, so be it.

This season got under way November 17 with a stunning performance of Balanchine's *Bugaku*, danced with exquisite clarity by Allegra Kent and Edward Villella and eight hand-maidens and men. *Bugaku* is a typically Balanchinian work: it shows where his mind has traveled after being stimulated by a very specific idea but doesn't elaborate on the process by which he got there. The stimulus in this case is classical Japanese court dancing; but the ballet looks neither Japanese nor Western, and the fabrication is so original that it demands to be believed entirely on its own terms.

Bugaku does have some oriental allusions—the ceremonial entrances and departures of the women, then the men; the narrow, angular poses that the women pour themselves into; the spreading samurai stance of the men. But then after all this introduction, Kent and Villella are disrobed to white tights and bikinis, and they do a slow, strange, entwining and stretching duet that is erotic and at the same time hypnotically detached. *Bugaku* is an astonishing ballet.

Symphony in C (Bizet) shows another side of Balanchine—his fascination with musical structure and choreographic design, his inheritance from the Imperial Russian ballets of Petipa's time. Each of the four movements begins with a basic module, a principal couple, two second couples, and a small corps of girls, but each group reapportions the stage space differently according to the music. I thought most of the principals looked a bit lethargic for the ballet's allegro pace, but Helgi Tomasson, who has joined NYCB from the Harkness Ballet, was outstanding.

Melissa Hayden and Jacques d'Amboise, two of my favorite dancers, gave an embarrassingly sloppy and labored performance of Balanchine's *Tschaikovsky Pas de Deux*. Perhaps Hayden and d'Amboise are getting too old for this rigorous ballet; their performance looked like something you might have seen in the declining days of Pavlova's company. But then, anybody's morale would be shaken by having to appear in a couple of hideous costumes that used to be blamed on Karinska, but that even she no longer acknowledges.

Jerome Robbins' *In the Night*, sometimes known as *Son of Dances at a Gathering*, doesn't seem to have enough to stand on, though I think it would look more substantial on the same program as its parent. Kay Mazzo and Anthony Blum, Violette Verdy and Peter Martins, and Sara Leland and Francisco Moncion were the three romantic couples who are so pointedly wrapped up in each other and with so little apparent reason.

November 23, 1970

Suite No. 3

In one sense, George Balanchine's choreographic career has been a process of continual refinement and elaboration of ballet's feminine ideal. He has elevated the pastime of girl watching to a classic art. His new ballet, *Suite No. 3*, premiered December 3 by the New York City Ballet, is as nice a job of embroidery on this familiar theme as I've seen him do.

One of the things we've come to take for granted about Balanchine is his elegant disregard for artistic proprieties. Though his whole creative framework is the classic ballet, he can bound away from that with startling unselfconsciousness when he feels like it. Balanchine had already choreographed the Theme and Variations finale of Tschaikovsky's third orchestral suite, in 1947 for Ballet Theatre. Without perceptibly altering that choreography, he has prefaced it with the first three movements of the suite. *Theme and Variations* is high-style Imperial ballet-ballet, while the first part is all scrims and moonlit romanticism. Instead of pretending it's all one ballet, Balanchine casually offers us two. Only one thing in the dancing links the sections together: the symbolic, eternal, everywoman organism known as the corps de ballet.

As the work begins, Anthony Blum is seen in a dejected-poet pose behind a scrim. Out of the frosty blue dusk comes a line of barefoot girls, dressed in lavender evening gowns with tight bodices to the hip and long filmy skirts. Almost before you've had time to be reminded of a 1930s movie musical, Karin von Aroldingen emerges from the group with Blum in rapturous pursuit. Their duet is brief and hectic—yearnings and claspings all seemingly done on one long, poignant intake of breath. Then she loses herself in the group once more and he is left alone. Like some of Balanchine's other Tschaikovsky works, *Suite No. 3* often seems to be an abstraction of *Swan Lake*, where the girl (swan), who is just like all the other girls, in an instant of transformation becomes a princess with a handsome cavalier, and then is doomed to return to anonymity.

In the second movement, with the sisterhood now dressed in toe shoes and grayish mauve gowns, Kay Mazzo has parted from the corps and dances a waltz with Conrad Ludlow. There is a suspended moment of hesitation, when Mazzo is alone, surrounded by the girls. She seems to be deciding whether she must or wants to rejoin them; then she breaks the spell and goes off with her partner. Marnee Morris, in the third-movement scherzo, is woman now fully grown from the chrysalis. Against a background of shadowy ballroom columns and chandeliers twinkling through the scrim, she dances a fast solo, and John Clifford performs a spectacular one for her.

The group of girls, now in white, dances alone, and after Morris and Clifford leave, they are joined by the flocks from the first two sections. Suddenly you see that they are not a nebulous mass of femininity at all but a formal working body, the foundation of a classic ballet. They leave, the scrim goes up, and there, in pink and gold tutus with sparkling tiaras, is the corps de ballet in formation for the first steps of *Theme and Variations*. I found the transition extraordinary.

The metamorphosed ballerina in *Theme and Variations* was young Gelsey Kirkland, partnered by Edward Villella. Miss Kirkland is small and quick and not quite imperious enough for this role. I like that.

Nicolas Benois designed the scenery and costumes for *Suite No. 3*, and Ronald Bates did the atmospheric lighting.

January 14, 1971

Kodaly Dances

John Clifford's *Kodaly Dances*, premiered by the New York City Ballet January 14, should have been in a 1930s movie. Except it doesn't even have the pretext of a spy plot or a middle European duke-and-slavegirl romance to explain its existence. Based on the Hungarian composer's *Dances of Galanta* and *Dances of Marosszek*, the thing isn't folky enough for a slick ethnic company, and it seems much too trivial for the NYCB to have bothered with.

I've never understood the NYCB's enchantment with young Clifford. This is his sixth work for the company, so it's no longer a question of their taking a gamble on new talent, as must have been the case with this season's other two young choreographers, Richard Tanner and Lorca Massine. And Massine at least attempted to express an idea of some depth. Clifford hasn't demonstrated any profound ideas in his works up to now, and it looks as if he's taken his most extravagant press notices to heart. He's getting better at glibness; he may even be making a profession out of not doing anything original. History may call him an Arpinoist.

Kodaly Dances takes place in what I suppose is a gypsy camp. (Gypsy Camp indeed!) Center stage is a giant bonfire exuding an inordinate amount of smoke, an effect that is guaranteed to make me jittery even though I know how and why it's being done. Some tall, straight trees are silhouetted against a dark-blue sky.

Colleen Neary is artistically crumpled on the floor in front of the fire as the ballet begins. She rises and stretches and does a solo with a lot of flinging around of arms and legs, a lot of ribbons and hair streaming out in all directions. Twelve couples come on and carry out some arm-waving, thigh-slapping, heel-stamping, and similar well-known Eastern European clichés.

Anthony Blum, wearing a mustache, purple tights, and a shirt designed to expose his chest, dances with Johnna Kirkland, who wears silver spangles on her eyes and more ribbons than the other girls. After their duet the sky turns magenta. Neary dances with two boys. Finally everybody dances in unison, shaking tambourines at the audience.

If there was one thing about the ballet that worked less well than anything else, it was style. If you're going to do camp, it's got to be full out and proud. Vulgar even. These dancers looked like what they are, nice well-bred ballet girls and boys trying to be passionate for no reason at all. Clifford's ballet contains very little drama and almost no danger.

I saw *Kodaly Dances* on a Sunday night, at the end of a program that also included *Scotch Symphony* and *Concerto Barocco*. One thing John Clifford's work does is make me appreciate more than ever the clean, sublimely simple, beautifully intelligent work of George Balanchine. Clifford and the pop-ballet mongers may be trying hard to rot your brain, but it's easy to resist them when you have Balanchine for comparison.

February 16, 1971

Home on the Back Burner

Dance companies troop in and out of New York these days in amazing numbers, like migrant birds. Only the New York City Ballet seems to be always around, holding down the home territory for fall, spring, and summer seasons totaling almost half the calendar year. In its present secure position, you might expect the company to set the tone for the city's dance life, to be a kind of source we would return to for stability and inspiration after experiencing the gimmicks and stars, the exoticisms and silliness of other attractions. That just hasn't happened.

Six or seven years ago, when the New York City Ballet was

moving into its posh Lincoln Center home and was hauling in the first multimillion-dollar grants ever for dance, from the Ford Foundation, a wave of resentment overtook the dance world. People thought a national monopoly was being created on behalf of Balanchine ballet and that no other organization could hope to meet such formidable competition. The Cassandras—including this one—were wrong, of course. Not only did the City Ballet's affluence fail to inhibit all rivals, it probably stimulated their growth. In fact, the condition of dance in New York today is so flourishing that many dance fans never go to the New York City Ballet at all, and even its former partisans are so busy sampling other things that they only find time for an occasional visit.

In the uproar that followed the NYCB's windfalls, I don't think anyone realized—certainly this observer did not—what an extraordinary venture was being launched: for perhaps the first time in history a major institution was being geared up where you could go night after night to look at some of the world's best choreography, performed by a company that had nothing else to do.

A dance repertory company that plays every night in its own theater twenty-four weeks of the year is probably unique in the Western world, for even the European ballets that seem so grand to us have to share their quarters, and often their performing schedules, with opera companies. Some of the big state ballets even have to dance in operas, an indignity Balanchine refused to undergo after 1949. And these companies may also have heavy touring obligations; New York City Ballet tours de luxe only, and when it chooses—summer festivals, Europe, selected American cities.

But it's not that simple. The European companies, for all the compromises they have to make, do have tenure. Culture is considered a national asset in places like Germany and Sweden, and ballet is on the government payroll. In dead-broke New York, the mayor goes into hock to buy a ball park, but you wouldn't catch him investing in any ballet company. NYCB, though better off than its compatriots, is still supported by a combination of federal, state, private, and foundation funds, none of which are permanently awarded. It still counts heavily

21

on box office receipts, which may explain its interminable sell-out seasons of *Nutcracker* and other extravaganzas, and its ticket pricing policies—an $8.00 top in the orchestra and a scale that puts every seat under $5.00 practically outside the hall—and its reliance on a large cushion of subscribers.

This exposes NYCB to the well-known pitfalls of subscription culture; lethargy, artistic conservatism, and the perpetuation of elitist forms. But ballet is not like theater or music. We haven't been Ibsened to death, or grown up in a bath of Mendelssohn. We're just learning what it's like to have *enough* dance around. The City Ballet's repertory includes some of the world's most important choreography, yet those students and balletomanes who can most appreciate it are unable to get tickets. The critics and scholars who ought to be immersed in it while it's offered are lured away by incessant promises of new genius and new styles. The people who *do* attend, I have the feeling, are measuring it by the inferior standards of the more transitory companies.

This fall NYCB was carrying about forty-two ballets in its repertory, most of them by Balanchine, but the other choreographers included Jerome Robbins, Antony Tudor, and Frederick Ashton. The Balanchine works went back to *Prodigal Son* (1929), *Serenade* (1935), *Concerto Barocco* (1941), and *Agon* (1957), all representing giant advances over any ballet that was being done at the time of their creation, and all having been so widely copied since their time that they look rather tame now.

I don't necessarily hold the audience responsible for knowing history, although we do presume a certain tolerance for the quaintness of any antique. What we can't count on this audience to see is the distinction of Balanchine's ideas, the breadth of his imagination, the serious dance qualities that are so understated in his work. I think the subscription audience is basically an entertain-me-it's-my-night-on-the-town kind of audience, which is not interested in the fact that this repertory offers a lifetime profile of a major twentieth-century artist, or that probably no choreographer in the world has been able to keep as many of his works alive and together in one company for so long.

The name of the game in New York dance today is new, with its corollary, swinging. Popular dance right now shares with much of American culture a monumental triviality. It's replaced the theater, and for many people films, as an escape hatch, upholstered in sentiment, thrill effects, and virtuosity. NYCB has permitted some of its younger choreographers a few lamentable excursions into this genre, but for the most part it doesn't deal in now dancing.

Production is decidedly secondary in NYCB's mind. When costumes are used at all they're apt to look as if someone ran out that morning and got together the makings at Woolworths. Decor runs to bare stages with timid lighting, or heavily romantic painted drops and old-fashioned effects like things rising out of the floor, and snow falling.

Though some of the great dancers of our time are in the company, they may share star roles with teen-aged unknowns. Where other companies like to finish off an evening by tearing up the place with blazing rock and strobe lights, NYCB's idea of a socko finale is *Stars and Stripes* or *Western Symphony*, which are just fast, dressed-up versions of old Imperial ballets.

It is, in fact, the heart of the NYCB repertory, the unsung, durable little ballets, that I find so exceptional. Little gems like *Four Temperaments, Bugaku, Divertimento No. 15, Monumentum Pro Gesualdo/Movements for Piano and Orchestra.* These are the dances whose intricate clarity I most appreciate after a surfeit of over-decorated, subintelligent now ballets. I love watching the sixteen-year-old wonders grow up, like Patricia McBride, and the great ones grow greater, like Allegra Kent and Violette Verdy.

Watching ballet can be a process as well as a single event. I've put down the museum approach to the performing arts as much as the next guy, but the fact is, you can find out a lot of exciting stuff in a museum. Balanchine ballet challenges me; every time I see it, I learn more about it, and more about dancing. This fall I couldn't get there often enough. I don't think the audience does either.

But there's always next season, isn't there?

April 4, 1971

The Goldberg Variations

Theme-and-variations as a musical form is a highly civilized, if not a positively intellectual activity, a basic building block for larger musical structures like the sonata and the symphony. But in its purest form it doesn't build cathedrals of sound, or paint pictures, or suggest psychological states, it just embroiders upon a musical idea. J. S. Bach's *Goldberg Variations* spins out these intricate little designs for well over an hour. Like Michelangelo's doodles, they've become classic.

In some ways, the *Goldberg Variations* is a very odd choice of music to choreograph, especially if the choreographer is Jerome Robbins. Robbins is not what I'd call the most musical of choreographers—in contrast to George Balanchine, for instance, who needs no other pretext for a ballet than some music he likes. Robbins' bag is theater—his most effective ballets use dance and music to delineate and color the various moods, relationships, and tensions of his characters. The simple, studious perfection of the eighteenth-century drawing room doesn't seem entirely his milieu.

The Goldberg Variations, premiered May 27 by the New York City Ballet, is, of course, too long—perhaps not even Balanchine could sustain a work of such length and compositional distinction—but Robbins does some new things in it that I liked very much. He's purposely left out a lot of the drama that comes so easily in his more romantic or contemporary works. There aren't so many changes of partners and odd-man-out groups— five boys against four girls—that pique our curiosity. The ballet doesn't seem so pent up, so fraught with things unsaid. In trying to match the candid artistry of the music, Robbins has made the danciest ballet I've seen him do.

Yet there's no doubt it's a Robbins ballet. What little formality of pattern and style it has is secondary to the casual development of steps and groupings, the willful rupture of the classic line, and the rhythmic variability that are so typical of him.

He's better with solos and small groups than with large ensembles, which tend to look like the ritualistically aimless walk-arounds in Anna Sokolow. As in *Dances at a Gathering* and *In the Night*, his other recent works for the City Ballet, the company performs Robbins with wonderful vitality and joy. I especially liked Sara Leland, Peter Martins, and Patricia McBride and Helgi Tomasson as partners at first viewing.

The Goldberg Variations has a lot of silly business about costume changes, period to modern and back again, which is unworthy of the ballet. It also has an unconscionable number of borrowings from the works of Eliot Feld—the last variation in particular looks remarkably similar to one section of Feld's *The Consort*. For a choreographer of Robbins' stature this too is unworthy; he appears to be delivering either the ultimate tribute or the ultimate put-down to Feld, but how is the audience to know which?

June 23, 1971

Square Dance

George Balanchine's *Square Dance*, choreographed in 1957, has had a rather limited performing life because it is so demanding for the ballerina. It was made for Patricia Wilde, one of the most spectacular allegro dancers of our time, and was later done briefly by the Robert Joffrey Ballet as well as the New York City Ballet. With sudden inspiration, Joffrey revived it in mid-season, for young Francesca Corkle. It's a beaut.

Not that it's a square dance. The title and the sketchy details of costume and setting—like having the shirt-sleeved musicians onstage on a platform under a wagon-wheel chandelier—are just the merest concession to the great American West. If you took away this setting and the "caller," Elisha Keeler, who recites a running patter of instructions and comments during most of the ballet, *Square Dance* would be indistinguishable from any suite of classic dances.

What blows my mind about Balanchine is that he refuses to disguise himself. He's an aristocratic Russian of the old school, and he knows as well as we do how ludicrous he'd look with bowlegs and straw in his hair. So when he makes a genre ballet like this one, or *Bugaku* (Japanese Gagaku) or *Who Cares?* (George Gershwin), he doesn't try to make it fit the particular style or period; he lets the style lead his own thinking. His ballet gets tinged with unexpected colors, but it's still his ballet.

So *Square Dance* is set to the music of Vivaldi and Corelli, and its dancing-ground is the sociability that characterizes both American folk dance and the eighteenth-century soirees where this music was played. From the Virginia Reel Balanchine got the idea of lining up his dancers facing each other and perpendicular to the footlights. He uses some of the partnering conventions of square dance, like the promenade position, and some of the floor patterns, but the steps are classical to the core.

The ballet follows the folk dance tradition that everybody dances nearly all the time, but without sacrificing the more showy moments customary in theater dance. Miss Corkle, partnered by Paul Sutherland, rips off the multiple entrechats and gargouillades for which this ballet is famous, and comes out standing up and smiling—endurance is as much a part of square dancing as virtuosity. Near the end Sutherland leads the men in a copycat variation, and Corkle follows with the women; then they all join for perhaps the fastest finale ever seen on a stage.

This clean, logical, and friendly choreography keeps the dancers so busy that they have no time to mug at the audience or try to create a period look. They just do the dance, and that's enough. I've been feeling for some time that the Joffrey dancers are getting so good they can do anything, and *Square Dance* proves it.

Rochelle Zide and Victoria Simon were in charge of this reconstruction.

March 20, 1971

PAMTGG

PAMTGG is not a ballet, it's a commercial. If it had words, they'd be something like: "Bal-an-chine . . . makes the going great." The perfect advertisement for the New York City Ballet's inexhaustible supply of gorgeous bodies in motion.

There is this duality about the NYCB, that its incomparable repertory of Balanchine, Robbins, and other choreographers qualifies it as an artistic venture of the highest caliber, yet, more and more often, it makes noises like some crass, complacent business concern. On the day of *PAMTGG*'s premiere NYCB co-director Lincoln Kirstein told *The New York Times*: "For 35 years I fought to be the Establishment. I want to be the Establishment. I glory in it." Perhaps *PAMTGG* represents some propitiatory offering to the gods of fashion, the ticket consumers and the culture wasters, but if Balanchine hadn't ever choreographed any better than this, they'd never have made it into the Establishment in the first place.

PAMTGG is very expensive and very slick, and—in the way of all Balanchine that adopts contemporary trappings—just misses looking really with-it. The score is a concoction by pop arranger-composer Roger Kellaway, based on themes from the Pan Am jingles, and the scenery and costumes are by those masterminds of bygone Broadway chic, Jo Mielziner and Irene Sharaff.

The piece is built a little bit like one of Balanchine's classical ballets. It has three sections, each with its principal couple supported by some secondary figures and a large corps, with a final ensemble that everybody joins. In *PAMTGG*, however, the scenario is movie fantasy: three earthling couples are whisked off on romantic adventures through the clouds by Olympian beings . . . but perhaps that's another airline. Or another ballet.

Finally, having arrived safely at their destination, all the travelers scramble for their luggage and rush off in different directions, a funny reversal of the standard ballet-ballet climax where everybody runs around madly until the last breathless instant of designed repose.

The principals, Kay Mazzo and Victor Castelli, Karin von Aroldingen and Frank Ohman, and Sara Leland and John Clifford, looked uncomfortable doing Balanchine's quasi-jazz movement to Kellaway's pseudo-music. I was intrigued, though, with their costumes, especially those of the three women: Mazzo's bare-midriff gypsy outfit, von Aroldingen in a G-string and some fringe, and Leland with a long, slit skirt and shorts. They looked so beautifully vulgar and exposed.

I kept thinking of Alvin Ailey all during *PAMTGG*. It had the same kind of high-octane but synthetic punchiness that Ailey uses so much. The music goes POW*POW*POW and there's a mass effect of lots of people changing level or running fast, but there's actually nothing very explosive going on.

Several New York City Ballet officials have denied that *PAMTGG* was subsidized, commissioned, or otherwise bought by anybody. If that's so, Pan Am has gotten an awful lot of free mileage out of the company; maybe they'll repay in kind someday.

July 4, 1971

Another Opening

The choreography of George Balanchine has great staying power. I was late in acquiring a taste for it, but now I find each repeated viewing holds unexpected delights. Accordingly, the New York City Ballet was most welcome when it returned for its long winter season November 16 with a program of three familiar Balanchine ballets, the strange, menacing *La Sonnam-*

bula flanked by two lightweight charmers, *Donizetti Variations* and *Who Cares?*

La Sonnambula borrows from Bellini's staple opera of the same name a mysterious lady sleepwalker and some musical themes on which Vittorio Rieti built a new, dissonant score. It's one of Balanchine's few story ballets, but the story has always been obscure to me.

Something melodramatic about a poet disdainfully attending a society party where he flirts with a lady in black who may be the host's mistress and then becomes infatuated with a beautiful sleepwalker he finds gliding around the premises. When the host discovers this betrayal of his family secrets, he kills the poet, and the Sonnambula carries the body away up to her tower.

Karin von Aroldingen, Shaun O'Brien, Nicholas Magallanes, and Kay Mazzo as the sleepwalker danced as if they weren't sure what was going on either. This ballet needs the mad, ghostlike transparency of Allegra Kent for all its hokum to work.

The NYCB insists on retaining a stereotyped Blackamoor dance in the party-entertainment scene of this ballet. It's amazing how callous the company is toward offensive trivia and social slights.

I like *Donizetti Variations* because it's small and amusing—a sort of pastel comment on music that is all simple tunes, fanfared and doubling back on themselves. Looking at it again, I realized that the very small cast—six girls, three men, and a solo couple—is the prime reason why the ballet never gets as cloying as the score. You can remember the dancers' faces, so it becomes a fascinating game to note new combinations of people—the three men each partner two girls, then half the girls dance, then the other girls, then two men do a duet and the third man attends all six girls. On and on. The possibilities begin to seem infinite.

Donizetti is one of Kay Mazzo's best roles; it capitalizes on her lightness and verticality in two Italianate solos, and on her smooth good humor throughout. Edward Villella jumped high and supported Mazzo with casual dependability.

Who Cares? is another happy save. With its Gershwin songs, cheerleader costumes, and jazzy-balletic movement it could so easily be pure kitsch. But it isn't because it's quite serious about the well-bred sweetness of the dancing that thousands of little girls in the thirties absorbed from Fred Astaire movies and mediocre dancing schools. They didn't become glamorous, only more like the girl next door. More lovable.

This has been Jacques d'Amboise's ballet since it was made—even when he's not dancing in it—and I was astonished to notice for the first time that it gives him only one solo. But his spacious, no-handed ease, his buoyant affability have set the ballet's style. The other principals were Sara Leland, Karin von Aroldingen, and Patricia McBride, who dances like the supreme girl next door of all time.

November 24, 1971

※◇※

Dancers Upstage Repertory

Up to now, I have most admired American Ballet Theatre, one of our oldest professional ballet companies, for its repertory. This is a company that I respect for reviving period pieces like Massine's *Aleko*, seen last summer at the Metropolitan Opera House, and one that I cherish for committing itself to gifted unknowns in its ranks, like Jerome Robbins and Eliot Feld.

In recent years, pressured by the competitive demands of our abundant cultural life, Ballet Theatre has invested a great deal in revivals of crowd-pleasing nineteenth-century story ballets—*Swan Lake*, a new *Giselle*, and, this winter, *Coppélia*. These quaint old parties dominated Ballet Theatre's recent one-month holiday season at Brooklyn Academy. If they managed to look more like festive roast goose than cold turkey, the credit must go to some unusually fine dancers.

Carla Fracci and Erik Bruhn, who have been guest artists with ABT for several seasons, are unquestionably among the brilliant dancing partners of our time. Fortunately, one need not pick *the* most brilliant; the Russians have their stunning theatrics, the English their exquisite technique, the Americans their extroverted athleticism. Fracci and Bruhn represent a complete fusion of dramatic and dance styles. Their characters are always believable, even in the most preposterous fairy tale, yet their technique is flawless. They never go out of character, even when a delirious audience insists that they stop to acknowledge an ovation.

Writing of his approach to dance in the issue of *Dance Perspectives* entitled "Beyond Technique," Erik Bruhn says he will never do another conventional *Swan Lake*, because "I couldn't believe in it." (I wish that Ballet Theatre had produced Bruhn's Oedipal version instead of the tintype they are doing.) His Albrecht in *Giselle* is the first romantic ballet hero that seems like a person to me, instead of an animated leaning post for the ballerina. Bruhn's own comments reveal that his commitment to the characters he plays is detached and intellectual. He never *becomes* the character, he never gets so involved as to disarrange his handsome Viking face. But if his artifice lacks passion, it is that much more finely wrought.

Fracci is a perfect match for him, though she ranges somewhat further along the emotional scale. As Giselle she is frail and reckless—half spirit even before she turns into a Wili; as Swanilda in *Coppélia*, with body widened and elbows out in a peasant stance, she is mischievously innocent. Fracci has a miraculous way of starting a movement with a quick impulse, and then sustaining it a long time, as if she had endless enjoyment to spend. Fracci looks the way people who don't dance think dancing ought to feel.

Of Ballet Theatre's own soloists, I find Cynthia Gregory most interesting. Tall and lyrical, but with surprising reserves of blazing attack and comic impertinence, she did a creditable Swan Queen, a regal Myrtha in *Giselle*, and even a distinctive Swanilda. Michael Smuin, whose small size rather than any lack of technique has limited his classical roles, is an exceptionally intelligent character dancer. As Dr. Coppélius he emphasized his diminutive stature with quick, strong movements of his whole body, creating a character that was both funny and touching, like a disturbed penguin.

Bruce Marks is regarded with special affection by many because he made it as a ballet soloist after starting his career as a modern dancer, with Pearl Lang. Increasingly, in his classical roles, he has taken on the glacial disdain of his wife and partner, Toni Lander. This attitude is never particularly communicative, I think, and it becomes Marks even less than most dancers. He is more sensitive in contemporary works like Eliot Feld's *At Midnight*, which, unfortunately, was not seen in Brooklyn. Among the younger dancers I especially enjoyed the musical Susan Casey and the boyish-bobbed but feminine Christine Sarry.

Ballet Theatre's repertory seems to make dancers flourish. Sallie Wilson's Hagar in *Pillar of Fire* (Antony Tudor) is one of the most moving performances of this or any season. Michael Smuin is a strong Billy the Kid (Eugene Loring), and Smuin, Terry Orr, and Ian Horvath made an agreeable new trio of sailors in *Fancy Free* (Robbins). Orr and Horvath are not known as dramatic dancers, but it is Ballet Theatre's particular grace to inspire versatility in its members. The repertory demands more of them than perhaps even they thought they had.

Yet the repertory in Brooklyn, aside from the story ballets, was heavily larded with plotless works of the romantic and neoclassic persuasion. Only four contemporary dramatic works were given, the three mentioned above and Birgit Cullberg's *Miss Julie*. The remaining nine ballets showed off an ultimately cloying variety of academic steps, floods of tulle, and music either so trite or so interesting you wished they'd left it alone. Unlike some of our other companies, Ballet Theatre does not have to be so one-sided; it has warehouses full of Tudor and de Mille, comic and period pieces, not to mention Robbins' tremendous though difficult-to-produce *Les Noces*.

One can only speculate that the season was calculated to attract an audience to the unfamiliar environs of Brooklyn. This company, soon to go into residence—but only for a miserly few weeks of the year—at the Kennedy Center in Washington, has been through a lot. Its insecurities sometimes show up in inadequate rehearsal and planning, or in unbalanced programming. But it is a company we need, and New York has got to remain its home. Except in its most elaborate works, the company looks fine at Brooklyn Academy, and something about the place seems to evoke an intimate, exciting comradeship among dancers and viewers. Negotiations are now being conducted to bring Ballet Theatre back to the Academy next Christmas, and I certainly hope they will prove successful.

January 27, 1969

Makarova's Ballet Theatre Debut

The Soviet ballerina Natalia Makarova has danced in New York before, but not since she defected to the West last summer. One could only guess at the accumulated passions—political, artistic, or just rubbernecking—with which she was welcomed on December 22 in her debut as principal dancer with American Ballet Theatre, in *Giselle*. Whatever its motives, the ovation was genuine, and the performance that provoked it was a fine one.

In looks Makarova is neither typically Russian nor a typical balletic beauty. She's small and blond, with huge blue eyes, wide cheekbones, and a generous smile. She has a flexible torso and a nice, suspended legato phrase. I must qualify my first appraisal of her by explaining that the critics were given seats upstairs in the City Center, way over to the side, which is something like looking for shoals off your starboard bow. What with incipient vertigo and trying to imagine how the ballet looked from a more reasonable perspective, I hardly feel I've seen the lady at all.

She does have exceptional feet—articulate, fast, clear in their beats and positions. Like Violette Verdy, Makarova uses her feet in a highly tactile way, actively relating to the floor through them. She seemed to be wearing softer ballet slippers than the heavily blocked, ramrod-stiff shoes most dancers use. Either for this reason or from nervousness, her pointe work was not flashy —no balancing for what seems like an hour on one toe—but otherwise she's admirably strong.

33

Giselle is one of those classic ballets that are laden with everybody's ideals of great productions and favorite dancers. Mine is Carla Fracci, who can't match Makarova's technique, but who is perfectly glorious as both the naïve, spunky peasant girl of the first act and the forgiving ghost of the second. Fracci, incidentally, is being allowed to fade in the Makarova glare. She was scheduled only for a few performances of *Coppélia* during ABT's three-week season, and I consider this foolish or perhaps even irresponsible on the management's part.

Makarova's acting is good; it's very good. It lacks the nuance and ethereal strangeness of Fracci's portrayal, but is more demonstrative and fiery. Russian dancers are supposed to be that way, and Makarova's conception of Giselle is clear and believable.

Partnering Makarova on opening night was Ivan Nagy, substituting for Erik Bruhn, who became ill a few days earlier. Nagy is an excellent, understated dancer and gracious partner. His acting is fairly shallow—all gallant smiles in the first act and Byronic suffering in the second, when the Wilis order him to dance till he drops. But the role, after all, has some depth. Albrecht must be a bit of a cad to go slumming with his peasants and trifle with Giselle's affections only to toss her away when his royal fiancée turns up; and then he is transfigured by remorse after Giselle's death. Nagy doesn't explore the possibilities of the role.

I enjoyed Diana Weber and Terry Orr's low-key, modest Peasant Pas de Deux in the first act, and Roni Mahler as Myrtha, Queen of the Wilis. Mahler is one of the few dancers I know who is both beautiful *and* womanly.

This opening night was definitely the snob event of the year. The City Center lobby resembled rush hour on the BMT, although it smelled more expensive. At the door, members of the press were handed lists with the seat numbers of various moneyed big bugs and show-biz celebs, either so that we could rush up and ask them how they liked being there, or so we'd feel we'd given up our accustomed seats in a good cause.

December 31, 1970

A Rose for Miss Emily

There are some ballets you wonder about afterward and some you don't, and the division isn't always predictable. Antony Tudor's works, which are considered "psychological," don't leave you puzzling about the characters' motivations and relationships; they are memorable for the intricate expressiveness of their dancing. But a big classic that you almost know by heart, like *Swan Lake* or *Giselle*, or an apparently abstract study, like George Balanchine's *Serenade*, keeps nudging your mind up new alleys.

Agnes de Mille's new work, *A Rose for Miss Emily*, presented December 30 by Ballet Theatre, is not one of the ones you wonder about. Like the Tudor ballets, it sets out a situation, develops with superb dramatic skill, and ends with a bang or a kiss. The melodrama fulfills itself before you can ask why.

A Rose for Miss Emily is based on William Faulkner's gruesome tale of a woman who kills her lover, then sleeps with his corpse until she dies. De Mille never arrives at this ultimate horror. Instead, her heroine, Sallie Wilson, preserves the unfortunate young man under a funereal mound of what look like decomposing roses. She is placed with him on the shrine by neighborhood children who find her body years later, and their discovery of the grisly object under the roses ends the ballet. Somehow the piece reminded me of Tennessee Williams more than Faulkner, but that doesn't make it bad theater.

The ballet takes a flashback form, opening with the children hooting outside Miss Emily's neglected house; right away we know she's crazy. When she first appears, to take a rose timidly offered by one of the children, she picks her way myopically across the room, and it's clear she's not in contact with the world. The rose triggers off a memory of Miss Emily's youth,

35

of the man who brought her a rose and became her lover, of his flirtation with another girl, and of Miss Emily strangling him in cold jealousy.

At significant moments, six women dressed in red emerge from the shadows, later partnered by six men who cover their eyes. The program calls these figures Mirror Images, and they seem to represent the treacherous fantasies of Miss Emily's romantic mind. I think they constitute the ballet's main flaw, not only because they look a little bit like a chorus line, but because they're such a trite way to solve a choreographic problem. Granted, de Mille herself may have invented this way of showing a character's emotional conflicts, in the *Oklahoma!* dream ballet, but it does look a little dated today.

There's a similar moment, just before all hell breaks loose, in de Mille's Lizzie Borden ballet, *Fall River Legend*. Lizzie has this fantasy of boys and girls going off together, leaving her the eternal wallflower. I remember thinking: You mean that's the only reason to dismember your parents?

Nevertheless, *A Rose for Miss Emily* is a good dramatic ballet, and Ballet Theatre has given it a considerate production. The piece is extremely handsome to look at. A. Christina Giannini's brown, gauzy sets and costumes and Tom Skelton's sensitive lighting create a decadent, moldy atmosphere, against which Sallie Wilson makes disquieting slashes wearing a crimson, accordion-pleated seduction dress. Miss Wilson gave a magnificent performance as the desperate spinster, and Gayle Young was dependably insincere as her lover. The ballet has a commissioned score by Alan Hovhaness.

January 7, 1971

ABT Ending Season

As American Ballet Theatre neared the end of its three-week winter season, the Fracci-Makarova fracas was simmering down, and one could settle back and enjoy the company, which looks better to me than it has in some seasons. Perhaps the battle of the ballerinas has enlivened things backstage as well as out front.

After Natalia Makarova's noisy debut in *Giselle*, she and Fracci shared seven *Coppélias* with Cynthia Gregory and Eleanor d'Antuono. Carla Fracci's fans struck back at the first of her two performances. A large poster of Fracci as, I think, Giselle, and inscribed "The Incomparable," from the balletomanes of New York, appeared all over the City Center lobby, most prominently in a small gallery where a Makarova exhibit was hanging. The remaining posters were distributed free after the ballet by a young man with an injured expression, who said they were a tribute from her friends. Fracci's performance that night seemed exaggeratedly comic, and she omitted some of the choreography, but she received adoring applause and a deluge of flowers.

Makarova's *Coppélia*, which I saw the following afternoon, was clear and complete. I haven't found Makarova as sensational as the skyrocket of publicity on which she arrived, but she's a dancer I feel I'm going to enjoy more and more, especially when she begins doing roles I don't associate with Fracci. In Antony Tudor's *Lilac Garden*, for instance, I felt her impetuously romantic Caroline was somehow the wrong period or the wrong type; a full-blooded, passionate girl like that doesn't get mixed up with marriages of convenience. Fracci, who did the role last spring, seemed more submissive to the commands of Tudor's uptight society.

I hope, by the company's summer season, all these temperamental rivalries will be patched up and both ballerinas can dig into Ballet Theatre's marvelous repertory and extend their range of interpretations. Makarova sat out front to watch a performance of Balanchine's *Theme and Variations* one night, and I hope that's an augury of things to come.

Erik Bruhn, Ballet Theatre's other superstar, recovered from his illness and did a few performances, including a *Les Sylphides* and the pas de deux from the second act of *Giselle* with Makarova. I was unable to see him, but he was reportedly not at the top of his form.

Dancing very well indeed, however, were Bruce Marks, who is developing a fine sense of style, ranging from the tortured Othello in José Limón's *The Moor's Pavane* to the suave and romantic Baron in Massine's *Gaîté Parisienne*; Michael Smuin as a crochety Dr. Coppélius and as the Peruvian dandy in *Gaîté*, and Cynthia Gregory, who is smooth as silk in everything. I also admired John Prinz's diffident elegance, Lupe Serrano's superhuman balances and flawless turns in the *Corsair Pas de Deux* with Ted Kivitt, Mimi Paui as the Other Woman in *Lilac Garden*, and the young dancers Karena Brock, Zhandra Rodriguez, and David Coll.

Ontogeny, a new ballet by Dennis Nahat, was premiered January 6, and I mention it last because it's less than least. It's one of those "modern ballets" of the grope, grab, and grind persuasion, illustrating all too viscerally the relationship between Biology I and boy-meets-girl, with a little Freud thrown in for extra pretentiousness. I thought it was exceedingly ugly, and the movement wasn't even interesting.

January 19, 1971

A Great Opening Night

It was June 29 at the New York State Theater, and it was everything a ballet opening night should be. The ballerinas were
beautiful, the programming was excellent, the music was spirited, and the audience warm. It was the beginning of American
Ballet Theatre's six-week summer season, and I was knocked
out. This occasion was one of those times that confirm an organization's greatness and sustain its reputation when the going
gets thin.

The evening began with the Michel Fokine classic, *Les Sylphides* (Chopin), a cornerstone of twentieth-century choreography. First performed in 1909, it captured the essence of
romanticism by using the idealized figures and movements of
the fairy-tale ballets unencumbered by a story. Carla Fracci and
Ivan Nagy were the enchanted couple, supported by Eleanor
d'Antuono and Diana Weber and a handsome corps of sylphs.

I hadn't seen Fracci do *Les Sylphides* before, and she was
unearthly as only she can be—withdrawn when dancing alone,
and smiling sadly when partnered by the elegant Nagy, but
always a spirit, dwelling in some remote pain that eludes human
understanding.

Closing the program like a neat parenthesis was a direct de-
scendant of *Les Sylphides*, George Balanchine's *Theme and Variations*. Balanchine made it for Ballet Theatre originally, in 1947,
just this year appropriating it for his own New York City Ballet
as the last movement of *Suite No. 3*. A glorious Lupe Serrano
was partnered by Ted Kivitt in this wonderful essay on the intrica-
cies of feet and arms, and again the Ballet Theatre corps gave
them fine suppport.

The Alvin Ailey–Duke Ellington ballet *The River*, with three
sections added since last year, was the big work of the evening,

I guess. I find the piece horribly pretentious, ungrateful for the dancers, and structurally obtuse though superficially impressive. Only a few of the dancers were able to assimilate Ailey's difficult movement, together with the changes of weight and flow that make it move. Most notable of these were Cynthia Gregory, Sallie Wilson, and William Carter. Natalia Makarova and Erik Bruhn, and Mimi Paul with Ted Kivitt and Ian Horvath appeared in the new portions of the work. They looked like comic strips.

Wilson and Gregory also danced, with Bruce Marks and Royes Fernandez, in José Limón's *The Moor's Pavane* (Purcell). Limón's Variations on a Theme of Othello is a masterpiece of American dance, and Ballet Theatre's decision to produce this work a year ago was a service to dance as well as an imaginative gift to its own repertory. The cast are now performing it with fine dramatic tension—aptly assisted by Akira Endo's conducting—and are finding the right suspensions and plunges of breath to animate Limón's courtly dance steps.

July 7, 1971

Paquita

Ballet Theatre's first new production of the summer season, a restaging credited to Rudolf Nureyev of the old Russian warhorse *Paquita*, was given at the New York State Theater July 6. This version contains quite a lot more of *Paquita* than we usually see, and significantly more Minkus music than I would voluntarily listen to in any given week.

Paquita is one of those big nineteenth-century ballets where they get the story out of the way in the first couple of acts and then settle down to the real dancing, the excuse for which is provided by the wedding of the main characters. It's usually this portion of the ballet that survives, sometimes intact—like *Auro-*

ra's Wedding, which is the last act of *Sleeping Beauty*—and sometimes in the form of choice dance segments lifted out of context.

This *Paquita* seems to comprise most of the original last-act divertissement, but no hint of the plot or characterization remains. It's basically a pas de deux, augmented by a corps of sixteen girls and solo variations by four other girls. Cynthia Gregory and Michael Denard danced the principal roles.

I thought the ballet was somewhat less exciting than things of this kind are supposed to be. Quite early on, I became aware how much I missed the aristocratic ladies with the fans, and the servants making the rounds with pitchers of glogg, who are background fixtures in the full versions of story ballets. Only when they're not there do you realize how much of this colorful byplay you take in, and what a relief it is to have something else to look at when the dancing doesn't happen to interest you.

A lot of the dancing did interest me, of course, especially that of Cynthia Gregory, who is turning out to be a ballerina for all seasons. Already this summer I've seen her do the sexy, sinuous duet in *The River*; an anguished Desdemona in the modern dance *Moor's Pavane*; a perfectly chiseled Queen of the Wilis in *Giselle*; and the romantic opening duet in Dennis Nahat's *Brahms Quintet*. In *Paquita* her adagio technique was flawless, her legato variation was beautifully clear and serene.

Partnering Gregory was Michael Denard, guest artist from the Paris Opera Ballet. In his solo he displayed a fluidity of phrasing and a feline pleasure in the stretching and flexing of muscles. Denard, who often dances in the works of Maurice Béjart, has the same sensuous inner concentration as most of Béjart's own male dancers. Also like the Béjart men, Denard is carefully aloof toward his partner in a duet. Gregory can play that game too, so their adagio looked more like a chess match than a love scene.

Of the four soloists, Karena Brock seemed most in tune with the style of the ballet. The others were Diana Weber, Ellen Everett, and Zhandra Rodriguez.

It seems to me these old-time ballets have to be incandescent to work, and *Paquita* looked as if someone had dampened its fuse. There's so much dancing around now, dancers are so eclectic, you can see technical feats tossed off every night of the week.

Maybe dancers need to adopt a more extroverted style for this kind of occasion. But then again, that Minkus music. . . .

July 20, 1971

La Sylphide

A balletomane is a person who reacts instantly if a step has been changed in a ballet, even if he hasn't seen the ballet in years. I am not one. So I cannot say whether Ballet Theatre's new production of *La Sylphide*, staged by Erik Bruhn and premiered July 7, is materially different from the old production, staged by Harald Lander. Nor can I judge how close this new version is to the ballet that was choreographed by August Bournonville in 1836. If anything this new *Sylphide* looks less authentic than the last go-around. For the life of me, I can't imagine why Ballet Theatre decided to revise it.

Of all the old-time ballets *La Sylphide* has the most interesting characters, I think; at least five of them have some psychological dimension. There's the Sylphide herself, a playful creature of the woods who falls in love with a mortal. There's James, so infatuated with the Sylphide that he gives up everything for her. There's James' jilted bride, Effie, and the faithful Gurn, who wins her by default. And finally the witch, Madge, who brings about the Sylphide's death in revenge for having been badly treated by James.

Bruhn seems to have added various symbols, portents, and devices to stress these relationships, but the ballet as now played is altogether broader and less subtle, more dramatic than mysterious. There's almost no sense left of its real theme, which is the ever-present attraction and conflict between the human and the supernatural.

Carla Fracci isn't creating quite the same magic for me this year. Well, we all grow less innocent, but, being as objective as I can, she doesn't seem to be performing with her usual resilience. Her changes of mood seem more calculated; she makes exits instead of vanishing; she assumes a pose instead of hovering. The Sylphide is mercurial; she uses every trick of feminine guile and sylph-charm to seduce James, but we can glimpse sincere love too. Fracci no longer has that unpredictable, expectant quality that made me believe in her artifice.

Ted Kivitt plays James as a rather selfish, impulsive young man who is overbearing with his rival, cruel to old ladies, and probably determined to have the Sylphide by force too, if by no other way. Dennis Nahat was a splendidly hideous witch, and the most exciting moment in the ballet came when the bent-over old crone rose to what seemed an enormous height (Nahat is about six feet tall) and spat out a terrible curse at James. Terry Orr was a sweet, dependable Gurn; I couldn't understand why Effie (Ellen Everett) didn't marry him in the first place.

About the actual dancing, the corps of Sylphides were pretty uninspiring, but there is a delightful Scottish reel in the first act for James and Effie's wedding guests. The ballet has several men's solos that are full of those big, open jumps with rounded arms and legs that definitely are typical of Bournonville. Kivitt and Orr performed them handsomely.

August 2, 1971

Romeo and Juliet

Antony Tudor's *Romeo and Juliet* is a beautiful ballet. An extraordinary ballet. I think it's the best new ballet I've seen this year, even though it's really a revival, originally choreographed in 1943 for the infant Ballet Theatre. Restaged July 22 by that company, with Carla Fracci and Ivan Nagy in the opening-night title roles, it's a deeply moving and interesting work. I don't know when I've seen a ballet with such clarity and distinction of detail.

Tudor saw the perennial story in quite intimate terms, encompassed in one act with several scenes. This makes for a tighter production—the story moves quickly, building to its powerful tragic end, without the long interpolations of swordplay and ceremony that pad out more grandiose Romeo and Juliet ballets. There's considerably less display dancing, smaller crowds, and less exposition, but I think this makes sense. Tudor's ballet is about the star-crossed lovers. The John Cranko and Kenneth MacMillan versions we've seen here in recent years are about the spectacular possibilities of a full-length ballet based on Shakespeare's play—quite a different thing.

Fracci and Nagy are splendid as the doomed couple. Fracci is one of our best actress-dancers, and Nagy, released by Tudor's unstereotyped movement from the conventional suffering nobility of his other roles, was more convincing, more alive to the dramatic situation than I've ever seen him. All their scenes together breathed wonder and changeableness, joy touched with disbelief, a sort of shining despair.

Tudor set the ballet in the Italian Renaissance, and much of the movement looks like the paintings and court dances of the period—the men with one leg turned out and pointing a fashionable toe, the women tilting back with their weight thrust mincingly forward. At times the company looked awkward with these stylizations, but Bruce Marks as Tybalt, Rosanna Seravalli as Lady Capulet, and Bonnie Mathis as Rosaline showed me immediately what the shape of the movement is, how it works. What intelligent character dancers these three are!

There's more in this ballet, both in its dancing and production, than I can discuss in one day, but Tudor's choice of Delius' music is indicative of his unusual concept. The elegaic, rich-textured, but not especially dancy score seems at first too impressionistic to support the tragedy. But in fact it reinforces the ballet's delicate romanticism and isn't overpowering as the more familiar Prokofiev *Romeo and Juliet* usually is.

Eugene Berman's multilevel set suggests both the scaffolded flexibility of a Shakespearean stage and the columns and perspective of an Italian painting. The costumes, also by Berman, I found ugly and distracting. Rosalyn Krokover's description of them in *The New Borzoi Book of Ballets* sent me to look at Botticelli prints, and sure enough, there they all were. But I can't see how authenticity ever justifies frumpiness.

August 11, 1971

Romeo and Juliet (II)

I went back to see Antony Tudor's *Romeo and Juliet*, given by American Ballet Theatre, and found it as fascinating as I had the first time. It's a ballet of ideas—not philosophical or moral preachings, but ideas about how to present a classic story.

Ballets are produced in such quantity here, and with so little atttention to durability, that they often seem to be a matter of choosing new spices to liven up the same old hamburger. Tudor's *Romeo* constitutes a rethinking of every aspect of the narrative ballet. He uses all theatrical elements to suggest the depth and universality of the theme, instead of just letting us recognize what we already know about it.

Eugene Berman's opening drop shows a small Romanesque building, possibly a tomb, suspended against a blue sea or sky, just hanging there, a door to something insubstantial and timeless. Classical allusions keep recurring quietly. You notice during the principals' first duet that the other guests at the Capulets' ball have seated themselves beyond some pillars, at a dinner table in another room. Their backs are to the audience; they are too close to the stage for realism. They look flat, like the background of a Renaissance painting. Juliet's friends, dressed like Botticelli nymphs, lift a shroud across the stage where Juliet's drugged body lies, and stand there throughout the funeral procession, echoing the statues perched atop the colonnaded set.

The changes of scene—there are about ten of them—are accomplished in a variety of ingenious ways, many involving characters in the ballet. In fact, two "attendants" watch the whole ballet from a bench downstage, moving around to draw curtains and even, at one point, simulating a wall. They are spectators of the tragedy who also help present it to us, and at the same time they belong to the House of Capulet as servants. This is an Elizabethan device as well as a classical reference. Realistic theater didn't come along till the late nineteenth century, and Tudor isn't offering us a modern romance. Other critics have objected to the extremely stylized quality of this *Romeo*, as if that were a drawback, and as if *all* ballet weren't a stylization to begin with. I suggest that Tudor's concept of production has the same elevating effect on the story that Shakespeare's poetry has.

The second cast for this revival was headed by Natalia Makarova and John Prinz; I found Carla Fracci and Ivan Nagy superior to them. Makarova plays Juliet without a shred of innocence, and with a slashing, almost petulant drive. I have to see some small frailty or sadness in Juliet for the tragedy to work. With Makarova, I don't. Prinz, candid and youthfully handsome, dances extremely well, but his coolly intelligent Romeo doesn't suit Makarova's passion.

August 13, 1971

The Miraculous Mandarin

Ballet Theatre has made a point of informing me that *The Miraculous Mandarin*, in its first production at Cologne in 1926, was banned for immorality. The difference between New York 1971 and pre-Hitler Germany may be that the present version is nothing but high-class pornography. I don't know whether that's a step forward or back in the long march of mankind.

All around me as the curtain went down July 29 on this last new production of Ballet Theatre's summer season, I could hear

46

men snickering, as if to say "Wow! How did we get away with that one?" I guess plenty of people will be turned on by seeing the great noble dancer of our time beaten, strangled, stabbed, stripped, and hoisted up virtually naked with his head in a blue silk noose. Or a favorite ballerina raped and thrown around by three masked thugs wearing yellow satin dance belts on the outside of their leotards. I regret I'm not so moved. Awfully unhip of me.

The plot, which is supposedly the reason for the ballet's survival, was unintelligible to me, something about a prostitute, Natalia Makarova, who lures victims into the clutches of her three masters. A mysterious, bald-headed Erik Bruhn is at first impervious to her advances. When he does yield, the thugs leap from their jungle gym hideout and chase him around a good deal. They catch him and kill him, at least twice if I've correctly distinguished the fatal blows from the purely decorative ones. But, in the preposterous words of the program note: "Crazed by his desire for the young girl, the Mandarin refuses to die." But finally he does and she does. Nobody can tell why.

The ballet must once have had a plot, or Béla Bartók wouldn't have bothered to write a big score for it. But now the story and the characters seem to be hidden in the gaps between episodes of reiterated violence, as Bruhn assumes new stances, Makarova cringes on the floor, the thugs coil around the jungle gym.

Actually *The Miraculous Mandarin* doesn't seem quite as vulgar as it is because of its striking decor by Hermann Sichter, a stark, menacing ladder and ceiling grid construction against a black background. The costume colors are handsome golds, blues, and beige, and the lighting is dramatic. It all takes place behind a scrim, which allows the audience to be titillated with convenient detachment.

The Harkness Ballet—with which the choreographer, a young Swedish dancer named Ulf Gadd, appeared at one time —used to specialize in these elegantly designed, insinuating sex fantasies. If they express anything it's the ordinarily private longings that many beautiful people have to do ugly things. *Swan Lake* in reverse.

August 30, 1971

Every Inch a King

A friend of mine was completely taken aback once when, noticing a Royal Ballet dancer in a drugstore, he thought he would tell her how much he admired her performance. In a pure Cockney accent she replied, "So glad you loiked it, ducks." What a jolt to hear that from the vision of aristocratic perfection he had seen on the stage!

The Royal Ballet must be the quintessential court ballet of the world. One can't imagine its dancers growing up in provincial dancing schools, living on yogurt, and washing their own tights; they all look absolutely born to the purple. We have nothing like it in this country. I'm not sure I'm sorry.

During its recent six-week stand at the Metropolitan Opera House, the company displayed seemingly unlimited reserves of dancing talent, from the principals to the character roles to the corps. If you tend to view those hordes of tulle-clad nymphs in the big story ballets as some kind of elaborate moving backdrop for the real action, as I often do, the Royal Ballet's corps is a revelation. In its anonymous precision, the corps becomes an organism unto itself, with a shape and a dynamic all its own. Instead of a lot of girls doing a dreary succession of steps in unison, it becomes a cloud, a circle, a magic wand.

I wish the evil eye of Publicity were not so relentlessly focused on Margot Fonteyn and Rudolf Nureyev, because the Royal Ballet has so many other marvelous dancers. There was a performance of *Romeo and Juliet* by Antoinette Sibley and Anthony Dowell that left this hard-bitten skeptic breathless. That was the night a rather silly lady I know from the suburbs reproached me before the curtain went up: "We're not going to see The Best tonight, are we?"

I don't know if Fonteyn and Nureyev are The Best (why on earth must we have such hierarchies?), but I do feel I have to

48

look at them differently. Technically they are not always fault-less. Dramatically they impose on our credibility. Fonteyn hasn't the spring or the innocence to be those enchanted young girls she plays, and Nureyev's face is a stylized mask, a representation of feelings rather than a re-creation of them. During the company's stay here, Nureyev was all over the city, attending dance concerts, roaming the streets, walking through crowds. I was touched by his apparent desire to see rather than to be seen, and I wish more of this quality would show up in his dancing.

Nevertheless, when these two dance together, we know we are in the presence of masters. Quite apart from the context of the particular ballet, they represent an ultimate achievement in one form of dancing.

The Royal Ballet itself seems consecrated to the classical form. Like all monarchies, it is interested in glorifying the past, in executing the given rules to such perfection that no one will notice how outmoded or limited those rules are. For all its opulence and refinement, the Royal Ballet tends to be colorless and slightly stuffy.

The traditional story ballets, *Swan Lake*, *Sleeping Beauty*, *Coppélia*, and *Giselle*, are not nearly so magical as the ideal fairy tales we might expect. Kenneth MacMillan's 1965 version of *Romeo and Juliet* is a pageant carried along on the momentum of its fine Prokofiev score, which refuses to milk the audience's applause in the usual bombastic manner; but finally the dancing in the ballet succumbs to the swordplay, pantomime, and incessant death agonies. The plotless works are either classical showpieces in academic style (*La Bayadère* and *Raymonda, Act III*), or the didactic, sexless, and to me utterly unappealing games of academic Chinese checkers represented by Frederick Ashton's *Monotones* and *Symphonic Variations*.

When the company ventures into what it considers to be the twentieth century, the results are disastrous. If Ashton's *Jazz Calendar* is jazz, we might as well call Paul Whiteman a soul brother. And if you are as steeped in the classical tradition as the Royal Ballet, I can see how you would think Roland Petit's twitchy, ugly, going-nowhere movement for *Pelléas and Mélisande* is modern. We in America know better, to the everlasting credit of our own choreographers.

The company did bring one work by an American choreographer, Antony Tudor's *Shadowplay.* (Since I seem to have opened up a Choreography Gap, I might as well claim Tudor for our side, as his genius wasn't really recognized until he emigrated here in the 1940s.) Tudor's works have so many emotional nuances that they should be seen repeatedly. But even on one viewing, I found *Shadowplay* a strange, intriguing piece. People discussed it in the intermission, an unusual event at the ballet.

For me, Ashton is at his best when he recalls the solid, brown days of Empire, as he does in *Enigma Variations.* Though the piece follows no accepted balletic form, simply portraying the friends Edward Elgar gathered together in his music, it brims with nostalgic, mannered, distinctive people, like the photograph one of the characters takes of the group at the end of the ballet. A rare and wonderful tintype. Ashton's mortals in *The Dream* (based on *A Midsummer Night's Dream*) are from the same Victorian period, and here he treats them with the same care, and a gentle ridicule.

Despite the Royal Ballet's occasional pomposities and bloodless purity, they have left me with beautiful memories. Sibley and Dowell, Fonteyn and Nureyev, Merle Park and Michael Coleman in the Bluebird variation in *Sleeping Beauty*, Kenneth Mason as Mercutio in *Romeo and Juliet*, Ann Jenner as Swanilda in *Coppélia*, and so many others. I look forward to their return.

June 25, 1969

Bread and Circuses

Britain's Royal Ballet ended its six-week run here May 31 with a gala performance in honor of the company's director, Sir Frederick Ashton, who is retiring from the executive post he has held since 1963. The nonsubscription audience that night appeared to contain more dance lovers and fewer culture hounds than usually patronize the expensive, official Metropolitan Op-

era House, and Ashton was given an affectionate half-hour ovation. New Yorkers like to create Occasions, but there was little
self-congratulation in this tribute.

Ashton's achievement has been not so much in the area of
innovative dance ideas as in having created a huge repertory of
durable, danceable ballets of every style, size, and intent. The
repertory for this visit, most of it by Ashton, included the usual
complement of classic and modern story ballets, plus shorter
works of various vintages. There were three Ashton revivals,
Birthday Offering, Daphnis and Chloë, and *A Wedding Bouquet,* plus
a single performance of *Façade* at the gala. The grandma of all
classic ballets, *La Fille Mal Gardée,* looking every bit of her 184
years, returned after a few years' absence from this country,
with Stanley Holden, who now makes his home in Los Angeles,
doing two guest appearances in the role of the Widow Simone.

Ashton's greatest choreographic gift lies, I think, in the creation of comic and period ballets. Perhaps only an Englishman
could conceive of a ballet like *Wedding Bouquet,* with its assortment of improbable characters gathering for the nuptial festivi-
ties at a country estate. The setting is provincial France, but the
whacky individuality is thoroughly English. Robert Helpmann,
in formal attire with brilliantined hair, watches the action and
drinks champagne and recites the verses of Gertrude Stein ("All
who call, call a wall") as if they made perfectly good sense and
explained everything. Ashton knows how to stage this kind of
madness, making his point about character through distinctive
dance movement.

Façade, a suite of dances to William Walton's music, accom-
plishes the same thing, without even the thread of a plot to help
it along. The Royal does *Façade* in a much more reserved, exqui-
sitely timed, and funnier way than the City Center Joffrey Ballet, which did a rather campy revival a couple of seasons back.
Considering what a pleasure it is to see these two ballets today,
it seems incredible that they were created in 1937 and 1931 respec-
tively.

One new work was presented in New York, Rudi van Dantzig's *The Ropes of Time,* a "modern ballet" created for Rudolf
Nureyev. I suppose in places where dancing hasn't advanced
very far beyond the nineteenth century they think this piece is

sensational—the British critic John Percival gave a reverent analysis of it this spring in *Dance Magazine*—but many New York ballet-goers were appalled. I can remember when we used to speculate what would happen if a modern-dance choreographer had all the manpower and scenic resources of a big ballet company to work with. Van Dantzig is not a modern-dance choreographer, since he only borrows Martha Grahamisms and glues them to the balletic body. But his attempt to amalgamate the two styles results in pomposity beyond all tolerating. Nureyev, as the Traveller (symbol of Man, Christ, Artist, or any other pretention you care to supply), does a few of his own splendid things—leaps, turns—and writhes around a lot, carefully, with Monica Mason as Death and Diana Vere as Life and a corps of thousands, in an intricately foreboding, beautifully, banally Freudian set.

The Royal Ballet is technically impeccable, probably one of the purest executants of classic style in the world. The dancers are so correct that everyone who is in the background, even momentarily, is apt to look carved out of stone. The corps in the story ballets arrange themselves into the proper positions and expressions, but they haven't the semblance of life that is allowed by the more natural, less planned crowd activity of our American companies. Even the soloists don't go out of their way for dazzling effects—the superhuman extensions one sees all the time at the New York City Ballet, for instance. Looking at these proper, poker-faced dancers in their proper, unexceptional ballets, one wonders if tradition always has to be dull.

But, perhaps because you aren't distracted by pushy personalities and showy effects, the real virtuosity comes through with an almost religious certainty. Margot Fonteyn's phrasing and line, Nureyev gobbling up space with his predatory legs, Antoinette Sibley skimming the floor like a water strider, Michael Coleman's turns and jumps tilting away from the vertical, and even Deanne Bergsma sprawling among the champagne glasses in *Wedding Bouquet*, and Merle Park as the glamorous tango dancer in *Façade*.

I saw the Royal Ballet season this year in a mise-en-scène of discontent. It is increasingly difficult to be only a dance critic in these days of revolution and cosmic catastrophe, to remove

Serenade (1935), choreography by George Balanchine. Group from New York City Ballet. (photo by Martha Swope)

Theme and Variations (1947), choreography by George Balanchine. Cynthia Gregory and Bruce Marks of Ballet Theatre.

Harbinger (1967), choreography by Eliot Feld. Christine Sarry and Larry Grenier of American Ballet Company. (photo by Terry Middleton)

Lilac Garden (*Jardin aux Lilas*) (1936), choreography by Antony Tudor.
Carla Fracci, Gayle Young, and group from Ballet Theatre.

Afternoon of a Faun (1953), choreography by Jerome Robbins. Helgi Tomasson and Allegra Kent of New York City Ballet. (photo by Martha Swope)

Trinity (1970), choreography by Gerald Arpino. Group from City Center Joffrey Ballet. (photo by Herbert Migdoll)

Revelations (1960), choreography by Alvin Ailey. Group from Alvin Ailey American Dance Theatre.

There Is a Time (1956), choreography by José Limón. Limón (center) and group from José Limón Dance Company (photo by Giese MU)

Deaths and Entrances (1943), choreography by Martha Graham. Mary Hinkson of Martha Graham Company.

(photos by Martha Swope)

Letter to the World (1940), choreography by Martha Graham. Pearl Lang, guest artist with Martha Graham Company.

Three Epitaphs (1956), choreography by Paul Taylor. Group from Paul Taylor Dance Company.

Winterbranch (1964), choreography by Merce Cunningham. Group from Merce Cunningham Dance Company. (photo by Jack Mitchell)

Tent (1968), choreography by Alwin Nikolais. Group from Nikolais Dance Theatre. (photo by Brynn Manley.)

Vessel (1971), directed by Meredith Monk. Monk (left) and Lanny Harrison of The House. (photos by Peter Moore © 1971)

Express (1968) *Bad* (1971) *Ajax* (1969) *Wail* (1969)

Choreographer and dancer, William Dunas. (photos by Edward Effron)

Walking on the Wall (1970), choreography by Trisha Brown. (photo by Caroline Goodden)

Dancing in the Streets of Paris and London, Continued in Stockholm and Sometimes Madrid (1970), choreography by Twyla Tharp. Tharp at Metropolitan Museum of Art, New York. (photo by James Kravitz)

oneself to the rarefied atmosphere of the theater every night and pretend the eruptions of the world aren't important. The opening weeks of the run were clouded by the unpleasantries of the New York City Ballet orchestra strike, which closed down the rival institution across Lincoln Center Plaza. Although it's sometimes hard to choose what to see when the two companies are running concurrently, I resent it even more when I don't have a choice. Especially since the Royal Ballet's orchestra was drawn from the same union that incapacitated the NYCB, playing under a separate contract with Sol Hurok that called for the same terms NYCB was offering.

While the musicians were still standing around Lincoln Center distributing aggressive propaganda, the Kent State strikes began, and the assembling ballet-goers were greeted by throngs of middle-aged petitioners and young militants. Inside the Met, however, the audience indulged in its own demonstrations, of vociferous rudeness, inattention, and extravagant adulation.

One warm evening during the last week of the season, three serious-looking Juilliard students sat on folding chairs in the middle of Lincoln Center Plaza playing a Mozart string trio while another student ran around the chairs turning pages and clothespinning the music down against the wind, and someone else distributed antiwar tracts and announcements for a benefit concert. People gathered around to listen with quiet smiles, and my companion whispered, "This is where the *real* art is." In a way I had to agree with him.

June 21, 1970

More Geese than Swans

More and more people nowadays must come to dance without any prior immersion in the classics. If you bathed in *Swan Lake* from the age of three, as some others did in Beethoven, you probably see it now through a whole process of cultural conditioning. It is, like the Eroica Symphony, a point of departure, according to which everything made before and since is judged. As a piece of work, it exists apart from any specific performance, and at the same time as an ideal conception made of many performances. It is simply—*Swan Lake.*

But what if *Swan Lake* is just another ballet? What if you go to see it, exactly as you go to see *Concerto Barocco, Pillar of Fire, The Green Table,* or *Astarte,* in search of beauty, escape, or that particular kind of transcendent truth that is found only in dance theater? If *Swan Lake* is not cemented into your aesthetic superstructure, it will be difficult to approach the piece with the necessary credulity. *Swan Lake* is nearly a hundred years old, and as produced today it offers a patchwork of choreographic bits, outmoded theatrical styles, and stagy effects from all over. Only the dancing is completely viable. Individual performances and ensembles throughout the piece are often exciting enough to provide a gratifying evening. But this is, after all, a full-length story ballet, and it ought to work as a theater piece as well as a showpiece.

In dance there are three ways to tell a story: pantomime, or stylized movement that is distinct from dance itself; the realistic imposition of a role upon the dance movement; and acting out by combining inner motivations *with* the movement. Pantomime is the favored method in *Swan Lake.* I submit that there is nothing more jarring to the sensibilities than Margot Fonteyn in the second act semaphoring to Nureyev: "Him Rothbart. Have heap big power from across water. No shoot um!" We have already extended our imaginations rather far to be able to accept all those girls as a flock of swans; now this beautiful creature—bewitched princess, wild bird, or ballerina, whatever she is—steps out of the flock and tries to communicate in a language that is neither hers, his, nor ours, and is funny-looking besides.

Sign language is unquestionably an expressive and utilitarian means of communication, but although there may be times when there is no substitute for it, its extensive use in ballets like *Swan Lake* goes down hard in the twentieth century. In the Ballet Theatre version staged by David Blair, during the party scene in the first act, Prince Siegfried repeatedly signals for a drink by miming "bottoms up." This gesture, through constant use in the saloons of Grade B Westerns and other low bars, has passed into slang, and is hardly appropriate for *Swan Lake*'s aristocrats, even if it were dramatically necessary, which it isn't.

Swan Lake may be a fairy tale, but some of the events that are devised for the purpose of spectacle are just plain silly on any level of fiction. No self-respecting flock of swans would mill around meekly while a troop of hunters kneel twenty feet away and draw their bows. And would the entrance of the Princess-Mother really cause as much anxiety and agitated motion among her own peasants and courtiers as Lucia Chase's arrival does?

When a more naturalistic role-playing finds its way into the production, we no sooner become dramatically involved than we are required to switch gears. In the Royal Ballet's *Swan Lake*, arranged by Frederick Ashton, during the ballroom scene the villain Rothbart stands on a stairway while Siegfried does a solo. Nobody is watching Rothbart, but he is raging; he is really playing a malevolent person plotting mayhem. Siegfried leaves, Rothbart is still seething—but then suddenly the audience begins cheering, and Siegfried, now Nureyev, comes back again and again to bow. Period, plot, and character have vanished during this dialogue between a famous dancer and his audience, and not the greatest actor in the world could maintain any dramatic continuity through such a lapse.

The star system works against illusion in other ways. Nureyev and Fonteyn are followed everywhere on stage by dazzling spotlights. When they dance alone or together, this makes sense. When Nureyev dances with a group of girls, it is absurd, for his limelight blatantly cuts his partners out of the picture. At other times a soloist is allowed to leave the stage for the purpose of making an entrance, whether or not there is any logical reason in the story for him to do so.

As for love scenes, those spectacular pas de deux that are supposed to demonstrate the acting skill as well as the dancing technique of the principals, the conventions of the dance style make it so difficult to sustain dramatic development that dancers most often resort to a set of stereotyped expressions that are symbolic at best. The movements of a pas de deux are presentational—both partners must face the audience even in their most ecstatic moments. Or else the man grasps the girl, usually in an indiscreet place, and lifts her high in the air, using every ounce of his strength and agility to keep his balance. The audience may be overcome by the beauty, grace, and brilliance of the picture, but for the dancers it's anything but a love scene.

George Balanchine's version of *Swan Lake,* consisting of the second act only, is a more acceptable solution. Without sacrificing the dance experience, he dispenses with superfluities of plot, spectacle, divertissement, and stereotyped character and concentrates on the encounter between the Prince and the Swan Queen. Balanchine's movement is economical. Pantomine is employed sparingly, and he lets his dancers make use of the expressive possibilities within the ballet technique.

The best thing about this season's New York City Ballet *Swan Lake* was Allegra Kent, who uses her face and body as one coherent expressive instrument at all times. No elaborate histrionic gesture spoils her portrayal; when she takes leave of Siegfried, for instance, she simply goes to him and gently puts his head down, conveying plot, character, and emotion in one lyric phrase. Allegra Kent is not a ballerina playing a swan, she is the essence of swan. She does not merely stretch her neck or flap her arms. All her dancing has the quality of floating, of unearthliness. She has the ability to do slow, sustained movement without visible tension, so that one is never sure where her extensions will stop. She could almost be about to fly. When she falls backward into Siegfried's arms, she creates a breathtaking effect of total submission that is beyond dance or acting technique alone.

This is the magic that *Swan Lake* should have. It is created by the infusion of expressive qualities into the movement itself. It speaks to our deepest kinesthetic sense, and so it surpasses all the theatrical gimmicks and pasted-on rapture. There is no magic in a fog machine for a modern audience, and there is no magic in a lot of dancers playing kings and queens and swans. Only the ballet in modern times asks for such unsophistication in a theater audience.

I would like to see some choreographer restudy the whole of *Swan Lake,* unify all its elements, throw out the pantomime and audience-wooing and old-time hokum, and create a clean,

dramatically believable story ballet out of the material of movement. But then, of course, it wouldn't be *Swan Lake*.

August 19, 1968

❧☙

Petrouchka: A Modern Fairy Tale

A few weeks ago I ran into a childhood friend with whom I used
to play a summer-long game called Desert Island, which utilized
a boxful of paper dolls and always began with a shipwreck. My
friend, oddly enough, ended up in dance too.

There is a certain kind of imagination that loves to people a
world. That seems to be what the great Russian choreographer
Michel Fokine was doing in his ballet *Petrouchka* (1911). *Petrouchka*
may be the first modern fairy-tale ballet. Into the lush, detailed
panorama of the pre-Lenten fair at old Saint Petersburg, it flings
an original story based on the archetypal characters of Petrouchka, the universal clown and loser; the exotic, brutish
Blackamoor; the fatally feminine Ballerina, and their despotic
but not quite omnipotent master, the Charlatan. *Petrouchka*, like
most story ballets, is a pretext for dancing to marvelous music,
but more important than that, both the dancing and the music
depict a period, an atmosphere, even a state of mind.

Plans for a new *Petrouchka* by American Ballet Theatre went
into the works two years ago, before the current Diaghilev
revival made everybody self-conscious about reactivating the
great golden days of the Ballets Russes. ABT has always been
an heir of the Diaghilev tradition in many respects, and *Petrouchka* has been in and out of its repertory since 1942. Before
Ballet Theatre could complete the remounting of *Petrouchka*, the
City Center Joffrey Ballet announced it too would stage the
work, having produced last fall a successful revival of Massine's
Three-Cornered Hat (1919) that duplicated the original Picasso decor.

Although a one-act ballet, *Petrouchka* is an enormous production. Its cast can run to fifty or more dancers and supers, all meticulously costumed. It requires three different sets plus a painted front curtain, and the main setting calls for such items as a Ferris wheel and a merry-go-round. Even the orchestration demands unusual forces in the pit for Stravinsky's colorful score. Two *Petrouchkas* in one season is testimony to the extravagant vitality of dance here, and while there are probably other things either company could have done with the money, it is a rare and edifying experience in ballet for a great classic to be available in the repertories of two organizations almost simultaneously. Having seen ten *Petrouchkas* since March, I've become very fond of the ballet. In fact, despite the reservations of many critics, including myself, about its problematical characterizations, its unwieldy scale, and its comparative lack of showy dancing, I think it is probably an ideal ballet of its type.

In the opening and closing scenes at the fair, the crowd activity is so rich that the stage pulsates like a huge animated canvas by Breughel. While the crowd in a work like *Swan Lake* only makes a kind of live backdrop for the main action, the crowd in *Petrouchka* is the main action. Fokine, and whoever of his descendants have kept *Petrouchka* together over the years, made the crowd both theatrical and naturalistic, according to the demands of the Stravinsky-Benois libretto. A lot of the time the gentry, servants and peasants, children and drunks, vendors and officials move around as if the proscenium opening that lets the audience in were not there. Early in the piece a coachman slips and takes a flying fall on the ice; I didn't see it until about the third Ballet Theatre performance, even though it happened down center—normally the most prominent part of the stage—because I was looking elsewhere. At other times the choreography and the music deliberately guide the attention to something. A festive theme in the orchestra is broken off and at the same time a commotion is seen at the puppet theater up center. The crowd surges toward it, away from the audience and actually hiding the spot from us; then two drummers come out and sweep the crowd aside so that both they and we can see the entrance of the main characters.

Although the story of *Petrouchka* is told by the puppeteer-

58

magician and his three dolls, it is the execution of the crowd scenes that separates Ballet Theatre from the Joffrey. According to their respective habits, the Joffrey stresses the surface beauty and excitement of *Petrouchka*, while Ballet Theatre treats it more as a human document.

The Joffrey's *Petrouchka* is like an exquisite picture book or a souvenir postcard. The colors are vibrant, the action is clearly delineated, even the snow seems gay. Ballet Theatre's version has less definition but more dimension. The Joffrey does subtle things to make incidents stand out, like having the crowd sway in mesmerized unison to the Charlatan playing his flute; in the ABT production the crowd breathes to the melody, but not all in the same direction. With Ballet Theatre, things are happening all over these two scenes, as they do in a crowd; some byplay even continues during the numerous little solo vignettes of the carnival celebrants and street people.

What I found so interesting about this approach was that at each performance I would notice new encounters among the crowd, and they all seemed to have a reason: two cocky cadets salute an officer and then duck away from his angry blow, the provincial merchant makes a deal for the company of two gypsy girls he spies on a balcony, a little street-dancer shivering with the cold suddenly warms to action as another dancer steals her audience. The famous Dance of the Nursemaids in the final scene is initiated by the nurses emphatically brushing back their voluminous skirts. In the Joffrey version this gesture looks like a way of showing off their costumes, as if the nurses were saying to everyone, now we're going to dance for you. In Ballet Theatre's version the movement is part of a flirtation; the nurses are literally brushing off the coachmen who are pursuing them. The gesture thus has a dramatic focus, not just a theatrical one. Ballet Theatre's crowd looks slightly disheveled and unpredictable, but it looks like a crowd.

Among the various principals, Ballet Theatre's Michael Smuin surpassed all the other Petrouchkas of the season. Smuin is probably the best young character dancer in America; he has not only the technique but the intelligence to portray a large spectrum of roles, and the ABT repertory encourages his versatility. The Joffrey's Christian Holder was my favorite Blackamoor. Perhaps only a black man can play this vaudeville-related part today without being offensive, and Holder did the stagy, strong/stupid primitive to the hilt. But Ballet Theatre's Bruce Marks gave the role with a savage dignity that also made sense. Susan Magno of the Joffrey was the only Ballerina I saw who was more than a mechanical doll. Magno seemed to contribute to the Blackamoor's eventual murder of Petrouchka by playing the two suitors off against each other. Dennis Nahat's Charlatan for ABT had a sense of mystery and especially of control over the puppets. With very small but unmistakable gestures he dictated their every move. Once the Charlatan establishes some kind of shabby power, the ballet's strange denouement takes on a convincing irony. When the Charlatan leaves the puppets to their own devices they go berserk, and after the tragedy Petrouchka's liberated soul mocks the cheap carnival magic of his former captor.

In all the *Petrouchkas* I saw this year I didn't find a single cast that I felt was evenly matched in dancing and characterization, and that also worked well as a team. Even if I could have this ideal combination of dancers together for one *Petrouchka*, I'm not sure they could invoke the necessary feeling that they are in cahoots, conspiring together and tricking each other eternally. This sense of ensemble, highly developed in the commedia dell'arte players from whom *Petrouchka* partly derives, comes only from constant performing together, and unfortunately *Petrouchka* is an expensive ballet. It can't be given often, and both companies have many leading dancers who want a crack at it. Nevertheless, the ballet is a challenge for them and a great gift for us.

August 16, 1970

The Green Table: Movement Masterpiece

One of the most noteworthy and imaginative achievements in the current alliance between government and the arts has been the New York State Council on the Arts' $25,000 grant to the City Center Joffrey Ballet for purposes of reviving *The Green Table*. Of all the twentieth-century choreography slipping ephemerally by us, Kurt Jooss' 1932 antiwar dance-drama is eminently deserving of preservation. Since its creation, *The Green Table* has never been long out of the active repertory. After the dissolution of the Jooss Ballet, Ernst Uthoff took the work with him when he became director of the Chilean Ballet, but American audiences could see it only when those companies visited here. The Joffrey revival, under the supervision of Uthoff, Jooss, and former Jooss dancer Ulla Soederbaum, was first shown at the New York City Center March 9, 1967, and its impact was immediate and stunning.

What makes *The Green Table* a work of art, and how does it manage to be revealing and radiant after thirty-five years? First, for a society preoccupied with information, it has a message: war is ugly, ruthless—and inevitable. The cynical ceremony of the conference table, which begins and ends the war, takes on a double irony for us. The peacemakers have learned nothing since 1932, as Jooss predicted; Geneva, like Versailles, resulted in gunshots.

But we are bombarded with antiwar art these days. Antony Tudor's *Echoing of Trumpets*, Anna Sokolow's *Time + 7*, and Richard Kuch's *The Brood*, based on *Mother Courage*, are three recent examples in dance. But although these works may be memorable, they are not immortal.

The Green Table has a tight structural logic that makes for extraordinarily good theater. Within its *a-b-a* form (the conference table—the war scenes—the table again) it builds in a crescendo of dramatic climaxes, until the final inexorable Dance of Death and the completion of the cycle in diplomatic stalemate. The characters are allegorical, and the action is a series of terse vignettes. With Death marking time in the background, the soldiers and wives, refugees and whores play out the panorama of war. The clarity of the dramatic line is preserved by a sparing use of the other elements of production. Aside from the grotesque masks and costumes of Death and the Gentlemen in Black, all the costumes are essentially practice clothes, with suggestions of detail, like the derby hat, white gloves, and dandified mustache on the Profiteer. Frederic Cohen's cabaret-style score is played on two pianos. There is no set, and the stark lighting of Tom Skelton provides all the atmosphere that is needed. In fact, my one reservation about the Joffrey production is that Skelton's Death-greens and destruction-reds are a shade overstated.

As an effective theater piece, *The Green Table* does all the things a classic is supposed to do: it tells a story economically and clearly, it has characters who speak for every age, and its message is of vital significance. Yet, after seeing it for the first time, a viewer may have an incredulous feeling that something doesn't add up. Clearly, the style of the piece is dated, no one makes expressionistic dances like this anymore, imagine doing a concert dance to a tango! Why, then, was he so moved?

The answer is in the movement.

American theater and most of American dance is symbolic in style. Where actors use words to convey a message, dancers use patterned sets of movements. I confess I am unable to respond, "Ecstasy," when the danseur noble lifts the ballerina high in the air, but this is the premise on which ballet has rested for a hundred years. Modern dancers rejected this artificiality and substituted their own vocabulary. Martha Graham's contractions and contortions originally may have been a realization of her own emotional states, but they are now dogma, and are most often used as a facsimile of the emotion that the dancer wishes to portray. The viewer has to translate these representative gestures into the terms of his own experience.

Central European theories of dance, to which Jooss adhered,

maintain that all movement has an expressive as well as a functional content, and that the qualities inherent in movement can be taken as a direct statement of feeling. In these terms, a ballet lift would be quite another thing than ecstasy because the dancers are using great strength, control, and precision, which are not the qualities of abandon. Alwin Nikolais' choreography, which has moved away from dramatic content, uses the whole gamut of movement qualities for visual and dynamic effect. He was recently asked by interviewers for a popular magazine what the dancers in a photo of *Imago* were doing. He answered, "Tilting," and, for him at least, that was sufficient.

The process of looking at one thing and perceiving another has become second nature to us, so that when we are presented with literal movement we immediately look for symbolic content. Even when the movement is in direct conflict with the words, we usually accept the words, allowing some remarkable things to get by on stage. In a recent production at the Vivian Beaumont Theater I saw a supposedly seductive girl beckon to a reluctant lover as she crossed one leg in front of the other. Perhaps the director thought of this as a slinky movement, or perhaps he judged that the audience would not notice a closing action where an opening one would have been more appropriate, but I was certainly confused.

The Green Table, on the other hand, deliberately chooses movement qualities that will reinforce the dramatic content. Its message is unequivocal and it evokes an emotional response even when the audience is not sure why.

The pivotal figure of Death gains its power from the varied use of two principal movement qualities, a purposefully channeled strength and a controlled use of energy that flows in toward the body. These qualities pervade all the actions of Death and define his character as one of self-centered, consuming appetite and implacable determination.

When Death first appears, he does a solo to a pounding martial rhythm, which he maintains with stamping feet. Keeping his torso expanded and immobile, he reaches out horizontally around his body and pulls in space with clenched fists. These— the strength being driven relentlessly to earth, and the energy gathered in from as far as he can reach—are the leitmotiv of

63

Death. In variation they appear throughout the dance. He will emphasize the gathering of his fists with a flourish. He will leap into the air, not to get off the ground, but to pull down more energy with him. He will await his victims firmly rooted with his legs together and crossed, his arms extended horizontally to his sides and his fists rotating with quick jerks, or with his arms wrapped around his upper torso, elbows pointing forward. In all cases he claims his victims by gathering them in, rather than striking them down, which would involve a release of energy. Each gathering is different: lustful, as he envelops the inert body of the Young Girl; almost tender, as he folds the Old Mother into his arms; predatory, as he swoops down from above the soldier, in one scythelike motion snatching the flag and hooking the soldier's arm; impatient, with the Profiteer, the last to survive, as he propels his arms quickly toward his body, as if he were hauling in a sail.

Occasionally the movements of Death appear to be contradictory, but these contradictions actually add to his character. His frequent extensions of arms and legs might not seem consonant with his inward tendency, but they usually end in a pulling in. When Death whirls the Young Girl in a huge circle around himself, her energy is outward—to escape—but his is centripetal. The extensions not only exaggerate their culminating impulse, but also add to the physical size of Death.

The other characters also have distinctive movement qualities that give them depth. The role of the Profiteer might be evident solely on the basis of his pantomimed stealing of a ring from a dead soldier's body and his introduction of the innocent Young Girl into the whorehouse. But how much more sly and sinister Jooss has made him through the use of lightness and indirectness! The Profiteer never approaches his objective in a straight line or on a single level; he circles, hesitates, crouches, springs, angles, reconnoiters, and finally makes contact with a deft and skimming touch. His movements are flexible to the point of sinuousness, and his poses are zigzag in shape.

The Young Girl, the Old Mother, and the procession of refugee women have a curious neutrality in their movements that suggests passivity. Carried along by the momentum of their forced march, they actively neither advance nor retreat, resist nor give in; they have been through horrors and can no longer feel. In a characteristic and poignant gesture, the Old Mother holds her hands slightly above her head, fingertips up, empty, weightless. When forced to dance with the soldiers in the brothel, the Young Girl narrows her body by keeping her arms at her sides, but she is too numb to make any complete body withdrawal. Only the Guerilla Woman still has the strength and resiliency to fight back, which she uses in her dance of defiance, and after her courageous murder of an occupying soldier, she deliberately embraces the feet of Death. In the enlistment scene, each recruit enters with a different quality, of eagerness, reluctance, determination, though they all have the same steps and rhythmic pattern. As each recruit joins the line of soldiers marking time, his own qualities disappear and he merges into the anonymity of the regiment.

The opening and closing scenes, with the Gentlemen in Black around the Green Table, have a tremendous pictorial and pantomimic effect, but even here the movement qualities contribute to the overall atmosphere. The diplomats, in their rusty black tailcoats, spats, white gloves, and senile masks, palaver back and forth in a continual discord that ranges from amiable to tense. They are devious, with weaving heads and wagging fingers, or aggressive, as they lean forward across the table. Their groupings are constantly shifting; one side of the table will work in a unit against the other, they scatter off into huddles, relax and shake hands with their opposite numbers, return to the table to argue as individuals in stiff, angular postures. The only time the ten men do anything in unison is when they line up facing the audience, draw their pistols, and fire into the air, thus by common consent precipitating the next war.

The Green Table works as a profound human statement because Kurt Jooss consistently selected the particular dynamic and spatial qualities that would best strengthen his narrative. I think most ballet and modern dance has become bottled up in its own movement conventions; it has nowhere to go but to repeat itself. Choreographers who use movement more fluently, for what it is, may have found one way out, and *The Green Table*, as a pioneer work in this genre, not only survives but surpasses a lot of later choreography in its vitality.

Fall/Winter, 1968–69

Maximiliano Zomosa (1937–1969)

People often think of acting as being allied to facial or vocal expression. Max Zomosa's masked portrayal of Death in *The Green Table* proved the dramatic power of the highly intelligent dancing body.

Kurt Jooss' expressionistic Death figure could so easily become caricature. In the hands of Zomosa Death was a superman —a composite of man's passions magnified to their ultimate destructiveness. Zomosa understood that Jooss' choreography was a design for a creature of gargantuan appetites and unyielding determination.

Tall and muscular, with rather less flexibility in his body than the average dancer, Zomosa was ideally cast as Death, and he exaggerated his natural strength, size, and tautness for this role. He dominated the stage, whether he was alone on it, dancing his warlike solo, or lurking in the background of a battle scene, marking time, waiting to claim his victims. Zomosa played Death not just as a dominant figure but as a selfish, consuming one. His energy when he chose a victim was always directed in toward his own body; he beckoned, embraced, grabbed. Never did he give anything of himself away, even in anger. Yet he played on this harvesting theme with great subtlety, ranging from a patient but confident stillness with the Old Mother, to a lustful softening with the Young Girl, to a sudden, machine-like hauling in of the Profiteer.

Zomosa knew how to use time, drawing it out triumphantly as he bent over the Young Girl's body and slowly lifted his face, or quickly swooping down to snatch the last soldier and the flag without breaking the inexorable tempo of the march. His attention to detail was superb, as he arched backward for almost a full beat to emphasize the arrogant momentum of his opening

66

march, as he drew attention to those greedy fists by closing them with a flourish or rotating them percussively, or as he wrapped his arms about his torso and then slowly, slowly raised two beckoning fingers.

The Green Table was probably Max's greatest role, but as he made it his own through inheritance, so was he also inseparable from the role he created, in *Astarte*. He was the moonstruck lover, hypnotically drawn to his partner, Trinette Singleton, yet always apart from her, deep in some inner contemplation of a duet that was larger than life and much more beautiful in its mutability, like the film that accompanied the dance. Most people associate *Astarte* with Singleton, but Zomosa conveyed its most profound meaning—the modern preoccupation with imagery and illusion that prevents so many of us from making contact with real objects and people.

Among his many other roles, Zomosa imparted special comic poignance to the poet Harolde in *Cakewalk*, the pencil-mustached, Byronic supplicant, forever spurned by the callous Hortense, Queen of the Swamp Lilies.

When a fine dancer dies, we are again reminded how ephemeral dance is. Remembering Max Zomosa, one sees the need to look more closely, to know more clearly what dancers are saying. That gift, that knowledge, at least, endures.

February, 1969

Dancing on a Precipice

Eliot Feld sits with his back to the mirror watching Christine Sarry and John Sowinski rehearse his duet *Cortege Burlesque*. Like a football coach, he unconsciously uses body English to support every play. Sowinski executes a solo with impeccable technique, and Feld stops the rehearsal. He asks Sowinski how he feels about this solo and what kind of person would do a dance like that.

"Come on, John, commit yourself," he says. "Get out of that gray flannel suit. You look like a prince, and I'm not interested in a prince in this dance. I'm interested in a Fuller Brush man. You've got seven minutes to sell the audience, you've got to sell it right away! Let's go on."

Then Feld stops Christine Sarry: "Look, it's an invitation to a party for two thousand people. You know how you feel when you get drunk and talkative. . . ." He waves his upper body around and smiles giddily. "You should be the greatest hostess, like Zsa Zsa Gabor on the *Tonight Show,* she laughs at the stupidest things, but she's very feminine."

Sowinski interrupts to say, "The pas de deux is dangerous when it's fast. . . ."

Feld flattens himself out against the mirror. "A pas de deux is a precipice! A *precipice!* I don't *care* if you miss the steps. The greatest success you had was when she fell down on the stage!"

"And she hurt herself," Sowinski says quietly.

"Then be healthy and be a bore. If you want to be safe you have to be in the corps of *Giselle.* It needs more personal bravado. It has nothing to do with the steps, it has to do with how you *feel* about what you're doing. If I'm a member of the audience I have to know you're the best male dancer in the company. You have to put me at my ease, I have to be able to sit back and enjoy you."

They finish the dance and Feld says, "Better. Now I have the sense there's a person behind the steps. You can't get dressed up in the steps and hide behind them. Every time you look at each other you smile. You have to leave yourself open for that. That's not performing a rehearsal, that's rehearsing the ballet."

This tyrant, this perceptive and gifted young man with the gaunt, pale face and the tired eyes, who doesn't believe in pasted-on smiles and vacant virtuosity, is considered by many to be the most impressive new choreographer the American ballet has produced in decades. He is about to take a tremendous gamble with his life and the lives of twenty young dancers. At twenty-seven he has organized a ballet company, which is probably the most expensive and least secure undertaking known to man. The American Ballet Company will have its U.S. debut next week and play a two-week season at the Brooklyn Academy. After that, Feld doesn't know what will happen.

"The whole thing is complete madness," he said recently. "It's against all the odds. Why are we doing it? The only reason to go through all this is if you're doing something special."

Feld is doing something special, and he hasn't the coyness to deny he knows it. His first two ballets, *Harbinger* and *At Midnight*, created in 1967 when he was dancing with American Ballet Theatre, were highly successful. They had something to say, and they said it with movement that was original, beautiful to look at, and very moving. For Ballet Theatre, the rise of a fine new choreographer from the ranks was a pleasant surprise, one that was often compared to the meteoric success of Jerome Robbins in 1944, via the same route.

In fact, Feld's relationship to Robbins was more than coincidence. As a teenager he had danced in both the stage and film versions of *West Side Story*. And it was Robbins who, after seeing Feld's ideas for *Harbinger*, persuaded ABT directors Lucia Chase and Oliver Smith to invest the dancers and the money for Feld to finish composing the ballet.

A few months later, after *At Midnight* had confirmed Feld's initial promise, his ballets were among the most popular in the repertory. But ABT is a big company with many irons to keep hot and an eclectic public to satisfy. In the spring of 1968 the company was to perform on the West Coast, and Feld wanted his works to be seen there more often than the company had scheduled them. Nor did he like having to show the poignant and meditative *At Midnight* as a curtain-raiser for *Giselle*. A prudent beginner would have quietly served out the terms of his apprenticeship, but Eliot Feld is neither prudent nor patient.

"I didn't feel I could make the kind of impression on the company that I needed to. It was hard to establish my authority with the dancers in rehearsals. I didn't want to play second fiddle to *Swan Lake*. When I left I didn't 'walk out in a huff' as Clive Barnes wrote that I did—I gave notice according to my contract. I was bewildered about what I was going to do with my life, but I wasn't angry. Lucia's a fantastic woman; she's done great things for the dance, but they're her things, not mine. My company expresses my thing."

After leaving Ballet Theatre, Feld created *Meadowlark* for the Royal Winnipeg Ballet and later set the same work for the Festival Ballet in London. Then last fall it was announced that Feld would form a resident company at Brooklyn Academy, and with the help of the National Endowment for the Arts, rehearsals began early in the year. The company made a successful debut in June at the Spoleto, Italy, Festival of Two Worlds, but October 21 in Brooklyn is the Big Apple.

"My biggest problem now is money," Feld said. "You know, Sol Hurok once said there are three important things when you're starting a ballet company. Money. Money. And money. And he was right. I don't see how we can exist after the Brooklyn season without support. I won't use anything but live music, and a company like this, with full orchestra, can run a $12,000-a-week deficit on a tour of one-night stands. We're counting on a smash in Brooklyn so we'll be offered some good bookings in places like Chicago and San Francisco. I have to try to make the most successful season I can."

The repertory in Brooklyn will include six ballets by Feld: *Harbinger, At Midnight, Meadowlark, Cortege Burlesque, Intermezzo,* and the world premiere of *Pagan Spring;* Donald McKayle's *Games* (1951), a work Feld performed early in his career, when he appeared with several modern dance companies; two ballets by Herbert Ross: *Caprichos,* choreographed in 1950, and *The Maids,* based on Jean Genet's play, a controversial work that was performed only once, in a Ballet Theatre workshop in 1957; and Michel Fokine's 1910 classic, *Carnaval.*

When the company reassembled after a short summer vacation, they moved into a spacious blue and white studio at the New York School of Ballet, which is the official school of the American Ballet Company and is run by ballet masters Richard Thomas and Barbara Fallis. As the rehearsal period entered its last few weeks, the atmosphere there became dense with concentration.

In the early stages of learning a ballet, the attention is on the steps, spacing, counts, and achieving a unified, clean line among the group. Later, when the dancers know the steps, Feld works almost exclusively on characterization and style. He is deeply concerned with this aspect of performance, and he often tells his dancers he would rather have them be less precise in their steps as long as they convey the dance's emotional quality.

"You're getting into position but it's highly manipulative," he tells a group of girls in *Games.* "You look like you're doing a good job of not bumping into each other." Later a boy comes out flipping an imaginary knife. "It doesn't *challenge.* I'm sure Donny is interested in what that's about, not whether your knee is straight." He stops a duet in *At Midnight* after the first eight measures. "I have no idea why you go away and why you come back and why you have that attitude toward him that you do. I mean, I don't *feel* anything about what you do."

Feld says he can think of only one pattern that runs through all his choreography so far. "My dance is always an expression of feelings. I think that's part of my talent. That's what makes the dance live."

In addition to trying to create movement that makes it possible for the dancers to feel the appropriate thing, he gives an unusual number of suggestions and images to help them. Working with Larry Grenier on a solo in *At Midnight,* he asks, "Have you ever read *The Brothers Karamazov?*" Grenier shakes his head and there is a long pause while Feld thinks of another springboard. Finally he says, "What do you think this is about? Look at all those other couples dancing around you. Everyone else has something you want. This guy is wild! He's angry. His anger is contained, but sometimes it breaks out." A few days later, still working on the same section: "It's not ferocious enough. You should be like a wounded animal. It's smoothly danced but that's not what this dance is about. You know the intensity you can get when you're just standing still. You see how I get sometimes when I'm angry—just seething in place. This gesture where you reach around your back with both hands, that's what the dance is about. It's unconsummated. That's why it feels uncomfortable."

Feld has a frightening way of seeing his dancers' private

71

thoughts and weaknesses, and sometimes he lets them know it. A couple stumbles, the boy apologetically indicates it was the girl's fault, she says she's sorry. Feld remarks, "Funny, you don't look sorry." Some days the studio is under a somber cloud. The dancers, when they are not onstage, sit as far away from Feld as they can get. There is no laughter and no small talk, and when Feld is displeased he says a few terrible words in a despairing tone, followed by a long silence in which no one moves, as if a disastrous mistake has been made for which they are all somehow to blame. Other days the mood is lighter. Feld makes heavily ironic jokes about himself, the dancers giggle and offer him jelly beans.

"If I have one weakness as a director," he says, "it's that I just don't see past the work. I'm so intent on what's being rehearsed that I sometimes don't see what's happening in the room, with the dancers. I know I'm hard to work with. I'm impatient, critical, crazy. They're subjected to the most intense scrutiny five, six hours a day. I have to grow too, I have to learn. I've never been responsible for so many people in so many ways."

Feld has a great affection for his dancers, and a faith in their ability to grow with him that lights his eyes whenever he talks about them. "If I'm asking them to do something that's beyond them, it's my job to get it out of them—I'm building a company. These are some of the best dancers in New York. There's an honesty about them."

Not surprisingly, this ambitious young man has been called immodest, arrogant, aggressive, and the dance world seems divided between those who consider him a brash upstart and those who wish him a brilliant future. Feld says, "It's very hard to separate dedication and selfishness. I like to think I'm dedicated. Art is not consensus; it's not doing what you think everybody will like. What the critics say has nothing to do with how I do my work. Of course"—and he grins—"I *want* to *succeed!*"

October 20, 1969

Esprit de Joie

There is so much that is new in Eliot Feld's work that one forgets how classical he is. On the other hand, his company is so natural and honest, one doesn't notice how revolutionary he is either. This poses a problem of categorization. People have trouble naming exactly what Feld does; they haven't got an easy reaction to pull out of some convenient psychic pigeonhole. This type of aesthetic confusion accompanies every significant advance in art, and there is no question in this observer's mind as to Feld's significance. Every other ballet company is putting the finishing touches to something old. Feld's American Ballet Company is beginning something new.

Feld's latest ballet, *Early Songs*, had its premiere last week at Brooklyn Academy. It doesn't equal his best works, the superb *At Midnight* and *Intermezzo*, but it still surpasses any new choreography I have seen this season. *Early Songs* is moving and beautiful and, like all of Feld's ballets, an original.

The first and most obvious departure Feld makes from the traditional ballet is his denial of virtuosity for its own sake. His dancers don't engage in the aggressive, egocentric performing that ballet is often about. Feld is more interested in the kind of statement dancers can make about themselves as people, and so it's perfectly natural for him to dispense with many of the balletic formalities that interfere with such a democratic idea. ABC has no corps de ballet, no arbitrary distinctions between principals and other dancers, like the one requiring that the soloist never be on stage unless he is the center of attention. The choreography doesn't constrict itself into the regimented lines and groupings, stops and starts of a royal occasion; it flows like breathing and curves like bird flight.

Feld's movement is firmly grounded in classical technique,

73

but he uses technique to say something about how the people in the ballet are feeling and how they are related to each other, not for mere display. This means he pays more attention to the people and the space outside the dancer's own personal self than he does to the placement or the design of bodies. If the feeling and the focus call for leaning away from the vertical, or jumping backwards, or sending the whole weight bounding toward the floor, Feld has no hesitation in using that, even though it may be drastically unclassical.

ABC dancers play to each other as much as to the audience. When they look at each other, they really see, and when they make contact, they touch. Their dance is about men and women together instead of the sexual idealizations and euphemisms of balletic custom. Feld's lifts are as spectacular as any choreographer's; but no one else's have so much to do with embracing and so little to do with acrobatics. His couples often use an open, arms-around-the-waists attitude for partnering that is reminiscent of the folk dance forms that preceded ballet. Boy and girl are more nearly equal here; they can look at each other and present themselves to the audience at the same time. You don't see busy preparations, grasping, arranging of limbs so that the boy can exhibit the girl like a piece of jewelry, with his head swathed in her costume. What you remember about Feld's lifts is that they seemed to flow effortlessly out of the music, or that they began or ended in a caress. The simple gesture, in *Early Songs*, of a boy cradling a girl's head in his hand, is as exquisite as the flights and raptures of *Intermezzo*.

Early Songs is set to fourteen love songs by Richard Strauss. The texts, almost objectionably romantic in translation, are sung—fortunately—in German, and Feld is faithful to their varying moods without being melodramatic. The piece seems to me less cohesive in its overall sensibility than any Feld has yet made. It has an odd shape, beginning and ending with solos, duets, and group dances about searching for and finding love; but suddenly Feld introduces a touchingly but inexplicably tragic Christine Sarry, who is comforted by John Sowinski, then five exuberant couples rush in and out, then Feld dances a playful solo and an interlude with three girls—one of his affectionate tributes to the classics, *Coppélia* perhaps. I don't question his

74

inventiveness or his accuracy of expression, but I wonder what these four dances have to do with the rest of the ballet.

Compositional detours bother me more in Feld's work than in other choreographers' because his ballets move so logically from one thought to another. This is not a kind of dancing that is constantly calling attention to itself by tight, unnecessary smiles, bravura entrances and exits, improbable dynamic switches. In the first of two ecstatic duets Feld and Sarry do in *Early Songs*, he lifts her high in front of him and her legs quiver as if she were a moth cupped in his hands. So complete is their absorption in one another that when two more couples come by doing the same thing, one doesn't think, "Ho hum, yes it's The Ballet, six people doing a beautiful thing is better than two." One scarcely notices them except as an echo, a way of holding on a little longer to this elusive, joyous energy.

Apart from being an extraordinary choreographer, Feld has now proven that he is also a gifted director. He presses his young dancers beyond their supposed limits, and has quickly molded a company with a maturity and a performing spirit no one had a right to expect. Feld hasn't danced in New York for two years, and I had forgotten what a fine dancer he is, what a splendid, masculine vitality he radiates. He infuses the company with an important kind of tension and awareness, while Christine Sarry touches it with something soft and swift and imperturbable, like a spring breeze—there is not another ballerina like her in the city. For that matter, all the members of this company look more like themselves than like the usual balletic types. John Sowinski and Elizabeth Lee in particular, whom Feld rescued from the ranks of Ballet Theatre, have become noticeably stronger and more confident since ABC's fall season.

Though its continuing existence is hardly secure, the company has weathered its sea trials. See them for fun, for love, for amazement, or as an investment in the future. But see them.

April 7, 1970

Eliot Feld and the Extinct Metaphor

When the curtain rises, a boy is crouched, low to the ground, in front of a huge, backlit, pastel-spattered sail. He slowly unfolds his body upward—and greets the empty stage with a flourish. The gesture has all the resonant confidence of a boat whistle saluting the harbor at dawn.

This is the first moment of the first ballet choreographed by Eliot Feld, *Harbinger.* It contains, in a way, everything one needs to know about why many people consider Feld the most important young choreographer at work today.

Someone recently told me that after seeing Feld's work for the first time he was puzzled because it didn't seem to be about anything but dancing. That, perhaps, is the fundamental point. The critic may suggest metaphors about it later, but that doesn't make the moment of performance any less complete. Feld's dance isn't a metaphor for anything, not emperors and princesses, or the demons of the psyche, or the vapors of mysticism, or dawn, harbors, boats, portents, or anything but a boy extending his arm. What you see is what's happening, and what's happening is precisely what you see.

Compare this to almost any other sort of ballet. Take a classical pas de deux. The man and woman enter, meet, dance together for a while; then one partner retires while the other does a solo. There are two reasons why he or she leaves the stage at this point: to breathe and rest before the next great exertion, and to give the entire stage to the other dancer. But the audience is not supposed to think of that. We are supposed to imagine that the first partner is really there, gazing fascinated on his beloved's performance, because this is after all an ecstatic love scene.

Or take a Jerome Robbins duet. There often seems to be much more going on between the partners than is evident. How else can we explain those ambiguous little gestures that seem so important, the loaded glance, the crackling pause, the sudden capitulation? Some unspoken contest has been simmering for ages between them, we're forced to suppose, but they're not telling us what it's about. And then they are gone, leaving us none the wiser.

Consider the colorful sexuality of modern ballet: the clutchings and acrobatic falls—the contorted embraces—someone's hand shoots up in the air—orgasm! Or the decorative anonymity of "abstract" ballet, where you are not supposed to see a man touching a girl at all, but an idealized depiction of a musical phrase.

What makes Feld's dancing different from all these is its immediacy, its refusal to adopt euphemisms, and its total reliance on the energy and sweep of the movement to convey meaning.

All of Feld's ballets take their impetus from the flow of the music that accompanies them. Events in the dance arise out of that flow and continue going with it, never stopping to crystallize a beautiful moment or point out some feat of agility. Feld works like a master of old-fashioned, cursive handwriting, achieving emphasis, shape, and character without lifting his pen from the paper.

Intermezzo begins with the music itself, Brahms played on an onstage piano, while the dancers stand formally, awaiting their cue. No pretense about a ballroom, gloves, bowing and curtseying, just dancers ready to dance to Brahms. A girl raises an arm and goes up on her pointes in one breath, and the dance is on. Carried along on the current of music, the three couples whirl and float, dip and rise, faster and more intensely, until suddenly their ardor subsides, and the men pick up the girls in their arms and rock them to a lullaby.

At Midnight poses solo dancers against groups, the way Mahler threaded his long, gorgeous melodic line through and over the orchestra in the Rückert Songs, which accompany the ballet. The group makes no statement of its own, but its presence, always surging and hovering in the background, determines the actions of the soloist. In *Meadowlark*, Feld matched the exuberant momentum of Haydn, and in *Harbinger* the frenetic pace of Prokofiev.

Several unusual things are implied by this highly developed musicality of Feld's. His dancing often has a folk quality. The vocabulary is classic ballet, but the impulse to dance, the vitality, the lack of restraint belong to European folk forms, where people dance just for the sake of dancing. In these forms, and often in Feld's work, the men and women partner each other to share something, rather than to show off. Their arms go around each other's waists companionably, one might almost say democratically. One seldom feels that fussy concern for placing and arranging so common in ballet, because what matters is the motion, not the stops.

The partners adapt to each other rather than dominate each other. A girl may be running or turning and the man can pick her up without disturbing her flow; you hardly notice she has left the ground. In the opening section of *Intermezzo* the man slips his hand under the girl's arm and across her breast, and she covers his hand with hers, as if to say, "That's nice, keep it there."

Responding to the pulse of the music, these dancers convey a real sense of the body's weight. Girls are thrown up and caught in midair; in *Early Songs,* Feld runs while carrying Christine Sarry high in the air, and she swings her whole lower body back and forth like a pendulum; in *Harbinger* the girls curl up into a solid mass and jump with their whole weight, backwards into the boys' arms. This kind of dancing is exciting to watch because it is closer to our own experience than the continuous withholding of weight that ballet dancers habitually do. We know the feeling of our own weight, rocking in a hammock, dangling from a handhold on a moving subway. Feld intensifies this experience for us instead of denying it.

Feld is incredibly good at the pure craft of dance composition —making up steps, patterns, group designs that illuminate the music, like the headlong six-part canon at the end of *Meadowlark*. He is daring, witty, intelligent. But his greatest gift is for making movement that authentically expresses feelings. The taut, jagged lines of distress and the roundness of embracing, the inquisitive stretches into space and the compactness of energy mobilized, the long delicate quiets and the furious, tumbling chases—these are the marks of Eliot Feld's choreography.

He is important because he is the first choreographer of this generation to break with the idea that ballet is about another world—a universe peopled with invincibly beautiful beings who are possessed of superhuman powers. Feld's ballet is about this world. We and his dancers are in it together, not separated by some great gulf of virtuosity. I remember my delight when the first astronauts stepped out of their hermetic, computerized capsule and began leaping around the moon. When I look at Eliot Feld's dancers, I get the same flash of recognition: Hey, they're like us after all! Or maybe even more exciting, we're like them!

October, 1970

✂

They're Alive. That Counts.

This is no time to be starting a major ballet company, but Eliot Feld seems determined to do just that. The American Ballet Company, in its fall season at Brooklyn Academy, looked far more confident and less precarious than it did in its debut season only a year ago. They may make it, and I hope they do because Feld is the best young choreographer in ballet, and he needs dancers who understand his style to perform his ballets properly.

The company is under tremendous pressure from the economic sledge hammer that is New York, and from the taste-brokers of the New York press. Obviously, no artist should have to bow to these pressures, but this is New York 1970, and integrity doesn't feed dancers. The fact that Feld made three new ballets for this season may have nothing to do with the peculiar but persistent idea that business at the box office depends on novelty in the repertory, but he himself admitted to *The New York Times* that two of them were done "by accident," after completion of what he seems to consider his major work of the moment. There have been other subtle shifts in the repertory that indicate the company is already discarding problems it hasn't time to grapple with, and trying new ideas that can in turn be tossed away if they aren't immediately successful. Too bad, but at least the company is still alive. That in itself is an achievement.

Of the two "accidents," *A Poem Forgotten* (Wallingford Riegger) seems the least fulfilled, because it promises so much. A family portrait of sorts, it presents a boy (Daniel Levins), his parents and sister, and some figures outside the family. The Making of an Artist or some similar poster-title suggests itself, but the ballet reveals little; the boy does not grow up after his encounters with a siren and three other boys, he returns to his infantile position next to his passive sister at the feet of their self-preoccupied parents. All my impressions of the ballet were static ones: the movement is posed, angular, masklike; the situations are descriptions, not developments; the people don't get anywhere.

Cortege Parisien (Chabrier) is a postscript to Feld's earlier ballet *Cortege Burlesque*. Both are parodies on dance styles, but where *Cortege Burlesque* is a gently amusing spoof on the ballet pas de deux, danced with disarming innocence by Christine Sarry and John Sowinski, the new work looks at French romanticism—the artists and dancing girls in the Toulouse-Lautrec cafés—and gives it a ripe raspberry. Overripe. The piece is one exaggerated rubato from beginning to end. That passionate but fickle embrace, where the man bends the girl dramatically backward and she looks down her eyelashes at him, is but one cliché and symptom of the period. Feld uses the whole familiar lot of them, as if he'd like to finish them for good.

With *The Consort* we have another bag of cats entirely. This is the kind of ballet that has made Feld a major artist. It has his stamp of sheer choreographic brilliance together with his sharp human observation. To a suite of fifteenth- and sixteenth-century music orchestrated—rather bombastically, I thought—by the young conductor Christopher Keene, the dance does a slow, insidious descent from the stately proprieties of the Renaissance courts to the roaring gluttony and lust of the tavern, exposing the peasant in patrician's clothing.

The Consort isn't a pretty ballet. Its comment on our skin-deep gentility is not easy to take, especially one scene in which the girls tie up their long skirts and take off some of their fancy clothes while the men rut around decorously. This scene, with its ritualistic quality—men and women preparing for an orgy with complacent, hospitable smiles on their faces—is incredibly decadent. So is the whole ballet, which, on a visual level, is about the raunchy outcome of some absolutely gorgeous dancing.

One other new ballet was given in Brooklyn, a first major work by the dancer Bruce Marks. *Clockwise* (Jean Françaix) is a charming, lyrical work that makes no demands except to be enjoyed. Marks uses movement in many of the same ways Feld does, emphasizing the swinging momentum of the body's weight, making accents by speeding up or prolonging time, sending his dancers off their vertical axis or into unexpected changes of level and direction. The difference between them is Feld's daring, his assured, personal approach to any idea. *Clockwise* would be considered a fine "repertory builder" in any company, but ABC is probably the only one that can perform it without turning it into peppermint candy.

November 8, 1970

Romance

Eliot Feld will never be an ordinary choreographer even though he tries. At least I hope not. Whatever is compelling Feld these days to make lots of negligible ballets in standard sizes and sensibilities, his originality shines through, denying him the right to be a standard success. Nothing seems to me more tragic than the pressures we put on artists to do what we think we'll like, and our refusal to prize what is most ornery and special about them.

Feld's American Ballet Company opened its spring season

April 20 at Brooklyn Academy with his remarkable first choreography, *Harbinger*. The brand-new ballet that followed it indicates that Feld has aged rather than matured since 1967. *Romance* has everything stylish going for it, and that's just what defeats it. Set to nine atmospheric Brahms pieces played onstage by pianist Harry Fuchs, *Romance* follows the trend Feld himself helped establish two years ago with his other Brahms ballet, *Intermezzo*.

By now, of course, we're so saturated with ballroom ballets that every new one gropes for a novel period or a quirky situation. *Romance* adopts the stiff-backed melancholy of Antony Tudor's world, where propriety is everything and regrettable attachments for the wrong people mustn't go beyond a timeless look or a furtive touch. Though they're heavy with the scent of old perfume, I've never really thought of Tudor's ballets as romantic, because the social comment is so much stronger. His lovers always give up their adventures for the approval of their friends and families.

Feld isn't at all interested in social customs, but he doesn't care much about developing character, either. His ballets are first and best about dancing, and somehow *Romance* works against itself on that level. It's full of checked impulses and suspended poses; it always seems on the brink of something that can't happen. How lovely it would be in one of these ballets if a girl for once went off with the forbidden man!

The music Feld has chosen for *Romance* isn't very dancy, and his choreography follows its indecisive harmonics, its unwillingness to be confined rhythmically. Instead of stating a phrase or a melody as he could do elsewhere, Brahms ruminates moodily, and Feld does likewise. One duet seems to be all about extended arms. In one quartet the dancers change partners running across a great distance, in another they change within a very close group. The ballet is always hinting, considering a possibility in its mind, never quite telling us anything.

Still, there's a marvelous windblown dance for Christine Sarry, who's as delicate as a dandelion seed, and a placid duet in which Elizabeth Lee and Daniel Levins weave smiling circles around each other. Anna Laerkesen, prima ballerina of the Royal Danish Ballet, appears as a guest artist with the Feld company this season; she suffers a lot in *Romance*, and dances very little.

April 29, 1971

✖✖✖

The Gods Amused

Some ballets are frankly about how beautiful the dancer's body is. They're made to show off finely modeled planes and surfaces, texture, and weight, just like a gallery for statues—except that, since the audience can't move around to see various angles and perspectives, the dancers change position now and then. I think Eliot Feld's *The Gods Amused* is that kind of ballet.

Premiered at Brooklyn Academy April 28, *The Gods Amused* is a trio for Christine Sarry, Elizabeth Lee, and Daniel Levins, set to Debussy's "Danses Sacrée et Profane" for harp and orchestra. The dancers, in white leotards and tights, move gently through a clear Mediterranean light, looking handsome enough if not supernatural.

Feld appears not to have troubled himself much over the choreography; in addition to striking heroic poses, these gods disport themselves by running and leaping back and forth, and impersonally admiring each other. Levins lifts each girl in turn while the other skips around. He fires an imaginary bow, plays imaginary pipes. They tire of their play, recline on the floor, arise, and end in another noble pose.

I guess *The Gods Amused* is Levins' ballet. It's unusual for Feld to favor one soloist over others in a small piece—he isn't given to the narcissistic sort of beating-on-the-chest male characterizations where the women are just there to provide a swooning entourage. But Lee and Sarry, two of the most individual ballerinas in the city, have to work here mostly in unison; Levins treats them both the same, lifts them the same way. Any two corps girls might have done.

83

Young Levins is turning into a fine dancer under Feld's tutelage, but he's being pushed too fast, I think. In *The Gods Amused* he's a boy trying to be a man, and it's not becoming. His upper body is almost too expansively developed, and here, where he's bare-chested, I noticed a straining around the neck and shoulders, a severe, held-in quality about his torso. Levins is most endearing when he listens with his mobile face and holds himself with the loose-jointed expectancy of his youth. I caught that for one moment in *The Gods Amused*, but I think the whole ballet will have to acquire that kind of serene enjoyment before it works.

Feld's American Ballet Company is looking remarkably well this season considering its exhausting battle to establish itself as a continuous performing unit. A particular joy has been the dancing of Edward Verso, an old friend from Feld's Ballet Theatre days who has most recently been underemployed in the City Center Joffrey Ballet. With the challenge of the Feld repertory, Verso's special qualities are most wonderfully in evidence —a high negligent jump, a bouncy flexibility in the lower torso, and a casual assurance in leaning away from strict verticality. Verso is also, like the best of Feld's company, a serious dancer. He doesn't allow facial acrobatics to sidetrack your eye from the movement he's doing. His smiles are rare and therefore important.

May 11, 1971

Theatre

Trying to get my thoughts together about Eliot Feld's *Theatre*, the most important and ambiguous of three new works being seen at Brooklyn Academy during the American Ballet Company's spring season, I kept hearing the Robert Schumann music to Michel Fokine's *Carnaval*. This overlapping of ballets is not as accidental as it seems. ABC revived the sixty-year-old Fokine work during its debut season in New York, fall, 1969, and although the production looked unfinished, its commedia dell'arte characters turned out to suit the company very well. Even then, ABC had acquired a reticent style of underplaying things that made the old pantomime figures look newly imagined instead of like the usual blatant stereotypes.

Carnaval didn't survive that first season, but Feld has returned to some of the same characters in *Theatre*. This is altogether a bolder work, using Richard Strauss's Burlesque for Piano and Orchestra, Frank Thompson's modish costumes, and a striking bare-lights-and-black-drapes scenic concept that's probably the work of lighting designer Jennifer Tipton.

But *Theatre* also has some of *Carnaval*'s structural lapses. There are odd pieces of a plot that don't add up to a story. There's a lot of miming and repetitious gestural movement, and too little real dancing. People seem to be diddling around a lot to use up music.

Commedia figures are, of course, lovable excuses for a clown show or divertissement, but they wouldn't have survived four hundred years if they didn't also represent some of mankind's universal aspirations and failings. *Theatre* seems unable to decide whether it's going to be a beautiful empty-headed showpiece or a serious essay on its characters. There are precedents for both in ballet—*Carnaval* and George Balanchine's *Harlequinade* are examples of the first genre; *Petrouchka* of the second.

Feld's minor characters are just barely sketched in. Pulcinello the hunchback is a duplicate of a Callot engraving, a pose with mincing steps in between. Brighella and his bandits are a swirl of multicolored capes in pursuit of a bag of money. Even the Colombina, danced charmingly by Christine Sarry or Elizabeth Lee, and the Harlequin, Edward Verso, are little more than bright transparencies.

But in the central Pierrot role Feld permits himself a deeper look at a character, hints that he could still carry out the promise of his introspective second ballet, *At Midnight*, even though he's been skimming the surface of human relationships ever since. It's a measure of how deeply felt this Pierrot role is that during its first week of performance, two very different, and very valid, interpretations of it were given. Feld played him as the doleful stepchild of fate, the eternal loser always determinedly in the act of scrambling up from the canvas in order to be knocked down again. John Sowinski was a waif, a lost nonentity who could only be confident with his buffoon's costume in place and a tear carefully painted on his cheek.

If Feld had invested all his energy in *Theatre* this season we might have had one memorable ballet instead of three minor diversions. There's already enough in *Theatre* to demonstrate what prodigious talent Feld is scattering into the wind.

June 1, 1971

⊱⊰

Noblesse Oblige

The Harkness Ballet's First New York Season: November 1–19, 1967

You can do practically anything with enough money. Ask anyone in ballet—without it your company is behind the eight ball. There is, of course, the question of talent, taste, innovation, goodwill. But American dance has these resources in ample supply. What artists need is the money to bring them together in stable producing organizations, and the story of dance in the sixties is largely the story of who found enough money and how, and what use was made of it.

For at least five years Rebekah Harkness, a lady with enough money, has been seeking to make a major ballet company. Entrenched as I am on the side of democracy, bootstraps, and the integrity of the starving artist, I might enjoy reporting that Mrs. Harkness's millions have only furthered the cause of Mrs. Harkness, but this is not so. By any standard that we have for the excellence of a ballet company, the Harkness Ballet succeeds. The dancing is first-rate at all times, and often superior; the choreography is occasionally interesting, and the productions are lavish.

I doubt if any ballet in modern times has received the kind of patronage Mrs. Harkness provides. The great state ballets of Europe and the tradition-laden companies of Asia have considerable resources at their disposal. But this support comes from government and is subject, presumably, to the bureaucratic influence that is tied to any state control. In this country, although the government has given partial assistance to some arts organizations, most theaters, dance companies, and orchestras subsist on a uniquely American combination of contributions from a wide diversity of sources: national, state, and local government, foundations, industry, individual donations, and the box office, with variations on the scheme ranging as far as the imagination can travel. This makes for a seemingly random pattern of operation, particularly among institutions in the dance field. What is often overlooked, however, is that those institutions which do survive have a remarkable vitality and organic sense of purpose. Their reasons for existence are strengthened because of their need to find congenial supporters, and their artistic goals can seldom be eroded by outside pressures. With Harkness, there is only one patron, and she is also the final artistic arbiter and the propelling force behind the company. She has provided handsomely for the organization, and it lacks nothing—except, perhaps the nagging drive to create. There is a subtle difference between this company and the many other groups that struggle along because of somebody's unbearable need to say something. The Harkness Ballet exists because Mrs. Harkness wants it to exist, and for that reason it has a precarious quality; the patron giveth and the patron can take away. She is the only person with any equity in the organization.

The Harkness Ballet was founded only three years ago. Before that Mrs. Harkness attempted to act as benefactress to an already existing company, the Robert Joffrey Ballet. But she reckoned without the tenacity of Robert Joffrey, who considered himself equally qualified to make artistic decisions. After two years of unspeakable luxury—salaries for his dancers, fully

commissioned new works, important tours and performances—
Joffrey felt his authority was threatened, and the relationship
ended. Inevitably, it was a messy breakup. For some time Joffrey
was in desperate circumstances, but he has fortunately survived
and now has a major ballet, with financial headaches.

Although Joffrey came out of the debacle with his soul intact
and the sympathy of a great many people who later helped him,
Mrs. Harkness also retained what she needed. Most of Joffrey's
dancers had been under contract to the Harkness Foundation,
and since Joffrey could offer them nothing at the time, all but
a few stayed put. Ballets that had been commissioned for Joffrey
belonged to Harkness, and Mrs. Harkness kept all of those except the ones created by Joffrey himself and his chief choreographer, Gerald Arpino. Simultaneously with the announcement
of the split, Mrs. Harkness pledged an initial $1 million to the
creation of a new company in her name, a company that had,
before the ink dried on the papers, all three essential ingredients: dancers, repertory, and money.

A few months later, with the glamour and fanfare that accompanies everything she does, Mrs. Harkness opened another
namesake, Harkness House for Ballet Arts. As a symbol of her
grandiose intentions Harkness House serves perhaps even better than the theater she has not yet invested in, because no
matter how opulent a theater may be out front, backstage, where
the artists live, it is always bare, efficient, and made for sweaty
service. Harkness House, on the other hand, is a showplace, a
plush paddock for the groooming of thoroughbred dancers, and
surely dancers have not been so pampered since the court of
Louis XIV.

Nothing is too good for the Harkness dancers. Their rehearsal
studios are decorated with cut-velvet walls, gilt-framed mirrors,
and crystal chandeliers. They have classes with famous ballerinas, their sore muscles are treated to massages and whirlpool
baths, and they are surrounded with books and paintings for the
uplift of the mind. They summer in the healthy sea air of Mrs.
Harkness's Watch Hill estate, and in spring they go to Cannes.
When they perform they play decent engagements in decent
theaters, and they travel first class. The care and attention that
has been lavished on them shows.

Nowadays excellent technique is expected from American dancers. The Harkness dancers are, in addition, well fed and confident. They are not subjected to the physical strain of constant touring and homelessness, as is Ballet Theatre. Unlike the Joffreys they do not have to fit their program into an assortment of projects contrived at least in part to meet their own payroll. They are not, like the New York City Ballet, cloistered from artistic infancy with one dominating genius; their range covers many styles and periods—they are sophisticated performers. On opening night it was a great pleasure to watch the aristocratic bravura of Finis Jhung and Helgi Tomasson partnering the fragile Lone Isaksen in *Zealous Variations*, the dramatic intensity of Lawrence Rhodes and Brunilda Ruiz in *Sebastian*, and the stylized brilliance of Elisabeth Carroll and the feline charm of Annette av Paul in *Firebird*. These are actors as well as dancers. They are not only with it and in it, but they are giving it as well. This quality of being not merely secure in a role but so confident in it as to be able to give it away I find consistently in only one other company: Martha Graham's.

In these seven soloists lies the real strength of the Harkness Ballet. I cannot say much about the corps because it seems to have no "personality." The choreography is built around the soloists. Secondary roles are nonexistent or so negligible as to offer few opportunities for outstanding performances. The corps as a supporting organism is ill-used—disguised in unattractive costumes, moving in the dark periphery of the main action, or, most often, dancing as a unit in imitation of the movements of the principals. Ruiz, Carroll, Isaksen, Paul, Rhodes, Tomasson, and Jhung are superb, each with his or her own distinctive qualities. They are delightful to look at, but the requirements of the repertory place a great responsibility and perhaps an undue strain on their talents.

In a recent *New Yorker* column Winthrop Sargeant described Igor Stravinsky as a "preeminent leader of musical fashion." I take this to mean that Stravinsky's preeminence has been based not upon innovation but upon his ability to fashion popular works using the innovations of others. In the field of dance many ballet companies are bringing into wider use the revolutionary ideas of not so long ago. If you use mixed media in the City Center, as Robert Joffrey's *Astarte* did recently, you can generate a good deal of excitement; the place and the focus are right for launching into the mainstream what has previously resided only in the obscure province of the avant-garde.

Ballet companies of every type nowadays recognize the important contributions of modern dance to choreography, and are reviving modern dance works to supplement the rather anemic output of classically trained choreographers. One choreographer described the phenomenon to me this way: "The management may not always appreciate my work, but I'm good for their repertory. I feel like some sort of special medicine." Pieces like Merce Cunningham's *Summerspace* and Anna Sokolow's *Rooms* have been revived more or less intact by big ballet companies. The Harkness, however, disdains to sanction anything as impure as real modern dance and therefore has engaged a number of modern choreographers to create new "ballets." These works illustrate what Clive Barnes calls the Third Stream, the true and hopeful reconciliation of the two dance forms. Contrary to Barnes' theory, I think these pieces usually do not work; they borrow styles from everywhere and have the blurred quality of double exposure. They are popularized modern dance; the bite and individuality of the real article have been refined out. Norman Walker's pointless exercise in the medium, *Night Song*, is just such a bastardized mélange, lacking in any sort of choreographic distinction.

Alvin Ailey's *Feast of Ashes*, based on Lorca's *House of Bernarda Alba*, is likewise caught between two disciplines, but instead of attempting to synthesize the styles, Ailey uses the resources of both alternately. By training and instinct a modern dancer would be economical, choosing only the essence of the dramatic theme to illuminate with movement. But ballet is not inclined to be so terse; it is not anxious to throw away opportunities for virtuoso dancing. Reiteration of an idea seems preferable to understatement. *Feast of Ashes* is encumbered with much that need not be there: much running back and forth, mass entrances and exits to signify changes of scene, a cliché "trap" scene—victim runs toward exit, finds a pursuer blocking the way, runs to another exit, another pursuer, and so on. (This scene appeared in three out of four ballets one night.) Ailey's free-swinging gestures and fast-traveling turns, while effective in his spirituals and blues dances, are not entirely appropriate for Lorca's repressed aristocrats.

In working out a dance based on a play, the choreographer can either abstract the themes and emotional conflicts of the original to make a completely new entity, or strip the original down to its plot outline and produce a story in dance form. Ailey has chosen the latter course, and I think has thereby lost much of Lorca's meaning. The story of *Bernarda Alba* is rather commonplace: a willful girl rebels against her family's wishes and brings destruction upon herself and shame to the house. But this is really a play about an angry nest of females, and its power lies in Lorca's delineation of the characters—the proud and cruel mother, the jealous sisters, the cynical servants—and the stifling atmosphere of a house dominated by death and tradition. Ailey's introduction of men and of prostitutes, who never appear in the play, creates opportunities for a more interesting production visually but almost entirely eliminates the terrible starkness of Lorca's tragedy.

Stuart Hodes' *Abyss* is another dramatic dance, based on a story by Andreyev, but in this case the story is reduced to its barest essentials, with the sole purpose of involving the audience in the emotions of the two central characters. Two happy young lovers, full of wonder and innocence, are set upon by thugs who drag the girl away and rape her. When she returns, dazed and unable to respond to the boy, he is at first bewildered; then, in a growing hysteria of sorrow and frustration, he realizes that she has become a carnal object for desires he has never realized in himself, and in the climactic moment, he falls on her. The simple intensity of the theme, and the fine performances of Lawrence Rhodes and Lone Isaksen as the two lovers who fall from innocence, make *Abyss* the most effective piece of theater in the Harkness repertory.

John Butler, a prominent Third-Streamer, works now in the modern idiom, now in ballet, producing a huge quantity of amorphous pieces none of which makes a unique statement. Butler's work often has a sentimental, androgynous quality that

91

takes the edge off the human conflicts it purports to examine. Whatever credibility it has is supplied by brilliant performances, such as that of Ruiz and Rhodes in *Sebastian*. *Sebastian* is big, well-made theater, with some of the ceremonial sweep of Butler's *Carmina Burana*. But it becomes painfully melodramatic in the death scenes, which is when you realize that it has been only another performance, like an expert Hollywood movie. Butler's *After Eden* is a skillful treatment of a familiar theme, really the same theme as the more interesting *Abyss*, and with the same stunning principals. (I was unable to see Butler's *A Season in Hell*, or Rudi van Dantzig's *Monument for a Dead Boy*, or the one comic piece in the repertory, Agnes de Mille's *Golden Age*.)

Cain, a first work by company member Vicente Nebrada, is conceptually modeled after Martha Graham's abstract dramas. Its sculptural set by Robert Davison is reminiscent of a Graham set. Its program is episodic, with dream sequences and flashbacks. It has a chorus that is meant to comment on the action without being involved. Its intent is to show the psychological motives of a crime. Helgi Tomasson as Cain is given some striking solos, but they might as well be solos in a divertissement for all they have to do with the other people in the story. Without Graham's genius for theater, Nebrada's piece is merely a frantic Freudian jungle.

Besides the narrative ballets, Harkness has a number of plotless pieces in its repertory. Brian Macdonald's *Tschaikovsky* is the kind of ballet that ought to have an exclamation point after its title. This would tell more about it than reams of critical analysis. Its choreography is high-tsarist muddied by modern quirks such as flexed feet where they should be pointed, turn-ins where there should be turnouts. The scenery and costumes, by Raoul Pene du Bois, are overdone and unbecoming in sickly shades of pink and green. The music is from the bottom of the barrel; I understand some of it was taken from scores even the composer wanted to throw away.

Variations for Four plus Four is another work in the classical vein, by Anton Dolin. This is more successful because it is cleaner in style and simpler in construction, a show-off ballet with fat, cheer-jerking parts for everyone. It has a curious fragmentary quality, however. The music (arranged from Verdi and M. Keogh) stops, starts, and changes key abruptly, and so does the action. This may result from the fact that *Variations* is a kind of pastiche that Dolin put together from some of his other dances.

Zealous Variations, by Macdonald, was a delightful, straightforward classical trio when it was shown on opening night. Later an entirely different *Zealous Variations* was given, and it developed that the two pieces were originally one ballet, which had been split because the entire work was too long to fit on one program. If this ballet had been a genuine artistic unity, I don't see how its creator could allow it to be dealt with in such a way. It would be like sawing the Venus de Milo in half for a traveling exhibit because the crate was too small to ship it in one piece. But I think many of the works in the Harkness repertory are not genuine—they seem often to be made to measure, and hence are fair game for any amount of tampering.

Richard Wagner's *Youth* is a lovely but slight little duet that one is inclined to pass off as a better-than-average student composition, until one learns that *Youth* is only a section of a larger work. New York never saw the whole piece, but no explanation was given to the public that only a portion of the choreographer's talents was being seen.

Canto Indio of Brian Macdonald, a pas de deux for Elisabeth Carroll and Helgi Tomasson, is entirely successful—a classical showpiece with a few modern surprises, a suggestion of Mexican costuming, and Carlos Chavez' exciting and familiar 1935 score, Sinfonia India. This is a dancers' piece. No overblown costumes or decor, no pompous music gets in their way. They can show off their most amazing tricks; they look as if they love it, and the audience always does too.

John Butler's abstract group work *Landscape for Lovers* once again reaches for a synthesis of the ballet and modern idioms and attains confusion. Butler uses erotic gesture, which would be taboo in classical ballet, in the same stylized way that ballet uses its own movement conventions. The girl will rub her buttocks against the boy's thigh, or he will clasp her breasts, in the

93

same cool, studied manner as if they were going through the rituals of a classical adagio. It has about as much relationship to passion, desire, or any genuine sexual response as the classical routine. Butler's stylized eroticism is ugly and, because it is unsupported by any dramatic motivation or kinesthetic logic, it looks campy and somewhat obscene. Butler further complicates the matter by continually switching his male protagonist's role from that of the danseur noble—with erect torso, sweeping arm and hand gestures, solicitous, elegant support of the girl—to modern partner with emotional expressiveness and distorted movements.

There is a disturbing thread of violence in the emotional content of much of the Harkness repertory. This is perhaps best summed up in Brian Macdonald's *Time Out of Mind.* From the first entrance of three boys leapfrogging each other in competitive urgency to the final exit of the last girl, still vibrating with desire, this dance is an orgy. Its terrific pace slackens once, without a release of tension, as the principal couple stalk each other, mentally squaring off for the next round; and once more before the final coda, when the couple are momentarily sated with their animalistic lovemaking and are almost able to feel disgust and pity before succumbing again to lust. Within the limits imposed by his one-dynamic idea, Macdonald has done some interesting things: the sexual tension that finds its outlet in vibrating hands and feet, the offensive—but consistent—lascivious postures and lifts, the boys' group with its energy widely extended into space as opposed to the contained, on-pointe fluttering of the girls.

Considered alone, I think *Time Out of Mind* would be quite an an effective dance, but within the context of the total Harkness repertory it becomes only the most capable delineation of an often-heard theme. The dramatic works of Harkness are almost without exception, destructive, lustful, perverted, and pessimistic about the redeeming possibilities of human love. I'm sure Mrs. Harkness did not commission her choreographers' viewpoints to order, and there is a lot to be depressed about in the world today. But there are still dances to be made about joy, delight, and the celebration of sex without resorting to Pollyanna clichés or escapism. I think *Landscape for Lovers* and *Night*

Song were attempts to do this, but their movement ambiguities reduced the idea to a parody.

In the October, 1967, issue of *Dance Magazine* Harkness artistic director Brian Macdonald reported that Jack Cole's *Requiem for Jimmy Dean* was not finished, but that everyone was proceeding in true show-biz fashion on the assumption that it would somehow be ready for the season. A few weeks later Cole sued Mrs. Harkness in an effort to stop the production because, indeed, it was not finished. Mrs. Harkness prevailed, and sections of the piece were shown in the season as a "work in progress." Clive Barnes thereupon reviewed it along with the rest of the repertory.

This sad little pyramid of indiscretion indicates a certain disregard for the artist's rights and a rigid attitude toward the creative act that is not in keeping with the realities of the theater. Production of the piece, in the face of Cole's problems and the nasty publicity of a lawsuit, does an injustice not only to Cole but to the dancers and the company as a whole. New York, which was seeing the company and most of its repertory for the first time, would never have missed *Requiem* if it had been quietly withdrawn before opening night. Choreographers are not commodities, to be ostentatiously placed on the menu and gobbled up raw. Sometimes a new piece does not work, or internal differences prevent its coming to fruition. Showing an incomplete work proves nothing, except that Mrs. Harkness owns it and can show it if she likes.

Rumor has it that each costume for Act II of Brian Macdonald's *Firebird* (which lasts about four minutes) cost $1,000. At that rate the price of the production alone for this extravaganza would probably support a good-size modern dance company or even a modest ballet group for a year. Mrs. Harkness, of course, can do as she likes with her money, but in times like these I consider *Firebird* a kind of social sin, like giving an elaborate coming-out party during wartime. I would gladly accept Mrs. Harkness's word for it that she could produce the world's most expensive ugly ballet, if only she had not made me a party to her theory of conspicuous consumption.

95

Although *Firebird* is the most flagrant example, many of the Harkness ballets are tastelessly overproduced, to the detriment not only of their visual attractiveness but sometimes even of their choreographic concepts. American dance is simply not accustomed to opulent productions, and over the years the financial exigencies that prevented us from using elaborate decor have actually worked to the advantage of our choreography. Without sets and costumes American dance has had to be doubly effective with its movement, themes, and performance. We have also developed some important substitutes for expensive decor.

As its alternative to florid romanticism, Harkness reverts to Spartan austerity. The inscrutable set pieces with which Rouben Ter-Arutunian has embellished *After Eden* look like *objets trouvés* from a giant's auto-parts store. These sculptures reminded me of the same designer's big eggshell fragments for Glen Tetley's *Ricercare*, except that the dancers in *Ricercare* use the set as a kind of cocoon in which they curl up, climb around, and do other acrobatics. The sculptures in *After Eden* are purely decorative, although not pretty. You can almost hear someone saying, "We can't have a duet on that big bare stage!" This is the kind of inappropriate thinking that minimizes some of Harkness's best assets. With Lawrence Rhodes and Lone Isaksen giving beautiful performances, no other decoration is needed. This kind of dancing can elevate a familiar theme and a merely competent score to the level of art, but it has to work hard to overcome a gratuitous scenic concept.

Modern dance has been much more imaginative in its use of design. In fact, I believe it was Martha Graham who first used the sculptural set for dance, in the thirties. But her designs are always a part of the dance, not merely decoration, and not merely serviceable props either. I cannot think of a more stunning yet simple and integral set for dance than Noguchi's tubular brass design for *Seraphic Dialogue*. Another point to be made here is that the moderns use light much more effectively, so that it becomes an element of design, often compensating for minimal sets and costumes. Apart from economic considerations, dance lighting has a valid artistic rationale: it complements the dance's own spatial and dynamic qualities because its intensity, color, and position are variable. Harkness does not list a lighting designer among its personnel, although Jennifer Tipton was engaged to light some of the ballets. Throughout the New York performances, at the Broadway Theater, there were dead spots in the lighting, misplaced cues, unmasked instruments, ominous noises during scene changes. All this could have been avoided by having some skilled technicians backstage accustomed to running dance productions flawlessly.

Opening night in New York was truly a glittering affair. The audience was filled with long evening gowns, jewels, and black ties. My escort remarked that we should have dressed, and I answered, "But I did." The dressiest thing in my closet was a nice wool print. I suspect a lot of the dance world finds itself in a similar state of deshabille, which is why the Harkness Ballet may be a little incongruous and hard to take.

According to Brian Macdonald, its artistic director since early 1967, the company has the best of intentions. It wants to be a workshop for new ballets of many styles, to give choreographers their every wish in casting, rehearsal time, and production. As a matter of policy, the company seems to oppose revivals in preference to mounting new works. But at the same time, Harkness presents itself to the world with all the trappings of a major company, and it is not unreasonable for the world to expect it will present major works. Since becoming director, Macdonald has purged the repertory of some of its excesses; he needs to exercise even stronger control. To encourage new works is one thing, but to present them with full, expensive productions in a big New York theater exposes their creators to the toughest public scrutiny. Even if a piece is later withdrawn because it was not successful, the damage has been done. The Harkness Foundation is a kind of fairy godmother of dance. Not only does it endow the Harkness Ballet and associated choreographers, composers, and designers, it maintains the Harkness Ballet School, supports the current Hunter College Dance Series and the annual free dance performances at the Delacorte Theater in Central Park, and helps various other worthy projects in small ways. It could also afford to present truly experimental works in modest tryout conditions, and to restore to the repertory some of the authentic lost treasures of American dance.

Not content with its immense wealth, the Harkness Ballet

also wants to be loved. The foundation distributed a questionnaire at the New York performances asking what the audience liked and did not like about its programs. The questionnaire seemed to indicate that if enough people voted for it, the Harkness would prepare a ballet with spoken or sung narration, with more elaborate sets and costumes, with emphasis on plot rather than performance, or with bagpipes and an animal act if we so desired. Unless it is a tremendous put-on, the questionnaire reveals a cardinal weakness in the company's philosophy. Art simply cannot be made to the order of a patron, an audience, or a critic. It must come first from the guts and vision of an artist, and this is the one factor to which the Harkness has yet to commit its fortune.

Summer/Fall, 1968

Ballet Patronage: How Not to Do It

On March 26, 1970, the Harkness Ballet was performing in Monte Carlo, about midway through a long European tour, when directors Lawrence Rhodes and Benjamin Harkarvy received a telegram from Milton P. Kayle, attorney for their patron and producer, Mrs. Rebekah Harkness. Citing financial pressures and ignoring the company's remaining tour commitments, Mrs. Harkness was ordering the company home on May 15.

Kayle's telegram continued: "The structure of the company will be reevaluated upon its return but the company will continue repeat will continue as a major group in the ballet world." Perhaps the only surprise in the destructive chain of events set in motion by that peremptory telegram was the fact that Mrs. Harkness still believed she could create a major cultural force by announcing it would be so.

98

Such is the naïve arrogance that has undermined nearly all the activities of the Rebekah Harkness Foundation, established in 1959, according to one of its early pronouncements, "to encourage and promote American cultural achievements throughout the world." After making a few special grants, the Harkness Foundation jumped heavily into the ballet field in 1962, when it assumed full responsibility for the support of the Robert Joffrey Ballet. Two years later Joffrey pulled out, claiming his authority as artistic head of the company was threatened. Typically, motives and plans went undisclosed behind a curt official announcement, but the message was clear enough: Mrs. Harkness intended to change the name of the eight-year-old Joffrey company to the Harkness Ballet. Some time earlier, dancers in the company had been signed to new contracts with the Harkness organization, and most of them elected to remain where their salary was instead of gambling on Joffrey's dubious future. All six of the 1970 Harkness Ballet's marvelous soloists were Joffrey principals at that time.

The new Harkness Ballet, with George Skibine as artistic director and his wife, Marjorie Tallchief, as prima ballerina, tried out in Europe and the U.S. provinces for the next few years, but Skibine was not to preside over its crucial New York debut. He resigned quietly in early 1967, and the Canadian choreographer Brian Macdonald emerged from a committee-led interregnum as director that June.

The frequent changes in command and artistic viewpoint were creating unrest in the company. With incipient mass resignations on her hands, Mrs. Harkness finally thought of entrusting the company to one of its own, and accordingly Macdonald was replaced in August, 1968, by Lawrence Rhodes. One of the finest young American dancers, Rhodes was respected by his colleagues, but running a ballet company and dancing several major roles at the same time was a job for a superman. A year later Harkarvy, who had just left his post as founder-director of the Netherlands Dance Theater, was brought in as co-director with Rhodes.

The company's morale and its artistic caliber improved, especially after Harkarvy arrived. At forty, he has maturity without condescension. Dancers respect him highly as a teacher, and his steady choreographic good sense acted as a leveler for the wildly gyrating Harkness repertory. Best of all, he and Rhodes formed an immediate, sympathetic partnership. The company at last began to coalesce, and their notices for the fall, 1969, season at Brooklyn Academy, and the tour that followed, were appreciative.

When Attorney Kayle's cryptic message arrived in Monte Carlo, Harkarvy and Rhodes were beginning to think they might have overcome their patron's chronic dissatisfaction with the stewards of her cultural enterprises. "If it's fame Mrs. Harkness wanted, now the company could give it to her," Harkarvy told me recently. "For the first time, reviewers were taking us seriously. The company was flourishing and growing, and the critics said so, especially in cities where it had played before."

The directors immediately wired New York asking several specific questions about what would happen to the dancers after returning home. Contracts ran until mid-July, but they had expected to be performing in Italy at that time. Would they be paid from mid-May to mid-July? Should they start looking for new jobs? And were Harkarvy and Rhodes to continue as "active and sole directors"? They stressed the demoralizing effect that Kayle's command, and the uncertainty of what was to follow, could have on the company's ability to function.

On March 28 they received the following answer: "As indicated in my telegram company is to return to New York to permit reevaluation. Only after this takes place can all questions you raise be answered. Individual contract commitments as well as union requirements will be honored in any event. Mrs. Harkness expects company to exhibit highest professional standards for the remaining European engagement. Anything less would be shameful disregard of her significant support of company over past years and will be a factor in reevaluation required under current circumstances."

At this point the dancers themselves offered to forego two weeks salary if they could stay in Europe long enough to do their Paris season, scheduled for the month of June. They were told another company had already taken over their booking.

Early in April the dancers' union, American Guild of Musical

Artists, began hearing from Harkness Ballet members. Joan Greenspan, AGMA National Representative in New York, told me: "I think Mrs. Harkness's attorneys wanted to disband the company on May 15. She hadn't made a final decision when she told the company to come home, but we forced the issue. There's no such thing as tenure in a ballet company. Our contract required the management to notify the dancers by May 15 whether they would be reengaged after July 15. During April they told us there would be a reorganization and ten or fifteen dancers wouldn't be renewed."

Gradually, information began to reach the company. In Barcelona, they were advised that sixteen of their thirty-one dancers would be asked to continue and were told who the sixteen were. Just before the final performance, in Lausanne on May 15, 1970, the chosen were instructed to report Monday morning at Harkness House in New York; the others were told to leave their addresses with the management and they would be contacted. In other words, with no notice, half the company was being laid off two months before the end of its contract.

The company scattered. Nearly all of the sixteen dancers Mrs. Harkness wished to keep refused to sign new contracts. A few did report to Harkness House, where they are attending class and rehearsing. Some of the company stayed in Europe looking for work and waiting till tenants moved out of their sublet New York apartments. All will get rehearsal pay until July 15; after that they go on unemployment, except, of course, those who turned down the chance to remain under the Harkness aegis. At no time up to this writing did Mrs. Harkness communicate directly with Rhodes or Harkarvy.

It was not until May 22 that the Harkness organization issued an announcement of the merger of the Harkness Youth Dancers and the Harkness Ballet. The new company, to be called the Harkness Ballet, will be under the artistic direction of Rebekah Harkness, with Ben Stevenson, former director of the Harkness Youth Dancers, as resident choreographer.

The Harkness Ballet has never been the sole preoccupation of the Harkness Foundation. In the past ten years it has sponsored numerous enterprises related to dance—lectures; concert series; schools; publishing ventures; the foundation's baronial New York headquarters, Harkness House; and many smaller projects. Harkness endeavors often seem engineered for some particular person Mrs. Harkness wishes to encourage, and since the personnel around Harkness House seems to go in and out of favor with great regularity, the projects often disappear too. One never knows which ones to take seriously.

Some, like the Ballet itself, have had a real impact on the dance climate of their time. In 1966–67 and 1967–68 Mrs. Harkness contributed to the Hunter College Dance Series, the first time modern dance was given large-scale, official sponsorship and presented as a major cultural attraction in New York. She has also sponsored the free late-summer dance concerts at Central Park's Delacorte Theater. Both these projects were used increasingly to showcase Mrs. Harkness's protégés, and when the Ford Foundation gave a big modern dance subsidy to another producer in 1968, Harkness support was withdrawn from Hunter entirely, and that series folded.

In 1968 at the Delacorte series, a group called the Harkness Youth Company made its debut. The company, consisting of trainees from the Harkness school, listed no director, but the next year at the Delacorte Ben Stevenson was heading a group called the Harkness Youth Dancers, which was described in a program note as "a versatile unit of expertly trained professionals." Some people assumed the Harkness Youth Dancers were to be a sort of apprentice company for the Harkness Ballet; others saw it as a complementary but not competing unit that would be smaller and more flexible than the main group. Harkness House, consistent with its habit of saying as little as possible about its enterprises beyond proclaiming their grandiose purposes, divulged nothing. But the company did announce a small tour in April.

Whatever it came to mean as a performing entity to its members and its audiences in its brief existence, the Harkness Youth Dancers will be terminated on July 15. Most of its dancers are leaving, according to AGMA. In fact, no Harkness contracts at all had been filed with the union by mid-June. So who will be left in the "merged" company and what will it do?

According to Robert Larkin, press representative at Harkness House, the size of the company is projected at from thirty to forty dancers, with the roster to be complete by the end of the summer. Dancers are auditioning now for Mrs. Harkness. The repertory will be "more classical." New works are being choreographed by the Spanish dancer Jose de Udaeta and by Walter Gore, who started with Ballet Rambert in the 1930s and has worked with various companies in Europe. Stevenson is working on a full-length *Peer Gynt*, and Mrs. Harkness plans to retain Brian Macdonald's *Time Out of Mind* and some other unspecified works from the original repertory. The new company will probably try out in Europe as its predecessor did, and no New York seasons are being planned at the present time.

If the new company survives, Joan Greenspan points out, it will only be the Harkness Ballet on paper. "It's dancers who hold the key to repertory. Mrs. Harkness decided to get rid of the dancers and throw out the repertory too. It's the most tragic situation that's ever occurred in the dance world. The company was built to a success and then dashed on the rocks. Every other company that's failed, has failed for *lack* of money."

Larkin explained the "merger" as a result of economic problems, especially the decline of the stock market. "When you have $500 million, it bombs hell out of your holdings," he told me. "It wasn't possible for Mrs. Harkness to support two companies."

So far the net result of all these manipulations is bitterness and an almost irreparably damaged Harkness image. The company's withdrawal has left a trail of disgruntled bookers and impresarios all over Europe. The British magazine *Ballet Today* reports that the cancellation of the company's season at Sadler's Wells Theatre, with a heavy advance sale of tickets, was a serious blow to the theater, then having its own financial troubles. A score or more dancers have been thrown onto the job market here, and it will take time for them to be absorbed into other companies. The brilliant Helgi Tomasson has already joined the New York City Ballet, and two other soloists, Rhodes and Lone Isaksen, will go with Harkarvy when he becomes head of the National Ballet of Holland at the end of the summer. Harkarvy said many of the dancers had wanted to stay together, but it was impossible to raise money for a new company at this time.

Those who cannot get work with the major American companies will probably filter off to Euope.

The Harkness Ballet repertory was never of the highest standard choreographically, but, partly because of the expertise of the dancers and partly because ample production money was available, it was a company that did things in the grand style. It looked elegant without trying to be fashionable, confident without pushiness. It could take chances; it didn't seem to be under any undue obligations to the past. It will be missed, for until its demise it had a freedom from poverty no other American company has known; and implicit in that freedom, the ideal persisted that creativity and artistic excellence need have no limits.

One woman was the key to this ideal. One woman had the power to dangle this opportunity for so long before so many artists and has snatched it away so often at whim. Rebekah Harkness's philanthropic adventures on behalf of dance date back only ten years. As a personality she is elusive, though it is known that she takes ballet lessons, likes to compose music (her scores, under various pseudonyms, have accompanied several Harkness Ballet ballets), and holds well-publicized conferences with people like Salvador Dali. Is that what she thinks ballet is about? Her works, if by those we are to know her, are an erratic succession of false starts, interrupted projects, thwarted hopes. The more creative a project is, and the more useful it becomes, the quicker it is apt to be derailed.

Rebekah Harkness's spokesman denies that she intended to destroy the Harkness Ballet. "She wanted to run the company the way she wants it run, not the way the directors wanted it run. Let's face it," he said. "She pays the bills. She has a right to exercise her own judgement and taste."

June 28, 1970

II

POP DANCE:
THE DISPOSABLE NOW

Pop dance as a phenomenon was first described by Arlene Croce in her excellent magazine *Ballet Review*, in the stunned aftermath of the Stuttgart Ballet's first New York season, summer, 1969. Although there had been popular ballets before that time —commercial, they were usually termed—up until the Stuttgart's huge success, dance, in a sense, called its own shots. Ballet companies needed audiences, but everybody assumed they were dance audiences, people who came to see ballet for the sake of ballet and who would try to understand it in terms of ballet. The Stuttgart seemed frankly to be making another kind of appeal, to another kind of audience. For the first time a ballet company scored a success for which the "ballet world" was not heavily responsible.

The Stuttgart's director John Cranko, whom Arlene Croce called "the bargain-basement Balanchine," astutely made his pitch to those bored theatergoers and culture samplers who were beginning to look to ballet for a new kind of entertainment. Where they might have found the New York City Ballet too esoteric, Ballet Theatre old-fashioned, or the Joffrey slightly adolescent, the Stuttgart was grown-up, professional, extravagantly produced, easy to understand, and still it retained the exotic demeanor of ballet. The uninitiated fans owned the Stuttgart in New York, and suddenly we all saw what a large, hungry public they represented. We became aware how frequently and in how many ways this public was being courted.

I've categorized certain companies here as being involved with pop dance, meaning that something I call pop dance seems to be their main concern. The New York City Ballet and Ballet Theatre have produced a certain number of pop ballets, but they aren't pop companies. The pop companies don't do pop dance exclusively, nor is all pop dance worthless. Pop dance takes many forms and claims many motives, some of them very high-minded. What all pop dance has in common, it seems to me, is a reliance on the most highly specialized techniques of dance and a use of those techniques to achieve theatrical purposes. But whether it seeks to entertain, to impress, to proselytize, to arouse, or to publicize something, pop dance is not preeminently concerned with a serious pursuance of the dance art.

Technique in dance is two things, really. It's a method of training the body to be able to accomplish specific movement tasks. Ballet technique is based on five positions, or shapes of the body, from which the dancer learns to move ever more proficiently into space, and through which he connects his steps, leaps, turns, and poses. But technique is also a systematic approach to the whole process of moving. Ballet technique has to do with a certain kind of presentation, with the hips and chest spread open, the arms framing the upper body, the feet pointed and continuing the body's line. This is the way a ballet dancer looks—the way ballet looks. Modern dance techniques look different in their various ways. I think technique eventually becomes as much a part of a dancer as his clothing or his diction, and it influences not only how he moves but how he conceives of dance—what steps can follow what steps, what actions are permissible and are not, what is his relationship to the ground, to the other dancers, to the audience, and so forth.

Perhaps ten years or more ago, the mechanical aspect of technique began to take precedence over its aesthetic implications for many choreographers. People who had been trained in both modern dance and ballet, notably John Butler and Gerald Arpino, began to use technical elements of both forms in their choreography, and soon a great blending of the two styles was being predicted. In traditional ballet and modern dance, considerable borrowing of movement possibilities has occurred without resulting in a complete blur. But many choreographers have managed to create whole repertories that can be classified as neither ballet nor modern, that use movement for its virtuosic appeal but that have no central stylistic attitude toward the movement process. Among the adherents of this combined approach are Glen Tetley and Lar Lubovitch.

The first time we saw this erosion of technique-as-aesthetic in wholesale practice was in the repertory of the early Harkness Ballet. The emphasis there was on balletic, presentational movement, together with the distortion of line that was part of Martha Graham's "look." The sexual wrangling and tormented eroticism seen in so many of those ballets was a simplification of Graham's efforts to find universal meaning in the conflicts of the individual psyche.

Whether it's dealing with narrative, polemic, or pure composition, pop ballet is always a watered-down version, because it has to be accessible. It has to present a clear progress toward its climax—an uncomplicated dramatic buildup, an unequivocal dynamic interchange. It can't be ambiguous or abstract; if one character is to seduce, attack, or abandon another, we have to see the act. Displays of violence, ritualized, stylized, even depersonalized, are endemic to this type of pop ballet. As the moral climate generally grew freer, pop ballet got more graphic, more extravagant in its perversions, nastier in its eroticism. This made it more popular, of course.

The same season that the Harkness made its New York debut, Robert Joffrey's *Astarte* had its premiere here, crystallizing another aspect of pop dance—its slick topicality. *Astarte* used rock music, film, psychedelic effects, near nudity, artifacts of Eastern mysticism, and a pervasive aura of drugs, to elaborate on what was essentially a conventional "modern ballet." The combination was so successful that the Joffrey, which had just become established in the City Center and needed to build a clear identity in the competition for audiences, embarked on a whole career of being mod. New ballets in the following seasons plucked ideas out of the headlines and the shops and draped them with matching movement.

These ballets look so unusual and contemporary that the audience mistakes recognition for enlightenment, name-dropping for profundity. A good example is Arpino's *The Clowns* (1968), a rehash of the old story of the last clown-everyman going down gallantly at the crack of doom. Arpino souped up the slapstick and sentimentality with inflatable plastic employed in various phallic ways, violent lighting and trick effects, and a huge, horrid plastic mushroom that finally swallowed the stage. The audience goes through so many sensual shocks and associations that it usually doesn't occur to them to wonder whether they've seen anything but spectacle.

Coming from a modern dance background and arriving, somewhat more demurely, at a similar point is Louis Falco. For the Boston Ballet in 1971 he choreographed *The Gamete Garden*, which featured an astonishing ten-foot stack of wooden cages containing live chickens, parrots, doves, ducks, turkeys; and aeons of desolate dancing. *Caviar* (1970) had a rock band in hippie garb singing about ecology, dancers clumping around in foam-rubber space shoes and playing with some life-size foam-rubber sharks. Falco and his company are playful and ingratiating, which gives them a different look from ordinary dancers. They seem actually to be the casual kids they dance about. The fact that his choreography is formless and interminable doesn't seem important.

Sloganeering par excellence is the mission of Maurice Béjart's Ballet of the 20th Century. Béjart has often stated that he wants to make dance everyone can understand, and he does it with a curious intermingling of virtuosic fragments and plain business. It's a kind of magic formula: the viewer sits there watching these superior beings who can coolly overcome all our prosaic afflictions of clumsiness and inertia—and suddenly they're showing us our thing! These supermen seem to have noticed *us* by appropriating our clothes, our dissatisfactions and lusts, even our pedestrian fantasies, and their flattery endears them to us.

Pop dance, while it is not the most creative or profound of all dance forms, is one of the most vital. Audiences love it. Dancers want to work in it because it challenges their technical skills. Choreographers enjoy its freedom from artistic restraints and pretensions. Maybe only critics find it hard to stomach. To me it is unbearably tame. For all its exploitation of techniques, its alertness to current events and processes, it never takes risks. It never makes me see something I didn't already know, and it puts too cheap a price on its own wares.

Creeping Orthodoxy

A few weeks ago a friend referred to the City Center Joffrey Ballet, more in sadness than cynicism, as an orthodox company. If true, this would indicate quite a metamorphosis. Consider that only twelve years ago the principal assets of the Robert Joffrey Ballet consisted of six dancers and a station wagon. And the station wagon was rented.

Orthodoxy in my friend's terms, I think, meant official sponsorship and the implicit responsibility for proving one's point over and over in the most persuasive, accessible manner. In American dance, probably only two companies would qualify for orthodox status, the Joffrey and the New York City Ballet, and they have a common tendency to stay away from the experimental, the controversial, and the idealistic failure. Neither company started out quite this way, but both have gradually accepted the tyranny of popular taste and economic pressure. Their job now is to produce, regularly and on a big scale, professional, inoffensive, and if possible stylish ballets.

This the Joffrey does extremely well. Its productions are attractive if not lavish, its dancers are excellent, and it even succeeds, through its evident enthusiasm for what it's doing, in establishing a warm rapport with its audiences. In choreography, though, the Joffrey Ballet offers little of substance. Its repertory is like some calorie-free soft drink—light and sparkly without the aftereffects, or the exhilaration, of champagne.

Novelties are always in demand by a press and public insatiably hungry for new flavor, if not for nourishment. This fall season three new works were prepared. At this writing I have not seen Gerald Arpino's *Fanfarita*, postponed owing to an injury to one of the dancers.

Arpino's *A Light Fantastic* is as vulgar as a big piece of junk jewelry. On paper it looks like a charming suite of court dances set to Benjamin Britten's Elizabethan music from *Gloriana*. On stage it is overdone in every way imaginable, from the elaborate costumes to the cutesy humor to the swarms of dancers diffusing the purity of the pre-classic line. Even the music, posing a small consort of amplified instruments against the full orchestra, makes too much of a simple thing.

The Danish dancer-choreographer Flemming Flindt revived *The Lesson*, based on Ionesco's play, for the Joffrey company. Although Flindt has transformed the philosophy professor of the play into a ballet master, the dance values in this work are surprisingly minimal. A naturalistic set establishes a mood of Broadway drama that is hard to shake off. Not until about the midpoint, when the professor's homicidal intent begins to assert itself, does the ballet begin to project the maniacal terror of the plot in dance terms rather than pantomimic ones.

The Lesson does represent a dramatic strain that shows up too infrequently in the Joffrey repertory. Almost half the company's twenty-five ballets are the work of Gerald Arpino, a serviceable choreographer who is inventive but seldom creative. He works primarily in a neoclassic vein of pure, lyric dance, and his more serious works, *Incubus*, *Nightwings*, *The Clowns*, and *Elegy*, take place within the already artificial structures belonging to dream, psychosis, or fantasy, where the audience doesn't have to become particularly involved with the tormented characters. Arpino seems unable to make a strong statement directly out of the material of life, as did Jerome Robbins in *Moves*, and Anna Sokolow in *Opus '65*.

Arpino's lack of choreographic gutsiness is consistent with what seem to be the aims of the company. Certainly they have an authentic, committed masterpiece in Kurt Jooss' *The Green Table*, but on the surface even this ballet can be seen as a period piece, like Ruthanna Boris's *Cakewalk* and Lew Christensen's *Con Amore*. The most uncompromising and disturbing human statement that the company has presented since its installation at the City Center was Anna Sokolow's *Rooms*. This stark document of loneliness wasn't pretty; it was powerful, and it said something genuine about the way we live. Revived last fall, it was dropped after two performances.

Apart from the dances mentioned, and Joffrey's own *Astarte*, the repertory comprises pleasant, plotless ballets by Joffrey,

Christensen, and George Balanchine. The dancers, most of them trained at Joffrey's highly respected American Ballet Center, perform everything lovingly and with spirit. If they seem a little light on the dramatic side, they probably haven't had enough practice.

There is a mod trend in the activities of the Joffrey Ballet, which, for me, somehow is symbolized by the use of amplification for practically all solo instruments, the cello in *Cello Concerto*, the consort in *A Light Fantastic*, and so on. I find the Joffrey's fashionable electronic gimmicks and plastic props fatiguing and superfluous, since they only dress up ideas that would look better in the flesh, or conceal something that might be unsettling if we really examined it.

The City Center Joffrey Ballet is the tourist attraction of the dance world. Like some air-conditioned Hilton Hotel in a tropical country, it keeps you away from snakes, bad food, and dirty natives, but you can look out at the scenery and pretend you've been there.

October 28, 1968

Moon Worship, circa 1968

What more can you say about something that has made the cover of *Time*? Quite a lot, actually, if the something is Robert Joffrey's mixed-media ballet *Astarte*. Thanks to *Time*'s astronomical circulation, the world now knows that *Astarte* is a psychedelic blend of film, lights, rock music, and dancing; that the hero, Maximiliano Zomosa, walks up onto the stage from the audience, strips to his shorts, performs some orgiastic rites with Trinette Singleton, and then strolls out the back door of the theater. Right out onto the street in practically his altogether.

Sex, nudity, and far-out effects. You couldn't invent a better formula for success in today's theater. The interesting thing about *Astarte* is that it's a good dance too. It not only conjures

III

up that total, turned-on involvement that seems to be so important now, but it also manages to be in itself a comment on the process.

Mixed media is not new in dance. In fact, since theater dance has always been a mixture of media, you might say that only the technology has changed. But since the advent of technological improvements in lighting, electronic modification of sound, and film projections, ten years ago or more, people like Alwin Nikolais, Merce Cunningham, and innumerable younger choreographers have been experimenting with these new elements of production, and have used them as constituents of some revolutionary dance forms.

Astarte does no such thing. While Nikolais transformed his dancers into elements of design, and Cunningham split up the scene into dozens of simultaneous discrete events, and the Happeners threw off all the structural proprieties, Joffrey uses an essentially conventional approach to production. The musicians are in the pit, the dancers have the stage, the film is their backdrop, and the audience watches from out front. The movement is a carefully choreographed duet that would probably have the same effect—less intense but the same idea—if you took away the film, lights, and music.

Like most other ballets, *Astarte* uses decor and sound as an adjunct to movement, to comment on and enhance the central idea embodied in the dancing. The total involvement part comes from an extraordinarily skillful use of some extraordinarily compelling theater devices. At a production cost of $60,000, it's also probably the biggest mixed-media dance ever done.

In a less sophisticated age we could become totally involved in a good book. Now we demand that more of our senses take part, and *Astarte* activates nearly all of them. Tom Skelton's flashing strobe lights impress blossoming rainbows onto our eyeballs and chop a movement sequence into stop-action photography. The Crome Syrcus' amplified beat pounds in our ears, leaving an almost sexual depletion when it stops. Gardner Compton's film transports us into a fourth dimension of image upon distorted image, all based on the actual movement that is tangible before us.

Astarte lures us, envelops us into its world of sensations. Each viewer's experience of the dance is intensely personal, not shared with the other members of the audience. The two protagonists likewise are almost entirely isolated from each other, almost entirely in the power of external stimuli. What is going on is not so much a love duet, or even a hate duet, as two people reacting to demands on their own nervous systems, the way we would brush away a biting insect or stretch out our hands to a fire.

When Zomosa rises from his seat, he is oblivious to the theatrical environment, which, as I have indicated, is for the benefit of the audience. He moves to the stage and slowly strips, with his whole focus riveted to Miss Singleton, who stands in icy stillness apparently giving off vibrations that he finds irresistible. The duet begins, a slow, controlled wooing in which each partner seems to be answering some internal needs of his own, rather than the demands of the other. Each one seems to be spiraling ever deeper into an accelerating and intensifying inner vortex.

Their two characters are very different. She is Astarte, the inviolable moon goddess, remote and unyielding. He is the seeker, the moth consumed in flame. His movement is sustained, strong, always directed to the object of his desire, but cautious, not too familiar. She moves with percussive emphasis and swooping assertion, never adapting her body to his embraces, but angling herself around him, or extending her arms and legs out of his reach. For much of the dance they occupy separate areas of the stage, but even when they dance together, they have little sense of each other's space. Each one, separately, reaches a climax that is expressed in destructive fury. Each one, in a sense, rapes the other. When they move apart at the end, neither one has been satisfied or changed.

Astarte has to do with the kind of atavistic, preintellectual experience that relies on an instinctive receiving of stimuli and an equally uncerebral response to them. It is the kind of experience that has been essential in primitive forms of religion and dance. In today's furthest-out theater it's the kind of thing that makes folks want to take their clothes off and embrace complete strangers. It's dangerous and it's healthy. If you're not ready for the more uninhibited variety, *Astarte* is a very good, very straight sample.

October 21, 1968

Spare the Confetti

With every season the nicest things about the City Center Joffrey Ballet get harder to see because the company is so anxiously pointing out the obvious. Robert Joffrey's own *Pas des Déesses*, for example, has slowly ripened from a gently amusing little tribute to three great nineteenth-century ballerinas into something close to satire. There's no reason why the romantic ballet style should be any more ridiculous today than it was in 1954, when Joffrey choreographed the piece. In fact, the Joffrey treats that very style respectfully in its revival of August Bournonville's *Konservatoriet*—too respectfully almost, as if they don't quite know what to make of an idea that isn't a biff-bam swinger.

One might ask, of course, how we know what the romantic style and period really were, or any balletic genre for that matter. In moments of extreme despair about dance ever learning how to hold onto its past, I think there's no use even trying to revive a period ballet authentically. Perhaps there wouldn't be so much hue and cry about whether the Joffrey's *Petrouchka* is or isn't the REAL *Petrouchka* if the Joffrey hadn't insisted so loudly in advance that it is. But the question, especially in reference to this ballet, seems academic.

In the nearly sixty years since its creation by Michel Fokine for the Diaghilev ballet, innumerable productions of *Petrouchka* have been mounted, each making slight changes that later became incorporated as gospel. The Alexandre Benois costume sketches that the Joffrey Ballet has so faithfully reproduced are conspicuously dated 1947 by the artist. They were done for a production at La Scala. Was that Benois' 1947 recollection of his original 1911 designs? Or a reconsidered, updated version? And if we aren't even sure about the visuals, when some drawings and photographs of the original do exist, how can anyone know what changes have come about in the choreography itself over the years? No reference book in my library tells me exactly what the famous crowd movement was that has been so agonized over in every new production. Nor do I know which particular artistic infidelity caused Leonide Massine to stage and then violently disavow the Joffrey production.

Maybe the best we can hope for in a new *Petrouchka* is that it live up to some of our imaginings about what kind of a ballet it "really" was, and what made it so celebrated. This one does and it doesn't.

It is extremely beautiful to look at and hear. The opening and closing scenes at the fair satisfy my inner vision of Old Russia, and the bits of character dancing Fokine (or somebody) wove into the swirling action of the motley crowd make dramatic sense instead of just being divertissements. When the whole stage begins pulsating to Stravinsky's memorable Dance of the Nursemaids and Coachmen, I can believe that Diaghilev's Ballets Russes was a stupendous moment in the history of dance, not just a nostalgic fabrication of some exiled aristocrats.

It is in the difficult portrayals of the three mysterious puppets with the almost human emotions, and their impresario, who may be either a clairvoyant or a con man, that Fokine left us the greater challenge. Something spooky is going on among these four characters, and the audience has to feel it, or else *Petrouchka* becomes just another spectacle or an expensive antique.

Christian Holder's Blackamoor came across most vividly to me, a crude primitive who scares the others not because he's bright enough to have any evil intentions but because he's so big and black and hungry. Yurek Lazowski, who assisted Massine in this revival, mimes the Old Showman with uninspired competence, as if he could do the part in his sleep. Both Susan Magno and Erika Goodman play the Ballerina with the requisite Coppélia-like automatism, though Miss Magno has a suggestion of a calculating glitter behind her unblinking eyes.

Edward Verso, the only Petrouchka I have seen so far (other members of the company are alternating in all three puppet roles), has grasped the choreography admirably, the character less so. Fokine made Petrouchka a rag-doll puppet, as opposed to the Blackamoor and the Ballerina, who are stiff, wind-up toys.

Verso is literally spineless: a floppy, agitated creature who is never able to impel himself by using his own weight, but instead gets going by kicking out his feet, shrugging his shoulders, dangling his torso from outstretched arms, collapsing into a rolling fall. But Verso doesn't yet project the suffering soul of Petrouchka as the universal buffoon, conscience, and fall guy that all great clowns are; so finally the ballet is unconvincing.

In its continual pursuit of amusing, inconsequential ballets, the Joffrey has come up with an early John Cranko piece, *Pineapple Poll*, which has almost everybody ostentatiously chewing the scenery at some point. Rebecca Wright, Burton Taylor, Gary Chryst, and Diana Cartier are very funny in *Pineapple Poll*, but the piece is drastically overstuffed with typical Crankovian borrowings from every conceivable variety of expressive dance, repeated several times, doubled and redoubled by having six or twelve dancers do it. *Pineapple Poll* makes you grin till your ears ache.

Meanwhile the Joffrey keeps offering new ballets by its resident choreographer Gerald Arpino. This season's premieres were in Arpino's well-known vein of flashy eclecticism: *Solarwind*, an inscrutable, pretentious, quasi-modern piece that seemed to be about a boy trying to choose between boys and girls, but may not have been about that at all, but I didn't care; and *Confetti*, a piece for three couples that featured beribboned tambourines and matched its Rossini score by making the least impression with the punchiest energy in the shortest possible time. *Confetti* did show a virtuosic side of the dancers that one doesn't often see, and I especially liked Francesca Corkle's subtle changes in tempo and dynamics; she doesn't do every step exactly like every other, which is a rarer attitude in a dancer than you might think.

You have to act fast to catch the best parts of the Joffrey repertory because they are scheduled so seldom. The magnificent *Green Table* has been recast and lovingly rehearsed back to life by its creator, Kurt Jooss, but it won't be done any more this season. Neither will Jerome Robbins' *Moves*. In the past few seasons, some of Joffrey's most promising dancers have left the company just as they started to get interesting. The present repertory is making notable underachievers out of several

youngsters, and you had better get over and see them while
they're still around.

March 30, 1970

※◇※

Trinity

Gerald Arpino's new ballet, *Trinity*, given its New York premiere October 7 by the City Center Joffrey Ballet, begins with
some pseudo-baroque chords played through a loudspeaker by
a brass choir. I couldn't tell if the music was live or not, though
there was a conductor in the pit making signals to someone. As
the whole synthetic exercise proceeded, I could see it was going
to be a typical Joffrey Ballet success: plugged in, turned on,
supersmart, and absolute superficiality guaranteed.

Trinity is a very noisy ballet, very big and punchy and calculated. It starts out at about Mach 9, slows down briefly to the
speed of sound, and then revs up again heading for home. Despite its loaded title and its pompous section headings—Sunday,
Summerland, Saturday** (here a footnote tells us that the word
Saturday is derived from the ancient "Sabbath")—*Trinity* isn't
about anything. It just wants the audience to be knocked out.
The fifteen dancers perform it with terrific oomph and sincerity, like the people who sing the jingles about how you can
satisfy your libido by driving a Comanche or whatever it is
down the New Jersey Turnpike.

When the ballet begins, boys are running and leaping hellbent
across the stage, for some reason. The grand jeté, a surefire
audience rouser, is usually saved for somewhere in the middle
of a piece, when everybody gets worked up to it. By starting
with jetés, Arpino might have been making a daring experiment, but subsequently it becomes clear that he hasn't a thing
on his mind except bravura—and if there's one thing Arpino is
good at, it's bravura.

Led by Christian Holder, Gary Chryst, Dermot Burke, and Rebecca Wright, the company races in and out, sometimes adding a jazzy twist or a few rock gyrations to movement that is basically classical. Every good turn is done several times, and in the slowish second section Arpino multiplies a pas de deux into a stageful of group acrobatics.

Besides the airborne virtuosity of those fast, near-collision jetés, the applause-getters include Holder turning and stepping straight down to the footlights while rotating his head—an old Alvin Ailey bit; the company locked in a circle with Holder hallelujahing in the center; boys running while holding up girls with one hand; and Gary Chryst's militant fist slamming into the air. There is the mandatory moment when the whole company lines up across the stage and advances, flinty-eyed, toward the audience. At last everybody comes in and places a lighted candle on the floor, while a long volley of pile-driver chords keeps firing from the pit.

Arpino has made much worse ballets than *Trinity*, but none, I think, so cynical. It uses the appurtenances of youthful communion and commitment to sell the idea that the Joffrey Ballet is youthful and committed. It disguises the same old tired ballet clichés in the dynamics of now, so that old tired businessmen can sit in their seven-dollar orchestra seats and yell, "Right on!"

October 21, 1970

Reflections

Gerald Arpino seems able to choreograph in any style, mood, or period ever imagined by Western man. In some of his recent works, like *Confetti*, *Trinity*, and the new *Reflections*, he also seems to be trying for the world's record at sheer number of steps per square inch.

Reflections had its New York premiere February 24 during the second week of the City Center Joffrey Ballet's spring season. Seeing it immediately after Jerome Robbins' stark, silent *Moves* only emphasized its force-fed quality. *Reflections* is all hormones and no bone structure.

The piece is set to Tschaikovsky's Variations on a Rococo Theme for cello and orchestra, and as the first girls flutter in wearing pale pink, skimpy little ballet dresses, you're unavoidably reminded of Balanchine—*Allegro Brillante, Suite No. 3.* Even that funny, rainstorm sound of many feet running in ballet shoes is Balanchinian. As the ballet progresses it recalls even more Balanchine's several versions of the last act of *Raymonda,* one of which, *Pas de Dix,* used to be in the Joffrey Ballet repertory and is regrettably no longer done.

Like the *Raymonda* divertissements, *Reflections* is a series of variations for a small ensemble of dancers, in this case ten of them. They are arranged in solos, duets, and trios, and everybody gets a chance in the limelight. The piece is introduced by seven girls and ends in a big, scrambling finale where they are joined for the first time by all three men, and everyone does as many things as they can before striking a decorative tableau just in the nick of time as the curtain falls.

The ballet is oddly out of focus. It's hard to see how it could be, since it's just an innocent string of dances. But it's busy, unpredictable. It looks classical but it has no refinement. It lacks the serenity of those ordered hierarchies of dancers, movements, parts of the stage that define the classical. It hasn't got the kind of good breeding that lingers over a beloved combination long enough to really see it, really develop it. Arpino throws in ideas sixteen to the dozen; too impatient even to wait for his music, he sometimes crams three solos into one musical variation.

Erika Goodman does a slow, reserved duet with Glenn White and later a more peppy one with Henry Berg. Since there's no ballerina in the work, one wonders why she ranks two men while five other girls get none. Starr Danias and Dennis Wayne have a duet in which they repeatedly cut into their own punch lines by getting to the end of a phrase and instantly shifting to do the same thing on the other side. Dana Sapiro, Charthel Arthur, Francesca Corkle, Denise Jackson, and Sue Loyd were the other girls, but they flew in and out so fast I'm not sure who did what.

Arpino's restless lack of discrimination is obtrusive in a pure-dance work with no message or narrative for glue. He has a good eye for style, and he obviously loves showing off his dancers, but once he gets style and execution together he thinks he's got a ballet, and the more the better. *Reflections* is like one of those fanatically complex machines or intricate watchworks built for display, whirring and turning in its own precision-tooled elegance and never making anything happen.

March 4, 1971

Valentine

We had this prizefight here the other day, you might have heard about it. Everybody here heard about it anyway. Women read the sports pages, knots of men gathered around radios, and political columnists wrote moral little essays about it. Barely two days later the City Center Joffrey Ballet premiered a new work by Gerald Arpino called *Valentine*, and it turned out to be a prizefight. It's not the Ballet of the Century, but it was certainly the most topical thing on a stage that week, so score another for the Joffrey Ballet, which has made a career out of being au courant.

The two contestants were Rebecca Wright and Christian Holder. Not unlike Messrs. Ali and Frazier, they played antagonistic types, the same types they do in other Joffrey ballets. She is the hard-boiled, kooky, dumb-like-a-fox female, and he's the rough, tough, sexy guy who's really like warm ice cream inside. Jerome Robbins invented them years ago.

The other character in *Valentine* is the music. This is Jacob Druckman's Valentine for solo contrabass, played, hit, scraped, sung, grunted, and hiccuped by Alvin Brehm, who wears a black and white referee's shirt and track shoes. He is not a stock character at least, though Druckman must have modeled him on the whacky, witty cellist Gwendolyn Watson, who's accompanied so many modern dancers over the past few years. I'd love to see those two in a battle or a duet sometime.

There isn't much more to be said about this trifle. Wright and Holder eye each other, dance around the ring, spar, go into clinches. They whiz through all sorts of awkward feints and holds, stop abruptly in midair, flop to the ground, jump up, and square off again. Referee Brehm keeps buzzing and twittering away, occasionally giving a strangled shout that the dancers answer monosyllabically. The fight ends in a draw, with Holder and Wright down but still punching and yelling, and Brehm also sprawled on the floor under his bass viol, still fiddling.

I'd swear Arpino whipped up *Valentine* while waiting for the returns to come in from Madison Square Garden, the way I might bake a pie on a snowy day. But I can't fault the piece for being what it is, just fun. Almost everything at the Joffrey Ballet is like that now—diverting, undemanding, good clean energetic fun. Fun, fun, it's coming out my ears. Help!

March 19, 1971

Real Rock Ballet: Why?

As the ovation was subsiding after the premiere of Gerald Arpino's *Trinity* last fall, a man behind me said in a deeply satisfied voice to his companion, "I've been waiting a long time for a real rock ballet, and I think this is it." I was amazed. Not because the man thought *Trinity* was a real rock ballet, but that he had been waiting for it.

What is rock ballet anyway, and why would anybody need one? Dance is experiencing a great surge of popularity today, and that tends to bring a demand for facile, showy, instantly absorbable, instantly forgettable new items. Though rock ballet isn't any more thrilling than ballet-ballet, gypsy ballet, nostalgia ballet, psychological ballet, or ballet of the absurd, none of these have the swingers losing any sleep. I haven't got any final explanations of the rock ballet phenomenon, but one thing I'm sure of: rock ballet has to look contemporary and with-it, but it isn't required to make a new artistic statement. In fact, it shouldn't.

All ballet is basically a traditional form. Over the centuries it has borrowed stylistic elements from almost every imaginable source—folk and Asiatic dance, commedia dell'arte, the ballroom, jazz, modern dance, rock—without losing its own character. Real innovation, in the sense of changing our concept of what the stage is for, who the dancer is, why or how the event is taking place, seldom occurs in ballet.

I think the last ballet of any kind to imagine the ballet performance in a new way was Robert Joffrey's *Astarte* (1967), and that innovation came entirely in its use of the stage space. With its huge, billowing screen and filmed images of the dancers, dematerialized, larger and more changeable than life, *Astarte* was able to comment on the tiny, hard-edge reality of the live performers. No ballet since *Astarte* has gone so far in revising the balletic concept.

Although it used no rock movement, confining itself to the vocabulary of modern ballet, *Astarte* was the first important rock ballet. It had a commissioned score by the Crome Syrcus, and dozens of ballets afterward picked up the big, warm, throbbing amplified beat and the nasal, unintelligible lyric, both of which you didn't have to go to a ballet theater for, but lots of people did.

The next thing that happened in rock ballet was *Trinity*, a plotless work in which Arpino attempted to translate the driving energy underlying hard rock into a modified balletic movement, instead of ignoring the music as *Astarte* had done, or using literal pop dances as many minor rock ballets did. *Trinity* added a visual electricity to the audible charge that the music had been providing all along. Aesthetically, I found it very effective and very vulgar, but that combination is always a possibility when you do too much of a highly specialized thing.

For the past two weeks Les Grands Ballets Canadiens have

been presenting their version of The Who's rock opera *Tommy*
here at City Center. Now *Tommy* is quite a different kind of rock
ballet again, most traditional and possibly most successful of all.
It's a dramatization, with choreography by Fernand Nault, of
a traumatized misfit who becomes a cult hero and finally a dis-
honored prophet. Except that there's not much dancing, I can't
see how *Tommy* is any different from *Swan Lake* or *The Nutcracker*. The dancers portray characters in a well-known story
with beloved music. The production is pretty, especially David
Jenkins' black and silver plastic Peter Max scenery. And of
course there's that beat.

As one of the few members of the audience who wasn't familiar with the music, I felt unusually innocent about *Tommy*, as
if I'd stumbled upon some tribal celebration in the jungle. I kept
seeing it in two or three ways at once. The ballet critic was
reminded of Antony Tudor's *Undertow* and its progeny, a long
string of lugubrious narratives about how a callous society
maims its sensitive young men.

The social critic thought how incredibly self-indulgent
Tommy is, how everyone in the story, especially the hero, is so
deeply into his own thing. "I'm a sensation," Tommy sings, and,
addressing a mirror, "At your feet I see the glory." Maybe all
the "new" religions are no more than the age-old wail of the
newborn: "See me, Feel me, Touch me, Heal me." I'm sure I
wasn't supposed to infer that the radiant love symbol, Tommy,
has a satanic doppelgänger in Charles Manson. But I did.

Unlike either *Astarte* or *Trinity*, *Tommy* is childlike in its
appeal and its sentiment. Like true pop art it's literal and a bit
reactionary. People look at it and see their hi-fi daydreams come
to life in kandy kolors. It's as good-natured and harmless,
though not nearly so clever, as *The Yellow Submarine*.

April 25, 1971

Louis Falco

Louis Falco is a popularizer. Reports of his emergence as an important choreographer are premature. They do a grave injustice to the real modern dance innovators whom he copies and the experimenters he hasn't heard of yet, and may even hurt Falco himself. Caught up in his own publicity, Falco is so busy doing faddy things that he doesn't even know when he's got something interesting.

Ibid, the first of two—or possibly three—new works seen at the ANTA Theater February 1, featured a strip of fluorescent lights reaching completely across the proscenium and suspended about three feet from the floor. This sensational decor had nothing to do with the dance, except to make it hard to see. Merce Cunningham and Paul Taylor, among others, have played with distorting our perception of dance by means of light or scenery, and no doubt there are still more variations to be rung on that theme. What makes it work, when it works, is the changing relationship between the dancers and the gimmick. Falco's idea is static. Once you've seen it you know everything about it.

The dance seemed to be a mild flirtation, with Georgiana Holmes doing academic turns and jumps, and Maathews Kheaann Khristiaann walking around playing a beautiful, long, wooden flutelike instrument. Miss Holmes finally snuggled up to Khristiaann and the flute. Later in the concert *Ibid* was repeated or continued. Mary Jane Eisenberg replaced Miss Holmes in the clinch. Dancer Matthew Diamond challenged the flute player, who won easily with a few musical blows. I liked the way Khristiaann looked—tall, thin, sinuous, and remote, with long arms cradling his flute.

The dance had the appearance of strangeness and improvisatory density that you often find in Cunningham. In this case, the garish light concealed the fact that nothing much else was going on, whereas with Cunningham if you can ignore the offending prop, the dancing behind it is fascinating.

The Sleepers, Falco's other premiere, also looked like an improvisation, an acting one this time. Four dancers, Holmes, Diamond, Jennifer Muller, and Juan Antonio, are lying on the floor among piles of feathers. They are evidently in bed together. They try to get comfortable. They pair off into couples. They fight. They tease each other. They make love. Talking all the time. The talking is funny initially, but even that goes on too long, while the dancing is mostly the same José Limón stuff Falco has been doing for years.

The Sleepers reminded me of Albee, Pinter, sexy movies where they run around the guy's bedroom naked, shouting obscenities at each other and laughing. It reminded me of James Cunningham's much more brilliant dance *Lauren's Dream*, done a year ago at Judson Church, and of Erin Martin's sensitive *The Day of the Dead*, seen at La Mama ETC last month. I don't believe in Falco's fun sex, or his now dances like the pious pro-ecology bore *Caviar*. He has craftsmanship, but he's an artistic parasite. He extracts the chlorophyll from healthier growing things and converts it to chewing gum.

February 20, 1971

※❦❀

Lar Lubovitch

Lar Lubovitch's choreography is more like marching: relentless, repetitive, and always waving somebody's flag.

Lubovitch and company opened a week of performances November 17 at Stage City, a big off-off-Broadway space in which a room-size ramp had been built for the occasion and upholstered with foam rubber. The audience lounged on the ramp, as if it were a soft hillside. The dancing had the same spectacular chic.

Lubovitch luxuriates in his dancers' bodies, especially those of the men, who are bare-chested as often as possible. The sensuality of rippling muscles and hard physical work and long, flowing hair is what claims your attention. That and the beat.

This dancing is inexorably rhythmic. Every beat is stressed, usually by pushing into the floor with the weight. The dancers seem always to be galloping or stamping or pressing themselves out of a skip or rushing across the floor with a regular downward impulse.

They maintain their connectedness with the ground by often walking low with knees bent, or digging into an exaggerated heel-first step, and they seem to draw upon some kind of gravitational strength as they pound on the floor with straight-armed fists or slap their own rib cages obsessively. There isn't any lightness or upward swing to this choreography, no sense of flying out into space.

The other characteristic of Lubovitch's movement style is its size. He's given to huge simultaneous body changes—on one beat the dancer drops to the floor and curls into a ball, the next beat he's propped up on one leg and arm, reaching for the ceiling. Or you may see just one big gesture, thrust out at high intensity in emphatic unison.

The movement is too active and forceful to become monotonous, but I tune it out after I've had enough pummeling.

Lubovitch's choreography follows the simplistic pattern of his movement style. He showed two new works in addition to his Handel oratory *Some of the Reactions of Some of the People Some of the Time upon Hearing Reports of the Coming of the Messiah,* and *Whirligogs,* a dance about dehumanization to a section of Luciano Berio's marvelous Sinfonia for orchestra and voices.

Social, to the soprano-contralto duet from Bach's Cantata No. 78, had four women in dated evening gowns posturing formally while a line of five shirtless men in black pants and cummerbunds stalked past, oblivious to their charms. At the end they paired off unenthusiastically, and the odd man looked relieved.

Clear Lake, with music from a Mendelssohn string quartet, was an "Ah, we are all swans imprisoned in human flesh" dance. After a lot of vehement group maneuvers, Lubovitch and Sally Trammell, idealized in amber light, twine around each other while the others jog and laugh—being people on a picnic instead of dancers. At the last moment they gaze wonderingly up at the sky and down at the water, and Lubovitch carries Trammell across the middle distance.

December 10, 1971

Béjart Opens

This is a big season for foreign dance companies—about ten have played here to date—but none was more heavily promoted or expectantly awaited than Maurice Béjart's Ballet du XXe Siècle. Its arrival January 25 at Brooklyn Academy overshadowed even the coming of Rudolf Nureyev with the Australian Ballet the following day. Rudy we've seen before, but of Béjart New York knew nothing but rumors, blurbs, and televised teasers. Béjart wasn't exactly modern and he wasn't exactly ballet. He didn't exactly do drama and he didn't do pure dance. He was definitely theatrical and unashamedly popular, so we were told. All of which could mean anything.

What it meant to me, on first look, was a very highly trained, hard-sell company doing eccentric, obvious choreography for all it's worth. "The dance is visual music," Béjart states in a program note. But after the long opening night program I felt I hadn't experienced very much dance *or* music.

Choreographic Offering, the curtain raiser, begins not with a curtain going up, but with an even more dramatic device. As the audience enters the theater, the dancers are warming up on the bare stage, with a white floor cloth and the Academy's brick wall newly whitewashed and lots of white light flooding the area.

Throughout the warm-up a girl in an army shirt, pants, and black boots sits at the edge of the stage looking out with a frozen stare. At the end of the ballet she reappears and offers the audience a rose. She represents LIFE, the program says, and she is

127

supposed to reconcile the classical and contemporary elements symbolized in the ballet. Accompanied alternately by portions of Bach's Musical Offering and some loud percussion by Fernand Schirren, the piece is meant to show off the company, and it does. I'd like it better if it weren't so doggedly clever.

Bhakti is a very long piece based on Hindu Themes, with a lot of ritualistic trudging around by men in devotional poses, and three blue-jeaned hippies tripping out on visions of Rama, Krishna, Shiva, and other deities. The choreography, combining suggestions of Indian postures with standard balletic movement, was executed well by all the soloists, but Paolo Bortoluzzi also caught the rhythm of Indian dance, the fluent distribution of weight that makes Indian movement so alive and rich. His solo made the evening for me.

As if the company's U.S. debut wasn't enough for one occasion, the program also included the return of Suzanne Farrell to New York. Miss Farrell, late of the New York City Ballet, has joined Béjart after a year of relative inactivity, and her appearance almost eclipsed that of the company itself. She danced *Erotica*, a duet, with Daniel Lommel. Though Béjart choreographed it in 1965, it might have been made to show off Farrell's spectacular extensions, the slow curvings of her back, and all her sultry little angularities.

In case we didn't get the point that Farrell is supposed to be a sexy superstar, a front curtain was covered with adoring graffiti, and the ballet's decor consisted of twelve-foot blown-up glamour photos of herself and Lommel. M. Lommel didn't have much to do except gawk ecstatically at Farrell or her picture.

February 2, 1971

Poster Art

Maurice Béjart's ballets remind me of Soviet music: you can't really say the artistic values are secondary to the propaganda values because the two have fused into a single, bombastic hammer blow. According to Béjart, I think, art is proselytizing, is utilitarian, is alphabet-clear, and that automatically makes it beautiful. According to Béjart, art is that which works. I'm not sure what he thinks dance is, except that he often puts down everybody else's dance as overspecialized.

Having sat through five programs of Béjart's Ballet of the 20th Century, during its celebrated U.S. debut at Brooklyn Academy, I can report that Béjart's ballets work. The audience always gets the point. However, I don't find them beautiful, new, or interesting. I find them, in fact, stupefyingly anti-dance and anti-intellectual. When Béjart announces the stripping away of all artifices of the picturesque in order to retain the essential forces of mankind—he, or the translator of his voluminous program notes, actually talks that way—it sounds to me more like a pious justification for a lack of dance ideas.

Béjart has created an aura for himself, and a fanatical audience for his work. He panders to them by claiming to have founded a new art form that, naturally, won't be understood by the sophisticated snobs but that the common people in their honest sensitivity can embrace; he stuns them with an eclecticism that borrows successful effects from everywhere and risks no inventions of its own; and he disarms them by the bravado with which he reduces tremendous ideas to their least common denominator.

Take Béjart's use of music, for instance. He doesn't waste much time hunting up innocuous little Drigo serenades that won't compete with the dancing. He chooses monuments—

Bach, Beethoven, some of the Western world's most popular classical music. But what he choreographs, inevitably, is the simplicity that made the music popular, not the complexity that made it great.

So in *Le Sacre du Printemps* you see big mass explosions and rushes of movement, underlining the dynamic exclamations of the music, but nothing of Stravinsky's savage rhythms, his orchestral complexity, his strange and subtle sonorities, his Slavic shifts of temperament. There is no trace of the ballet's original scenario, and no suggestion of what Lincoln Kirstein has called the "seriously ugly" look of the Nijinsky version that scandalized Paris in 1913.

What Béjart substitutes for all of this is effects. Twenty men spinning in the air while one man in the center does a spread-eagled jump. Twenty girls in faultless unison changing level or direction, unwinding from a line to a circle or a plastique formation. Couples doing pelvic rotations and other simulated eroticisms in unison and on the beat, then lifting the lead couple and clustering below them for a final tableau that is nothing if not picturesque.

It's all very intense and visually pleasing, but shallow and in a curious way lifeless. The dancers aren't spontaneous and personal, as the best American dancers are. Most often they seem conscious of themselves only as an element of design or a tool of the drama. Whether in masses or small groups, they dance as though before a mirror. They're so preoccupied with their own stage power that they never play to each other.

I think another reason Béjart's work seems static is that he's so short on ideas or a point of view about anything. He presents you with a fact and doesn't develop it. The *Sacre* touts sexuality, in *Actus Tragicus* he shows you that death is sad and it's happy, *Opus 5* is a supposedly subtle variation of a few academic steps. He's heavily into rituals and political allusions, but his idea of liberated practice is to have his one black dancer do only barefoot parts and roll on the floor a lot.

Béjart movement features endless repeats of the same few positions. The beat is inexorable, the phrase nonexistent. His language is so impoverished that he seems unable to do two things at a time or connect those ever-present poses. He ar-

130

ranges Bach, the master of counterpoint, so that only one dancer or group moves at a time, or at best devises a plain little canon. In *Bach Sonata* he gave Suzanne Farrell a solo in which she seemingly had to change every body part at once, on every beat. This resulted in a sequence of such illogical twitches and posturings that Jorge Donn repeated it, as if to prove we really had seen it happen.

Béjart's emotional content seems to revolve around the satisfactions of religious trance and unisex. His well-publicized version of *Firebird* has incredibly pretentious notes jumbling up revolution, art, and several other holies, but the ballet is almost completely abstract. The only reason I could see for doing it was to replace the ballerina with a boy-firebird. It was not an improvement.

There is a contemptuousness for the audience that runs close to the democratic surface of Béjart's polemics. He obviously thinks they are too dumb to understand any art that is deep and connects with real feelings. So he gives them tracts and spectacle. The closest thing we have to Béjart in this country is at Radio City Music Hall, which holds three times as many people as Brooklyn Academy. I think Béjart should have played there.

February 21, 1971

I Can't Hear the Music

This is the year of Stravinsky tributes in ballet. Eliot Feld is choreographing two Stravinsky ballets for Ballet Theatre, to be seen this winter in Washington and New York, and the New York City Ballet plans a huge retrospective for spring.

Maurice Béjart's Ballet of the 20th Century, returning to the United States for a second smash-hit visit, opened a two-week season at City Center November 24 with an all-Stravinsky program. I'd call that blasphemy if Stravinsky's music weren't too alive and immediate to be considered sacred.

Béjart uses music like a pair of boots, for its utilitarian strength and support. All nuance, color, intelligence is crushed by his dance rhetoric. We had already seen his pictorializations of the *Firebird* and *Sacre du Printemps*. Completing this program of remakes from the fabulous Diaghilev Ballets Russes was *Renard*, a stylish vignette in the form of a cantata.

Renard is a homosexual hors d'oeuvre that Béjart tries to dignify with a philosophical program note about the eternal treachery of Woman. The setting is 1920s-French-silent-movie-playground, all slicked-back hair and becoming tank-top bathing suits.

The Fox, Jaleh Kerendi, furiously bats her eyelashes and wiggles her hips at the Cock, Victor Ullate, who is horrified but too weak to resist. He is saved from her clutches by his two friends, the Cat and the Goat, who beat her up cheerfully. But she's not dead; at the end they all go off chummily in a real antique car.

I don't know if Stravinsky intended *Renard* as an outrageous camp or a giddy nothing. Or whether there was some subtle message that escaped me and Béjart. Maybe pansies and predatory females were funnier in those days.

Béjart choreographed *Renard* as a cantata, the dancers literally miming and mouthing the words of the singers and freezing in pretend invisibility when their characters were silent. The pop-art backdrop, the animal figures hovering around upstage like movie extras, even the spectacular auto, were nothing but furniture. I found it curious that with all the resources of dance to choose from, Béjart deliberately imposed the visual restrictions of the recital stage on this ballet.

Also seen in New York for the first time was *Les Fleurs du Mal*, to Debussy's "Five Songs of Baudelaire." Like the Renard, the songs were sung by a mostly incomprehensible tape recording. In a dim light four women and three men pair up with various partners of any sex, make love to themselves in Mylar mirrors, and daydream narcissistically.

The movement was academic ballet except for some academic modern done by Dyane Gray-Cullert who, I guess, doesn't dance on pointe, and who acted as a sort of fantasizing Martha Grahamy protagonist for about half the ballet, until she joined the figures of her dream in languid, erotic play.

I couldn't help thinking how much more was said on the same subject in Jerome Robbins's exquisite miniature *Afternoon of a Faun*, which was danced beautifully by Patricia McBride and Edward Villella around the same time at the New York City Ballet.

Symphonie pour un Homme Seul, the third Béjart work having its initial U.S. performances, was set to Pierre Schaeffer and Pierre Henry's musique concrète score. Jorge Donn, as the man alone, was very good in the overwrought Béjart manner, and Suzanne Farrell, as the desirable, threatening female who besets all Béjart heroes, had more to do than she has anywhere else in the repertory. Which isn't saying much, but it's the season to be thankful, and I was.

This time around I found the Ballet of the 20th Century really dreary. Last winter each piece of poor choreography was a new outrage; one could marvel at the heights of propaganda and pomposity to which the company climbed. Now I'm no longer even aroused by that.

The least one can expect from a major dance company is to see dancing, and Béjart frustrates me in this respect. Cheats me, if you like, with his poses and reiterations, his literalness and his clichés fired off with super-intensity. It's big, it's powerful, but it doesn't move me. At best he can create a kind of visual charge, as in the *Sacre*—an explosion of sensational effects that hits your senses with a kinetic rush but leaves you unscathed. Even this seems automated and unbeautiful to me. There's more life and humor in a graffiti-strewn subway car than in these calculated assaults on our contemporaneity.

I guess this is the real place where I part company with the Béjart fans. I won't buy prepackaged togetherness and joy for the masses just because it's sold to me as the latest style in revolutions. Béjart's soft, sensuous movement and heavy-handed kitsch may be the new turn-on, but they mask a virulent antifeminism and a rerouted sexuality that seem to be his real message.

A writer for a popular magazine has extolled Béjart's manipulation of standard dance forms as great iconoclastic art because he's doing something nobody else in dance has done before.

Well, nobody has choreographed the mating habits of turtles either, but I can wait.

December 19, 1971

Dance Muzak

The success of the Stuttgart Ballet this spring sums up a year in which dance enjoyed unprecedented popularity—at the same time as it suffered an appreciable drop in quality. Let me put it another way: values are shifting. Superior-quality ballet is still around, but it's underappreciated and underattended. You have to make some investment in it—of your time, intelligence, taste —just as you do to enjoy any art. No such investment is required by the Stuttgart. In fact, the more you demand of it in dance terms, the more tawdry it looks.

In the tradition of the old-fashioned European opera houses, the Stuttgart and its artistic director/chief choreographer John Cranko don't see the dance as an end in itself. In their world, dancers were the darlings of rich noblemen, and a ballet was a sensual bath, taken between the more serious exertions of watching opera.

It's amazing how tenaciously this air of escape and triviality still clings to European ballet. Even more amazing is how, cut off from the blasé benefactors and the decadent ways, American ballet developed a depth and creativity to rival anything being done in music, art, or theater. Yet it's the best of American ballet —the ballet of Balanchine, Tudor, Robbins, Feld—that's presently being sneered at as elitist by the defenders of Cranko.

Cranko's basic premise seems to be that dancers can be made to do anything, and it's all in the service of spectacle. Not the minimally choreographed, overpoliticized spectacle of Béjart ballets, but the opulent kind, festooned and plumped out with riches. Cranko choreography has too much movement for what it has to say—too many turns and jumps, wrists and ankles flapping, elaborate preparations, exaggeratedly contrived lifts and effects, with the juicier bits repeated in case you missed them. The dancers are oriented as if by magnets to face the audience, and there is a monotonous flamboyance about their attack.

Where Cranko must establish his point succinctly, in his shorter ballets, the result is disastrous. I think he must be one of the world's most unmusical choreographers, yet he chooses some of the most challenging music—cerebral Webern, rhythmically complex Stravinsky and Milhaud, atmospheric Debussy. Then his restless steps and interrupted phrases go their own way, as if the orchestra and the dancers are conspiring to bury each other. The divertissements with "modern" themes tend to be ponderous, and the light ones are unremittingly clowny.

What I miss most in Cranko's choreography is flow—the sense that the movement is going somewhere, that it can change and blend into itself, pause and hurry, that it can expand into limitless space and shrink to the head of a pin. For me, the best dance has to have this kind of lively connectedness, no matter what technique is being used. Cranko's dance emphasizes placement, not even design.

Cranko has built a reputation here for his full-length narrative ballets. These, in most cases, are Cranko versions of literary works, and the dancing takes second place to the exposition and to the depiction of a grand, autre-temps style of living. Jürgen Rose's beautiful decors for *Eugene Onegin*, the superb Prokofiev *Romeo and Juliet* score, even the rough-and-tumble slapstick pace of *The Taming of the Shrew* are stunning accomplishments in themselves.

"Theatrical" is often used to describe these works, as if theater were the main thing you go to the ballet to see. The costumes are lush, the ballerinas have flashing eyes and steely extensions, and the men are bursting with passion. But these ballets subordinate even the dramatic clarity to the stagy effect, and the human statements of the original plays are reduced to cartoons.

Juliet drapes herself, facing the audience, across the outstretched arms of Friar Laurence, the gaudiest crucifixion symbol I've seen this year. And it's jarring, because religion has played only a perfunctory part in the ballet up to that point. Onegin and Tatiana's last duet, climaxed by his pulling her up from the floor so that she can kick the back of her head while she's in the air, is just as sensational as any other Cranko duet, and just as oblivious of who the two characters are. A bunch of gypsies dump a pile of booty in the middle of Carmen's bedroom and do a little celebration dance there. In duel scenes, the swords clash exactly on the beat of the music.

The Stuttgart does anodyne ballet, and its popularity at this moment is not an accident. It's part of the whole cultural scene that administers to people's frantic attempts to get out of this difficult world, to crawl back into some safe yesterday, where the furnishings are elegant and it doesn't matter how the plot comes out.

June 6, 1971

III

BLACK DANCE:
A NEW SEPARATISM

BLACK DANCE is the most emotional issue in all of dance. Now that the stakes are higher for everyone, now that it's possible we are talking about huge, commercial successes and cover-of-*Time* recognition instead of a job here or a commission there for a black dancer, it seems that the accolades are getting sillier and the defenses more paranoid.

All serious white critics are self-conscious about their power over black art. We know many blacks don't consider us competent, but the few qualified black critics either don't want or can't get jobs in the white press. I think we all at some time have asked ourselves whether we must adopt special positions from which to view black art. While people were hurling their hatred at us from the stage, we cowered in our guilty shoes and thought of "social relevance" as a possible standard. When we saw amateurish performances or half-finished ideas being cheered hysterically, we wondered if we could slip out of our telltale skins and see this art as black people see it, or if we should duck the problem and not try to cover it at all.

Yet at the bottom of these questions are only more questions. What do black people really get from black dance, and are all blacks in the audience alike in their response? The black dance movement and its militant publication *The Feet* boosts all black dance and puts down nearly all white dance. What kind of standards lie beneath this bravado? Until blacks themselves are able to make basic distinctions about quality and originality, I don't see how the distinctions made by whites can be declared invalid.

I am interested in discovering what is authentic and fine in black dance. That means trying to understand all I can about it and then finding out in what way it moves me. I have been and no doubt will be attacked as an insensitive bigot for this attitude, but there's no other way I can arrange it with my conscience.

The general condition of black dancers has improved as all dance has improved with the increased subsidies of recent years, but in addition black choreographers and companies have come in for special attention. Large infusions of money have been pumped into black dance from the white establishment. It's always been conscience money to some degree, but at first it was spurred by idealistic hopes and the tunes of fraternal progress into the great windswept American beyond. Long after that dream disintegrated, the white guilt lingered on. The money began to be tinged with fear, appeasement, and a kind of tolerant laissez-faire. But it didn't stop.

Distinctions between art and sociology got harder to see. New companies began springing up everywhere, many to serve legitimate needs of nonwhite communities. But in New York, where there's so much of every kind of dance, and where the nonwhite communities are less isolated from the whole community, no one could tell who these companies were serving a lot of the time, or if they *were* serving or just doing what all other dance companies do.

In place of Brotherhood and Integration there's come a new kind of segregation, an acceptance of blackness as the main reason for a dance company's existence and the main criterion for its success. Now that the white companies are belatedly opening their ranks, black dancers say they would rather belong to their own companies.

This trend has many positive aspects, apart from the raw advantage it gives to artists who have previously been excluded from the performing world. It's imparted to black audiences a sense of pride about black physical characteristics—the way black people move has become something to be admired rather than stifled under white proprieties. For the white audience there's insight into customs and ideas that are unfamiliar, and even more important, a recognition of a different dynamic, a different energy, a whole different way of performing.

If it were possible to think of black dance without considering its race, I would characterize much of it as pop dance. It's directed to a novice audience for one thing—blacks who have never seen concert dance before and whites who have never seen concert dance of such vociferous blackness. So it shares the same desire to be explicit, uncluttered, entertaining. A large quantity of this kind of dance also has political overtones. It's selling black consciousness or black revolution or black anger, and it tends to do this by means of literal gesture, narrative, and stereotyped characters. At one time every black choreographer seemed to have a piece that ended in a riot, with people pitching hand grenades out over the footlights as the sirens shrieked. More recently the messages have been of aggressive pride in the sorrowful past and the florid present.

Alvin Ailey, Talley Beatty, and Donald McKayle were working with this awareness over ten years ago, and Ailey has succeeded in making an identifiable style, creating a repertory, holding a company together, and building a huge audience. The black dance world seems to have ambivalent feelings toward Ailey. He's not angry enough. His enormous success is resented, his commercial slickness is scorned, and his importance as an originator of style is downgraded. Yet dozens of young dancers have appeared with Ailey over the years and have been indelibly marked by his aesthetic.

I can think of almost a dozen people in their twenties and early thirties who are choreographing in a sort of neo-Ailey vein now. The high-heeled, short-skirted, hip-wiggling girls with the saucer eyes and the flapping wrists; the men frantically spinning, crashing to their knees, stretching heavenward in an ecstasy of religious repentance; the couples casually Susy-Q-ing, stopping, glaring at each other, backing away mad, relenting, and bobbing off cheek to cheek, these have become as stylized as the ballerina-princess or the procession of neurotics that strode through modern dances in the fifties.

Neo-Ailey, when it's done well, is irrepressibly strong, vivid, and exciting. As we watch it, the style seems to sweep us along, substituting for content or profound feeling. In his 1969 work *Radiance of the Dark*, Eleo Pomare sketched a marvelous, sinister evangelist-crook, Prophet Jones. For the most part, this was a toy "character"—swaggering around dressed in white robes with silver trimming, hidden behind dark glasses, waving his arms in exhortation and grinning slyly. But what was Pomare's attitude toward a person like this? To me his portrayal seemed to have been skimmed off the pages of a tabloid newspaper. Like Ailey himself, Pomare is a serious choreographer who can make such clever portraits that he often neglects to explore his subjects to any depth.

Other Ailey alumni, such as George Faison, have frankly accepted the charge of commercialism and intend to exploit its possibilities for all they're worth. If Ailey still feels slightly compromised when his company appears on a bill with a pop singer, Faison is proud of it. Pop is big business today, profitable business, and I think some black artists have decided to cash in on it. This is both an interesting and a refreshing idea to me.

For all their determination to have a "mass" appeal, the ordinary pop dance purveyors never reach more than a tiny fraction of the people seeking live entertainment—it's rock, folk, and pop music that command the huge audiences. Except for the dying vaudevillian strain, we have no legitimate models of dance as a popular art form. We either write it off as Broadway or grope for serious standards we can apply even when it's clearly not serious art. Music has a quite specific category situated between "classical" and mindless Muzak-music, a category largely descended from black music. Jazz and traditional folk music have always had nearly universal appeal as well as the individual expressiveness we associate with serious art. No matter how slickly professional pop music becomes, it draws vitality from its jazz-folk roots, and I'm not surprised to see a similar dance form growing out of jazz-Afro and black vernacular movement.

A choreographer back from some travels has reported to me that in certain colleges the physical education departments are now running rock concerts in the field house—thus no doubt garnering nice dividends for the volleyball curriculum. The kind of dance that Faison's highly theatrical, dynamic company does would certainly not be out of place in this kind of concert. He's already taken a suitable name: The Universal Dance Experience. Probably, with the advent of videotape cassettes, this trend will really take off.

While these popular forms are being perfected and extended, another breakthrough in the serious realm seems imminent. The problem, as in all dance, is getting past the easy adulation, not letting the theatricality, the shouts of recognition, the humor, and the rhythm substitute for a personal statement. Talley Beatty and Donald McKayle both had a keen eye for black forms and the black experience, but weren't able to sustain their early visions. Since Ailey there hasn't been a black choreographer of major importance.

Sometimes I have to remind myself that as recently as the early 1950s, when Ailey, McKayle, and Arthur Mitchell were getting started, there were virtually no openings for black dancers in paying jobs. It may be that some of the energy that went into the struggle for just getting a living can now go back into creative exploration. I'm fascinated by people like Clyde Morgan and Gus Solomons because they seem to have finished with their need to prove political and social points, and have now looked to more personal questions. Their work is less broadly applicable, less easy to grasp, and also tougher-fibered. It reaches me on a deeper level and tells me new truths about blackness.

Starting with Dance

The building wasn't hard to find. Its square, yellow-brick new-ness made it stand out from its dilapidated neighbors. Above the door was a red neon sign reading *FRATERNAL CENTER*. A church billboard announced services for Tingman's Esoteric Temple. And another sign on the front wall said: Brownsville Community Council, Inc.—Head Start Child Development Center.

This all-purpose community gathering place in the heart of the Brooklyn slums was chosen as one of ten locations for mod-ern dance performances last spring by the Rod Rodgers Dance Company. The lecture-performances were directed primarily to preschool children in New York City's Head Start program and were cosponsored by the Harlem Cultural Council and the Parks Department Office of Cultural Affairs. Other perfor-mances were to take place in schools, housing projects, and a church, in Harlem, Bedford Stuyvesant, Queens, and the Bronx. The project represented one aspect of New York's effort to coordinate the resources of government, private capital, profes-sional talent, and community leadership in an attack on the massive problems of the ghetto.

Inside the center, in a large basement room, several rows of chairs had been set up at the back for parents, and in front of them dozens of tiny children sat on mats facing the cleared portion of the room that would serve as the stage. The atmos-phere was subdued, as it was everywhere in the city that day, because it was the day after the assassination of Martin Luther King. The local Head Start people had decided not to cancel the performance, and the room was filled to capacity with parents, older children, teachers, and some seventy-five four- and five-year-olds in their best party clothes. Before the program started, a white priest offered a prayer for reconciliation and forgiveness.

Then Rod Rodgers came forward to introduce the first dance, a Folk Suite that he describes as a modern version of festive men's and women's dances in Afro-modern folk style. Rodgers, a thirty-year-old native of Detroit who has three small boys of his own, spoke to the children simply but not condescendingly about why people all over the world dance, and how much he and his company enjoy dancing for others.

"When we decided to do this Head Start program," he explained later to an interviewer, "my idea was to present concert dance material, not kiddie-poo material. Even though these are very young children, there's no reason for them not to understand or to be bored and restless. They won't behave like adults, but they shouldn't. I take my work very seriously, but the audience should enjoy it in whatever way they can. If the kids want to talk during the performance, that's okay. They're so alive and responding all the time to what's happening. They'll take a little break to chatter about what they see, but when the high points in the dance happen, the faces come around and the eyes are riveted."

After the first dance Rodgers showed the children two long, thin sticks. He demonstrated how the sticks would be used by the dancers in the next piece, *Tangents*, to create designs in space, and to make sounds by tapping on the floor or swishing through the air.

Rodgers is interested in developing a set of concepts that can be used to relate dance to the experience of children at different ages from preschool through high school. "Anybody could do a lecture-demonstration using these points applied to his own material, even if the director isn't particularly education-oriented," he says. "Teachers can also take these ideas back to the classroom and use them in connection with other activities." For the age level of children in the Head Start program, Rodgers stresses the emotional and ritualistic aspects of dance, he explains some of the theatrical devices the choreographer employs, such as costumes, lights, and music, and he shows that dance can either tell a story or merely make beautiful designs. The concluding dances were a narrative piece based on a traditional primitive theme and a Percussion Suite in which the dancers created their own accompaniment with bells, cymbals, and other instruments.

The dances on the Head Start programs, although less elaborately produced, were the same choreography the Rod Rodgers company presents in concert performances on tour and in New York. "It's important for these kids to see things that represent a maximum artistic possibility, otherwise we can't even talk about developing discriminating taste," Rodgers says. "Most of what they see is done in a compromising way, like TV and grade B and minus C movies—things that are made to be sold to an audience that's ignorant. All kids need to rise above this TV mentality, but especially in the ghetto, where children have so little other stimulation."

Rodgers knows about commercial art first hand. Before coming to New York in 1962 he choreographed musical shows for night clubs and resorts, and he was resigned to the idea that the only opportunity for a Negro in dance would have to be in the field of jazz. Now, however, he is evolving his own movement style of abstract modern dance, and, with growing confidence in himself as an artist, he refuses to rely on the stereotype of either the grinning tap dancer or the stridently black protester.

"One of the worst things the contemporary black artist can do," he says, "is to confine himself to oversimplifying the black aesthetic image, to implying that Afro-American art is either primitive or jazz dance. I'm an Afro-American, and any dance I do is Afro-American. Each dance that I create has grown out of my personal experience as a black American. My function in the revolution will be to share my vital and growing experience, not to show only old stereotypes or create new ones. It's important for children to see me experimenting, to see that there are no limitations to what the black artist can do."

Ed Taylor, executive director of the Harlem Cultural Council, believes Rodgers is one of the most promising young black choreographers, and that modern dance, America's primary dance form, is also the form of black choreographers. The council is a cultural umbrella for the black arts community, with the goal of providing employment for artists and making their work accessible to wider audiences. One of the council's early projects, the Jazz Mobile, has toured the city for the past two summers and is now an independent program. Last summer the council sponsored a Dance Mobile, which is expected to be duplicated in other cities this year. An exhibit, "The Evolution of the Afro-American Artist," at CCNY created a stir of interest in the art world.

"We aren't a producing outfit," Taylor explained, "but when we have to produce to get something going, we do. We want to let the arts develop in their own way, we only require that the work we sponsor be of the highest quality. If we had more money, there are a number of other projects we'd like to undertake, such as providing artists-in-residence at city schools."

The Head Start project was engineered by dancer Carole Johnson, who is the dance representative on the Harlem Cultural Council, and Liz Wiener, who administers arts programs in the ghettos for the New York City Office of Cultural Affairs. Miss Wiener, a former teacher, helped organize the first Central Park Happenings three summers ago under former Parks Commissioner Thomas P. F. Hoving.

"We work with different agencies in poverty areas," Miss Wiener said recently. "There are nine preschool centers that we visit every week with the Cinemobile, which was originally funded by the U.S. Office of Economic Opportunity. We show the kids experimental films and then have classroom sessions with discussion, painting, music, and so forth. These dance performances are being shown to all the children in the preschool groups, about two thousand, plus about five hundred in Harlem who aren't part of the regular Head Start program. Rod's kind of dancing is great for kids of this age group. I think they can respond to its abstract quality more fully than to work that is pointedly all-Afro. This reaches them on a beautiful level, which is the kind of thing they don't normally get enough of."

The city's underlying philosophy in sponsoring arts programs was described by Doris Freedman, director of the Office of Cultural Affairs. "We want to expose kids to the mainstream of art, to bring the most creative work to the places where they're isolated and locked in. The universal quality of the arts speaks better to many of them than the structured experience of the classroom, where, if he can't respond, a kid will drop out or just sit there in apathy and anger. The nonverbal expression of the arts communicates like nothing else does. We had a tremendous success with our film-making program last year—kids really worked hard and produced their own films, which were later shown in other parts of the city on the movie bus. Every kid has a need for expression, and the arts often make it possible. If you can make something, you have a feeling of accomplishment, you can say 'I am someone.'

"We're not a social agency," Mrs. Freedman continued, "but the arts as a social tool haven't been explored enough. We take the long-range view that people who are involved don't get in trouble. It's not our purpose to keep the city cool—there are other agencies that do that. But we can be a preventive agent if we're in there all along, getting people to participate in rich activity. In summer the city outdoors is a great place. There's a neutrality in the streets, people don't feel uncomfortable attending a concert or an opera in the park, as they might in an auditorium. This city is driving with the greatest creativity in the world, and fifty blocks away people are unaware of it!

"A great thing is that the artists are coming to us offering to help. Last summer a priest, Monsignor Fox, started a Summer in the City program, where he just turned artists loose in different neighborhoods and let them make contact and do their thing. There were block parties, mural painting projects, shows —people became involved in a most positive way.

"Of course, in a city like this, the arts aren't given a very high priority in the budget, but our office is able to supplement some of its programs with contributions from private funds. Rod Rodgers' dance performances for the Head Start children are part of what we call the Youth Opportunity Creative Workshop program. Along with the Dance Mobile, some school appearances by Merce Cunningham, and other dance events, it was partly financed by the proceeds—$25,000—from a special benefit performance given last fall by the Harkness Ballet and run by our office. We'd love to encourage more participation of this kind from private sources."

It may be years before anyone can tell what impact programs like this are having on the ghetto, before audiences are built, identity is discovered, talent is revealed. But one response was immediate and gratifying that afternoon last spring, as the children in the Brownsville Head Start Center filed out past the dancers, staring up with eyes round in awe and shyly saying, "Thank you."

Fall/Winter, 1968–69

✄ᛒᛯᚷᚷ✄

New York Goes Tap-Happy

Tap dancing?? Well, yes. I have no intention of being a purist when I can tell you about one of the happiest, liveliest, and most thoroughly enjoyable events of this or any year.

The Tap Happening, a celebration of old-time hoofing organized by Leticia Jay, has been quietly happening Monday nights at the Bert Wheeler Theater in the Hotel Dixie since early spring. Owing to the pressures of an unusually busy dance season, critics and audiences have only recently discovered it. The run has now been extended through July, and I wish the show an even longer and more prosperous career.

Sunken amidst the fleshpots of Times Square, the Tap Happening has an innocence, an almost mystical honesty that is astonishing and beautiful to see. Even the dirty jokes are clean, flung out as they are with a mock-seductive joy that reminds me of Suzanne Farrell doing *Slaughter on Tenth Avenue.* The entire show has an ingenuous, unrehearsed quality—sometimes a dancer outdoes himself, to his own and everybody else's pleasure, and, prompted by his fellows, holds a hurried consultation with the band and launches into an encore. The dancing styles range from raw intensity to polished precision to casual virtuosity.

The Tap Happening is part nightclub act, part vaudeville, part dance concert, part family reunion. There are sweet, wilted old jokes like the one about the cross-eyed judge and the three cross-eyed prisoners, and songs you haven't heard since what used to be called The War, like "I Cover the Waterfront." The theater is tiny, and the atmosphere is intimate. No microphones are used. The performers play directly to the audience, not into some spotlit void, and the audience yells back words of encouragement: "Work out, baby, work out!" and "Yeaahh!"

Holding the show together is Chuck Green, a tall, trim man with a benevolent smile and what must be the world's most expressive forehead. After leading all the dancers on in a tribute to Bill "Bojangles" Robinson, Green does a little turn with Miss Jay and then introduces the "acts," reminiscing about dancing on the streets of Harlem and the golden days of the Apollo and the Savoy Ballroom. Following the intermission he joins the others in the traditional "Battle of Taps," a spirited though good-natured competition.

Now you may not think tap dancing would be interesting enough to look at for a whole evening. But each of these performers has his own distinctive approach. Raymond Kaalund, whom Chuck Green calls "an eccentric stylist," is a serious-faced man continually glancing around and bounding away on rubber legs from some imaginary threat, nervously touching the microscopic brim of his gray slouch hat. Sandman Sims is a wild extrovert, constantly mugging and imitating the other dancers. But when his own turn comes to perform, he is a miraculous artist, whether scuffing out rhythms in the sand, or tapping them into the stage. Sandman works in silence, the better for us to appreciate the intricacy of his sound patterns. There is Rhythm Red, who looks like one of those enormous palace guards with the broadswords in an exotic Cecil B. de Mille picture, but who dances with an unexpected, almost flirtatious lightness. Jerry Ames uses the "modern tap" style popularized by Fred Astaire and Gene Kelly. Tony White accents his tap rhythms by driving his whole weight into the ground, and he can reverse directions in a series of turns, something very few ballet dancers can do. Jimmy Slyde alternates between quick percussive taps and gliding movements that look like ice skating. The cast of characters also includes singers, musicians, joke-tellers, and colleagues in the audience who come up for a bow and then perhaps dance a few bars themselves.

On the two occasions when I attended, the audience was almost entirely white, and there were virtually no young black people. Tap dancing, of course, has had unpleasant connotations of shuffling and Uncle Tomism, and the youngsters have denied all that. But the performers at the Tap Happening are proud of what they can do, and they love showing it to an audience. In fact, the beautiful thing about them is that they remain themselves; they haven't sold out to the commercialism that is today's sophisticated black—and white—slavery.

If you wanted to see black stereotypes this spring, you had only to visit the Stuttgart Ballet, where the only blacks in the company were carrying spears in period ballets, never dancing; and where an entire tasteless number in the *Nutcracker Divertissements* was done by whites in blackface. There must be something wrong with people who will go to the Metropolitan Opera House and hysterically applaud a foreign company that is hurling ancient bigotries in their faces, while they allow the last survivors of an indigenous art form to fall into oblivion.

The Tap Happening has a strange fascination that makes people want to see it again and again. Is it the personality of Chuck Green and his relationship to the other dancers—straight man, father confessor, admiring colleague? Is it the knowledge that we are looking at a lost art? Or is it the spontaneity that we find so refreshing in a world of slick, packaged entertainment?

July 21, 1969

Selling Soul

The early modern dancers didn't go in for glamour. During the "long woolens" period, the British ballet critic Arnold Haskell remarked, rather unchivalrously, "Not one of them has given me the impression that anyone could ever wait for her at the stage door." Well, they didn't want to be stars; they shied away from theatrical flimflam. They wanted to be loved for their movement and their ideas alone. Strangely, the attitude persists, even though this year Broadway has become an exacting fact of life for dance, instead of a remote symbol. The homespun costumes and sketchy sets of some of the major companies look unnecessarily austere, even to those of us who always said we didn't care because it was the dancing that counted.

The Alvin Ailey American Dance Theater has been accused of commercialism by some dance purists. Ailey, schooled in the revivalist dynamism of Southern Baptist churches and the dance-theater ideas of Lester Horton, has never been an advocate of the earth-brown-leotard type of dancing. He loves vibrant colors, spangles, fringe, floppy hats, and umbrellas. Visually, his concerts are dazzlingly alive even when a bit vulgar.

Ailey's revival of Lucas Hoving's *Icarus*, shown during the company's recent engagement at the Billy Rose Theatre, proves that a viable modern dance need not suffer if it is richly mounted. *Icarus* (1964) is probably the last good traditional modern dance based on a Greek myth, and when Hoving created it for his own trio, it looked spare and stern, with intimations, for me, of Stonehenge or medieval woodcuts. Now it has opulent costumes by Beni Montresor, and the iconography is high Renaissance or Byzantine. But the structure of the legend and the slow inevitability of the action are still intact.

The Alvin Ailey company also has an opulence of movement that comes uniquely out of its black heritage. Ailey himself choreographs in a striking blend of free-flowing African dynamics and the slow, spacious Horton technique. Talley Beatty, whose works were also seen at the Billy Rose, combines the percussive tautness of the modern idiom with an easy jazz or Latin rhythm, to make some of the most exciting movement I can think of. Any academic dancer could tell you he choreographs too literally, using every beat of the music, so his turns, kicks, changes of direction are twice as fast, or twice as many, as you would expect. But watching it, one is about as aware of good form as of the shape of the track during a horse race.

Both Ailey and Beatty employ the tribal gestures of the ghetto, the assertive upward thrust of the head, and the expressively rotating shoulder, the gliding pelvic step, and these evoke delighted recognition from blacks in the audience, and bemused fascination from whites.

The choreography underlying this lush immediacy of movement and production varies in its degree of truthfulness. Before
he had as large or as technically proficient a company, Ailey
used to build his dances on the bodies and personalities of his
people. Method choreography, I used to think, watching rehearsals. Probably no one who saw them will forget the jaunty
James Truitte and the bustling Thelma Hill, for instance, or
Ailey himself and Carmen de Lavallade, exuding sex appeal.
The ideas they crystallized in the *Blues Suite* and *Revelations* are
still evident, but the company is more disciplined, less spontaneous and effervescent.

Ailey's new *Quintet* is a reworking of this old exuberance and
intensity, instead of a new thinking through of the material. If
the slinky, red-gowned, blond-wigged singing quintet is revealed here as an empty-headed banality of TV and Motown,
what they express when they strip down to their true selves is
just as fictitious, it seems to me, because it is based on the stereotypes Ailey himself created when he first depicted the strutting
insolence and ancient melancholy in the black experience, ten
years ago.

In *The Black Belt*, Talley Beatty has done the obligatory riot
piece, more skillfully than some, but without the organic development of madness and rage found in Eleo Pomare's *Blues for the
Jungle*. *Black Belt* is romanticized, cinematic stuff, with its big
bad Ku Kluxers conveniently martyring the sweet little church-
goers so that everybody can lose their cool and take to the
streets. Violence was more convincing in Beatty's *The Road of the
Phoebe Snow* (1959), which wasn't about riots, but which contained the same dynamics that eventually bred them.

The company performs with the utmost spirit and com-
municativeness, but only sometimes with deep conviction. The
whole of *Revelations*, Dudley Williams in Ailey's old solo *Reflections in D*, and Alma Robinson in the "Poverty Train" section
of *Quintet*: these have poignant beauty as well as pizzazz.

This most theatrical and probably most successful of modern
dance companies has been abroad touring for much of the past
few years and may be out of touch with current American
realities. The business of performing night after night to houses
full of strangers in foreign cities has taught the dancers how to

make instant contact. Under their electric spell, even American audiences forget to ask whether they are contemporary, relevant, profound, or even honest. But, for this company especially, these questions matter—this kind of commercialism cannot be justified.

March 10, 1969

A-Changin'

Things used to be a whole lot simpler. Not so long ago if a critic set up categories like black choreographer or black company (the word would have been "Negro" then), he was automatically considered a bigot. People like Alvin Ailey, Donald McKayle, Pearl Primus, Katherine Dunham, and Talley Beatty were expected merely to make good dances and perform them professionally. It was assumed that these dances would reflect the American milieu and the black heritage to whatever degree the particular artist chose to use and synthesize those cultural ingredients. And some remarkably good work came out of that approach, work that we would have called unselfconsciously black, if it had occurred to anybody at that time to make such a distinction.

Today all black artists are self-conscious about blackness, and many white critics, exuding a smug tolerance, tend to gloss over defects as if a work's color were all that counted. I think we are all betrayed by that kind of tolerance—artists, critics, audiences, and students alike. Discrimination is unconstitutional, but it is a critic's job to be discriminating. All the goodwill in the world cannot make a bad dance good, and no matter how sincerely I may wish to see more black dancers employed, I can't make myself blind to the inadequacies of students thrust on stage before they are fully trained.

This is the slippery position from which I was assigned to

153

look at three black companies that appeared this spring under the impeccable auspices of Brooklyn Academy. There is nothing that can explain anyone's appraisal of a black company today better than the fact that we're all in the new American revolution together. Don't expect us to make sense of it, or even to be consistent and logical. In five years, perhaps, we may be able to tell what has been happening. Now I can only relate some wayward facts and opinions.

Alvin Ailey, in one of his periodic fits of discouragement, announced he was disbanding his company. The company, surely the most popular modern dance organization in the world and a pioneering one artistically in many ways, has the most varied repertory in all of dance and the dancers to perform it. As a resident company of Brooklyn Academy, it performs about four weeks a year in the city's best dance theater, and it benefits from the fund-raising that the Academy, as a major cultural institution, is able to do for its constituents. The Alvin Ailey American Dance Theater's lot otherwise is the same as that of all modern dance companies—rigorous touring, periodic layoffs, and, in between, rehearsing new works and breaking in new dancers. Ailey evidently doesn't want to put up with it anymore. Perhaps he thinks a black company is entitled to better treatment. I think everyone is entitled to better treatment. At this writing I'm not convinced that Ailey will carry out his threat to quit. At least I hope not, for I'm fond of this company although it disappoints me these days.

Ailey's two new works for the spring season lacked the personality and eccentric joy of his earlier pieces. Even when he was leaning heavily on stereotyped black characterizations, Ailey's wit and honesty came through. *Streams*, his new group work, is very "white"—plotless, balletic in its formality and seriousness, skillful but undistinguished. *Streams* is a more than acceptable example of the hybrid, balletic-modern style, a kind of dancing that makes few emotional demands on the audience but employs an expanded vocabulary that looks interesting to the classically trained eye.

Ailey's other new work, a solo to Satie's three "Gymnopédies," had a similar remoteness. Choreographed for Dudley Williams, it was danced by guest artist Keith Lee when Williams became injured. Built on the familiar pretext of a dancer improvising in the studio, *Gymnopédies* has the kind of supertheatricality that often glistens from simple situations in the work of Jerome Robbins—the dancer is so intent on his own activity that the audience is forced to conclude it must be important. If Ailey himself were dancing it, or Williams, it might have the humor or sophistication to match its program note, a derisive remark from the composer Ernest Krenek to the effect that Satie succeeded in making trite material look pretentious. Lee doesn't seem to perceive the sarcasm of this observation.

Three company members, John Parks, Kelvin Rotardier, and Miguel Godreau, choreographed solos that served mainly to show themselves off as dancers, and this was especially pleasant in the case of Godreau, who was returning to the company after two years on Broadway. The rest of the season looked stylish, perhaps a little too professional—as if the dancers have been trying so hard they've learned every nuance by rote. What this company does now, usually, is called hype. They play for the big effect, the breathless ovation. And it works.

Eleo Pomare also tends to have a galvanic effect on his audience, but in his case it comes from pent-up anger, generated new every time and contained at just below the explosion point by the structure of the movement. Take away his own seething presence, and you notice that his choreography isn't very good. Or perhaps I mean it gives many indications that it ought to be better.

When Pomare seems most determined to prove that he doesn't need his modern dance precursors—Ailey, McKayle, Graham—his work is most uptight, least original. His new duet, *Movement for Two*, was a series of diagonals and gentle curves for Diana Ramos and Strody Meekins—another bland and balanced example of balletic-modern. Pomare in recent years has created a spectacular array of tense Harlem types who fend off the world with lifted shoulders and silent obscenities. But the most exciting event of this entire concert was Pomare dancing an ecstatic, timorous monk in a revival of his 1959 solo *Cantos from a Monastery*. Only in this piece, it seemed, both Pomare the choreographer and Pomare the performer had their mind primarily on the dancing.

Down in Philadelphia Arthur Hall has been training a young company that pays special attention to "Afro" material. African dance, enriched as it has been in the Western Hemisphere by Spanish, French, Indian, and other cultures, is a particularly fruitful area of study and expression, especially for blacks, if the ability to achieve its polyrhythmic fluency hasn't been trained out of them by Western dance teachers. Hall's Afro-American Dance Ensemble did some spirited African dances and a theatricalized Caribbean suite in the style of Dunham or Geoffrey Holder. In the final portion of the program, however, Hall ventured into modern dance and revealed not only his own choreographic ineptitude but the elementary level of his dancers' technique.

At least ten other predominantly black companies are now operating at varying levels of competence. I've seen only one this year, Joan Miller's, that seems to have real choreographic promise and a healthy approach to its own hang-ups. The others don't yet demonstrate such high potential, or else they have passed their highest potential and slipped into a kind of blasé aggressiveness. It may or may not be significant that Miss Miller has taken the independent route traditionally followed by modern dancers, rather than relaxing into the pattern of large subsidies and official sponsorship that seems increasingly possible for blacks now.

July/August, 1970

Flowers

If you didn't know Alvin Ailey's history of innovations in modern dance production, you might be tempted to think that in choreographing a work for the Royal Ballet's Lynn Seymour and his own company, he was merely staging a pseudo-event to attract customers during a week when his company was playing against Nureyev, Béjart, and a dozen other events. Fortunately, the piece has more than curiosity value.

Dance has never been on such a high, and I for one am ready to come down. *Flowers*, which opened January 25, was the ninth new ballet I had seen in five days. The fact that it made a vivid impression on me is some indication of its worth, if not the wisest, most considered opinion you've ever heard from this critic.

Flowers is about the self-destruction of a star. The music, the ambience, is rock and the allusion is to Janis Joplin, but there's no generation gap here. It could be Jean Harlow or Judy Garland or Marilyn Monroe just as well.

Miss Seymour prances out in a yellow jump suit, puffing on a cigarette while photographers' flash bulbs explode in her face. She digs it . . . at first. But they won't let her alone, even when she starts drinking; even when she slumps over in her chair, someone with a camera slides to the floor and shoots up at her face. She dances a TV-type routine with a group of men, then a duet with Ramon Segarra in black and silver cowboy clothes, shades, and an Afro wig. Segarra soon has her sniffing something in a red kerchief, and the next thing you know the kerchief is tied around her arm and she's mainlining.

The lights get dim, and in her freaked-out mind she plays ugly sexual games with her chorus boys, now nearly naked. Segarra presides over the orgy with satanic cool. Finally, in a deranged fit of writhing and shaking, she passes out. The photographers scurry to the scene immediately to take pictures of her body. Flowers of excited mourning rain down on the stage. The audience—us—applauds hysterically.

There are things wrong with *Flowers*. The movement, especially for the men's group, often looks like textbook sensuality designed to fill the stage while the star changes clothes. Miss Seymour isn't loose enough in the hips to be convincing in the jazzy idiom, though her final solo and her acting throughout were superb. The ballet frays a bit at the climax, which doesn't make it clear whether the star has OD-ed, fallen in front of an oncoming car, tumbled out of a window, or what.

What is clear, though, is that Lynn Seymour gave a stunning performance, and that *Flowers* hits at the very consumerism we're all taking part in by watching it and applauding it. Just a few blocks away, an exhausted Rudolf Nureyev, dancing every night on the Australian Ballet's tour, was proving Ailey's point.

February 6, 1971

Choral Dances

Barely three months after finishing a highly successful ANTA Theater season, the Alvin Ailey American Dance Theater returned to City Center April 27 for another two-week run, with three new works on its schedule. Ailey's company now and especially his new piece, *Choral Dances*, represent the most theatrical and popular form modern dance has ever taken.

Ailey's work is undoubtedly commercial, but he doesn't vulgarize and cheapen the modern dance idiom as so many other choreographers have done. I think he picks out features that are most distinctive and appealing about the modern dance and heightens them—its concern with the dancer's relationship to space, for example, or the adaptation of movement to dancers' individual styles rather than the subordination of the individual to the demands of the movement. He avoids the strangeness and choreographic idiosyncrasy that made people think modern dance was "difficult" and presents a very clear, unambiguous event. Accessible and basically honest, which in these ersatz times may compensate for its lack of depth.

Choral Dances is set to some modern madrigals from Benjamin Britten's opera *Gloriana*, sung by a small, regrettably miked chorus under the direction of Ronald Isaac. The songs tell of ample country pleasures—concord and harvest, time and tribute. Rather than illustrate each musical theme, as did José Limón's *There Is a Time*, to which it is related, the dance discloses a community of idealized people going through some life rituals with all the solemnity and timelessness of a church service.

Kelvin Rotardier, as a sort of patriarch, leads the processions and focuses all the action with big gestures of accelerating strength. Rotardier is a commanding physical presence anyway, but all the dancers look more heroic than usual. Nicola Cernovitch's lighting and A. Christina Giannini's costumes—long-sleeved jump suits for the men and long crepe dresses with hoods for the women, in shades of purple—emphasize their long bodies and the way they swing in wide arcs out into space.

Ailey's movement language here is almost pure Lester Horton technique, with its satisfying stretched-out line, its diagonal tensions, its long-held balances and suspensions. The torso provides a consistent center through which everything flows, whether the gestures are straight and linear or spiraling in smooth curves. It's not an idiom with much subtlety or expressive range, but it's peaceful, harmonious. It doesn't contradict itself or take you by surprise. Ailey's dancers perform at high intensity without seeming to show off. I think *Choral Dances* is visually pleasing. It offers no intellectual challenge. To me it's tame—a bit sanctimonious and remote, perhaps—but not trash.

May 17, 1971

Child of the Earth

For many years Alvin Ailey has been committed to the idea of repertory, and even though his company carries his name, it's not his exclusive instrument. In addition to commissioning and reviving works from outside choreographers, Ailey has begun showing dances by members of the company. Kelvin Rotardier's second work, *Child of the Earth*, had its premiere May 5 at City Center.

Set to music of the exiled South African trumpeter Hugh Masekela, it's a duet for Rotardier and Consuelo Atlas, in the theatricalized modern dance style that this company does so well. In this kind of dancing the performers have to imagine themselves as superior beings—as personification of man's magnificence and suffering—and the effect depends as much on their acting skills as on the expressive power of the choreography alone. In contrast, Martha Graham's dancers, for instance, while they also represent heroic figures, don't have to "pretend" at all because their movement is so overwhelmingly communicative.

A program note for *Child of the Earth* explains that the couple is on a journey to a new country after escaping from their oppressed homeland. This kind of message invariably spoils the dance for me if I read it beforehand, by placing too specific a meaning on the dance and telling me how the people feel and what's going to happen. A more descriptive title for the dance would have told everything necessary.

The choreography is fairly simple and clear. Rotardier enters with long, leaning-forward strides, scooping up armfuls of space. He makes a sort of clearing of the stage, a temporary stopping place, by pacing off its boundaries and peering warily out beyond them. Atlas then appears and they dance together with a slow, grave strength. When it's time to go on, Rotardier falters and she encourages him until he's able to lead again.

The dancers gave a feeling of great protectiveness and endurance, as if by being together they were creating an enclosure of safety. Atlas in particular, squatting on the ground with rounded, rocking arms, seemed to be planted there, more like a tree than a fugitive animal.

May 25, 1971

Cry

Some of Alvin Ailey's most memorable works have been solos. Early in his choreographing career he was able to capture an emotional climate with very little help from costumes, plot, or other dancers. Although he did rely on words sometimes to provide initial motivation, solos like "Sinner Man" and "I Want to be Ready" from *Revelations, Hermit Songs,* and The Boy in *Knoxville: Summer of 1915* were poems rather than narratives. They elaborated on an idea rather than showing a type, as Ailey can also do, in his character dances.

I haven't heard the word *soul* used lately, but I'd definitely apply it to Ailey's newest dance, *Cry,* first shown at City Center on May 4. Dedicated to black women, *Cry* moves from oppression through sorrow and pain to a kind of anguished liberation. This kind of mood dance works best when the dancer is strong enough to live in the choreography, to wear it like his own skin, which is the way Ailey himself performed solos, and probably still conceives of them for others.

I saw *Cry* performed by Judith Jamison, and she tore the place apart. Jamison is a statuesque woman with close-cropped hair and incredibly long arms and legs, who can do dumb-broad comedy or an indecently beautiful arabesque. She's an original, she's gutsy; she causes a sensation just by walking out on the stage.

In *Cry* she does much more. Dressed in a white top and long ruffled skirt, she dances first to music of Alice Coltrane with a big white cloth that becomes a scrub rag, a turban, perhaps a shroud, as she reminds herself of black woman's sometimes sad, sometimes proud inheritance. She writhes and bends double in agony to Laura Nyro's drug lament "Been on a Train," and finally she raises her arms in sobbing, stamping joy as the Voices of East Harlem sing, "Right On, Be Free."

In a piece like this you don't remember specific choreography —steps and floor patterns and designs. You remember a presence and a sensibility. Besides stage magnetism and an intense dramatic projection, Jamison can do astonishing movement of African derivation such as head swivels, neck snapping from side to side, undulations of the torso in spirals and curves. You could say *Cry* is just Judith Jamison doing her things, which is all right too. Ailey knew the right way to pull them out of her without allowing the piece to slide across the delicate boundary into nightclub or TV entertainment.

June 8, 1971

Modern Dance—with Pizzazz

A year ago the Alvin Ailey American Dance Theater seemed on the point of extinction. In a burst of dissatisfaction over the company's perennially shaky finances, Ailey threatened to disband it entirely, and soon afterward he ended the company's residency arrangement with the Brooklyn Academy of Music, which he felt wasn't giving the company enough rehearsal space in exchange for the exclusive right to present all its New York performances.

The company did not die. Money came in. There was an African tour and one to the Soviet Union. And this winter the company played four sold-out smash weeks at two Manhattan theaters.

The stakes are higher now and the gestures more dramatic, but this is not a new story for Ailey. In the early sixties his company would come back from dazzling tours of Europe and the Orient—and play its annual New York concert in the drab, ill-equipped auditorium of Clark Center in the West Side YWCA, which was then its home. All modern dance companies live precariously, but with Ailey the contrasts between fame and poverty have somehow always been more intense. Perhaps they just seem so because his sense of the theatrical pervades everything he does.

Alvin Ailey comes out of that side of modern dance, represented by Lester Horton and Denishawn, which accepts theatricality and showmanship as a means of bringing serious dance to the public. Ailey's teacher and hero Lester Horton was not above taking his company into nightclubs to perform, nor does Ailey disdain sharing a bill with pop singers or rock groups if he can reach a wider audience that way. "Four thousand people is four thousand people," he told me recently, explaining the apparent artistic ambiguity in his company's forthcoming performances at Los Angeles' Greek Theater, on a program with Vikki Carr.

Although the AAADT seems commercial compared to the old, threadbare but pure modern dance companies, it has actually been grafting to itself many of the practices common to ballet. Ailey himself may never have stated it in precisely these terms, but for years he's been pushing his company toward a performing style, glamour, and accessibility that make it resemble the big ballet companies, without their unwieldy size.

Where modern companies worked in a single, very individual style and expected their audiences to appreciate the personal, often introverted qualities of their dancers, Ailey wants a company of virtuosos. His dancers are highly trained in all the major modern styles, and most of them in ballet too, and one thinks of them as performers rather than interpreters, a subtle but significant difference.

What comes across in an Ailey company performance today is like the excitement we get from the ballet. Maybe more so. We're conscious of beautiful dancers, marvelous technique, high-intensity motion. The costumes are handsome, the music is loud, the message is blammed at us, big. This is true of the jazz and soul pieces, like Ailey's *Blues Suite* and *Cry*, where you would expect it, and also of the more serious works in the repertory, where you wouldn't.

I'm sure that the gospel churches in Ailey's background are partly responsible for this stomping, joyous approach to dance. As a choreographer Ailey uses not only the outward themes of the black experience but its inner passion. He was, I think, the first to explore both these phenomena—the first to translate the uptown mannerisms and shapes, and the looseness and tensions into a dance form that wasn't straight jazz, and he has been so widely imitated by young black choreographers that even his own originals are beginning to look stereotyped. Whether it is strictly a black quality or not, the highly charged style of delivery that's characteristic of the AAADT is almost never seen in white modern dance companies.

The other important lesson Ailey has garnered from ballet is that of repertory. Long before other modern dance companies began incorporating works by outsiders, Ailey was mounting a wide range of works by young and older choreographers, black and white, men and women. This gave a variety to his programs and a challenge to his dancers that no other company could offer.

Beyond merely satisfying the demands of program-building, Ailey also has a strong instinct for preservation and documentation. He's aware how fragile the dance repertory is, and that the best archive for dance is live production. AAADT has revived works of choreographers who don't have their own companies, like Talley Beatty and Pauline Koner, and has shown dances that could be compared with other current productions—Paul Sanasardo's *Metallics,* for instance.

Periodically in the dance world people talk about how ideal it would be to have one repertory company that would do the classics of modern dance. Although not officially sanctioned or subsidized, it seems to me the Alvin Ailey American Dance Theater has been doing this job. It gives us a fascinating opportunity to see how modern dance repertory would work—whether modern dance, so much more dependent on individual movement qualities than the technique-rooted ballet, can really survive the generation that gave it life.

I've seen works in the AAADT repertory go through a gradual evolution until they are not the works originally choreographed. Some of these transformed versions work, others are distortions of the dances as I first saw them. I'm not sure that such changes are an inevitable result of continuous performances over many years, or if the choreography has been affected by the particular Ailey company stylistic tendencies I've been describing.

Lucas Hoving's *Icarus* is a piece that has been radically altered during the three years AAADT has had it, but somehow it adapts itself to Ailey's altogether more lush interpretation without getting lost. *Icarus* as originally performed by Hoving (Daedalus), Chase Robinson (Icarus), and Patricia Christopher (later Nancy Lewis and others took the role of the Sun) was like a desert—choking hot, with clothes the color of ashes and movements that seemed to be conserving their energy and scope for the ultimate moment of doomed flight. Ailey's version is also hot, but blazing, rich with all the scintillating colors of a Mexican cathedral.

Ailey's dancers—this spring I saw Clive Thompson and Kelvin Rotardier as Daedalus, Ramon Segarra as Icarus, and Judith Jamison and Consuelo Atlas as the Sun—are physically more muscular, more opulent than the spare, sinewy Hoving and his cast. Dressed in Beni Montresor's majestic costumes, they've made the movement more rounded, more expansive in space, and also more pantomimic where Hoving's was abstract as a primitive carving. Rotardier looks like a man trying to fly, Segarra floats and skips with flapping wrists, Atlas seems consciously seductive. I remember the original Sun especially as implacable, indifferent, plucking a tear from her eye like a cinder as Icarus tumbled to his death.

I preferred Hoving's version, and I hope it's safely on film somewhere because some of the movement sequences are now omitted—I recall Robinson doing a long series of agonizing, snakelike Graham falls at the end; they're gone now. But Ailey's *Icarus* stands up well as a theater piece and still says basically what I think Hoving intended.

What's happened to Ailey's own *Revelations* (1960) is less tolerable. I used to think this beautiful, moving suite of spirituals was choreographically perfect. Now, without actually changing many of the steps, Ailey has turned it into an escalating thrill trip, a buildup to the screaming, jumping ovation that ends the show every night.

Throughout *Revelations* the movement has become clearer, more designed-looking. Where it once looked almost improvised, almost as if the dancers weren't sure it would work, it's now set and calculated. The tender, devout "Fix Me Jesus," which had a fatherly James Truitte making benedictory gestures over a rapt woman (originally the late Minnie Marshall), now looks as romantic as a ballet pas de deux. And as technically exacting. Little nuances of focus and phrasing that used to seem spontaneous have been choreographed in now, and you see a dancer fulfilling a shape rather than answering some inner impulse.

Ailey has also given in to the temptation to make *Revelations* a big show-biz piece. At the finale six people used to be able to lift the audience out of its seats for endless curtain calls—now Ailey has sixteen doing it. An expansion of this magnitude makes such a drastic change in the stage space, the energy with which the same movements are performed, and the audience's whole image of the dance that I can see only the most superficial connection to the dance Ailey first choreographed.

In both these dances, *Icarus* and *Revelations*, one can see an evolution toward a more theatrical, vivid experience, even in kinetic terms. Ailey is not, like some contemporary dance companies, going overboard on the scenery, costumes, and sex appeal to the detriment of the movement. Perhaps the reason one dance still works as art and the other does not is that *Icarus* had pared everything down to the bone and could stand a little padding. But *Revelations* began in the human emotions, and every attempt to program that process moved the dance further away from where it was meant to be.

June 27, 1971

※⌘※

Dance Theatre of Harlem Debut

The Guggenheim Museum on Fifth Avenue and Eighty-ninth Street is about as close as you can get to Harlem and still be downtown. That's where Arthur Mitchell's Dance Theatre of Harlem held its official debut last week with three performances and a couple of lecture-demonstrations for schoolchildren. What follows is some sober reflection on a remarkable achievement.

Mitchell, who is a principal dancer with the New York City Ballet, organized the company only two years ago with a little quiet help from the Ford Foundation and visible encouragement from the likes of Lincoln Kirstein and George Balanchine, the directors of NYCB. The project has grown into a flourishing arts school in Harlem and a company of about twenty high-spirited dancers.

Once, to explain the formation of a black classical ballet company, it was said that there weren't enough black dancers in the major companies because they couldn't get the proper training. But the NYCB's School of American Ballet, with generous scholarship funds at its disposal, does accept black students. You see them every year at SAB recitals, but somehow they never graduate into the company. Even Mitchell, who remains the only black in the NYCB, dances only "exotic" roles—the fantasy character Puck in *A Midsummer Night's Dream*, the tap dancer in the show-biz romp *Slaughter on Tenth Avenue*, the leads in modernistic works like *Agon* and *Episodes*.

Dance Theatre of Harlem, in understandable reverse snobbery, doesn't accept whites, although they can study at its school, where some of the best dance teachers in the city are on the faculty. It's been said that blacks don't have the right bodies to do classical ballet, and the company easily disproves this assumption. But that doesn't get me much closer to understanding the company's purpose and intentions.

At the Guggenheim they showed three ballets by Mitchell, all in a basically classical idiom, all derivative of the Balanchine style. *Tones*, done in black and white practice clothes, was reminiscent of *Agon*; *Fête Noire*, to a Shostakovich piano concerto, was a bright ballet-ballet, with the girls in Degas dresses and the boys in cadet uniforms; and *Rhythmetron*, a kind of initiation rite, introduced a barefoot Priestess who did some energetic, not-quite-African gyrations while the rest of the company adhered to the standard vocabulary.

Mitchell choreographs with the limitations of his youthful company in mind. The boys especially impressed me as needing to develop more strength and technical assurance. But there is in all of them a sense of suppressed fire, of dynamic, dramatic potential, contained—sometimes awkwardly—by the simple, facing-front patterns Mitchell gives them to do. They need the challenge of real Balanchine and the depth of inspired modern and Afro choreography to express who they are.

Which brings me to the queasy feeling I had at the chic Guggenheim watching opening night unfold—wondering what is black about the company besides their skins, thinking how ludicrous it is that dancers like these are barred from the NYCB and most other big ballet companies. If we accept that a black face in *Swan Lake* is aesthetically incorrect, then a black company doing a Western aristocratic dance form seems to me equally wrong.

January 22, 1971

Home to Harlem

It was cold in the studio. In fact, it was cold everywhere in New York that afternoon, the kind of cold that slows down a city's vital juices and hangs gray gauze over the sun. James Truitte was teaching a class in Lester Horton technique, and it got under way late. As the last few children straggled in, he rapped his baton on the floor and directed the first series of the long, flat stretches and slow, rounded unfoldings that make you think your muscles will either have to thaw out or break. Before the exercises had gone very far, Truitte had banished quantities of jangling silver bracelets from several teen-age arms and had established the businesslike regimen that typifies all his classes, whether they are for professionals or spindly ten-year-olds.

Watching the class, I forgot that this was the basement of a shabby little church in Harlem, and that these youngsters pay only fifty cents or a dollar a week to take classes every day with some of the best dance teachers in New York. I also began to forget the misgivings with which I'd come to talk to Arthur Mitchell about his company, the Dance Theatre of Harlem.

Founded only two years ago, DTH has been giving lecture-demonstrations, out-of-town tryouts, and parts of performances for some time, but I had missed them everywhere until their official debut January 8 at the Guggenheim Museum. That evening left me with some strong and confused emotions. Anger, first, at the persistent prejudice that keeps black dancers out of the classical ballet. Disgust at the opening-night patrons who gurgled their praises throughout the performance, as if they were showing off their poodles. And the puzzling feeling that DTH was somehow out of its time, that a black separatist dance organization should be doing black dance—whatever that is—and not carrying on the legacy of the seventeenth-century French monarchs.

Arthur Mitchell came in and took me up to a big, dark room adjacent to the church sanctuary. He turned on some ceiling lights and we sat down on folding chairs at the end of a long table, while he told me about the new home the company and school expect to move into next spring. "It's on 152nd and Amsterdam. It's a plumbing and heating place now, three floors; we'll have three studios there instead of the one we have here, and we'll be able to start our classes in sewing, scenery building, and photography. We take any kids in the school—black, white, fat, skinny. The gifted ones are put into special preprofessional classes, but I think everybody who wants to dance should be able to."

Mitchell said he had two main objectives for the company: to provide an outlet for young black performers, and to disprove the theory that black dancers can't do classical ballet. DTH has received help from Lincoln Kirstein and George Balanchine, directors of Mitchell's own performing home, the New York City Ballet, and gets its major financial backing from the Ford Foundation, which has invested heavily in NYCB and its School of American Ballet. By creating a black classical company, do the culture barons hope to divert attention from the fact that there continue to be no blacks in the NYCB besides Mitchell? He doesn't think so.

"I think they'll change," he told me. "Some of our dancers have already had offers from the bigger white companies, but they prefer to stay here. They feel this is their own company." Even the Harkness Ballet, which had probably progressed further beyond token integration than any American company before its reorganization last summer, did not offer its best opportunities to blacks, Mitchell said.

"I can't tell you how many fantastic people have tried to get me to integrate Dance Theatre of Harlem. White dancers who want to come with us. But my goal for now is to keep it a black company, until we prove our point everywhere that it needs to be proved. Till there are enough jobs for black dancers. And that'll be a *long* time."

Mitchell understood my reservations about the style of dance his company does. "I'm against pigeonholing," he said. "We start with classical training because it gives a strong technical basis, but then I'd like to include everything in the repertory— modern dance, jazz. I want to do a rock symphony. Anna Sokolow is going to do a piece for us, and we'd love to have Alvin Ailey's *Revelations.* Balanchine's *Concerto Barocco* is already in our repertory. We've had black militants in here asking why we don't do black dance. But I'm a ballet dancer, I couldn't teach 'Afro.'

"We're creating a new audience for dance, and their response to us is terrific. Last year we did eighty lecture-demos and forty-four performances. It's a problem with kids, talking their language. Like you have to convince them it's not precious, that the artist isn't some inhuman, untouchable, ephemeral thing. In my lecture-demonstrations I don't come on and say, 'Now we're going to do ballet.' " He stuck out his elbows and clenched his fingertips together, like a club lady dispensing culture.

"Ghetto kids can identify with us because we show them how their dances are in *our* steps. Contrary to just coming out and doing . . ." Mitchell swung his shoulders and snapped his fingers for a jazzy minute. "We carry it to a higher level. We can always do their thing. Last year we went to this *tough* school in Newark. You know, like we were afraid to get off the bus? And the principal only let the younger kids come to the lecture-demonstrations, right? Well, by the time we got home afterwards, they had already called and said they had voted to bring us back, and if the school didn't have enough money, the kids would chip in their own money. They have dance classes in that school now. Even if they aren't going to end up dancers, the discipline transfers to whatever you do."

I asked Mitchell if he ever thought about the long-range future, and he admitted that he didn't often. "Of course, I want to have a theater here in Harlem. This project has changed a lot since it began. We were just a little school, and now all kinds of people want to exploit us—managers, producers. I have to choose the things we'll do carefully and not go too fast. I don't think in terms of *the* greatest company, or being *the* greatest choreographer or school. We just do what we have to do. We don't have any stars. We don't preach. But if the core is right, it'll work."

Katherine Dunham has written: "For myself, I insist upon the meaning of negritude as the effort to create a community of men, who happen to be black but must belong to the world around, no matter what kind or color. . . . I do not admit to a spiritual or cultural poverty in black people which would make it necessary to coin a word or system of thinking of oneself outside the human division." Dunham expresses an important theme in American dance, one that has been followed by Pearl Primus, Donald McKayle, Alvin Ailey, and now by Arthur Mitchell. It may be a political anachronism, but artistically it still makes sense.

February 14, 1971

The Pattern-Breakers

Some of modern dance's cherished convictions are fading these days as new patterns get established. There was the formula that a young dancer, after spending a respectable time in a well-known company, would begin to choreograph on his own, get his friends together now and then for concerts, and eventually start his own company. Often this process seemed to demand either a complete, rancorous break with the parent company and style, or an all-too-slavish imitation of it.

Clyde Morgan and Carla Maxwell, members of the mostly inactive José Limón company, have been making dances since their student days, as is the custom for traditionally trained modern dancers. This season the husband and wife team gave two series of their own works here, last fall at the Cubiculo and more recently at the theater of the Riverside Church. What you notice immediately about their work is that they're exploring new dance ideas without renouncing the past. They seem to believe, as I do too, that modern dance forms and techniques can still serve contemporary ideas, without the assistance of glossy decors and balletic fireworks. They are also preserving the works of other choreographers such as Anna Sokolow, Daniel Nagrin, and Limón in the best possible way—by performing them.

Perhaps even more important is the unique way the Morgans have combined the modern dance and "black dance" aesthetics. As an interracial couple, they find themselves somewhat outside the heavily political, often defensive circle of black dance advocates here. Their work neither ignores nor propagandizes for the identity of the black dancer. Together with a few others, the Morgans may be—consciously but not self-consciously—inventing a true Afro-American dance.

Up to now, black dance has tended to be either a narrative form sympathetic to the black experience—ghetto and slavery dances incorporating jazz and vernacular movement—or a reproduction of more or less authentic African or Caribbean dance material. The Morgans see choreography according to modern dance tradition, as a probing, searching journey into the human experience; they use basically the expressive language that they know, but they're going beyond the Western sensibility for their resources.

Maxwell's *Function* is a dance of exorcism, a ritual that occurs in many cultures. It begins with a little procession—Maxwell in a scrap of a dress, her long wiry brown hair streaming out loose, pale as a ghost herself; and three men in outlandish finery, parts of a Civil War uniform, the motley robes of a ragpicker king, green velvet knickers and a derby. All the men have things with them or on them that make noise—bones, bells, a tambourine—and, using these implements and their voices and bodies, they incite her from trance into whirling, thrashing frenzy. After they have scared the demon out of her body, they all leave as ceremoniously as they have come.

In this work as well as her more recent duet *Improvisations on a Dream*, Maxwell is successful in evoking many kinds of images without being so elaborate that she loses her central idea. *Improvisations* is a rustic duet with both Morgans in overalls and T-shirts. Some musicians at the side of the stage play light rhythms and harmonica riffs. Morgan recites a few spare lines: "Among a hundred and twenty snowy mountains the only moving thing . . . was the eye . . . of a blackbird." They dance together coolly.

Morgan's work, especially his new dance, *The Traveler*, is more ambitious and less clear. But it also has a kind of integrity that one doesn't always see in the work of more popular black choreographers. He seems to be digging for who he is as a black man in a white culture, and his answers are not the stereotyped ones.

The Traveler, based on Amos Tutuola's novel *The Palm-Wine Drinkard*, is a series of scenes in which Morgan confronts the various aspects of himself—African god-figures and medicine men, a tall, beautiful black woman, a contemporary couple, two white vaudevillians, and the sweaty athleticism of a track team. It doesn't resolve itself easily; as a program note comments on the final scene: "Hard to salute each other, harder to describe each other, and hardest to look at each other at destination."

The Morgans have a special kind of theatricality, and both are superb dramatic dancers. Morgan is especially imposing in *The Traveler* when he transforms himself from a loose-limbed sprinter to a wary, half-animal, half-human creature of the bush, and when he carries on a long African-style dialogue with three drummers that hasn't a bit of literal African movement.

These gifted dancers are also teachers—together with their colleague Ze'eva Cohen they will conduct the dance program this summer at the Boston University–Tanglewood Institute. Morgan is a painter of considerable talent, and they make many of their own costumes, decors, and masks. On a trip to Africa they were taken with the people's scavenging habits. Miss Maxwell once told me, "At the airports you see them carrying home junk—old oil drums that they'll use for something. We got the idea, and now we're picking up stuff around our neighborhood. Soon we'll make a dance out of it." They will, too.

May 23, 1971

IV.

MODERN DANCE: THE PROCESS OF REDEFINITION

From time to time I hear young modern dancers ranting about ballet as if it were the world's biggest cultural disaster and tyranny. While I'm amazed that this ancient animus still survives, I'm grateful for it in a way. As long as there are dancers who would rather die than do ballet, modern dance will not disappear completely.

There's never been an adequate definition of modern dance, except that it usually implies change—a search for new forms, new themes, new movement. In fact, what is generally thought of as modern dance is not the most modern dance being done: nearly all of those choreographers I've called experimental are modern dancers whose work has not assumed a conventional shape or direction. Modern dance is not a technique—it comprises several techniques and some eclectic non-techniques—but everything I've learned about it leads me back to the theory that the first modern dancers were simply answering an instinctive, almost blind determination not to do ballet. Whatever it was about the ballet that they hated—its intellectual poverty, its conservatism, its restriction of certain parts of the body and its overdevelopment of others, its formality and tradition, its emphasis on physical beauty—the moderns demanded freedom of expression, temperament, and aesthetic values, and they decided to make dances that wouldn't refuse them that freedom.

This pronounced individualism was the easiest target for people who opposed modern dance. You could say somebody's style was too personal, which conveyed several kinds of disapproval and discouragement. The choreographer was acting out his own psychological problems and/or cleverly devising a way around his failure to possess a balletically perfect body. If a modern dance role was successful, it became identified with its creator, and nobody else was supposed to be able to reproduce it, except with slavish, and inevitably futile, imitation. This meant that success in modern dance would be even more transitory than in other kinds of dance, and that the only way to survive was to codify one's work into a system so rigid and impersonal that it could be taught by people who understood nothing about it except its mechanics. When you characterize any dancer as personal, you are tacitly acknowledging the fact that more of him is present than in the work of other artists—he can't put a medium like paint or a tool like a piano between himself and his work. So modern dancers, who don't even have the security of a three-hundred-year old technique, could always be put down as cultists or—perhaps worse—idiosyncratic personalities incapable of contributing anything to the Ages.

All this, of course, is beside the point of what modern dance is doing, but rather than argue the case, I wonder whether we ought not to relax and accept the charge. All the best art is personal. Perhaps we're only suspicious of strong identities in dance because we don't know how to trap them for our museums. We tend to distrust any experience that really says anything to us until it's been suitably embalmed and displayed in less threatening form. "No, he can't have moved me so deeply," we say about a dancer, "it must have been a trick. I might let myself be taken in again, but I know it's not *really* really art." Modern dance offers almost no way of checking on what did happen, no way of repeating the experience, so it gets neatly condemned to the status of an unusual but ephemeral phenomenon.

Modern dance developed like every other art form: the inventors devised techniques, crystallized their styles, acquired followers and imitators, and saw their work gradually become diluted and combined with other styles as other innovators took their place. Some modern dance, principally that of Martha Graham, became almost as formal in technique and as pronounced in style as ballet itself—and thereby lasted longest. The most individual of the early moderns, the ones who cared least about founding dynasties, left no trace when they died. One film and memories are all we have of Helen Tamiris, who enlivened modern dance and musical theater with her vitality, warmth, and glamour—who was determined to find truly American dance forms—from the Depression years till her death in 1966.

In recent years, the incentives for modern dance companies have run heavily on the side of less experimentation and more predictable, perfected work with broader appeal. Even the surviving styles and repertory of Graham or Humphrey-Weidman have suffered a gradual attrition over time. Those early styles, so insistently antiballetic in their emphasis on the ground, their denial of vertical stress, their awkward or contorted shapes, their rhythmic complexity and spare designs, have become smoother, prettier, airborne. The generation that followed Graham has ranged much more freely into the detested provinces of ballet.

I don't think we can demand that artists cease growing or changing when they've arrived at a moment that strikes our fancy. Modern dance, by its nature, must be constantly renewing itself. But we diminish the modern dance out of all conscience by assuming that the whole thing is only a phase. Why this failure to examine or even identify styles of modern dance, to preserve anything but its most anecdotal history, to capture it by whatever admittedly inadequate means are available? There must be a way to say modern dance *is*, now, at this moment, instead of always shoving it into the corner of not-quite-being.

Ballet has its long tradition and its universally accepted vocabulary to ensure an artist's or a work's longevity, and Americans will spend money to perpetuate ballet institutions whose job is that kind of conservation. Pop dance has never pretended to be of more than momentary relevance; it doesn't concern itself with history. But modern dance is only beginning to realize that it's been doing something over the past forty or fifty years besides self-expression. Efforts to preserve modern dance have been as individual as the forces that created it. And because nothing broader in scope has been instituted than a company school or an annual festival of several choreographers, the agencies that support dance feel it necessary to help modern dance only in the short run—underwriting a season, commissioning a new dance, picking up a year's deficit, trying to reclaim a bit of the past long after its sharpest outlines have eroded.

Modern dance repertory seems to me one answer to this spendthrift process. Suppose there were one or more companies of national stature, each with teaching facilities for a variety of styles, and a serious research and archival department for the analysis and preservation of dances in their original form. This would allow the choreographer to get on with his job and at the same time would "freeze" his work so it could continue to be seen after he stops wanting to perform it himself. Ballet companies haven't been too successful in capturing modern dance styles, and the few modern companies that do repertory, such as Alvin Ailey's, are inadequately financed to undertake the large-scale effort that is necessary. Repertory Dance Theatre of Utah, created in 1965 by the Rockefeller Foundation to do this job, listed no notation, film, or research people when it made its New York appearance in late summer, 1969, and its execution seemed competent but stylistically rather bland to me. Nevertheless, this is a start.

It seems absurd to be talking of trailing after the artist, gathering up dances as if they were crumpled memos he'd made to himself and discarded. I don't know of another art form where the act of serious creation doesn't produce, simultaneously with the art work, both an artifact and a record of the work. A musical composition is, synonymously, music and a written score. Only dance requires such elaborate procedures to effect the simplest type of retrieval.

I'm not willing to consign forty years of creative achievement to oblivion without protest. Nor am I willing to see strongly personal styles get smoothed out and homogenized in the interest of more accessible theater. Modern dance is the most eloquent and humanistic of theater dance forms. In its several stubborn ways it speaks of and to the individual. For this reason most of all, we need to spare it from the increasingly mass-minded pressures of a depersonalized society.

Are Graham's Gods Dead?

Martha Graham today is more of a national monument than a shrine. Once she represented an exclusive cult where the insiders worshiped in awe, but now she belongs to all of us. And since this is so, we take a proprietary interest in her preservation. What she does with the company and the repertory she has devoted her life to create is a matter of concern to everyone who believes that dance is part of a continuum and not just an ephemeral moment in time.

In its Broadway season just concluded, the Graham company seemed to be in decline. Among all the possible reasons for this, foremost are the attitudes of Miss Graham herself. For some years critics and dance lovers have been suggesting that Miss Graham should not be dancing, and the Graham forces counter with the dictum that the public wants to see Miss Graham, that she has an obligation to appear. The issue is no longer solely that time has drastically limited Miss Graham's movement capacities, but that she continues to be the focal point, psychologically and theatrically, of all that appears on stage, and as the focal point has weakened, so has the company.

Choreographically, there appear to be two options available if a dancer of Miss Graham's restricted mobility must be the star, and these were displayed in two of the season's new works, *A Time of Snow* and *The Lady of the House of Sleep*.

A Time of Snow depicts a retrospective life, in this case the legend of Heloise and Abelard viewed by Heloise at the end of her life in the convent. This approach utilizes Miss Graham's technique of rearranging time in flashback form, and it permits most of the story to be enacted by other members of the company while the main character muses apart from the action. Perhaps because Graham has done this sort of work so often before, perhaps because it unavoidably merges with the reality of her present life, *A Time of Snow* is sentimental, even decadent, stressing the theatrical elements she invented long ago, to the detriment of the dancing. The score, by Norman Dello Joio, is indulgently romantic. Rouben Ter-Arutunian's sculptural sets consume a large part of the stage, not only reducing the playing space but actually obstructing the diagonal and forcing the movement into the confinement of limited areas and straight alleys across the front and back of the stage.

Thus not only time but action is disjointed, and, lacking the sweep and freedom of dance, the piece is closer to drama. The moments of dance excitement come in the solos of Noemi Lapsezon as the young Heloise, and in the encounters between the Abelard, Bertram Ross, and the men's group, first in the role of his fellow scholars and later as accomplices of the avenging Fulbert, played by Robert Cohan. The story is carried along by the familiar Graham device of dialogues and soliloquies, but with the dance values diminished the piece is more narrative, less poetic and ritualistic than *Night Journey* and *Cave of the Heart*, two earlier works in a similar style. *A Time of Snow* is sad but not tragic, dramatic but not epic.

Miss Graham taxes our loyalty even more in *The Lady of the House of Sleep*, where she actually is the central figure, not just the remembering mind that triggers everything off. A long philosophical program note failed to illuminate the murky symbolism of the piece, or perhaps this viewer did not try hard enough to fathom its meaning because watching it was so difficult. Miss Graham's physical limitations require that if she assumes a central role, certain conventions will have to be observed. She must be a commanding, almost totemic presence who activates the sequence of events without leaving her throne or pedestal. By witchcraft, hypnosis, or some other power, she must motivate the other characters, and correspondingly they must be drawn to her in hate, fear, desire, or any other relationship.

But—notwithstanding her influence off the stage, her status as a legend in the history of dance, the respect we owe her as an artist—this commanding presence on stage is exactly what Miss Graham lacks. When she gazes at her minions in mute assertion, or when she pulls one of them to her, there is no tension, and all that her dancers do to compensate for the missing strength cannot convince us kinesthetically that it is there. As deity or seductress Miss Graham is inappropriate, and structurally the dance has no other support. There isn't much dancing, but there is a great deal of struggling and moving around, so that the dancers can maneuver each other into new positions on the stage, or arrive at Miss Graham's feet. There is also an inordinate amount of apparently unmotivated activity with some mysterious and complicated props. I doubt whether Miss Graham has ever made a dance without an inner logic; in *The Lady of the House of Sleep*, because we are required to concentrate on her, what we see contradicts or obscures her intent.

In gratitude for all she has given to dance, perhaps we should bear with Martha Graham now and try to forgive, but she has taught us by her own example to be uncompromising, to demand much and to reject the nonessentials. Are there alternatives to the present course? I think there are many, but the first step is up to Miss Graham.

She can still make fine lyrical works for the company: *Plain of Prayer*, new this year, is one. In recent seasons there have been *Dancing-Ground* (1967) and *Secular Games* (1962). Graham's Greek cycle entered a new phase with *Circe* (1963), the only dramatic work she has made recently in which she does not appear. These dances show a still-superior choreographic mind at work, one that can give its attention to using the qualities of a new generation of dancers.

Martha Graham's company is her creation in as real a sense as her dances. It is the well-tuned instrument for her choreography and probably the best example anywhere of her technique. From it have emerged many of our best dancer-choreographers and teachers, and in it today are some notable talents. But they need to be given challenging roles, not to be always cast in support of Miss Graham and the perennial male leads, Messrs. Ross and Cohan. The new works this season provided welcome opportunities for Robert Powell, Takako Asakawa, and Miss Lapsezon. For the senior women in the company, Mary Hinkson, Ethel Winter, and Helen McGehee, the natural sequence would be the re-creating of roles Miss Graham can no longer perform. These have been discouragingly few: Jocasta in *Night Journey* and The Bride in *Appalachian Spring* for Miss Winter,

Medea in *Cave of the Heart* for Miss McGehee.

Martha Graham has said, "I do not know whether my dance will live. This is not my concern. If the ideas and principles of movement that I have created pass into the general stream of dance, I shall feel amply satisfied." It is well known that Miss Graham detests revivals, that every one is a painful process for her and for the company. She seems to feel that her works should not survive her own participation in them. She has allowed none of her dances to be notated, so each reconstruction has required the intensive efforts of any dancer who can remember some part of the work. It took seventeen dancers in addition to Miss Graham to revive *Primitive Mysteries* (1931), *Frontier* (1935), and *El Penitente* (1940) for the American Dance Festival in 1964. They have all been dropped from the repertory, as was *Herodiade* (1944) after two performances at the Juilliard School in 1963. Miss Graham may feel that these early works were conceived on a scale less grand than the one she now envisions, but it is precisely because they show the lineal development of her genius that they ought to be shown. Imagine if Haydn had thrown away the eighty-two symphonies he wrote before composing for a big orchestra!

This tragic disregard for history afflicts nearly every major figure in dance today, from Balanchine to Cunningham. In part it may account for the paradoxical condition of American dance, that as the most creative and prolific of our indigenous arts, it is also the poorest and the least appreciated. If dance is to become truly a part of our cultural frame of reference, it must be seen, and seen not merely at its present point of development but in the context of the past. In a more civilized country there would be a major dance repertory company to perform this service, but in America today the task of holding the territory must fall to the same artists who broke the ground.

The direction in which the Graham company is moving—toward lightweight group dances and extravagant melodramas—can only work to its disadvantage in comparison with the important dance innovations of other groups. More serious, this trend diminishes Miss Graham's previous accomplishments. Many in her audiences can remember her glorious early days, but every performance also draws newcomers to whom Martha

Graham is only the greatest name in American dance. I would have them see the "real" Martha Graham who revolutionized the art, even if she has to be represented by others. After a performance of *Primitive Mysteries* in 1965, the last time the work was seen in New York, a young dancer of avant-garde persuasion told me of the impact the piece made on her: "It's brilliant! I can't believe it, it was made so long ago, and everything is *there.*"

June 24, 1968

Graham in Brooklyn

Probably the least original thing anyone could say about Martha Graham is that her choreographic range and inventiveness are truly astonishing. That has been established long since. And yet the recent Graham season at Brooklyn Academy, with three revivals and a few omissions, reshuffled the jigsaw pieces of Graham's choreography so that they fell together in a new way. In this perspective, it is impossible not to marvel all over again at the scope of her mind, and to wish more desperately than ever that we could go back over the entire body of her work and study its development, instead of having to snatch our impressions from the examples of it that she can show us at this moment on stage.

Thematically, I think all of Graham's work stems from two great, interrelated preoccupations: that of mystery, religion, myth, man's rootedness in the earth and the supernatural; and that of the psyche, the inner conflicts that set man apart from nature and God. Although her dances are often considered abstract, Martha Graham never makes dances about abstractions.

The oldest work in the fall season was *Dark Meadow* (1946), revived after a fifteen-year absence. Like so many other Graham works, *Dark Meadow* examines the interior emotions of a man and a woman, in this case linked together by an Earth-mother figure and sprinkled with Freudian references in the props and the Noguchi set. The movement content of *Dark Meadow* most closely resembles the stylized ritual of *Primitive Mysteries*. This is echt-Graham of the earliest vintage: the sculptural designs of the body, the controlled flow of movement that is often cut off before completing its path, the flexed-footed, straight-legged jumps where the body pushes its energy into the ground, the violent, angular thrusts into stillness. All of this has a severe, monolithic intensity that even today we find strange and ascetic, and purifying.

By what mysterious means was Graham able, only two years later, to create the intoxicatingly lyrical *Diversion of Angels*? Or more recently the even more exotic *Part Real–Part Dream* (1965) and *Plain of Prayer* (1968)? The idea is the same: the discovery, the joy and pain of love. But the movement in these latter pieces is more fluid, seemingly less contrived to achieve a design in space than impatient to fulfill itself in time.

The earthbound, primitive religiosity of Graham was translated into Christian terms, more spiritual and intellectualized, with *Seraphic Dialogue* (1955). Already into her most theatrical period then, Graham told the story of Joan of Arc by using a device that has become almost a trademark. She had more than one dancer play the same character in different times or states of mind. Other theatrical ideas used by Graham in this piece, but not invented by her—some of them probably go back as far as the existence of theater—are the rearranging of time into a nonlinear sequence, the personalizing of one dancer's action by having everyone else go blank, and the use of a chorus (in this case Saint Margaret and Saint Catherine) to signify the passage of time or the change of events.

All these devices allow the telling of a story without interrupting the dance form by a spoken narrative or other audiovisual aid, and they are essential elements of Graham's Greek cycle. The earliest and simplest of these now in the repertory is *Errand into the Maze* (1947), in which Graham surprisingly transformed the character of Theseus into a woman. Only a mind like Graham's could have reset the myth of Theseus and the Minotaur in terms of man's, or woman's, struggle against

184

the nameless forces of fear and darkness. Similarly, she saw the legend of *Alcestis* (1960), the queen who sacrificed herself to save her husband and was restored to life by a repentant god, as a parable of the seasons, with spring triumphant.

The universality of theme is less apparent in *Cortege of Eagles* (1967) and *A Time of Snow* (1968), because the choreographer seems to have concentrated more on narrative values than on personal ones. Perhaps the vast sweep of the Trojan War is too complex, and the sentimental tale of Heloise and Abelard is too anecdotal, to permit the kind of cosmic revelation through personal witness that is the key to her greatest works.

But in these as in all Graham dances there is that distinctive vocabulary of hers, which has remained pertinent through the years. It is an expressive language in which the body is almost always in conflict with itself, reaching out with the arms and retreating in the pelvic area, opening with one side and closing with the other, striding firmly across the floor while sending a different energy upward with swinging arms. Graham wanted to move this way not just because it looked different, but because it makes visual the very real conflicts of the human spirit that are her concern.

Martha Graham has been celebrated and publicized into an American article of faith, like Lincoln or eating an apple every day, but as we look at this choreography, her genius becomes more, not less, momentous.

November 18, 1968

Martha, or Mother

At the end of Saturday night's performance of the Martha Graham company at the Connecticut College American Dance Festival, some voices in the audience began calling for "Martha! Martha!" Amidst the applause and bravos, it almost sounded like "Mother!" Modern dance has been heading away from the dictates of the Graham matriarchy for several years; indeed, it has frequently been in open revolt against this most enduring and demanding of its parents. But the Martha Graham mystique persists, accompanied by the classic love-hate familial patterns. Saturday's Graham revivals showed the great choreographer at her most creative, and her company as an obedient if not always inspired instrument.

Diversion of Angels, the latest of the three works, was created during the first American Dance Festival in 1948. A plotless company work, it was one of the first in which Graham did not create a role for herself, and it contains an entirely different kind of focus and tension from those tortured epics in which she was the center. Takako Asakawa as the Girl in Red, Mary Hinkson as the Girl in White, and Yuriko Kimura as the Girl in Yellow flash and glide among three serene couples like brilliant tropical fish in quiet waters.

A lucid, lyric piece of choreography, *Diversion of Angels* has a relaxed flow and a suspended, cartwheeling expansiveness that seem to point toward a later, softer Graham style. *El Penitente* (1940) and *Every Soul is a Circus* (1939) belong to her uncompromising early era.

El Penitente, a sort of peasant mystery play, based on the rituals of the flagellant sects of the American Southwest, was last seen in 1964, when it was revived in New London in memory of its composer, Louis Horst. The movement is stiff and linear, growing out of the procession that introduces the piece, and the music is spare and naïvely ceremonious. As Mexican peasants enacting a little pageant of sin and forgiveness, the dancers stamp and run with angular hips and flexed feet, holding their upper bodies in poses like the crude frescoes on the walls of Indian churches. There is a cruelty about their faith and an unyielding devotion about their play-acting.

The Mary role was originally Graham's and is now danced with compassion and knowing sorrow by Mary Hinkson. Moss Cohen plays the stern Christ figure in a black velvet robe and triangular death mask with a crown of thorns. Bertram Ross, the penitent sinner, is a stoic, self-despising religious fanatic.

Every Soul is a Circus has not been performed in about ten years, and Patricia Birch, who supervised this revival, plays Martha Graham instead of Martha Graham's role. This observer had never seen the work before, but I kept thinking it was Graham up there, so faithfully has Miss Birch re-created her. Few of Graham's roles have come to life on their inheritors; to follow her must seem a sacred trust, and it is a delicate undertaking to preserve Graham's style without merely reproducing her mannerisms and timing.

Circus is one of Graham's famous spoofs on the performer's profession and, incidentally, on Graham herself as Empress of the Arena. Graham's wit and visual originality are there, down to the last detail of costume and ogling chorus girl. So far the company has not found a way to be comfortable in the work— one feels they are imitating it, not dancing it new. Miss Birch carries the piece, staggering around the stage, hurling herself into plastique poses, fluttering and mugging in the mock derangement of Graham-as-artiste. The company prances indifferently about her, but they seem less the cause of her distress than the stage setting for it. Bertram Ross is one of the most immobile dancers dancing; as the Ring Master he makes a good Mexican church painting. Robert Powell as the "juvenile" Miss Birch supposedly covets is not much more than pretty.

The production has a curiously lifeless two-dimensionality, perhaps a result of its having been reverently reconstructed from a film. By the company's fall season, perhaps they will have stopped looking at the film and started learning how they feel about the dance.

August 11, 1970

Mailing Her Letter to the World

By now it's as difficult for anyone involved in dance to look at Martha Graham's work with equanimity as it is to regard one's own photograph. So much of ourselves is invested in it, one way or another, that though we study it persistently, squint at it from every angle, or try to sneak up and catch it fresh, we can never really get outside it anymore. The problem has now become crucial, because unless someone can do this, Graham's work is going to disappear very soon.

On the day the Graham company opened its season at Brooklyn Academy, Miss Graham made front-page news by declaring she would not dance again. That night, accepting New York City's Handel Medallion for distinguished cultural achievement, she denied it, saying she plans to appear in one piece next spring.

This kind of vacillation is understandable; Miss Graham has spent her adult life on the stage and it must be agonizing to give up that role. But the necessity of doing so has been evident for some years, and Miss Graham's continuing indecisiveness has gravely affected her company. There are so many ways this woman of genius could have remained at the center of her own life's effort, without literally playing the central role. Dancers are the only artists who can keep the world from owning their art, and Martha Graham of all people should not be permitted that luxury.

The Graham repertory, even the limited one offered during the short season in Brooklyn, has extraordinary range, from the spacious romanticism of *Appalachian Spring* to the harsh iconography of *El Penitente* to the heroic passions of *Cave of the Heart*. Everyone knows Graham for her psychological probings, but we often neglect her gift for color and costume, her wit and timing.

Now that she seems to be freeing all her roles, the body of her work takes on an entirely new perspective. It may not be necessary, as we have always thought, to see all her choreography as a projection of her own emotional or intellectual states. It may even be, dare I suggest, that there's more than one way to dance a Graham role. There were, after all, things Martha Graham knew about the world that she could not dance herself.

Most people seem to associate Martha Graham's choreography with her doom-ridden, vengeful Greek heroines—Clytemnestra, Medea, and the rest. In these roles the dissonant energies, the earthbound strength, and the devouring intensity that were her most notable performing qualities found appropriate expression. The Martha Graham Myth began here, I suppose—the idea that the performer and the choreographer were fused into one indissoluble organism. Yet a different aspect of *Phaedra* is revealed now by Matt Turney, a tall, beautiful, soft woman, about as different physically and temperamentally from Miss Graham as any dancer in the company. Turney's Phaedra, distraught and yielding, is the classical figure imagined by Racine —truly possessed by Aphrodite, the goddess of love, unable to express any will of her own.

The present *Phaedra* is a drama of more equally weighted forces pitted against each other, with Mary Hinkson as the implacable Venus, Richard Kuch as Theseus, Robert Powell as Hippolytus, and Phyllis Gutelius as the rival deity Artemis. I never saw these other characters before, except as streaks of light refracted off the prism of Graham's obsession.

Even in the early days Graham had an elegiac side—an unsentimental, lyric reverence for life, for air as well as the ground, for the renewing part of death as well as its finality. These were present in *Alcestis* and the company work *Canticle for Innocent Comedians*, and this season in the luminous *Letter to the World* (1940). Guest artists Pearl Lang, Jean Erdman, and Jane Dudley have revived the two-sided, dancing and speaking poet Emily Dickinson and her oppressive, puritan Ancestress. Pearl Lang, in Miss Graham's original role, is delicate and quick, like the Emily who can rhapsodize to her New England world: "I'm sorry for the dead today!" Miss Lang's grief over the loss of her lover may be fluid and quietly personal while Graham's was, I'm told, Promethean. It doesn't matter. *Letter to the World* moves me now, perhaps because I'm not haunted by any other view of it.

Deaths and Entrances (1943) seems less amenable to reconstruction. Perhaps it's just not a very good dance—its three main characters are modeled rather tenuously on the Brontë sisters, but only one, now played by Mary Hinkson, has much chance to establish an identity. The others, with assorted lovers, friends, and remembered selves, run in and out a lot on possibly spurious errands. Mary Hinkson's acting and dancing are magnificent. Yet I feel the tenacious grasp of Miss Graham on this role more than any other now in the repertory. When Mary Hinkson goes mad with unrealized love, her torso arching and sinking, her upper arms pressed tightly to her sides while forearms splay out into thin air, or one hand flutters weakly at her throat, I feel I'm looking at some very private purgatory, and I want to run out of the theater.

Patricia Birch makes a good job of the silly, vain Empress of the Arena in *Every Soul is a Circus,* but here again is a piece I feel cannot really be revived. The Empress is Graham's mocking portrait of Graham; someone else dancing it is a sawdust heroine. It's as if Johnny Carson in all seriousness tried to do Jack Benny.

The thing about revivals is that we can't know until they are produced whether they will live up to our memories. Martha Graham revivals are probably more difficult to achieve than most because of the resistance, not to say opposition, their creator has always posed to any attempt at saving her work. Yet, after an old work has been laboriously reconstructed, it's apt to disappear after a season or two. Is *Letter to the World* going into the same limbo as *Dark Meadow* did a couple of years ago?

October 18, 1970

Ex-Post-Graham

Choreographically, the Martha Graham epoch is declining, and Israel's Batsheva Dance Company, in its two-week run here, displayed all the excesses and conceits of a weakening line of succession. The company, however, appears to regard choreography as the vehicle instead of the driver. It takes some adjusting to accept the increasingly prevalent idea that modern dance means dancing perfection instead of creative insight. I can't help suspecting this is happening because dance is so much in demand and real choreographers are so scarce.

The Batsheva dances in a strongly dramatic, full-out style that stresses immediate impact rather than the more reticent, introspective qualities often associated with modern dance. Rina Schenfeld demonstrated how effective this approach can be in every role she danced. Thin and fine-boned, she moves with the fluidity of a Pearl Lang and the acting authority of no one I've seen in modern dance for ages. Leading the men was Moshe Efrati, a muscular, aggressive dancer whose self-centered agility I found more offensive than dullness.

Efrati's *Sin Lieth at the Door* relates the Cain and Abel story from a male chauvinistic viewpoint that I think of as Siegfried's Revenge—a retaliation for men dancers' years of boredom and eclipse while the ballerinas held center stage. The men, Efrati and Ehud Ben-David, dance up a storm in preparation for the usual disastrous denouement, except that instead of two contentious brothers, they symbolize a creative misfit and a doomed conformist, with a well-meaning but seductive lady Demon (Schenfeld) getting the blame. In Efrati's *Ein-Dor*, a narrative of King Saul, a woman is again the death-bearer, but it is the king, played by Efrati, who gets to do the emoting.

Maybe we have had enough female protagonists in the Graham era, but one thing Graham was never guilty of was showing off. These he-men do their tricks at the audience like a TV chorus line. I should add that most of the psychological stuff I just told you about came from the program notes, not from what I saw on stage. Rina Schenfeld's *Curtains* could have been replaced by its program note entirely. Or, preferably, by Graham's *Every Soul is a Circus* or *Acrobats of God*, which the said note might have been describing. The Artist torn between the life of contemplation and the glamour of the stage. *Curtains* has a marvelous wrought-iron, spidery trapeze set by Danny Karavan that could have decorated a French ice-cream parlor, but the dance had neither the wit nor the fantasy to match it.

Batsheva's artistic director Norman Walker contributed *Baroque Concerto #5* (Vivaldi), and the Englishman Norman Morrice choreographed *Rehearsal! . . . (?)* and *Percussion Concerto*. I put these works together because they all seem to lack a point of view about movement; the dancers always look unmusical and off-center somehow, and confused about which direction they are going next. Walker follows conventionally the neat lines of his music; Morrice is oppressively cute.

Glen Tetley, who is about five years closer to the mother lode than any of the choreographers mentioned, looks far better than usual when seen in this perspective. Tetley's *Mythical Hunters*, a kind of semiprimitive fertility rite, shows a richer movement vocabulary, a more inventive use of imagery, and a greater range of dynamics.

But it is in the works of the "originals" that the Batsheva really shines. It's always a pleasure to see good choreography done by a new set of dancers, and this company gave additional dimension to all the oldies I saw. Jerome Robbins' *Moves* is given on pointe by the Joffrey Ballet, and that company is far better equipped to tackle its movement difficulties. But what the Batsheva lacks in technique here it supplies in theater intelligence. They do *Moves* not as an enigmatic ritual but as drama. They performed Graham's *Diversion of Angels* and José Limón's *The Exiles* with similar vibrancy.

Rina Schenfeld gave a brilliant performance as the woman who traverses the path of fear to the center of her own heart in Graham's *Errand into the Maze*. Not only is she dramatically intense, but she is very clear about the shape and path her body makes in space, something modern dancers often de-emphasize. As a result, the dance is as much about the confines of space— and the breaking of those limits—as it is about emotions. Rahamim Ron, incidentally, was the first dancer I've ever seen play the Minotaur as if such a creature could conceivably do battle with a woman.

Embattled Garden, Graham's sophisticated quadrille about eternal sparring partnerships, was given a superb, alive performance by Nurit Stern as Eve, Moshe Efrati as Adam, Rina Schenfeld as Lilith, and Ehud Ben-David as The Stranger. Though Efrati rather overbalanced the symmetry of the piece with his mugging and acrobatics, I haven't seen men move this well in a Graham piece since Robert Powell was a boy.

December 27, 1970

Early Floating and Twilight Turbulence

Probably no two approaches to modern dance are more radically different than those of Anna Sokolow and Erick Hawkins, who shared a week at Brooklyn Academy. The one similarity between them is that they maintain a consistent level of intensity. Both choreographers have, really, one dance, one theme. I find Sokolow emotionally exhausting, Hawkins progressively soporific. In effect on the nervous system, it's the difference between a fast run around the block and a tranquilizer.

Miss Sokolow's programs included *Tribute*, a short memorial to Martin Luther King; an extensively revised version of *Memories*, choreographed in 1967 for the dance students at Juilliard; *Odes*, also done first at Juilliard, in 1965; and a new major work, *Steps of Silence*. Anna Sokolow's choreography is intensely theatrical, loaded with emotional content despite its deliberate ambiguity. Its themes are dark—Miss Sokolow once told me: "I haven't got that happy philosophy, but what the hell's to be happy about?"—but it is beautiful in its despair and its passion. The movement is like breathing in all its variants—sobbing, choking, sighing—as it builds or explodes to a climax, subsides, builds again from the stillness.

Steps of Silence opens in the dark, with the dancers reciting passages they have chosen to illustrate the condition of Anna Sokolow's world, and presumably theirs. "If life presses down on me and I don't take it in, don't push it out, don't do with it —if I don't transmit life, then no one will know that I existed," says the first one. "Nothing exists except myself," says another, and "This is a place where nothing is happening."

Nothing is happening except the terrible aloneness of the individual. Anna Sokolow may be the inventor of the dancing-without-seeing convention that so many choreographers use to

193

signify isolation—the lovers who never make visual contact, the running in circles with the body completely open and the face tilted up toward an empty sky, the boy who lifts his hand, not to stroke the hair of the girl in his arms but to clutch his own face. Whole sequences are choreographed in unison but are executed in each dancer's own impulse and style.

This is dancing of frantic movement, and of indelible images. In *Steps* a boy stands in a spotlight shuddering, grabs his ankles to stop the spasm, falls backward, and looks back at the pool of light in bewilderment, like a stricken animal. Though you may hate it, you can't take your eyes off this choreography, and you don't forget it in a hurry either.

Erick Hawkins' new dance, *Tightrope*, may or may not be about balance and imbalance. So may *Early Floating*, and *Cantilever*, and *Naked Leopard, Lords of Persia, Geography of Noon*. Whatever the title, this kind of bodily sensation is pretty much Hawkins' whole bag. Hawkins and his dancers are concerned with weight and flow, with the gently shifting energies the body can generate by giving little pushes to itself and catching itself again. It looks very sequential and pretty, and it feels good, like swinging in a hammock or ice skating. It's just not very interesting.

A striking contrast, even an aberration, is *John Brown*, now revised but originally made in 1947, when Hawkins was dancing with Martha Graham. Whatever its shortcomings as a theater piece, *John Brown* has a much more expressive and communicative range of movement. It is exactly this expressiveness that Hawkins seems to have rejected since leaving Graham in the early 1950s.

Hawkins has flattened out his dancing by taking away its response to time and space. If you remove the scent glands of a skunk, or clip a dog's tail, you may make a more aesthetically pleasing object, but you've also destroyed some of the essential skunkness or dogness of the thing. Time to a Hawkins dancer means how long it takes to complete a movement, the body's own time, not the urgency or delay of time that makes movement exciting. Because the dancer gives in to time, none of the insistence or conflict of rhythm and counterpoint can develop. Lucia Dlugoszewski's scores are written after the choreography is made, and minutely follow the counts, which have no pattern. Similarly, space is not a separate entity that can make demands on movement, or into which the dancers might focus. They are simply poised in space, placidly making their way through it.

When a Hawkins dancer leaves the ground he becomes curiously awkward. He is no longer in contact with his own weight, and since he has no space or time factors to govern his movement, everything, in a sense, just flies around loose until he lands again.

Hawkins' dancers are sunken into a pleasurable, trancelike sensation that is subtle in its variation and limited in its scope. Nothing can touch them or interrupt their continuum. Anna Sokolow's dancers are engaged in a constant battle with time and space, with the sluggishness and momentum of their bodies. They commit themselves completely to the movement, even when it's dangerous. Sokolow reveals what is crucial about emotion by doing it. Hawkins tells us in pretentious program notes what we should feel, and shows us no feeling. Hawkins makes me restless. Sokolow makes me care.

December 16, 1968

Zone of Safety

Erick Hawkins seems to have deliberately cut himself off from most of the expressive possibilities used by other choreographers, particularly Martha Graham, with whom he danced for many years. Where Graham's dances are narrative or psychological, Hawkins' are abstract. Her dynamics are strong, exciting; his are soft and limpid. Her dancers cut through space, writhe, leap, struggle, stretch out to get somewhere; his are comfortably undulating along inside their own bodies, gently shifting their weight with no desire to take it anywhere. Graham exploited the tensions that can be created when the body works against itself, twisting into dissonant shapes or defying the stabilizing center of gravity; Hawkins and his dancers let the energy flow sequentially through their bodies, operating always in the safe zone directly in front of themselves, never allowing themselves to venture off balance.

Having dispensed with individual danger, conflict, and surprise, Hawkins also isolates his dancers from one another by treating them as elements of design. A boy touches a girl in the crook of her elbow or behind the knee. No reaction. No sex. In his new work, *Black Lake*, premiered in a week of performances at the excellent little theater in the Riverside Church, various individuals appear to be related to each other. We can tell this because the program note gives them names (stars, birds, night people), because they wear similar costumes, because they move in unison to counts or to Lucia Dlugoszewski's complicated score for violin, cello, clarinet, percussion, and prepared piano. But not because they are making contact as people. As a matter of fact, the entire cast is masked until they advance in a line to make their final bow.

Black Lake has moments of terse, haiku-like poetry. In one section, a girl bathed in silvery light wafts a white disc through the air in smooth arcs. Two figures in black run swiftly around her with rustling sheets of tissue paper, like wispy clouds blowing across the moon. Because Hawkins' movement range is so restricted, this kind of imagery cannot go very far without becoming literal—lightning is represented by a girl with a jagged white stripe down her back being chased by a rattling cardboard-sheeted thunder.

Hawkins' choreography in itself has no thunder and lightning. His kind of abstraction may be suited to the graphic or literary arts, but dance is about people; it can never be abstract. Hawkins' movement looks, and probably feels, pleasant and harmonious, but a whole evening of it on the stage is about as interesting as a lullaby. Some people think it's beautiful. I prefer my beauty less refined.

January/February, 1970

Something Beyond Steps

The four choreographers who prepared the spring concerts of the Juilliard Dance Ensemble, March 20–22, represent vastly different approaches to dance, but they agree on one thing; Juilliard students are a rewarding group to direct, even though they are not yet professional dancers. For their own special reasons, the gifted young dancer/choreographer Michael Uthoff and the three veterans Anna Sokolow, Antony Tudor, and José Limón seem to find Juilliard an important place for personal growth and refreshment.

Michael Uthoff is not very far from being a student himself, having left Juilliard after two and a half years in 1965 to join the Robert Joffrey Ballet. Uthoff, the son of former Kurt Jooss dancers Ernst Uthoff and Lola Botka, was not encouraged to follow his parents' career, and only decided to study dance after seeing a performance of the José Limón company in Buenos Aires. By then he had completed high school. He came to the United States from Chile, where his parents headed the Chilean National Ballet, and after studying briefly at the Martha Graham School and School of American Ballet, he began taking classes with Limón and Antony Tudor at Juilliard.

Uthoff feels Juilliard is an excellent place for students who begin their dance training late, because of the opportunity it offers to work with outstanding choreographers and teachers, and because students can perform while still in school. Uthoff danced in the Juilliard touring company, with José Limón, and in the two seasons of the American Dance Theater at Lincoln Center before joining Robert Joffrey. During the next three years he gained rapidly in strength and sensitivity, until he was dancing several solo roles. In the summer of 1968 Uthoff and his wife, Lisa Bradley, resigned from the company.

Uthoff says he is at a point in his career where he wants to stop and think about the future. He intends to continue dancing and to choreograph, and he is also teaching at Brooklyn College. "I don't want to have my own company, or even do whole concerts of my own choreography," he says, "but I would like being part of a company where I could participate in the artistic direction."

Last spring Michael Uthoff choreographed his first work, *Quartet*, which was shown at a special performance by the Joffrey Ballet. Since then he has done a new piece for a civic ballet in Houston and choreographed a ten-minute film by Gardner Compton, the photographer of Joffrey's *Astarte*. His piece for the Juilliard students, *The Pleasures of Merely Circulating*, using a combination of balletic and modern movement, has thirteen dancers and a score by Handel.

Uthoff believes the scarcity of new choreographers coming out of the ballet field is due primarily to the scarcity of real talent. But the economics of ballet companies, he feels, discourages them from taking the risk of producing a new choreographer's work. He mentioned with admiration that American Ballet Theatre was performing a first work by Juilliard alumnus Dennis Nahat this spring.

"I want to keep dancing and choreographing—do both as long as I can," Uthoff says. "I don't want to wait to choreograph until I stop dancing. By then, if you're forty or so, you have preconceived ideas. I can still grow now; I'm open to new ideas. I'll experiment with anything that stimulates me, if it comes from Alwin Nikolais, Murray Louis, or anyone. I wish there were more opportunities for young people who want to do choreography. You have to work with other bodies than your own, or else your work becomes too personal. Each dancer has his own qualities, which should be used. The chance I'm getting to work at Juilliard is fantastic. The students are marvelous people. I had no trouble communicating with them. They honestly work very hard—they're doing what I wanted them to do, and they look good doing it."

It was Antony Tudor's idea to ask Michael Uthoff to do a new work for Juilliard. Uthoff says of his former teacher, "Not many people get a chance to work with Tudor. It I ever become something big, a lot of it will be because of what he has to say. He makes you think of what is essential for a dancer to become greater. It's something beyond steps that makes you an artist."

Antony Tudor found a few minutes between a class and a rehearsal to talk to this reporter. Dressed in rumpled street clothes, with a tie and rolled-up shirt sleeves, he looked more like an engineer or a government official than the famous choreographer and teacher that he is. He explained that he had decided to teach the first-act Pas de Trois from *Swan Lake* as a final examination piece for Anthony Salatino, who will be graduating this year, and juniors Sirpa Jorasmaa and Maria Barrios. The idea for showing the Pas de Trois on the spring concerts came from Martha Hill, director of the dance division, he said.

Tudor learned many of the Russian classics as a dancer in England, and this version of the *Swan Lake* Pas de Trois was taught to the Royal Ballet (then the Sadler's Wells) by Nicholas Sergeyev from notes made at the Maryinsky Theater, where he had been regisseur-general. "With these classics," Tudor said, "you can't really pin down which is the original choreography. Certain steps are obviously always the same, but others are changed from time to time by directors and gradually get accepted. I think this Pas de Trois is pretty close to the original Petipa, but even Sergeyev may have made a few changes. But that's all right, as long as the steps remain in the period."

Over the years Antony Tudor has choreographed new works and revived his own ballets for Juilliard concerts as well as directing the classics. He says he finds making dances exhausting. "This year I'm saving my energy for a new piece I'm going to do in Australia. It's more fun reviving the classics than my own ballets. They bore me badly by now—the same movements day in and day out. But people surprise me. Sometimes it becomes a different ballet. Once we did *Pillar of Fire* at the Teatro Colon [Buenos Aires]. Everything was the same—the steps, the costumes. But the family looked slightly seedier, poorer. Why? The posture of the Hagar's body was waif-ier. It changed the whole quality. That's very interesting to rehearse. That's a lot of fun."

Asked how he feels about working with Juilliard students, Tudor called over some embarrassed dancers and tried to get them to answer for him. Then he said, "I think they've had trouble with the Pas de Trois, it's terribly hard, but they're learning more than they would if we hadn't been planning to perform it. I don't consider them amateurs. Everyone, even professional dancers, can do better. Teaching people with polish you have less to get your teeth into. Students bring more enthusiasm into the work. I'd infinitely prefer to teach a lot of rough clods like this." Tudor's eyes twinkled and the students giggled. "There's not much difference between teaching class and setting a piece. I rehearse this exactly like a combination in class. When they've learned it so well it does itself, that's a performance."

The dancers ran through the difficult Pas de Trois once, and Tudor said, "That's a killer. But it's a very good training piece. If you can stagger through that you've really learned a lot."

Echoes is the tenth piece Anna Sokolow has choreographed for the students at Juilliard. Most of these works were later staged for Miss Sokolow's own company, or for one of the many ballet and modern dance companies who want her as a guest choreographer. "I always do new pieces for Juilliard," she said recently, "never revivals. The students are well trained, and I don't find them much different to work with than a professional company. And here you get a chance to work with a live orchestra."

Music is very important to Anna Sokolow. She says, "I don't have choreographic ideas. I just keep playing the music. If the music evokes an image, the image will evoke movement. Then when you see the people doing the movement, you know why you're doing the piece. You have to feel the musical phrasing and timing as well as the movement. The music we're using for *Echoes* is very challenging—you can't count out bars. But the more unplanned the dance looks, the more planned it has to be."

A friend had suggested that Miss Sokolow should listen to the Concerto for Harp and Chamber Orchestra by John Weinzweig, who teaches at the University of Toronto. When she heard the piece, she was fascinated by it and decided to make the dance that became *Echoes*. The title was suggested by one of the dancers. When asked its theme, she answered in the oblique way that is typical of her, "Everything's about something. I hope it's not considered sad, though. I'm tired of people always thinking my pieces are sad. This is supposed to be a 'lyric piece'—I'm saying this in quotes. It's what the music evoked, purely that."

Miss Sokolow, who always seems to be in several places at once, expected to join her own company on a tour of the Midwest during the last week of Juilliard rehearsals. Leaving Janet Soares in charge, she would return just before the performances. "I feel I can trust the kids by the way they've responded to how I work," she said. "I like working with students. They're very alive and seem to understand what I'm doing. Maybe because I work differently. There's the excitement of the unexpected— what am I going to ask them to do next. And I like to know how the dancers, especially at Juilliard, feel about doing my movement. I stop and ask them once in a while what their images are, and they must be specific. I'm against this anti-feeling school."

Later in the spring, while rehearsing her company in a new work set to Edgard Varèse's "Intégrales," Anna Sokolow will teach movement in the Juilliard acting department. She feels her choreography has a direct link with acting, and has frequently taught movement for actors, although she never teaches technique for dancers. "All art involves technique," she says. "When a group rehearses with me, they learn."

For José Limón *La Piñata* is a nostalgic reminiscence of his childhood in Mexico, where the birthday of a child's patron saint was celebrated with games, pranks, and the breaking of a beautifully decorated *piñata* filled with presents. He calls the piece a romp, but he adds, with the awareness of the contradictions in human nature, the sinister beneath the gaiety, that often shows up in his work, "Breaking the *piñata* caters to the destructive in all of us, the latent vandalism, especially when it's something very beautiful and carefully wrought. It's like the mischievous delight of Halloween."

La Piñata has an original score based on several children's folk songs that Limón sang to the composer, Burrill Phillips of the Juilliard composition faculty. The dance is a huge one, using over thirty dancers. Limón says he tries to provide students with performing experience to the limit of their capacity. His ideal is always to choreograph for "incredibly gifted dancers," and he has to keep reminding himself to simplify his ideas so that students can execute them.

However, he has warm praise for the hard work and enthusiasm of the students, some of whom were also to appear in other works on the spring program. Limón enjoys large groups—"I want to learn how to work with them"—and the students at Juilliard have provided the raw material for his mass-movement experiments over the past ten years. Many of these students later graduated into his professional company.

Like young Michael Uthoff, whose dance career he inadvertently ignited years ago, José Limón feels he is at a kind of crossroads in life. This year he gave up his technique classes at Juilliard to concentrate on directing and choreography. After twenty-one years in residence at Connecticut College School of Dance, Limón and his company will take a sabbatical this summer. Most of the dancers will be teaching and performing elsewhere, and Limón and his wife, Pauline Lawrence, will stay at their farm in New Jersey. "It's the first time I won't have to force things, rush to finish a piece for the American Dance Festival. I'm looking forward to it."

The man who is considered among the giants of American choreography stated with a look of determined idealism, "I want to learn to be a good choreographer. I want to rearrange myself. I have a lot to think about, and I plan to do a lot of gardening. This moment is a kind of continental divide of our century. We all have to make certain choices about what we are and where we're going. I mean everybody, not just the artist. We can't exist inside a safe egg—nobody has that luxury. We have a lot to do, and we have to find out how. Nothing may come of it, but that is the risk we take for being alive."

March, 1969

Spoils of Success

In the space of a few short years, the modern choreographer Paul Taylor has gone from iconoclast to classicist. Make no mistake about it, Taylor's choreography at its least adventurous is significantly more interesting than the reshaped and tinted segments of the same old wallpaper that so often pass for new ballet. But we have come to expect a certain satirical punch and kinesthetic challenge from Paul Taylor, and his evolution from calculated chaos to refined order has disappointed many of his old admirers.

As recently as 1963, Taylor electrified the audience at the American Dance Festival in New London, Conneticut, with the world premiere of *Scudorama*. Tortured and enigmatic, *Scudorama* was beautiful as only violence can be beautiful—a thunderstorm, a four-alarm fire, or Times Square on a rainy night. Anonymous dancers, dressed sometimes in street clothes and sometimes in leotards, struggled and writhed in the impotent fury of nightmare. With its strong, distorted movement, empty relationships, and shocking images—like a squirming pile of bodies on the floor—the dance gave an impression of the futility and isolation of modern life that was at once realistic and abstract.

After *Scudorama* came two lesser works of social comment, *Post Meridian* and *Party Mix*, and the bitingly sarcastic but less dancy *From Sea to Shining Sea*. At the end of 1966, *Scudorama* was given a sabbatical from the repertory, its descendants were to appear less often, and Taylor entered his neoclassic period with *Orbs*, a two-act allegorical ballet set to Beethoven's late string quartets. The Taylor company's appearance at the 1968 American Dance Festival last August featured the return of *Scudorama* and, in dramatic juxtaposition, two post-*Orbs* pieces, *Lento* (Haydn) and *Agathe's Tale* (Surinach).

203

Lento could be the exact antithesis of *Scudorama*, a serene urban landscape with well-planned streets and gentle inhabitants who don't believe in littering. The substance of the piece is lyric movement, danced with a cool extroversion that resembles the work of George Balanchine more than Martha Graham. Taylor divides the company into small choric groups that move about an essentially passive central figure, Bettie de Jong. Making a focal point of a dancer who hardly ever dances is typical of Paul Taylor's mind; even in his most logical works he refuses to do entirely what the audience expects.

Watching *Lento*, I thought of *Aureole* (1962), Taylor's abstract work to music of Handel, and wondered why the two were so different. Humor is one answer. In *Aureole*, Taylor puts non sequiturs into the movement with great ease and charm. A line of three girls glides downstage on the diagonal with a movement pattern that begins almost classically, but on the last beat of the measure, as they go into attitude, the line of their bodies crumples into a hilarious zigzag. A girl comes out of the downstage wing, facing the audience, and with little sideways jumps she circles up to the next wing, disappears for a moment, and comes back trailed by another girl doing the same thing; then the two jump down to the first wing and blossom into three girls. For all its immediate beauty, there is a hidden dimension in *Aureole*. *Lento* has the same kind of visual appeal—the interesting patterns and groupings of dancers, the fluent movement—and the same intelligent musicality that distinguishes Taylor from many of his more far-out colleagues, but it lacks the subsurface life that made *Aureole* brilliant.

Taylor seems to be after a tighter theatrical effect in his recent work. He is less concerned with the expressive qualities of movement, less willing to dangle any perplexities or loose ends. In *Lento* the dancers' arms and legs are prominent, with a gestural theme of reaching high overhead, palms parallel. The arms lead the upper torso in a diagonal across the body or from side to side. The hips follow the thrust of running or jumping legs. The prevailing dynamic is one of tranquil mastery.

Contrast this with the movement of *Scudorama*: percussive contractions and rotations of the upper torso against the lower, arms and legs flailing in dissonant shapes, energies that shoot out from the center as if they would tear the body apart, twisting of a closed body with perhaps a hand or foot hanging useless from the sinuous central mass.

One might argue that *Scudorama* was simply a different dance with a different theme, but an indication that Taylor really is thinking in a new way comes from the manner in which that piece is currently being performed. When it was made, Taylor augmented his company of six dancers with two extra girls for this dance. His present group consists of eleven dancers, and all are used in *Scudorama*. The original choreography had a basic group of three girls, soloist Bettie de Jong, two boys, and the two extra girls who provided peripheral embellishments and gave weight to the crowd scenes. The two men were especially strong, partly because they *were* the only two men, and partly because they were given incredibly difficult and striking things to do. Dan Wagoner walked very slowly, with arms in the horizontal, bent knees, flexed feet, and a spread-out stance, and a girl draped on his shoulders. The movement had a quality of laborious effort, of the girl being an intolerable burden and the man exerting all his force to drag their weight across the ground. Now the girl-on-the-head sequence is done by two couples in unison, and it merely looks virtuosic.

Where once the dancers' faces remained impassive while their bodies ran the gamut of expression, they have now been told to "look ugly," and their resulting masks draw attention away from the movement. This distortion of faces and multiplication of forces occurs throughout *Scudorama* and in almost every case depersonalizes and overstates the original idea.

Where *Scudorama* is grim and *Lento* is glowing, *Agathe's Tale* is funny in a highly stylized way. Paul Taylor's sense of humor was always one of the most joyous and individual elements of his choreography. He developed comic sequences out of the movement itself, often with a kind of naïve astonishment, as if the wayward foot or whirling arm had suddenly acquired a life of its own over which the owner had no control. The explicitly stated *Agathe's Tale* lacks the freshness and surprise that come from taking risks with the audience's comprehension.

Agathe's Tale, probably Taylor's first story ballet, is a bawdy account of a chaste young maiden who is deflowered by Satan and finds it good. Similar to Callot engravings in its exaggerated passions and physical grotesquerie, *Agathe's Tale* is an expert piece of work. I find I like it better with each viewing, but not, as with some dances, because its ambiguities grow clearer. In fact, *Agathe's Tale* has no ambiguities. At first sight it is so graphic as to be almost offensive. But after one has assimilated its hard-sell farce, one can look closer at the skillful choreography and timing, and the way Taylor uses movement to delineate character. Before her seduction the maiden Agathe moves with proper mincing steps—and a suggestive undulation of the hips. The Angel Raphael, her protector in the guise of a unicorn, operates in a plane of pious verticality. The orphan Pan, a ward of Satan, is earthbound, and beguiling as a serpent. Satan himself is mocking and relentlessly phallic.

In its very perfection *Agathe's Tale* exemplifies the new Paul Taylor. Gorgeously costumed and flawlessly danced, the piece is immediately accessible to the least sophisticated audience. Its humor and symbols, like the slapstick wedding section of *Orbs*, leave little to be discovered. Structurally, *Agathe's Tale* is probably the best dance Taylor has ever made. Its narrative is clear, and it has little superfluous movement and no problematical shifts of focus or role. Unlike the earlier choreography, *Agathe's Tale* does not require the audience to supply meanings or act in any way as the choreographer's partner.

Orbs and *Party Mix* were revived for the company's fall season at Brooklyn Academy. *Orbs* is big, programmatic, and very balletic; in fact, its more abstract moments remind me of Balanchine's *Four Temperaments*. *Orbs* explores the related ideas of the planets in their orbits, the seasons in their cycle, and the tug and ebb of human relationships.

Taylor has set up the piece in a rather complicated structure that superimposes celestial bodies and seasonal characteristics on their human counterparts. The choreographer himself plays the Sun, and in the abstract, formal opening section he dances the central figure in a pattern that includes four solo Planets and four choruslike Moons. Things become more specific in the next section, Venusian Spring, as the Sun introduces the Planets to flirtation and love-making. He later returns with an angry mask on the back of his head to dictate a Martian Summer that is by turns violent and exhausted, depending on which face the Sun shows to his galaxy. Everything comes down to earth in the modern-dress Terrestrial Autumn section, with its farcical wedding where two former Planets are married by Taylor, now a minister. The structure then reverses itself, peeling off the layers of meaning, through the sunless Plutonian Winter, where the Planets are detached and slow-moving as icebergs, and finally back to the single motif of the concluding/opening section.

One can't help but admire the almost Copernican logic of a dance like *Orbs*. But the grandiose structure, together with the majestic music, is too much to take in. If you go out and look at the stars on a clear night, you aren't much going to care *what* Copernicus figured out about them. They're there, is all that's important.

In *Orbs* the dancing itself is constantly being overpowered by the logic. To me, the humor is often forced, the movement labored, the plan too insistent. Possibly I wouldn't mind this if Taylor were revealing some cosmic truths about the human condition, or even some trivial insights. Love and hate, power and dependency, nervous brides and tipsy bridesmaids. *Orbs'* significance is both too profound and not original enough.

Party Mix is a strange little piece about the games of courtship and conquest, put-on and put-down that are played at a cocktail party. Like most cocktail parties, the piece is inconsequential, there is no thematic or character development, it just bubbles on until it's over. As if to underscore (or perhaps distract from) the triviality of the dance, Taylor has given it a succession of outlandish costumes. When it was first made in 1963, the dancers wore zany wigs in every color of the rainbow. Now the wigs are gone, but the girls have new bare-midriff, pedal-pusher costumes that look as if they are made out of a patchwork quilt. After you've taken in what everybody is wearing, this party is only an amusing diversion.

At the Academy Taylor also gave the New York premiere of *Public Domain*, a piece that demonstrates he has neither lost his gift for nonliteral comedy, nor run out of things to say that aren't banal and obvious. Basically an affectionate view of the foibles of dance, the piece has a tape score by John Herbert McDowell that opens with the overture to the second act of *Swan Lake* and closes with Brahms' Variations on a Theme of Haydn, and in between skims through Gregorian chant, marching music, Puccini, a polka, baroque organ music, Arabic music, Elizabethan music, and possibly everything else ever composed for which a choreographer does not have to pay royalties. The way Taylor uses and abuses these gems may be in itself a comment on the economic difficulties of dance-making, and the artistic disasters that can result from dipping into the public domain. For example, an actress says, throatily, "Medea, beware! Some great person is coming!" In the suspenseful silence that follows, a large white ball rolls across the stage. Three beats. Then a small white ball scuttles after it.

Public Domain, like its score, is an eclectic string of ideas put together in no particular order, in which the dancers gamely go through the paces of choreography that is by turns diabolically difficult, glib, showy, or just plain terrible. Taylor has a great fondness for his dancers, and his view of them here is compassionate even when they are called upon to make fools of themselves. Their apologetic faces seem to be saying, "I'm trying my best, but this body of mine just won't cooperate," or "I know this is silly, but we'll muddle through it somehow." The comedy is sometimes hilarious, sometimes gentle, as when a girl in purple does a slow, introspective solo to an utterly inappropriate Dvořák folk song, holding aloft a tiny white flag. Some sequences are not funny at all.

I had a curious reaction to *Public Domain* at its first showing. The more serious parts seemed unbearably slow—I wanted the piece to be fast and funny all the way through. I have concluded that this difficulty is not the fault of the piece, but of the context. Taylor's Brooklyn repertory, consisting of *Orbs, Party Mix, Agathe's Tale,* and *Lento,* was so light that I was unprepared for *Domain*'s shifts of mood. One of his stronger or satirical dances, such as *Scudorama* or *Sea to Shining Sea*, would have tipped off the audience that everything was not going to be pure pleasure. But it is precisely these darker works that have always puzzled and disturbed Taylor's critics and some of his audience.

This recent tightening and purging of Taylor's style is, I think, symptomatic of a larger trend throughout the modern dance field. Like Taylor, Merce Cunningham, Alwin Nikolais, Alvin Ailey, and others are finding life rather easier these days —and more demanding. Their audiences are growing, they perform almost continuously, and they pay their companies almost year-round. Concurrently, they are under pressure to produce more successfully and to please more universally than when they gave that one infallible concert a year for their New York fans.

It would be easy to say that Paul Taylor is just going through one of his phases, and if we wait long enough a more creative period may come upon him. *Public Domain* may be the beginning of such a period. But the growing institutionalization of modern dance will make it difficult for the leaders of the field to retain or regain their innovative powers. We may be in for a period of conservatism in modern dance, and then it will be up to another generation of choreographers to rise and break the icons of the 1960s.

December, 1968

Food for the Eye

In a program note introducing his concerts at the Brooklyn Academy dance festival, Paul Taylor has called his choreography food for the eye. In his recent work Taylor seems to be aiming for the most immediate and accessible of our responses. We don't need to do much more than sit back and enjoy his easy visibility, or, as two different people remarked to me during the Taylor week, he's wonderful to look at when you're tired.

Public Domain, Taylor's new work, offers just this sort of entertainment, relying on two of the things Taylor does best, movement and humor. The piece opens with Taylor and two couples up left, the couples doing some adagiolike combinations and Taylor doing the same thing with an invisible partner. A girl in purple reclines on the floor to their right, but no one pays any attention to her. From there, they're off on a spoof of the perils and pomposities of just about every style of dance you're liable to encounter on a New York stage this year.

There are the two competitive ballerinas who miscalculate their grand finale, crash into each other, and, unable to extricate themselves, hop off in a ghastly tangle of arms and legs. There is the earnest soloist in a female interpretive dance number who suffers from an uncontrollable tremor that could be contagious. There are the three neophytes who try to do a complicated Russian-ish routine and fail spectactularly. There is the eager performer whirling and smiling through the last hurrahs of a verbose production number, long after the bored departure of her comrades.

Taylor's affectionate humor in *Public Domain* occupies the middle register of a range that extends all the way from the broad slapstick of *Orbs* and *Agathe's Tale* to the merest whisper of surprise in the lyric pieces like *Lento*, where the central figure practically never dances. Whatever he is choreographing, Taylor seems unable to suppress this comic strain. I think he is more interesting when he lets it grow directly out of the movement than when he derives it from a situation. For instance, *Party Mix* is rather a one-joke dance about the casual flirtations, rivalries, and disappointments of a cocktail party. Although Taylor makes a funny comment by having the dancers continually shift partners, he is even wittier when he has a sexy girl enter and quickly transfer her throbbing expectancy to the entire assemblage.

There is, of course, more to Paul Taylor than his humor. He is one of the most musical people in dance, and this quality is expressed as much in his movement as in his attentiveness to the accompaniment itself. Taylor's movement style encompasses a large variety of changes in body shape and direction, from the smooth, almost classical line, to fluent curvings and twistings, to contorted angles and knots. Throughout all their modulations in space, his dancers maintain an unusual degree of lightness, even the men, who are built along more muscular, even stocky lines than the average male dancer. The dancers glide or skim across the floor instead of running, and each action seems to spring out of the one before without interruption. Their response to time is highly developed; they can make sudden changes of direction with the whole body, come to a complete abrupt halt in the middle of a very fast sequence, or do sustained jumps that seem to float on air. Their faces are serene and alert, only occasionally tinged with surprise or perturbation, as if what's going on in their bodies is all happening to someone else.

This constant use of the unexpected—the lightness where you would look for strength, the discontinuity between the dancer's action and his reaction, the improbable changes that seem so logical after they have been done—always occurs within Taylor's overall command of phrasing, composition, and musical structure and provides a cornerstone of his work.

Taylor's intent has not always been as clear as it is now. Some of his earlier work had ambiguities, loose ends. Mysterious people drifted in and out, ominous things happened that seemed to have no reason or consequence. It wasn't quite perfect, and I liked it better then. A programmatic piece like *Orbs*, with its concentric themes of planetary revolution, seasonal cycle, and human relationships, is so big, so well planned that it leaves little room for the viewer to speculate. The narrative *Agathe's Tale* is bawdy and colorful as a Punch and Judy show, and just about as deep. And the plotless *Lento*, tranquilly elaborating on its Haydn score, is bland and bloodless.

With *Public Domain*, Taylor may be moving back to some of his former complexity. It has, deliberately I think, moments that are not funny, but it was difficult, within the slick context of the Brooklyn repertory, to experience them as anything but ponderous flaws in an otherwise up-tempo divertissement. I hope Taylor will not "fix" this piece by making the comedy broader and trimming the introspective parts. He is too good a choreographer to forget that dance is best when it supplies food for the mind as well as the eye.

January 6, 1969

211

Big Bertha

Paul Taylor isn't clever, chic, mod, or zingy. His dances aren't particularly with-it, they don't try to clear up all your doubts before you realize you had any. They are only crammed full of movement and ideas and originality. They are, in fact, a perfect antidote to too many mediocrities, and a reaffirmation of the great but rare American art of choreography.

Of course, Americans didn't invent the art of choreography, but we do seem to have a corner on the special breed of dance artists who owe nothing to anybody except with thanks, who don't bother to explain what they're doing because often they don't exactly know, and who don't give a damn for fashion or history and end up making both. Paul Taylor is one of them.

Taylor's new work, *Big Bertha*, was first shown February 9 at the ANTA Theater. The piece is funny, macabre, garish, low-keyed, and provocative, all at the same time. It's about an all-American tourist family mesmerized into bestiality by a nickelodeon. Out West I've seen these weird contraptions, with cymbals clapping together, the bass drum going thump, and the piano keys being pressed by invisible fingers. There's something freaky about the idea that all those robot instruments can play together and succeed in making music.

Big Bertha is represented by Alec Sutherland's gaudy cutout set, John Herbert McDowell's collage of sound effects and authentic music from the St. Louis Melody Museum, and by a well-padded Bettie de Jong, costumed as a turn-of-the-century majorette doll, who conducts the music and gulps nickels when the machine runs down.

Taylor and Eileen Cropley, as the folks next door, Mr. and Mrs. B, come sauntering in with their cute daughter, Carolyn Adams. They are all scrubbed and holiday-smiley, pretending there's no inconsistency about the fact that Miss B happens to be black and Mr. and Mrs. B are white. They are a typical bloodless, 1946-nice family that doesn't have problems.

Taylor puts a coin in Bertha's hand and as she begins to play, the family dance for each other, shyly at first and with polite nods of appreciation. Suddenly Big Bertha points her baton and Mr. B goes goggle-eyed and slaps his wife. Then he's his old bland self; you hardly think it happened. But it did happen, and as Bertha pulls them into her power, the whole family turn into fiends. Mr. B starts fondling his daughter, then drags her off to the bushes. She's shocked at first, but later she likes it. Mrs. B meanwhile strips to her red undies and stands on a chair wiggling, something she has no doubt considered shameful all her life.

As the orgy is building up, you remember that at the beginning of the dance you saw some exhausted red-clad figures crawling away, and you realize that Bertha is going to wring out the hapless B's the same way. She does.

Paul Taylor has a merciless eye for this kind of Americana. His 1965 satire *From Sea to Shining Sea* comes out of the same dusty carnival trunk. I think these dances say more about us as a people than all the romances of Agnes de Mille or the jazz of Jerome Robbins.

February 18, 1971

The Theater of Vision

Alwin Nikolais, whose "sound and vision theater pieces" *Somniloquy* and *Triptych* had a four-week run late last fall at the Henry Street Playhouse, is one of the few innovators in the American theater today. Unlike most playwrights and choreographers, Nikolais does not try to reshape traditional theater forms to fit his ideas. He makes up his own forms. Nikolais' theater is different from a play, a dance, or a happening. It is most closely related to film in its visual flexibility, but because it is live and three-dimensional it has a breathtaking immediacy that film can never achieve. Some of today's most far-out theater still makes use of symbolic devices such as language, connotative movement or sound, and the metaphorical conventions of the stage space. Nikolais believes, as do many contemporary choreographers, that the artist should not try to impose his emotions or opinions on his audience, but instead of breaking up the plot or the message with random sequences and simultaneous unrelated events, his theater is ordered and planned, to give the viewer an experience that is coherent and beautiful as well as open to interpretation.

The term *dehumanization*, which has so often been applied to Nikolais' work, is misleading because it conjures up ideas of robots dancing in a chrome-plated, computerized laboratory. Nikolais rejects the symbolic-psychological premise on which most modern dance has rested, but his ideas are always founded in the human experience. He sees man not as a heroic figure struggling to realize some personal truth, but as a creature who exists as only one part of an environment no less complex than himself. Nikolais does make extensive and often novel use of technology. He composes his own sound scores on electronic synthesizers. His methods of lighting break every rule in the stagecraft books. His use of projections is advanced far beyond anything else being done in dance. But Nikolais' mechanical devices are a creative means, not an end in themselves.

Both artistically and technically, *Somniloquy* is a brilliant, mind-blowing achievement. It is charged with insight though it has no "meaning." Its impact on the senses is anything but transitory. As a unified whole it surpasses anything Nikolais has done so far.

Instead of accepting the stage patterns traditionally implied by the wings, the cyclorama, and the edge of the stage, Nikolais has divided his stage horizontally into an almost infinite number of planes by the use of a scrim and bands of light. The action takes place within any one of these areas, or in more than one area at a time. The lights and projections can make the spaces appear and disappear. Like the spaces, the people in them materialize in a variety of ways: as silhouettes growing larger and smaller on the scrim, as disembodied faces or limbs, as figures that suddenly appear out of the darkness and then fall away into the void, or as complete bodies weirdly lit by projections. The people sometimes cross from one dimension to another, by leaping through shafts of colored light, or by drawing up the scrim. Viewed through these layers of perception, the dance is a play on the degrees of reality and unreality, and the thin line that divides the two.

The piece opens with a design projected on the scrim that looks like the mouth of a cave or a cross section of a geode—one of those strange rocklike formations lined with crystals. A man's torso appears in silhouette behind the scrim, growing to giant size, then shrinking away. Then another man appears, far away, deep inside the cave. Then he is gone and the cave is gone, and the area behind the scrim is filled with dancers, illuminated in bright colors by flashlights that they hold on their own faces. Later, other people take the flashlights and shine them all around on the scrim, to make it look like a field of psychedelic fireflies. The whole dance is a succession of images like this, created by the rearrangement of these few basic technical devices—pools of light, atmospherically shifting blocks of color, and projections on the scrim, the cyc, and the floor.

Some of the environments thus created are spectacular. In what I thought of as the tent caterpillar scene, there are figures behind the scrim, pressing against it and moving back and forth, as if they were trying to break through. They are lit from behind by bright beams of color reflected off sheets of foil. The color changes from red, silver, and blue, to green and purple, to blue and green, to all red, while the movement of the dancers against the scrim intensifies and the electronic sound becomes more frantic. At last the whole scene is a pulsating inferno of sound, color, and movement. By interposing a scrim between the audience and the action, and then making the scrim a part of the action, Nikolais transformed a conventional stage climax into fantasy.

Nikolais is often criticized for making his dancers subservient to his technical effects. Actually, his dancers are employed in three distinct ways. They may be the insignificant manipulators of props or lights. They may be the center of attention, dancing in solos or small groups. Or they may fuse with a total environment. One should not go to Nikolais only to see great dancing, for his intention is to show something beyond the dancer's capability. But when they do dance, his people exhibit the finely honed style, the precise control of space and dynamics that Nikolais has preserved and developed from the Mary Wigman–Hanya Holm school of modern dance. This German style was more analytical and less introspective than the American modern dance of Martha Graham and Doris Humphrey, and for twenty years it has served as the springboard for Nikolais' "total theater" experiments.

In *Somniloquy* the duet between Murray Louis and Phyllis Lamhut is almost a bare-bones version of the entire work. It is a dance showing the discovery of space, and of the self in space. The dancers feel and explore the space around the body, and when they touch, they become part of one another's space. When they embrace, the feeling is not so much one of contact as of enclosure. With a movement technique that deals with the body as it relates to space, Nikolais' choreography is by nature environmental and objective. The critic John Martin once looked at Murray Louis dancing a piece called *Dark Corner* and recognized that he was not dancing about how it felt to be in a dark corner, he simply *was* dark corner.

In the final scene of *Somniloquy* Nikolais creates one of the most astonishing effects I have ever seen in the theater. Using the full stage and all the dancers, he projects an overall design of white dots, so that the whole picture resembles a snowstorm in a Japanese woodcut. The dancers, who have been moving about, suddenly freeze. The projection goes completely out of focus and at the same time the dancers tilt into new positions. Almost before we realize what has happened, they tilt back and the projection comes into focus again. This abrupt switch from all the previous color and movement to a milky white silence is repeated two or three times. It has the stunning impact of a hallucination or any unexpected glimpse of the world from an entirely new perspective. Before we can recover, the dancers begin moving again through the snow, the scrim comes slowly across the stage, and one by one they disappear behind it. The curtain comes down on the snow-covered scrim and a looming figure in silhouette.

The other half of this program at Henry Street, *Triptych*, consisted of three rather unrelated sections that illustrated some of the theatrical devices with which Nikolais has experimented. Each section used the dancers in one of the three ways I described earlier.

Scrolls seems to return to Nikolais' earliest work, which explored the use of props as extensions of the body. Here the dancers play with all the possibilities of six-foot wide scrolls of brown paper. They hold them aloft in V shapes, they hide behind them, they conceal themselves inside them. These particular props are rather clumsy to move with, and they are most effective as settings for Nikolais' elegant projections, which resemble delicately colored tapestries and glowing stained-glass windows.

Putti is set in an eerie world of the imagination where nothing is quite real, and everything is beautiful and slightly scary. In the foreground of a dark stage three pairs of acrobats revolve slowly on ropes, lit only by many pinpoints of colored light. From the murky green distance behind them, two couples gradually emerge. They are dressed in street clothes, all in white. They are still and aloof. One couple embrace, the others link arms. They all recede into the darkness. But they return several times, becoming more curious about the acrobats, who continue to exercise on the ropes. The couples walk nonchalantly down to the acrobats and gaze at them as if amazed and envious of their strange beauty. Then the couples slowly retreat to their empty twilight and the acrobats revolve on the starlit ropes.

Idols employs the mechanical device of three huge, whirling cylinders made of string. Sometimes they are empty, with designs and lights projected on them, and sometimes there are dancers inside. *Idols*, however, is a dancers' piece; the props could be of another type or could be dispensed with altogether. The dance has a ritualistic quality, especially in Murray Louis'

217

solo, where he works himself into a dervishlike frenzy that can only be calmed when the others impale him with sticks.

Critics have had a lot to say lately about the ideal theater—if it's not the Lincoln Center Repertory, is it the APA, or the New York City Ballet, or the Martha Graham company? If a theater is a place where artists can experiment with new ideas, develop and perfect them, and use them to discover still newer ideas, then Henry Street Playhouse has to be one of the most important theaters in this country. While other dance companies spend most of their time on exhausting tours, build up their repertory in hasty rehearsals at rented studios, and continually alter their productions to fit an assortment of unsuitable stages, Nikolais and his followers have a permanent home where they can rehearse and perform. Nikolais' output is not large. Sometimes he works a full year perfecting all the elements of a new piece. In the admirable little Playhouse, with its understanding administration, Nikolais has been able to apply his enormous talents and has created a unique and visionary theater.

December, 1967

Deus ex Machina

If you go to the theater several times a week and have a speaking acquaintance with light plots, cue sheets, and all the backstage machinery that makes the theater work, it's hard to believe in magic. But Alwin Nikolais flips me out every time. Nikolais, of course, is the choreographer-composer-designer who made words like *mixed media* and *total theater* obsolete, and whose company gave its only New York performances this season during Thanksgiving week at Brooklyn Academy. Nikolais is visual, funny, nonliteral, and absolutely unique.

His work is always evolving, and the Brooklyn season covered a five-year span that I think represents very great progress indeed, from the full-length *Imago* (1963), a suite of dances in which the dancers are at different times merged with their environment, dominated by it, and aloof from it; to *Tower*, a section of the longer 1965 work *Vaudeville of the Elements*, in which the dancers, chattering inanely, build a sort of Tower of Babel out of aluminum pipe, with suitably apocalyptic results; to *Somniloquy* (1967) and *Tent* (1968), where, with consistent and concentrated imagery, the dancers appear in an almost ecological relationship to their dreamlike environment.

Nikolais is traditional about one thing: he confines his theater to the stage. None of this audience-participation, break-down-the-barriers, we're-all-performing-together sort of thing for him. Nikolais' theater is carefully planned and controlled, but it is at the same time wide open to interpretation by the viewer.

Within the playing area, Nikolais achieves great spatial flexibility, often breaking down the dimensionality and perspective that the proscenium stage imposes on our understanding of a theater event. In *Imago*, for instance, in the section called "Fence," bands of tape are stretched horizontally across the stage, creating two narrow upstage corridors through which the dancers pass in a seemingly endless stream. Our orientation to the stage as a boxlike enclosure is destroyed, and we can then imagine the horizontal corridors and the dancers in them traveling an indefinite distance out into the wings. This extension of the imagination through a restructuring of space is carried even further in *Somniloquy*, where the entire dance takes place in several horizontal planes across the stage.

In *Tent* the playing space expands and contracts around a womblike shelter to which the dancers relate in various ways. When they bring the tent out at the beginning, furled like a sail, they inspect the stage and the audience jauntily, like circus performers coming into a new town. But as soon as the tent is pitched, no other space has any meaning for them. They gather inside it, venture out—but not very far, arrange it into new shapes, dance underneath it, and finally are crushed by it. Nikolais' gorgeous lighting and projections intensify the idea of the tent as the center of a growing and shrinking universe by sometimes focusing on the tent against a blacked-out background, sometimes adding light so that we can also see the area around it.

Nikolais' movement style, from which all his choreographic ideas have developed, is highly spatial. His dancers are trained to move in relation to space, not according to arbitrary demands of body alignment or motor strength. In *Imago* there are still traces of the "dehumanization" for which Nikolais is, wrongly, I think, sometimes condemned. Even when his dancers are the most disguised, the most subservient to props, costumes, and effects, even when they become objects, they relate to each other in human ways. The cumulative effect of ten depersonalized dancers in *Tower*, alternately at voluble cross-purposes and in inexplicable harmony, building their aluminum fortress, is both very funny and very human. But with *Somniloquy* and *Tent*, I think, Nikolais has reached the most impressive and meaningful realization of his contention that man and his environment are inseparable. For some people this may mean that man is diminished. For me, the human spirit comes off immeasurably enriched.

January 13, 1969

Nikolais' Theater of Marvels

One afternoon a couple of weeks ago Alwin Nikolais sat on his own home stage at Henry Street Playhouse and told a group of people from the U.S. Institute for Theater Technology, "In two years multi-media will be finished. In fact, I'm getting a little tired of it myself." These may seem fateful words indeed, coming from an acknowledged master and originator of the multi-media craze. However, if a lot of imitators and faddists are going to be left stranded when the tide turns, Nikolais himself will probably have no trouble figuring out what to do next.

Even now, Nikolais uses the term *multi-media* with a certain ironic undertone, because to him theater has always meant a fusion of dance and sound with whatever visual elements were technologically possible. He probably could not pick out if he had to the moment when his work stopped being a theater of masks, props, and mobiles and became a theater of multi-media.

So, although his recent works have relied heavily on film and slide projections, color, shadows, the whole transitory gamut of images evoked by light, it isn't surprising to find him now going back to dancers manipulating props, and achieving equal success. *Structures,* which received its premiere last week during the Nikolais Dance Theatre performances that opened the City Center American Dance Season, has a lot in common with the best of his previous works, regardless of modus operandi—it is beautiful, funny, constantly surprising, and almost diabolically simple.

The basic elements of *Structures,* are ten dancers in plain leotards and tights, and ten rectangular screens about four feet high, with smaller hinged panels at the sides that allow them to stand up alone. Each dancer has his own structure that he can hide behind, push around, jump, lean or fall out of, and in general have a ball with. Colored lights and projections are used in the piece, but not to the same extent as they have been in Nikolais' recent work. The predominant shapes and patterns in *Somniloquy* and *Tent* were fluid, curving; in *Echo* (1969) they were hard-edge silhouettes of human body parts; in *Structures* they are straight lines and angles that suggest the man-made linearity of a warehouse or an urban landscape.

As usual, Nikolais is working on several levels at once. Sometimes the dance is all design, especially when the screens glide around the stage and form into ranks and fences without visible means of propulsion. Nikolais' color sense is one of the most acute in the theater today, and in *Structures* he uses a lively palette of blues, greens, pink, orange, and lavender that is stated in the dancers' costumes and that later recurs when they turn the white screens around to reveal mosaic panels on the inside.

Then there is the idea of the transformations that the dancers can make by using the screens as props. They can appear to be taller than they really are, disembodied hands can clutch at incorporeal heads, people can emerge from places where no people are supposed to be. One marvelous scene reels off a long series of fast optical jokes and non sequiturs based on just this possibility.

Nikolais' dancers are exceptionally well trained to use certain parts of their bodies in isolation while the rest is still, and to control the flow of movement so that they can achieve a very smooth, almost mechanical kind of locomotion or can come to a dead halt in the midst of nearly any activity. They are thus astonishingly good at producing all kinds of kinesthetic illusions, but they are less effective in those "pure-dance" passages Nikolais choreographs into every new work. To this observer Carolyn Carlson alone has the compelling solo qualities that in previous years made Murry Louis, Phyllis Lamhut, Gladys Bailin, and Bill Frank as interesting to watch as the most grandiose of Nikolais' theatrical inventions.

Beyond their immediate reality, Nikolais' works usually carry some imagistic suggestions for the viewer to take home and ponder. *Structures* is at least the third of his dances to end with an apocalyptic pessimism. Suddenly the sight gags are gone and the dancers have built a city out of their screens, and the city is burning, and bodies are flying through the air. When we think it over later, the scene should not have been so unexpected; the screens could have been alleyways all along, and those scurrying, posturing, grinning people could have been ourselves, couldn't they?

Nikolais is a genius. Not because he is so clever with media, but because he can show us how closely related are the apparent polarities of the world. With the sophisticated skill of a grownup, he dares to play out the games of our childhood, when we imagined our bodies to be different shapes and sizes than they were, when we had fantasies of becoming invisible, or everywhere, or superhuman, when we built a house of cards and pretended it was a city that we could blow down with a huff. Nikolais' work perpetually hovers around the blurred line of demarcation between the real and the unreal, the prank and the retribution, the delight and the horror. It is utterly fascinating and utterly unique.

May 7, 1970

Scenario

People are probably going to think Alwin Nikolais' new dance, *Scenario*, is a radical departure for the great abstracter and "dehumanizer" of movement, but it isn't. *Scenario* does use emotions—or the physical properties of emotions—in a more specific way than Nikolais has done during his mature career, but it uses them in the same way and for the same purposes that he previously used color, the shapes of natural forms, and the sound of words.

Nikolais long ago outdistanced the myth that he doesn't make works for dancers, that his people are the servants of props and devoid of individual expression. As far back as *Tower* (1965) he was working with the pop-art, collage effect of many people talking, moving, and emoting all at the same time. *Tent* (1968) is as pure-dance a work as anyone has ever made; Nikolais' stunning concept of a circus tent that can change shape, color, and design was meant to—and did—enhance the dancers rather than override them.

The works that followed *Tent*—*Echo, Structures,* and now *Scenario*—all concentrated on the dancer as the main event in a potentially threatening landscape, the dancer laughing, whistling, jigging, with a corner of his eye on the shadowy distance. *Scenario*, premiered February 25 during the Nikolais company's ANTA Theater season, sets out four emotional territories or weathers that the dancers create with voices and movement, and intersperses them with a diagrammatic commentary of slide projections.

The dancers start out in a lineup, pinned against a dark backdrop by projected cubicles of diminishing sizes and then by straight and wavy stick-figure designs. In a jagged lightning-split background the men punch and yell at each other. Girls spar with ghostly figures in the dark. There's a hysterical orgy of crying and another one of laughing. People grope around a brightly lit stage as if they can't see, and frighten each other into screaming fits with the slightest move. At the end they mix up their fight, fright, laughter, and tears at random in a madhouse of temperament, and finally they line up again and shuffle toward the audience, holding little speakers that emit scratchy mechanical guffaws.

I found *Scenario* disturbing, and I'm not sure why. Though there are some dazzling visual effects, the piece isn't primarily an essay in sensual images as many other Nikolais works are. It doesn't flow as smoothly from one idea to another, or sustain ideas; it's constantly being broken up by blackouts and by the dancers freezing in a posture, their faces twisted in mid-shout.

The dancers handle the technique of sobbing or giggling with great facility, yet I balked at the idea of such strong emotional manifestations being under such tight control. Is Nikolais saying here that emotions are just another theater element, to be turned on and shut off at will? He's often stated as a keystone of his whole aesthetic that "art is motion, not emotion." Somehow, while I can buy that joyfully in his other work, it seems contradictory and even cynical when the subject of the work is emotion itself. If anything, *Scenario* seems more dehumanized than its decorative predecessors, not less.

March 29, 1971

The Reluctant Showoff

Katherine Litz is one of the more underappreciated people in dance. Soloists often are, especially if their style isn't big and extroverted. A Pauline Koner or a Helen Tamiris could fill a stage with passion and project it out across the footlights so that you'd feel that energy flowing all around you. With Litz the process is reversed: she pulls our attention in to the place where she is, doing something very small and detailed and compelling in its intensity.

Katherine Litz has a reticence, a certain self-deprecation. She seems to sense an absurdity in the idea that such a private individual as herself should have gotten into such a public line of work. Her best choreography occupies the two extremes of riotous farce and understated, even cryptic, sincerity, but she strenuously avoids didacticism. This year Miss Litz has been evolving a sort of lecture-demonstration in which, with her group, she shows what her dancing is about. She calls it *Harangue and Inner Thots with Big Sister*. The choice and spelling of those words are entirely consistent with the shy, half-joking way she deals with the most serious ideas.

Earlier in the year, during the *Harangue*, Miss Litz made some intriguing comments on herself: "In order to find out how to deal with the earth, I had to come to New York where the pavement is," and "I say it's never so very impressive but it comes from the gut." For two more recent concerts at Brooklyn Academy she discarded these teasers. As if she has realized the futility of trying to convey her own essence in words, she tells us straight off, "The total look of what I do—it would be like explaining me to you, and that I cannot do." There is no one anywhere who has quite the look of Katherine Litz dancing. Her solos are intensely personal but not self-indulgent, internally focused but still aware of being watched. Like some madwoman presiding at a tea party, she seems to be warily inviting us to meet characters and situations that she knows are ridiculous, but that she cherishes just the same.

In *Fandango*, she makes her entrance through a backstage door held open by the stage manager, a slightly vain, slightly faded artiste wearing too much costume. (This pathetic/hilarious lady is a familiar Litz character; she reappears in other dances as a singer, actress, cocotte.) She executes a minimal Spanish dance, giving herself little jogs of energy in the head, the upper back, the torso, and then ignoring them with the rest of the body as if to say, "Don't bother me; I'm concentrating." Some irrelevant props bombard her; she ignores them. Then, as a voice on tape callously advises her over and over to "get with it," she turns frantically to the growing pile of inscrutable junk around her, feverishly unfolding sheets of paper that she takes from plastic cups strung on a wire, scanning them for an invisible message. She gets up, tries to dance again, by now swaddled in tulle and foam rubber. But it is too late. The stage manager is holding the exit door and the curtain is coming down.

All of Katherine Litz's best work seems to make some similar comment on this deadly serious and at the same time absurd business of performing. Sometimes it's just the endless, steadily declining, but bravely dissembling performance of life itself, as in the autumnal solo *Fall of the Leaf*, shown in January at Judson Church. Sometimes it's the sham yet earnest world of the Theatah, which she satirized in *Recitativo: Aria (Duettino)*, at the same Judson concert. In that piece, with music Al Carmines set to lines from her own *Harangue*, she was the egotistical soprano, majestically overriding the musical intrusions of David Tice. Her daggerlike glances of jealousy, almost imperceptibly wrong timing and pitch, and exaggerated emphasis meant to conceal, but only drawing attention to, some horrible mistake had the kind of sophistication and innocence you might find in Anna Russell doing a takeoff of Florence Foster Jenkins.

In *The Glyph*, seen at Brooklyn, she alternately flirts and struggles with a piece of long tubular jersey. Others have explored the possibilities of confining, stretchy fabric, but I don't think Litz meant to satirize Nikolais, Graham, or anyone else. I think she was, once again, describing the state of the performer, who finds herself enmeshed and disguised in her costume or role. She pushes against it, tries to break out, but also finds it snug and protective, and when she finally wriggles free and becomes figuratively naked in front of an audience, she flees offstage.

Katherine Litz's vision is so personal it doesn't transfer well to a group. Moreover, her dancing style is neither strong enough nor definable enough to be copied. Martha Graham codified her way of moving into a technique and then taught it to a company that now, in gross outline at least, moves like Martha Graham. Miss Litz seems to work more with the motivations and sources of movement than with its outward form. Her choreography for the group alone, a piece called *Adaptations*, is somewhat academic and slow to develop its theme, though it does have some of the quirky Litz humor. But when she does theater pieces with herself as the central figure, like the *Harangue, Recitativo: Aria,* and a full-length work called *Continuum* that she gave two years ago at Hunter College, the presence of other dancers, actors, or singers seems to inspire the reluctant showoff in her to new heights of whacked-out surrealism.

April, 1969

The Real McCoy

This week someone asked me whether a certain young choreographer was doing modern dance or ballet, and I couldn't answer. So many young dancers are using a kind of stylistic Esperanto that movement is no longer a distinguishing factor in their dance. What Charles Weidman is doing is unmistakable, authentic, and as pure as anything being executed by young bodies today. For this reason if for no other, it's very important that he keep on working.

Seeing Weidman and his company, I realized with a jolt how far the style we think of as modern dance has moved, by imperceptible degrees, away from its sources. We critics try to pick out these changes when we see them, but the experience of the moment is so strong, so much more real than what we might remember, that we end up describing a gradual evolution toward theatricality, we talk about the incorporation of balletic techniques and the diminution of this and the deterioration of that. But we probably don't make the point strongly enough that a whole approach to dance has virtually disappeared.

"Modern dance" is talked about almost exclusively today as if it had been merely some catalytic influence that freed dancers from the confines of ballet, for the purpose—depending on the critic's bias—of either expanding the range of ballet, or triggering the creativity of the post-1950 avant-garde. People seem to value Martha Graham most today for having spawned Gerald Arpino and Merce Cunningham! This attitude of detachment from our immediate past, of devaluing our precursors, scares me a lot. Mostly because in dance, unlike any other art, we have no real system of retrieval. Forty years from now, when a new generation begins to appreciate Doris Humphrey again, how will they know what she did?

The program I saw was one of the six Charles Weidman is giving at state hospitals, under a grant from the Cultural Council Foundation. Though it was short, it encompassed many of the ideas that have been forgotten or have passed, diluted, into the mainstream of dance.

Opening Dance from *Opus 51*: Everyone programs something special to open a concert, but I think it was only the early modern dancers who conceived of the opening dance as a direct welcome to the audience. Today an evening starts out with *Les Sylphides*, because it's a period piece; or *Harbinger*, because it's upbeat; or *Petrouchka*, so the large cast and extra musicians don't have to wait around all night; or other dances for a variety of business or show-biz reasons. Those early dances of greeting made a more personal bargain. Today they look somewhat naïve —and very ingratiating.

The Moth and the Star: Weidman's Thurber fables are unique because they represent a perfect meshing of two artistic sensibilities. Weidman's comedy is as delicate and clean as Thurber's drawings and prose. Chuck Wilson dances the moth trying to reach the star instead of hanging around lampshades and getting singed, and Weidman, as the moth in his old age, told the story.

Palms: I believe this is an excerpt from a relatively new work to the *St. Matthew Passion*. In it Weidman employs the architectural kind of choreography that Humphrey and Limón also used to do. What makes this style different from any contemporary pure-dance work that explores music is that it doesn't rely entirely on a predetermined vocabulary. The movement grows out of the music pictorially as well as dynamically—more than counts and phrases are important. In *Palms* Weidman places his stress on the dancer's legs, with odd, even funny-looking, articulations that I've never seen before. He's not always concerned with making the dancer look long and beautiful.

Kinetic Pantomime and *Submerged Cathedral*: Weidman's performance, of course, is limited, but I feel the essential quality remains—the idea of lightness and seriousness at the same time. I think young dancers would be embarrassed to do the kind of tender comedy Weidman does in the kinetic pantomimes; in fact, it probably wouldn't even occur to them, though many dancers and mimes took this approach at one time, with their own individual results. Katherine Litz is one. *Submerged Cathedral*, where Weidman, draped in a painted sheet, more or less acts out the Debussy tone poem, is a bit too old-fashioned even for me to appreciate, but I think it's an idea that should be preserved somewhere.

Brahms Waltzes: I was fascinated to see this pre-Romantic version of the same music Eliot Feld used for *Intermezzo*. Danced by four girls, Chuck Wilson, and Weidman, it is almost completely unconcerned with sex—the only time the men and women dance together they slide, as if by accident, into a hitch-hiking pantomime. Yet it fulfills the lyricism of the music just as well as choreography that is more specifically suggestive of the nineteenth century. Maybe I'm saying Weidman is more modern than Feld—modern in the art sense of daring, unusual, unadorned.

I had the impression here, as I did at a concert at the Weidman studio last fall, of unintentionally low dynamics. I think this comes partly from the minuscule size of the studio; dancers get used to holding back their energy and not projecting intensely when they work in a very intimate space. But also Weidman himself has a reduced force, mobility, and range of speeds, and most of the dancers are not authoritative enough to put these qualities back into the movement he teaches them.

I wish there were a place where groups like this could really perform—a salon-type atmosphere that would allow an audience that cares about them to participate in their efforts, where the conditions could be adequately theatrical but the whole aim wouldn't have to be Broadway-competitive. It's not that I don't appreciate the subsidies to modern dance in recent years, but they have exerted sudden and demanding pressures on the dancers. Some companies have adapted to these pressures; others have not; still others wouldn't even know how. The setting up of one performing situation to which all companies must conform or else become invisible may make easier handling for the bureaucrats, but I doubt if it benefits most dancers.

July, 1971

Reaction and Vanguard: Which Is Which?

There are many differing views about what is new and what is old-fashioned in dance. We plug it into our own aesthetic and personal orientation first, then take into account what we know of the artist and what we think contemporary life is about. Some people who loved Merce Cunningham when he was the original alienated bad boy of dance are bored with him now that he's made it to Broadway. Others find him unbearably far out. People who see modern dance as an inherently evolving process think José Limón qualifies as an antique by at least ten years, while to that portion of the audience which has been deafened by the verbal conventions of theater, Limón is intensely revealing.

Perhaps if dance were not such a passing phenomenon, if we had more dance repertory, films, scores, or other methods of preservation, we might not place such a high judgmental value on its immediate relevance. Perhaps we might be able to say that there is such a thing as a good dance or a bad dance, apart from fashion or contemporary thought. But even now, we should be able to tell with some accuracy whether a piece is authentic *for its time*, and that quality might give it staying power over the many reconsidered versions of old dances that we see.

These thoughts are occasioned by the performances, in two successive weeks at the Billy Rose Theatre, by Cunningham and

Limón. Both of them, I think, were once of, or ahead of, their time, and both have continued to make dances out of their earlier sensibilities. We can hardly expect them to do otherwise, but neither choreographer is really new for today.

Limón tried to break with his past in *The Winged*. Limón, who wrote in 1965, "I reach for demons, saints, martyrs, apostates, fools, and other impassioned visions," had worked in what we might now call the classical modern dance, devising triumphant essays of dramatic, choreographic, and musical commentary. In 1966 he put aside plot, accompaniment, and thematic development, and made *The Winged*, a suite of dances with incidental jazz and sounds. This is the first Limón piece I know of that turns away from the architectural design and construction of his precursor, Doris Humphrey. For Limón *The Winged* was quite a remarkable achievement.

Two things happened, or didn't happen, to it. In order to work as a repeatable experience, instead of just an experiment, *The Winged* needed to be cut, by about a third. This Limón was unable to do, and insisting on some lingering divine right of the artist to be wrong, he commits a greater wrong: he lets the audience get tired of the work before it's over.

More important perhaps, Limón did not feel comfortable enough in this style to develop it. He went back to his heroes and visions. But heroes and visions are in decline at the moment, and even Limón knows it. He dressed his subsequent works in jet-age fabric, but they are masquerades, not masterpieces. We have to look further in the past to find the great Limón works, and *There Is a Time*, *The Moor's Pavane*, and *Missa Brevis*, seen at the Billy Rose, are great. Not new, but great.

Now consider the interesting case of Merce Cunningham. Once he was the iconoclast of all time. He broke every rule anyone could think of fifteen years ago. Now people are breaking his rules. Cunningham's "dance by chance" idea does not describe an improvisatory performance situation, as many people think it does. Rather it refers to the random methods by which Cunningham composed many of his early works, in his desire to avoid the ancient artistic role of consciously or unconsciously imposing his will on the piece. Further relinquishing the artist's traditional dictatorial powers, Cunningham allowed

231

his designers and audio people to add their own input to his choreography.

For the viewer, the resulting pure-dance works could suggest surprise or boredom, excitement, joy, or humor, but seldom drama, until *Winterbranch* (1964). La Monte Young's catastrophic sound track and Robert Rauschenberg's manic-depressive lighting injected fear, rage, despair into the piece by requiring that if the viewer was going to sit there at all, something more was going to happen to him than just the pleasure of watching movement. The sound and light actually distorted the movement, rather than just coexisting with it. Interpretation was still open, but some psychological fingers were being pointed.

Cunningham then took this added possibility (call it theatricality for lack of a better word) and made *Place* (1966). Now *Place* has been universally acclaimed as Cunningham's masterpiece, and I myself think so, because it moves me—through a wide range of emotional and intellectual response. *Place* is a clear departure from Cunningham's other works in that it has a beginning and an end, a theme, a development, and even a main character, however nonspecific all these may be.

Whatever we think about *Place, Winterbranch* was a far more innovative piece. For Cunningham, *Place* is really a throwback. Both in his actions onstage and his choices of what was to be staged, he resembles the traditional artist more than the antihero he has so vehemently styled himself. But maybe this in itself is a contemporary development. After all, what nineteenth-century hero can exceed the charismatic and mythic dimensions of today's dropout gods: Che Guevara, Tim Leary, John Lennon, or Gene McCarthy?

February 17, 1969

Cunningham's Here and There

Don't let anyone tell you Merce Cunningham's choreography has no content. Despite all the disclaimers, the talk of Dada and "dance by chance," and the obvious fact that a Cunningham dance never has a plot or any identifiable characters, both kinesthetically and theatrically his work presents a point of view about the human condition. Or, as was demonstrated in the season of repertory recently completed at the Brooklyn Academy, two points of view.

Cunningham's outlook shifts from dark to light, from despair to a quiet kind of joy. His dark pieces seem to arise from the confinement and frustrations of the urban experience, while the light ones are expansive and athletic, like some of their titles: *Field Dances, Scramble*, the new *Walkaround Time*, and *How to Pass, Kick, Fall and Run*.

The light pieces are anti-ballets. Cunningham's use of the balletic style is prominent in these works. Movement is often initiated in the limbs, with a correctly held torso following through. The body is often symmetrical, especially when the arms open out through space. But as if to make fun of any academic pretensions they might be displaying, the dancers will casually drop whatever they are doing and saunter offstage, or break up the pattern with sudden, large body changes. The dancers use space the way a swimmer uses water, as a medium through which to achieve locomotion. They are contained and confident, and they are neither apprehensive nor curious about their environment; they are masters of it, it does not penetrate them. In the lighter works the choreography brings pairs or groups of dancers together briefly, but, as is literally true in *Field Dances*, they only touch each other lightly and then gyrate off again into their own orbits.

These works are collages in which each dancer goes through his movement combinations independently of the others. A Cunningham dance bears much repetition because of this—you can never assimilate all the movement in one viewing. Besides, the scenic, aural, and kinesthetic elements of the collage never fall together quite the same way from one performance to another.

At times the resemblance to ballet is even more pronounced. Twice in *Walkaround Time* everyone leaves the stage, the music stops, and in a fanfare of silence Carolyn Brown performs a solo of enormous technical virtuosity. In *Scramble* and *Suite for Five*, she and Cunningham have duets that are possibly the nearest equivalent to the ballet pas de deux in modern dance, complete with poses, lifts, and pleasantly competitive solos.

These all-outdoors pieces often have improvisatory elements that contribute to their mood of relaxation and self-confidence. *Walkaround Time* has a long pause that might be the break between a dance class and a rehearsal, when the dancers do exactly what dancers do when they are given a few moments' rest in the studio—they chat, they go over their parts, they do a few stretches to keep warmed up. In *Variations V* there are moments of play with a rubber plant, a bicycle, and a mat wired for sound, on which Cunningham works out—primarily, it seems, for the pleasure of the bizarre noises he can produce.

The setting for *Variations V* is provided by six projections at once, showing in rapid juxtaposition scenes of war, food, politicians, dancers, riots, trees, prizefights, and many other things, together with a cacophony of electronic, instrumental, and vocal sound. This environment parallels the clashing tempos of modern life, fragmentary, irrational, and racketing by at a deafening speed. Yet through all this the dancers remain serene. In *How to . . .* John Cage reads droll stories to amuse the audience, but the dancers smile for the pure enjoyment of their own movement. *Nocturnes*, like its Erik Satie score, is beguiling, moonlit, and gently surrealistic. The dancers give no sign that their zany costumes and deranged poses are anything unusual.

In Cunningham's dark pieces, *Winterbranch*, *Place*, the new *RainForest*, and his own solos, *Untitled* and *Collage III*, man is no longer in control. He alternately pits his energy against the nameless forces around him and submits to them while gathering courage for another bout. These works are more tightly choreographed and take place in settings of planned menace, like the merciless light glaring down on a bare, lonely stage in *Winterbranch*, and the subterranean chamber of *Place*, shut in by grub-white gratings with old newspapers blown against them.

The movement in these works is tense and spasmodic. The body is closed, contracted, fractured into terrible angles. There is a series of slow, controlled falls in *Winterbranch*, where the dancers defy gravity until the very moment they touch the floor. In *RainForest*, they try to play in an oversophisticated world where the "forest" is only a thicket of silver plastic pillows and the animal calls they hear come from the throat of a machine. The dancers crawl on the floor, their hands are inarticulate, they butt the pillows with their heads, they twine around each other, but after all they remain human beings trying to be animals.

Cunningham uses the dancers to support each other, but it is not always easy to tell whether they are locked in combat or embrace. In *Winterbranch* and *Place* they rush at each other, struggle, achieve a moment of balance, and ricochet apart. At one point in *Place*, they cross the stage slowly in a tight group, moving one at a time, avoiding contact, but always bound together, like a crowd on a subway.

Cunningham himself is prime mover in *Place*, an unquenchable ego absurdly struggling to affect some change. He rearranges the scenery, sets the dancers in motion, dances out his own frustrations on legs that give way under him, jumps up again to punch at the shadows. Finally, earthbound but still rebelling, he rolls on the floor in a plastic sack, a cocoon, or a giant condom, kicking and flailing his way across the stage and out through the gratings to another ominous place.

Cunningham portrays the common man as hero, beset but indestructible, in *Collage III* and *Untitled Solo*. In the latter piece he uses the persecuted, almost psychotic movements of fear. He focuses almost entirely on the area directly in front of him; he raises and lowers his gaze, but doesn't glance behind or to the sides, as if he were afraid of taking his attention for a moment from the main threat. His hands make nervous clenching movements, his body retreats or sidesteps, but the danger is always there in front of him, he leaps from the floor as if it were hot, and he falls on his back, spreading his limbs as if he were being flattened by a huge rolling pin. He stands facing the audience, and in one sudden convulsion of fright his entire body folds forward and the curtain falls.

John Cage, who often acts as literary spokesman for Cunningham, has said many times that these dances are not "saying something." Nevertheless, this choreography, together with its ostensibly unrelated music and decor, is deeply expressive of modern life. I like to think of Merce Cunningham in the metaphor of John Cage sound that ended *Field Dances* this time: a man's voice intoning, "*This is high fidelity,*" a yawn, and a few bars of a swinging clarinet. High fidelity indeed!

June 17, 1968

Come in, Earth. Are You There?

Somebody said it's okay now to hold your ears at a Merce Cunningham concert. I saw several people doing it during his spring (1969) season at Brooklyn Academy. In his good-natured way, Cunningham has always been in the forefront of the rape-the-audience crowd, and it is perhaps a measure of our acceptance of him that we no longer feel compelled to submit to all his brutalities. Certainly his choreography itself is no longer revolutionary. Without the music it would probably be either pure entertainment or pure boredom, depending on your degree of kinesthetic sophistication.

I don't know if the auditory documents of John Cage and his colleagues are becoming more violent, or if urban life has had a sensitizing effect on our hearing, but I find I have less tolerance for Cunningham's noise today than I had five years ago. Opening night at Brooklyn was performed in silence because of a dispute between the musicians' and the stagehands' unions as to who had jurisdiction over the indefinable activities in the pit. Several of Cunningham's most ardent admirers who were there remarked how lovely that concert was. And their impression of his new work, *Canfield*, was quite different from the one I got when the sound had been restored.

When you look at Merce Cunningham you can either separate the various events that take place—the dancing, decor, lighting, accompaniment—or you can see them as a whole unit. Separating a Cunningham dance into its component parts is perfectly valid because the parts are created separately, often coming together only in performance. Not only do the dancers not dance to the music, they don't know in advance what the quality and sequence of the sounds will be. In some dances, sections of the choreography are shifted around from performance to performance, so that there can be no set narrative or dramatic line. Cunningham's dancers don't attempt to relate to the decor in which they move, except in the most practical sense. When Andy Warhol's gently floating silver pillows get in their way in *RainForest* they plow right through them. Or the visual imagery may change drastically from one performance to the next, as in *Scramble*, where Frank Stella's brightly colored rectangles of cloth stretched at different levels on aluminum frames are moved around so that whole sections of the dance might be invisible to some of the audience. In *Variations V*, six projectors throw a cacophony of moving and still images onto the stage, but the dancers act as if nothing were happening. (Compare this with Robert Joffrey's popular but conventional mixed-media ballet *Astarte*, in which the music and the film/lighting sequence begin together and are precisely timed to coincide with and complement the dancing.)

Never to my knowledge has Merce Cunningham given an "interpretation" of any of his dances, nor do any of his associates. They will talk about the movement, what it is like, how it was made, what chance operations were used in putting it together, but they won't divulge the message or even the mood, as if it wasn't their business to be concerned with those things. Since I have no reason to believe that Cunningham and his people are either so naïve as to be unaware that they are always creating some kind of theater event, or so cagey as to pretend that they are not, I can only assume that they are deliberately maintaining their neutrality. There is in their attitude a certain fatalistic cheerfulness; they intend to do their job no matter what goes on around them. If every member of the audience has a different idea of what they're doing, or if the stage environment changes, still the integrity of their own task is constant. You can imagine them completing their appointed rounds in the dark, or if a dancer were injured or the theater were in flames.

Nevertheless, a Cunningham dance *is* a theatrical entity, especially in contrast to the work of some younger choreographers who have distilled his theories into more austere and concentrated forms. Judith Dunn uses nonsequential movement, Yvonne Rainer stresses the simultaneous, antiemotional quality of events, and Twyla Tharp turns chance operations into mathematical monotony. None of these choreographers uses other theater elements to the extent Cunningham does, and where their work seems cold and abstract, his takes on a dramatic life that he apparently neither dictates nor denies. The audience does have to find its own specific metaphors and relationships, but each piece usually has an overall sensibility that is apparent to everyone.

For me, Cunningham's dark pieces have suggested more specific "meanings" than his brighter works. The latter, which include *Field Dances, Scramble, Walkaround Time,* and others, are expansive, flooded with light and color, pervaded with a general air of good fellowship and the joy of movement. In the dark pieces the lighting and colors are somber, the movement is more restricted, the dancers seem more isolated from each other and at the same time more submissive to their environment. I feel in these works, especially *Winterbranch, Place, RainForest,* and now *Canfield,* that Cunningham is responding—perhaps unconsciously—to the ugly demands of civilization, rather than ignoring them.

There seems to be a progression from *Winterbranch* (1964), where the dancers are crushed by merciless light and total darkness and a maniacally screeching sound track; to *Place* (1966), where they rush frantically at the boundaries of some nameless enclosure and finally break out of it into some other unknown darkness; through *RainForest* (1968), where they seem poised between their humanness and some nonhuman existence that could be either animalistic or artificial, and that they cannot attain in any case. Now, in *Canfield*, the dancers seem to have become resigned to a bland, computerized state in which both the joy and the rebellion have been diminished to faint emotions that can be easily countermanded by the more powerful hand of technology.

The dancers are in gray leotards against a white cyclorama and ungelled lights. The legs and borders masking the perimeter of the stage have been flown out; the space is enormous and the dancers look insignificant in it. A huge vertical boom travels constantly back and forth across the proscenium, with lights inside it, projecting onto the cyc. Sometimes the dancers are pinned in its glare, like escaping convicts in a searchlight; sometimes they drift in the gloom beyond its reach.

The movement seemed pale, the dynamics easy, without much thrust or conviction. There was rather more unison movement than in the average Cunningham dance, and an occasional theme of brushing past each other, making contact at the shoulder but without enough impact to upset each other's direction or momentum. Toward the end a huge bare leko bulb is projected on the cyc, then an indistinct man's face, then the lights in the boom begin to fade, looking somehow not like stage lights dimming but like the brown fatality of a power failure—and the curtain comes down on moving gray ciphers.

But it is the sound that dominates *Canfield*, a sound devised by Pauline Oliveros ("In Memoriam: Nikola Tesla, Cosmic Engineer") that by its literalness and its overriding force insistently calls attention to itself in an unequal competition with what is going on on the stage.

Ever since Merce Cunningham began choreographing in 1942, his musical activities have been directed by John Cage. The two work amiably yet quite independently together. Each pursues his own inventions; the moment of collaboration is the moment of performance; and it is either a recurring accident or a figment of the critic's orderly mind that the two disparate parts seem so frequently to be in consonance with each other. Cunningham seems to have no egotistical notions about the dance being more important than the music, and on occasion the musical event was so shocking that it drowned out the dance until we became accustomed to it. At first we hated the catastrophic din of *Winterbranch*, but now it's hard to imagine that dance without it.

For the past couple of years Cage and his colleagues David Tudor and Gordon Mumma have been experimenting ever more radically with sound, and *Canfield* once again pushes us beyond endurance. We may grow used to this too, but now we feel like the exasperated stranger who grumbled to me during intermission, "It's a secret pact to obliterate the dance."

What Cage and his cohorts are into now goes back, I think, to *Place*, when Gordon Mumma played around with distortion. That is, instead of distorting sound as Cage and many others before him had done via prepared piano, *musique concrète*, and other devices, the distortion *became* the sound. Radio feedback, hum, static, excessive amplification, and manipulation of other sounds generated by the equipment itself, not any sounds being fed *into* the equipment. Gradually the dial-twisting has become the primary concern; the original sounds, whether they are vocal, instrumental, or electronic, are important only as a medium for producing distortion, instead of the distortion being a means of modifying the original sound. In current performance of Cage's piano and orchestra score for *Antic Meet* (1958), there are now hardly any sounds left that even resemble a piano and orchestra.

In many ways this is a logical development. If you mike all the instruments and then ask the musicians to blow through the wrong end, put a trumpet mouthpiece on a bassoon, and bring along transistor radios and alarm clocks, as Cage did with *Antic Meet*, why not put the whole thing on tape and then reshape those distortions? Is there any difference between Cage climbing all over a theater, rubbing the mike against different wall surfaces, chewing aluminum foil with a mike in his mouth, to find sounds for *Story* (1963), and sending people all over the theater in *Canfield* with walkie-talkies to speak into the main sound system?

Well, there is some difference. More than ever the machine is in control. The chance activities that were produced by human beings doing unpredictable things have been submerged under the more powerful unpredictability of electronic equipment.

The human input is simpler and less noticeable—all that's needed now is one long and two short blasts on a trumpet from the top of the balcony, or a voice-over test (testing one-two-three), or simply throwing the mike open. The tubes do the rest.

No matter how awful or boring or nerve-racking it was to listen to an amplified belch or the squeaks of a stool being dragged along the floor, there was a certain childlike charm in the idea of Cage doing it. That kind of sound could often arouse one's curiosity as to how it was being produced, what kind of transformations were being worked on common objects or activities to make them come out sounding the way they did. The effects of the intervening circuitry never quite obscured the fact that somewhere at the beginning of it all there was a complex and original mind searching for new ways to make sound, notate it, and get others to produce it.

In *Variations V* there was an elaborate system of antennae set up on the stage that were supposed to be activated by the dancers moving near them. Though I've seen the dance at least three times, I've never been able to detect any relationship between where and how the dancers moved and what sounds occurred. I was always interested to see how it would work out—something like an electrocardiogram maybe—the radios or whatever the antennae were hooked up to would, I supposed, get louder when the dancers approached them, suddenly louder if suddenly approached; but how would other dynamic and shape changes affect the sound? Two dancers instead of one? What would happen if somebody bumped into one and it whipped back and forth? I never found out. Whatever the antennae picked up was swallowed and digested into all the other sounds that constituted that score, or it was so misshapen at the controls that it couldn't be connected with its initiation when it came out.

There was a certain pleasant camaraderie between the dancers and the presiding technicians in the first version of *Variations V*, at Philharmonic Hall in the summer of 1965. The technicians, though somewhat patronizing, I felt, were always interested in what the subjects of their experiments would do next, sometimes consulting with them. On their platform behind the dancing space they presided but they also performed—they controlled the dance to some extent, but it was the *dance* they were showing off.

Now, in *Canfield*, with the arrogant competence of Rocket Control, they are running the show. Their cool, anonymous engineer's talk dominates the dance for much of the time. No matter how I tried or how uninterested I was in their matter-of-fact voices talking about unimportant things (John, where are you now? I'm under the stage. Give me a reading. One. One. Hmmmm, we didn't have that buzz in rehearsal), I couldn't focus on the dancing until about halfway through, when the jargon subsided into squeals and static—I couldn't get free of the busy multitude of disembodied taxicab drivers and policemen and disk jockeys who kept floating in and out on the walkie-talkie band. (Lotta guys on the line tonight.) Like all true radio nuts, even after they have obtained their tunings and levels, Cage and Tudor and Mumma keep fiddling. No pattern satisfies them. Nothing is good enough, or loud or unusual enough, to keep and use for something—it only serves to be surpassed by the infinite capabilities of their electronic superbrain.

It has been said that the visual sense is stronger than the aural, and in most instances at dance concerts I'm not specifically conscious of the music, even when I'm making an effort to relate the structure and phrasing of what I see to what I hear. The visual takes over. But not in *Canfield*. If you've ever been on the BMT when it grinds into those curves near City Hall station, or driven past Kennedy Airport when a jet was taking off over your head, you know that extreme noise can reduce or otherwise alter your perceptual powers. But even when it is not physically uncomfortable, the *Canfield* sound is literal, which can be even more distracting. What is it about words that makes us pay attention to them? There are ways of de-emphasizing a verbal dance accompaniment, as Cunningham does in *How to Pass, Kick, Fall and Run*, where Cage and David Vaughan read low-key selections from Cage's writings, sometimes overlapping each other. Then we can choose to listen to one or the other, or to neither, letting their combined flow of words make an abstract background for the dance. But in *Canfield* the drama behind those banal dialogues is inescapable. How *could* I be interested in those efficient, faceless men with their dreary talk of inputs and readings? But I am, I'm fascinated, I strain to make out the words when the tuning drifts away. I hate myself and I hate the sound, because I'm missing the dance.

Well, maybe this *is* the dance.

A few days after the Brooklyn Academy season, *The New York Times* reported that an eminent biologist told Senator Muskie's committee investigating pollution that "in the process of creating new goods and services, technology is destroying the country's 'capital' of land, water and other resources as well as injuring people." In fact, scarcely a day goes by that we are not offered pronouncements, pamphlets, threats, warnings, and predictions of disaster resulting from the masochistic and perhaps irreversible course of technological exploitation. Intentionally or not, Merce Cunningham is going beyond the tracts and the vague dread. He is showing us postmillenial man—wired for sound, dissolving into his colorless backdrop, ineffectually and without regrets, alive. The image is more vivid and more terrifying than all the dead fish in the Hudson and all the polemics in Congress. And our response is to cover our ears, as Merce Cunningham, wise as a stone, probably always knew we would.

Some time after this article was written, the astronauts landed on the moon. After watching their televised performance, Merce Cunningham's manager, Jean Rigg, told Merce Cunningham that the lighting effects on the moon were exactly what they had been trying for in *Canfield*. Merce Cunningham said, "Yes! And the sound too."

Spring/Summer, 1970

243

More than the Museum

Merce Cunningham's work always surprises me. I always find it even more enjoyable than I remembered from the last time. Although the technique may be familiar—the characteristic combinations and attitudes in which Cunningham employs the body—one is never quite prepared for the changing energies, speeds, and interactions with which his company executes a work. In most of his dances there is, also, the element of "chance," which allows the sound, lights, projections, scenery, or sometimes the dance sequences themselves to appear in different relationships. One never sees a Cunningham dance quite the same way twice.

Throughout his choreographing career Cunningham has been preoccupied with immediacy, with the richness of the spontaneous moment. You could say all his choreography has been an attempt to free dance from the metric, spatial, and theatrical restrictions that tend to deaden the art while making preservation or repetition of it easier. As he says in his own book, *Changes,* "More than the museum I like the actuality."

This may account for the relatively low value Cunningham puts on "repertory." Except for one performance of *How to Pass, Kick, Fall and Run* (1965), the oldest work seen in the company's fall season at Brooklyn Academy was *Scramble* (1967). Though I got much pleasure from the pieces they did present, especially *Walkaround Time* and *RainForest,* I wish we could see a longer span of Cunningham's ideas. What seemed to be missing were the darker, more menacing implications carried by such earlier works as *Crises, Winterbranch,* and *Place.* The Cunningham repertory now is low-keyed, spacious, and amiable; there's hardly a pierced eardrum in the house. It's a soothing trip, but the terror was also beautiful.

Signals, the first of Cunningham's two new works, has a lot of very prominent, built-in variability. Three of the dance's four sections can be done by different numbers of dancers. The score is assembled—it seems absurd to use the word *composed* any more in regard to Cunninghamusic—by one of four sound men, David Behrman, John Cage, Gordon Mumma, or David Tudor, depending on the day of the week and month. The lighting can also be varied. Curiously enough, these changes don't have much effect on the piece from one performance to another. It keeps its basic intensity and design, beginning with one, two, or three solos and increasing in size until a group of six dancers is playing a game that looks like a cross between Follow the Leader and Red Light.

I often have the feeling that the dancers in a Cunningham piece are in the power of someone or something else without being particularly resentful or submissive about it, and this is true of *Signals*. Cunningham dances a solo with weights strapped to his ankles. In the section "Trio for 3 or 4" one dancer "conducts" two others with a large baton. Cunningham signals a series of position changes to the group with barely audible gasps. Finally someone seems to make a split-second decision how to end the dance, and they all follow suit as the curtain falls. At one performance there was a quick contest for two chairs, ending with Mel Wong teetering on the edge of one and Valda Setterfield in possession of another, Cunningham perched on her knee. Another time, the girls keeled over one by one, their bodies in stiff straight lines, and the men caught them at different levels.

Objects is a longer and perhaps more serious piece, although it contains some literal comic elements—Cunningham doing a very short mimed scene as a sweeper turned partner for ballerinaesque Sandra Neels, a group sitting in a circle on the floor miming a game of jacks as Carolyn Brown takes slow poses in the center, three dancers walking heavily around the stage coughing to themselves. The dancing itself proceeds like any Cunningham dance, with solos, duets, and group sections following one another and sometimes overlapping, according to the unspoken rules. I especially liked one continuous sequence in which there were always three dancers moving in unison, but the people kept changing as one dancer would join and then one would drop out.

The score for *Objects,* Alvin Lucier's "Vespers," consisted of the sounds made by scanning different parts of the theater with sensing devices resembling Geiger counters. It's amazing how musical four things ticking simultaneously at different speeds can be.

One other important element of *Objects* was Neil Jenney's four aluminum frames with black cloth draped on them. These objects looked like the scenery they used to have in 1925 Middle European plays when they wanted to show the times were out of joint. Something has obviously gone wrong in the design of them; they are put together so lopsidedly that they can barely stand up; they have a wheel on one corner; no one of them looks like any of the others. The dancers push them on and offstage, not quite accommodating to their presence. They're like some big clumsy pets without any personality. You wonder why you ever gave them house room, but you can't exactly throw them out on the street.

November 29, 1970

V

EXPERIMENTAL DANCE:
FIREBRANDS
AND VISIONARIES

SOME OF THE MOST interesting dance of our time is classifiable as dance only because it doesn't fit anywhere else. For that matter, it doesn't fit as dance either, in any of the common usages of the term. As radical as many earlier developments seemed at the time—Isadora Duncan daring to dance barefooted, Graham and Humphrey integrating the spoken word into their dances, Jerome Robbins putting jazz movements into ballets—at least the revolution was taking place in the same ball park.

Today's experimental dancers frequently do not dance. They seldom employ music, and when they do, they don't use it as accompaniment for their dancing, or non-dancing. They hardly ever dance, or non-dance, in theaters. Their structures, content, methods, and means not only exist outside the usual channels of dance production but call into question the nature of dance itself. Yet this is not a destructive revolution. Its practitioners don't even despise the more traditional modern dance as the modern dancers despised ballet. Experimental dance today is affirmative and challenging. It is trying to push out the boundaries of what we consider dance.

The dance avant-garde is no longer a Merce Cunningham

generation. It seems quite clear that Cunningham made it possible for this group to work, but their relationship to him for the most part is philosophical now, rather than stylistic. Cunningham was the first to explode the old concepts of stage space, phrasing, sequence, and determinacy in dance, but with the lead he gave them, many younger choreographers are exploring these areas more deeply than Cunningham cared to go, and making new discoveries.

There was a period of a few years in the early 1960s when the dance avant-garde centered around Judson Church in New York. Most of the participants were Cunningham devotees, and Cunningham's attitudes were reflected in their work; they were also heavily influenced by the Happening movement of the same period and by the idea of collaborating with painters. The Judson Group seems to have been a rather tightly knit, like-minded community that did things for their own enlightenment and showed them to their friends. Judson was like a growing, ripening milkweed pod. When it popped open, things got planted all over the place. Today's experimental choreographers are far more visible and less exclusive. Where Judson was the Underground, working almost in secret with an almost fanatical desire to destroy the dance conventions of its time, today's experimental dance is very much in the open, not a Movement in itself but representative of and spokesman for the social and political movement of our time.

Some months ago Yvonne Rainer, taking part in a television panel, expressed genuine amazement when portions of a black-militant dance by Rod Rodgers were shown. Rodgers was using the now-literal vocabularies of modern dance and stylized jazz-Afro movement to express the anger, fear, and alienation of the black man. Rainer's reaction—how could a dance be political while using the languages of its oppressors?—dramatically clarified the difference between the politics of content and the politics of form. Many black choreographers and white populist choreographers such as Maurice Béjart want to get across a message; they show the audience the sentiment or the slogan in the quickest, clearest way. Rainer and the experimental choreographers want, rather, to show the audience something about the process of dance. You might say that though their work is nonpolitical their whole life-style—their artistic posture —is a political statement.

I think this generation of experimentalists view themselves and their work very differently than do all other American dancers. They don't, for one thing, see their output as part of a progression toward a certain standard success. Their aim is not to become good at making dances that are solid, assured, and repeatable, or to install themselves as masters of increasingly structured, programmed organizations. Their "companies" might consist of three or four regular dancers, augmented when necessary by students or even by people summoned through classified ads. Some people work almost entirely outside the established routines of teaching, touring, and producing; others are organized only to the extent necessary to receive financial help and reach wider audiences.

The formal company hierarchy in some cases has been virtually eliminated. People as far apart artistically as Rainer and Twyla Tharp and Daniel Nagrin, who since 1971 has been working with an improvisational Workgroup, incorporate the contributions of company members in their work, not listing themselves as choreographers at all but as directors or leaders. Quaint communal-sounding groups are beginning to replace the one-owner dance company, although the founders continue to dominate our image of those groups—James Cunningham's Acme Dance Co., Deborah Hay's The Farm, Rainer's Grand Union, Meredith Monk's The House.

This democratizing tendency is perfectly visible in Rainer's work, and Hay's and Rudy Perez's for example—in the underplayed costumes, production, dance proficiency. They are attempting to put the performer more on a par with the spectator —not, as in the Judson days, by figuratively handing round peeled grapes in the dark or reciting "in" formulas—but by recognizing their common humanity.

This worries me somewhat, because all antielitist movements that I know about in the arts have resulted in a downgrading of art. But so far, experimental dance seems to be in vigorous health—I suppose because there's still such a remarkable flow of creativity among its practitioners. Of course, the traditionalist would argue that dance *is* being downgraded because most of these people are not obviously dancing, and even those who do something recognizable as pure dance—Twyla Tharp, Dan Wagoner, Viola Farber—use the devices invented by Merce Cunningham to defocus and understate the dancer's virtuosity: the spurts of everyday movement borrowed from sports, games, rehearsals, mealtime; the working against or without music; the presenting of several key events at the same time so the viewer can't concentrate on any one of them.

I find it interesting to note how many experimental dancers did not come from the major companies. The modern dance always accepted, and even welcomed, the possibility that young dancers might go off on their own after dancing for a suitable time with a major choreographer. It may be their firm grounding in post-Graham dance that keeps Tharp and Wagoner, who danced with Paul Taylor, and Farber, who danced with Merce Cunningham, as attached to pure dance as they are. A surprising number of important people on this scene, however, went straight from their dance training into their own creative work, and some, like James Cunningham, had considerable experience in other theatrical forms. They seem to be freer from preconceptions about what can or cannot be done in the name of dance, and they're also refreshingly without the anger or rebellion that often hangs over the dropout for a while after he's declared his independence from the system.

Perhaps the most important difference between the present avant-garde and everybody else is their attitude toward continuity. Up to now I think most choreographers saw themselves as descended from certain artists, thought they were adding something, however modest, to the development of dance, and hoped, however secretly, that others would follow them. Those who judge are always wanting to wait and see if a new idea takes—and so withholding their real esteem until the work has grown senile hanging around. I don't think the people who make today's experimental dance necessarily see their work as part of a linear progression; it simply exists because it needs to be done at this moment in their creative lives, and at the next moment it can cease to exist. Repertory is almost unheard of among these artists—not only because they want to avoid its confining demands on their time and energy, but because they don't see the need for repeating a work after the doing of it in the first place. Their work is truly disposable, not in the planned obsolescent, chromium-plated manner of the pop companies, but like some useful, biodegradable product that has its place in the life cycle.

Critics and conventional audiences are bothered by this attitude, which aggravates all the familiar difficulties of dance manyfold. If we don't know what dance is or how to look at it or how to contain it or keep it or value it, at least we can look for precedents, relationships, likenesses. We can discern lines of heredity and expect certain kinds of effects and experiences to come from certain previously defined situations. Now experimental dancers are telling us to forget all that. Nothing can be taken for granted; we can't expect a new work to look like anything that came before, and the difference may be in light years, not just minute stylistic advances. Nor can we hope for another chance to see the work; this *is* the experience, and this is the only time we'll get for taking it in. But there's reassurance too—that even if this is the end of this particular line, it isn't going to be the end of dance.

Young people have accepted experimental dance in gratifying numbers, not just young intellectuals and artists, but students and working people who may never have seen any dance before. Wherever I go to see experimental dance, at colleges, in museums, in churches, parks, and plazas, there's an open, giving atmosphere on both sides. No one is condescending or putting on airs for anyone else. Performers and audience are there to explore experience together, and in this most thorough sense, without slogans or testimonials to promote it, the new dance belongs to the people.

Televanilla: Theater in Two Flavors

It's very likely that within a few years some of the technological devices employed in Susan Buirge's *Televanilla*, given at the Martinique Theater recently, will have been sufficiently perfected and glorified to serve as the basis for a popular ballet uptown that will be considered very new. But there is another reason for taking note of Miss Buirge's concert. During the evening two distinct events were taking place simultaneously, each representing one of the important currents of change that are influencing dance theater.

Described as an improvisational theater dance piece, *Televanilla* consisted of three short episodes performed by Miss Buirge and a number of television sets, which were placed around the perimeter of the Martinique's thrust stage. In this unusual media mix the audience had its choice of watching Miss Buirge dancing on the stage, or watching televised pictures of Miss Buirge dancing, or watching the cameraman photographing Miss Buirge. In one section there was also a film showing some of Miss Buirge's movements in close-up, and in another a device called Videosketch allowed the dancer to produce patterns on a screen by manipulating lights in front of what seemed to be a sort of electric eye or radar.

On a modest scale, *Televanilla* explored new ways of fragmenting time and space. The dancer appeared on the stage and the television screens at the same time; and the viewer could watch her from his own seat as well as through the spatial orientation of the cameraman. Techniques of movies and still photography were employed, such as blurred focus, grainy textures, and negative images, in effect telescoping the creative process by showing both the raw material and the finished product together. Time was arrested visually, as the camera captured

253

the path of the dancer's body in ghostly traces across the screen. At moments the camera caught the dancer's kinetic pulse by rhythmically zooming in and out during a series of jumps.

With more money for experimentation and development, this form of intermedia might grow into a theater experience at least as viable as film-dance. Even at this early stage, however, *Televanilla* exhibits some of the characteristics of all mixed media work. Intermedia's purpose is to heighten one's sense of participation in the event by stimulating, often violently, as many of one's sensory organs as possible. It creates an overlapping series of stimuli in order that the experience, taken as a whole or selectively, will be more intense.

The intermedia experience is super-self-involved. The kind of response it generates doesn't have to do with joy or hate or the world or other people; it has to do with me and that strobe light, with eyeballs that are blinded to everything beyond their own hallucinatory images. The extended sense of self ("awareness") that one may experience with intermedia is really not self, but a projection of self into another sphere of time or space. If this projection of self begins to seem real, then the actual reality, the actual moment, has been obliterated. In *Televanilla* the live dancer became less real, and less interesting, than the multiple versions of her that were being projected onto the screens.

The other event that occured during *Televanilla* had to do with something that might be called the humanistic theater. An outgrowth of the early happenings, it is headed, through psychology, movement exploration, and group interaction, toward a greater consciousness of self—in relation to the world, not in isolation from it. The extent of the audience's or the performer's participation depends more on what he gives to the other elements of his environment than on what he takes from them. A word or another person's movement may provoke a response as easily as an electric shock can.

The San Francisco avant-gardist Ann Halprin, whose company is trained in ensemble responsiveness as much as in dance technique, has recently invited her audiences to share in such experiences as carrying each other down a passageway, and standing for an hour in silent atonement. Since the humantistic theater makes you open your pores in order to let something flow out, rather than to take something in, it is almost always a threatening experience in some sense. It can also be a very beautiful one.

Televanilla turned into a happening of this sort. Upon entering the theater everyone received a real flower and a neat packet sealed with a sticker in the shape of a butterfly or some other design. Inside the packet were a program, a press release, and three small squares of colored gelatin strung together, which could be used for technicolor viewing of the television. During the first of the two long intermissions ice cream and soft drinks were served, and for the second, bulletin boards were brought onto the stage and everyone was given paper and magic markers and invited to compose graffiti.

There is apt to be a certain amount of resistance to this sort of games-playing, even among the supposedly hip off-Broadway audience, but when it became clear that nothing would be required of us except to have a good time, the mood relaxed. Instead of a formal concert, the evening became a happening in which a lot of people became rather intimate in a pleasant place. The traditional distinction between the stage space and the audience was broken down by allowing the audience to take over the stage when the performers weren't using it. Cameramen literally became performers. Friends visited comfortably in their seats instead of being herded out for the usual hasty smoking break, and the technicians and artists who had worked on the concert were on hand to answer questions. At the end of the concert the audience was invited to experiment with the Videosketch process by creating their own designs on the radar screen. They went home reluctantly, as if they were leaving a party.

Much of the theater today is in rebellion against the type of ritual in which the audience is conditioned to sit in decorous neutrality and receive signals from the stage. The intermedia people want to revive the apparently lost art of feeling, and they have upped the volume and variety of their signals so that it will be impossible not to react. But because its audience is still essentially passive, and because there is no requirement, often no possibility, to reach out beyond whatever is turning you on, intermedia appeals to the same instinct for blocking out the world that it is supposed to counteract.

255

Intermedia is approaching the limits of sensory excitation. If it is not to nullify itself by pushing us over the threshold of pain, oblivion, or total chaos, intermedia will have to go in the direction of bigger and bigger spectacles that are increasingly dehumanized. The humanistic theater, on the other hand, presents a seemingly unlimited range of possibilities. It can be based on loosely structured dance movement, or it can grow out of improvisational group activity. It can be used in combination with intermedia or other theatrical devices. The humanistic theater confronts the environmental and interpersonal elements of the world, rather than transporting us out of the world. It is the theater of therapy and of the streets. It could be the theater of the future for dance.

June 10, 1968

Working Out

It's hard to tell exactly where the dance avant-garde is at right now. In fact, it's quite possible there isn't any. At least, the days of standing still and other conceits seem gone for good. Mixed media has become so popular that the cognoscenti think it's boring. Films are everybody's bag, and nudity doesn't arouse even the cops. Perhaps, having experimented with every kind of anti-dance, the dancers are working their way back to movement. The restrictions on technique and structure that characterized the Martha Graham–Doris Humphrey–Louis Horst ascendency have relaxed somewhat, and today's dancers are rediscovering their own ways to move. During the six-week summer season just presented by Dance Theater Workshop, ten choreographers demonstrated ten distinct personalities, ten approaches to movement. In that sense I found the series truly experimental.

Most interesting of the newer choreographers at the Workshop is William Dunas, a curly-haired blond young man whose cherubic face has a suggestion of malevolence, like a discontented Bob Dylan. His solo, *X*, was a frantic study in resisting the weight of the body. In the opening section, Dunas dragged himself along the studio wall to a pole, considered the pole, and returned to his starting point. He repeated the pattern over and over, accelerating each time, and each time grappling more intensely with the pole, until he was climbing it to the ceiling like an ape, dropping off, and scrambling home again. In the second section he repeated the same dynamic sequence with different movements, slowly, then rapidly, pulling his body upright and falling straight into the floor. Instead of giving in to the fall, he fought space, as he did the pole, and there was violence in the confrontation. The piece concluded with variations on this lacerating mood of determined self-mastery.

In contrast to Dunas (or to almost everyone else), Rudy Perez is a cool choreographer. He loves to investigate things carefully, even microscopically. When the study turns inward, as in *Center Break*, choreographed over a year ago, it can be static. In his new quartet, *Loading Zone*, it is more interesting. To the burbling vibrato of Tiny Tim and an Irish shaggy dog story, Perez takes apart each dancer's movement pattern and tries it in all sorts of positions, planes, and relations to the others, rather like an interior decorator with a roomful of furniture. Perez is bright and witty, but his work will not be fully realized until he digs into the dynamics of movement as deeply as he probes its spatial orientation.

Art Bauman confronts life with an attaché case in one hand. His 1966 work, *Errands*, explores the competitiveness and insecurities of three grown men with football letters engraved on their backs. Barbara Roan, a lovely lyric dancer, is also a comedienne, with a mobile face and a fine sense of timing. Her *Up Cover Under Off* is a wistful exposition of the security-blanket syndrome.

That's That, Elizabeth Keen's new solo, comments on the kind of popular dancing that I am told no longer has a name but is just called Doing Your Own Thing. Miss Keen, doing very much *her* own thing, catches the essentials of this kind of dancing and the kids who do it; the beat that starts in the periphery and throbs up the arms and legs into the whole body, the progression toward abandon halted by a sudden turning off, the guarded awareness, the mocking seductiveness, and the off-balance vulnerability.

Janet Soares' *Z6508 Times*, a collage of want-ad clippings and scraps of movement, and Tina Croll's series of rambling phrases, *One Space, One Figure and Occasional Sounds*, both needed a clearer choreographic focus.

James Cunningham is a slope-shouldered Canadian who is very good at the kind of harmless nuttiness displayed in his *Skating to Siam*. Where Cunningham's Dada is almost slapstick, Jeff Duncan's, in his 1957 *Three Fictitious Games*, is playful and more classically structured, and Jack Moore's, in *Parsley All Over the World* (1966), has some serious overtones.

Moore and Duncan are the co-directors of Dance Theater Workshop, but, with Moore away a good deal of the time teaching at Bennington College, Jeff Duncan really holds the place together. It is greatly to his credit that the Workshop has been hospitable over the past three years to so many choreographers of such diverse persuasions. The Workshop was organized after the decline of the Judson Dance Theater's most revolutionary period, and it follows a less deliberately iconoclastic course. Or perhaps the choreographers who work there are less intent on overthrow just now than they are on developing what they have. Clearly, they have a great deal.

August 26, 1968

Marathon at Manhattan School

There are limits to how long a Western audience can sit in a theater and enjoy dancing. Dance Theater Workshop, which has maintained an outstandingly high level of professionalism in its studio programs, scheduled six long pieces for its concerts at the

Manhattan School of Music in November. DTW had received grants from the Rockefeller Foundation and the New York State Council on the Arts and probably wished to stretch the funds as far as possible among its participating choreographers. Good intentions, however, could not rescue the three-and-a-half-hour program from the eyeball-glazing effects of fatigue and hunger.

The program foraged among most of the current ideas of anti-Establishment dance without offering any striking new insights. While all six numbers were announced as premieres, two have been seen before in slightly different form: Tina Croll's *Ground-Work* (first called *Fields*) and Rudy Perez's *Arcade* (formerly *Match*). The omission of these two pieces might have thrown the other four into bolder relief.

James Cunningham's work has always interested me, as much, perhaps, for its non-dance theatricality as for its movement ideas. He himself is a marvelous mover, full of rebounding energies, odd angles, and unexpected initiations, from the hip or elbow, for instance. But one feels he uses movement, both for himself and the group, as an explosive, almost unintentional kinetic comment on other matters, rather than as the substance out of which commentary is built.

The Sea of Tranquility Motel was a disorderly sequence of ideas that somehow, despite their wild diversity, added up to a logical statement of where young people are at today. The piece began with high camp—a Woody Woodpecker silent cartoon about a mad professor and a rocket ship—and ended with low camp— a filmstrip of the *Apollo 11* flight to the moon, the astronauts' return to earth, and their welcome home by President Nixon, who was absentmindedly hissed by the audience, like any ordinary celluloid villain. The trip in between included music from the Japanese Gagaku theater; mass movement games by a large group dressed in miniskirts and blue jeans; a few subdued orgies; an elderly garbage-picker, played by Leslie Berg in blue velvet and pearls, who later climbed into the garbage can and rubbed out each boy in the group to the accompaniment of taped machine-gun fire; a soft-shoe song and dance routine by Cunningham and Linda Tarnay; a heavily symbolic oriental-modern-dance Sun and Moon duet; and some rock dancing.

There was also a return visit from an endearing character, whom I'll call Aunt Agatha, that Cunningham has created to pronounce the doddering phrases of Authority and Good Form over a degenerate world. Aunt Agatha, who may be a man or a woman but who is clearly a spinster, has lectured us in the past about religion, elocution, and the futility of looking for one's contact lenses in the dark. Now he/she surveyed the raffish proceedings and querulously demanded, "Is this dance? Let's get a grip on ourselves! All this screaming and yelling and jumping over garbage cans . . ."

Sorry, Aunt Agatha, dance can be jumping over garbage cans and a lot more these days. Take Kathryn Posin's *Guidesong*. It seemed to be just a duet between Miss Posin and Andé Peck, accompanied by live chamber music—one of those earnest "music visualizations" of dance's romantic younger days. But the musicians, led by composer Kirk Nurock, wandered all over the stage, some of them shyly playing from offstage a good deal of the time, instead of occupying the neat arrangement of chairs and music stands that had been provided for them. The dancers couldn't seem to get in tune with each other, or with themselves for that matter. Leading with one stiff arm, they would pivot their bodies around like boards instead of yielding to the shape of the movement. When they tried to embrace, they couldn't unravel the knots they had made of their own arms and legs.

Miss Posin is a choreographer who can never seem to make an entirely serious statement because she is always aware of the ridiculous implications of the human frame in motion. Just one wayward impulse or muscular kink, if obeyed, can turn a harmonious phrase into a jangling discord. In this she reminds me of Paul Taylor. She doesn't always probe into these physical idiosyncrasies, or use them in the service of a profound message, but then, neither did Taylor when he was doing his most original and least self-conscious work.

Deborah Jowitt's *Zero to Nothing* explored the familiar theme of Make Love Not War, or Look How Dehumanized We've Become, without advancing much beyond polemics. Six dancers, divided into two teams, engaged in formal combat, or encountered each other in highly charged duets or trios that the others witnessed impassively. At the end of each encounter, a piece of clothing was removed from the victim by the victors and ritualistically draped on what might have been a clothesline or an altar. Finally, in a sudden enlightenment, the dancers stripped to their skivvies and blindly groped for each other, until an anonymous voice reading war reports brought them back to their senses and their normal state of clothed belligerence.

Of all the DTW choreographers, Jeff Duncan is the most traditional, and since he is the director and motive force of the workshop, his adherence to form and content provides a steady, solid ground base over which the others can pursue their more or less outrageous variations. Duncan's *Resonances* was a suite for five dancers that examined the idea of starting with an impulse, like a swing or a rising attitude, and letting it spread through the body and then subside. Duncan's movement resembles that of Merce Cunningham, with overtones of strong but unspecified emotionality.

Critics talk a lot nowadays about the coming together of modern dance and ballet. I still find few points of creative fusion. But I note with a certain irony a growing number of similarities in the peripheral areas like organization, presentation, and program building. *Resonances* is just the sort of piece—skillful, well performed, not particularly new or significant—that every ballet company would be happy to add to its repertory at least once a year.

January/February, 1970

Smut and Other Diversions

I really wasn't going to deal with Yvonne Rainer's pornographic movie at all, since it seemed so unimportant at the time. Unquestionably, it was the filthiest thing I ever hope to see in a theater in terms of its explicit rendering of the sex act. On the other hand, I don't consider it any more obscene than some of the symbolic allusions in Graham's *Phaedra*, Limón's *Comedy*, or Balanchine's *Don Quixote*; perhaps less, because of its intent and its context, which I'll discuss in a minute.

When the film was shown, as a last, unscheduled, but leeringly rumored gesture to spite the bourgeoisie at the so-called avant-garde week in the Billy Rose Theatre, nothing happened. Nobody leaped to the stage in righteous wrath, no one fainted, no one even booed. Hardly anyone I spoke to at the intermissions or afterward even bothered to mention the film.

But a scandal has been made of it just the same. In a fit of outraged decency, Clive Barnes has attacked not only Miss Rainer but the Ford Foundation, which supported the entire four-week Billy Rose season (eleven choreographers) and is sponsoring modern dance at the Brooklyn Academy and City Center this year as well. Even if the rest of the audience had been as offended as Mr. Barnes, the onus would lie on Miss Rainer and Charles Reinhart, producer of the Billy Rose series, not the foundation.

For a major critic to hold a foundation accountable for the artistic quality of its beneficiaries, it seems to me, reopens the whole question of censorship that has only in recent years become desensitized enough to permit productive alliances between government and foundations and the arts. The best a patron can do is to know the artists it endows, or entrust the program to responsible administrators, and then let the process happen. The goofs, the failures, even the bad taste are part of the process. Whatever we may think about one pornographic film, the Ford grant is having a widespread and largely salutary impact on dance this year, one that critics should examine in its entirety and with reason, not out of momentary pique and boredom.

The fact that Yvonne Rainer's audience was *not* offended has to do, I think, with her concept of dance. Her aim is to defuse all events that occur. She purposely takes the dynamics out of movement, the portent out of props like a book, a tray, a package. As she wrote in 1965, she is simply opposed to all theatrical trickery: "NO to spectacle no to virtuosity no to transformations and magic . . . no to moving or being moved." Cunningham-like, she makes many things happen at the same time, but she has gone beyond Cunningham by saying that none of these things are important; one is as neutral as the other, be it pornography or play, or a deadpan Lenny Bruce lecture on snot.

The effect of all this is, of course, boring, and Rainer knows it. Her outer limit of emotionality is a kind of flowerchild euphoria that the dancers feel when they skip together or touch. I would like to see this go somewhere, and it has some elements of ritual and group interaction. But just as it is, this work can be purifying. Without ignoring the world, Rainer is noncommittal in a badly overcommitted, overstimulated age.

Of the others in this ill-assorted Billy Rose week, Don Redlich is not far out at all. He has his own organic sense of space, time, and theater elements, but someone with a personal style and statement is not necessarily a revolutionary. Redlich is in advance of his Billy Rose colleagues in that he enjoys dancing and shows it.

Twyla Tharp and her company avoid theatricality like the plague. In a whole concert of pure dance, if the dancers betray no expressiveness toward each other or toward the audience, everything begins to look like a rehearsal. Tharp has rich movement. After two hours it becomes a surfeit. However, she never works in a stage, and perhaps her preferred environment of a railroad station or a gymnasium would give her work a different character.

At the intermission of Meredith Monk's concert, "exhibits" were set up in the lobby, consisting of corrugated cardboard cylinders with holes cut in them. Inside were people, reading by flashlight. They never moved when you scratched or knocked on the outside of their huts, or stared in at them. They made me feel like a peeping Tom. So did the concert.

I fail to see what was accomplished by lumping these people together, calling them avant-garde, and bringing them to Broadway. Those who have had it with the phoniness and excesses of conventional dance will follow Rainer, Tharp, and Monk to Judson Church or any of the places where they can be seen to better advantage. The avant-garde label is ridiculous anyway, since the moment you can catch up with something and define it enough to give it a label, it's no longer *en avant*. But audiences and some critics who now think they've got it pinned down can damn the whole experimental scene if they don't like what's been placed in this particular category. As Clive Barnes said, again blaming the Ford Foundation, "It has damaged the cause of dance in America." With some respect, I reply, "Nonsense."

March 24, 1969

Radicalizing the Dance Audience

Steve Paxton is a thin, serious man in his thirties, who has a lot of dark curly hair and a sparse beard and mild, steady blue eyes. He speaks softly and reasonably, without the strident emphasis of those who consider themselves oppressed. If the word *Christlike* seems too extreme a description, at least you would never pick him out of a crowd as a troublemaker.

A few weeks ago Paxton staged what was probably the first instance of guerrilla theater in the dance field. The event was deliberately ignored by the press—a tactic that tends to legitimize protest instead of nullifying it. Paxton delivered his shocker, *Intravenous Lecture*, in place of a scheduled concert at New York University, as a protest against the university's refusal to let forty-two naked redheaded people walk across a room on a Sunday afternoon.

Paxton had been invited to perform on the NYU School of Continuing Education's dance series, a project that has also presented concerts this year by the companies of Pearl Lang, Rudy Perez, and Louis Falco. Paxton says he has no idea why he was chosen to be in the series, since he has no regular company and, for the past five years or so since he left Merce Cunningham's company, has been working at the outermost boundaries of experimental dance.

"I don't like to regard the sponsor as an antagonist," he told an interviewer recently. "I inform them of my intentions—it helps me to verbalize my ideas anyway." Before signing his

contract, he had presented the university with a written description of his plan for the concert, including the three-minute nude
sequence, *Satisfyin' Lover*. Putting provocative titles on low-key
events is a common practice among experimental artists; perhaps they intend a mocking appeal to the audience's prurience.

Paxton is interested in the phenomenon of performing, in
whether the performer can hold on to some small part of his
own private self while being looked at by several hundred people. For this reason he has simplified movement to the basic
elements of walking, sitting, rising, turning, and has used non-
dancers, because he feels they retain more of their own personal
characteristics and aren't marked by that attitude toward performance known as technique.

"My aim is hardly ever to make people uncomfortable," Paxton said. "My work isn't audience-oriented. It's a train of
thought. Sharing it helps you to get on to something else, and
the audience presumably comes with the same spirit. NYU had
an opportunity to let the nude body be seen in a good way. This
infantile repression of the human image prevents people from
growing and changing—it was depriving me of my connection
with the audience."

Three days before the first of the two scheduled concerts
Paxton was notified that nudity was out. He canceled both performances. "But by then there was no way to reach people who
had bought tickets. I didn't want them to come and not find
anyone there, and so I did *Intravenous Lecture*. I would have
preferred to cancel the whole thing."

Intravenous Lecture is a review of various experiences Paxton
has had with performing situations and sponsors, good and bad,
and his musings on the ideal performer/sponsor relationship.
As he spoke, a doctor appeared and began taking equipment out
of a pink shopping bag. Paxton ignored him, but they sat down
together on two chairs facing the audience, and after preparing
to give an injection, the doctor plunged a needle into Paxton's
arm, taped down some tubing, and gave him a bottle filled with
a colorless liquid.

For another twenty minutes or so Paxton walked up and
down talking, while the unknown substance dripped into his
vein, and sometimes his own blood oozed up the rubber tube.
He took no notice of this intrusion on his body, or the violence

of the metaphor he was creating. Later he said, "I always do *Intravenous Lecture* that way. It wasn't a protest lecture until I had something to protest. I just wanted to tell the people what happened, I don't want to burn down NYU."

Paxton's anti-performance raises some crucial questions about censorship and permissiveness in the arts, and about the great gulf that often stretches between artists and the institutions that sponsor them. NYU officials, reacting with Pavlovian simplicity, decided that nudity would automatically be bad for the community, and that Paxton's wrath could be soothed by giving him his day in court. In effect, they were treating this artist like a militant sophomore.

One has to sympathize with today's university officials, squirming under the pressure of continual hard decisions, bargains, and adjustments. But the needs of the artist are not those of the student, and noncommunications between artist and academy were established long before the campus upheavals of recent years. For dancers and choreographers the university has always been an important place to perform, teach, and even create new work. Yet performance conditions are still frequently below professional quality—theaters that were not designed or equipped for dance, inadequate rehearsal time, ill-informed publicity.

Why do college administrators fail to see that the difference between art and pornography turns on something besides the amount of human flesh exposed? And why, having exercised their right of uncomprehending censorship, are they surprised when the artist doesn't spew out his anger in a few harmless laps around the debating table, but instead restates the issue in a harsher and more obscene way than anyone had intended?

Does anybody really like guerrilla dance? Most of the people at NYU that Sunday afternoon would probably have preferred to see Steve Paxton's concert. If they had been looking for titillation they could have gone directly to Forty-second Street. NYU's position was very civilized and quiet—what Paxton calls "soft-sell censorship"—and Paxton responded in kind. Who then was the destroyer and who the destroyed?

April, 1970

Progress in a New Environment

It began in an open field, wandered through a gym, and ended in a dark room with a party going on down the hall. It was the evening shared by Twyla Tharp and Yvonne Rainer that initiated a revitalized American Dance Festival at Connecticut College. Using the spatial resources of the New London campus, and students with whom they had worked during the previous two weeks, Tharp and Rainer carried their ideas into a larger scale and a greater environmental unity than has been possible before. Their conceptions certainly had far more shape and distinction here than in the narrow confines of the Billy Rose Theatre, where they performed last winter.

Twyla Tharp's portion of the program, called *Medley*, took place on a huge parade ground, about the size of two football fields, with the audience seated on a slope at one end. It was a pleasant country evening, cloudy, with warblers singing in the trees bordering the field. The darkening grass was very green, and dense, fragrant patches of thyme were in bloom.

When we arrived, the dance was already in progress. The six girls in Miss Tharp's company were way off at the other end of the field, looking very tiny and remote. There was no accompaniment, and the audience was very quiet. Gradually, the group moved nearer, but they never got close enough for the audience to see the intricate detail of Tharp's movement.

Later, about thirty students rose from the audience and swarmed down the hillside into the field, where they formed into ranks and files to do unison movement, with a member of the company leading each squad. One couldn't help comparing these precise formations with the marching bands who sometimes drill on that field, or the cadets from the neighboring Coast Guard Academy. But how superior to armies these danc-

ers were, with their big, free-swinging, and—even at that distance—individual movement. The climax of *Medley* came when
the entire group dispersed all over the field and commenced
doing one long sequence, each person moving at his slowest
possible speed. The effect was extraordinary—a field full of
statues in a continuous but imperceptible state of change.

Finally a bagpiper in full Scottish regalia appeared under
some trees, walked slowly up and down, and played some tunes.
The concert was over—except for one dancer who continued
her adagio set after the audience and the other performers had
left. According to the program each member of the company
was to dance a half-hour solo out there for anyone who cared to
watch.

Most of the audience repaired to the college gym at the other
end of the campus, where Yvonne Rainer had apportioned various spaces for various activities—film showings, a continuous
performance of her *Trio A*, a studio where people could listen
to taped lectures and discussions.

Miss Rainer, especially in her work for the students in this
piece, called *Connecticut Composite*, seems interested in the execution of given tasks with a small number of choices being left to
the performer. A wide pathway down the center of the big gym
was assigned to a "People Wall," lines of people walking perpetually back and forth. Their instructions were to keep their
shoulders touching and to proceed until forced to turn around,
either by a real wall or by another oncoming part of the People
Wall, or by some fractious member of the audience who would
not get out of the way. Rainer's People Wall was as inevitable
as a juggernaut, although an amiable one.

Sections of *Composite* had a certain similarity to Tharp's
parade-ground maneuvers—the mass following of instructions,
the linear floor-plan groupings. But where Tharp's movement
is complex in its use of dynamics, space, and body parts, Rainer's
is very simple—limited to walking, sitting, running, and so
forth, usually focused to the front of the performer's body and
often symmetrical.

In *Continuous Project—Altered Daily* Rainer and four dancers
from her company carried the task-accomplishment idea into a
group activity where a good deal of spontaneity, play, and vari-

ety could develop. After some discussion Rainer took a running leap and swan-dived over two big cardboard cartons into the arms of two men. In another part, one dancer would call out another's name and run to catch him with a pillow as he fell backwards into the ground. Sometimes the dancers had to cooperate to complete their task, other times they engaged in friendly competitions.

All of these games and performances were going on at once, the audience moving around from one to another, sometimes joining in. Where Tharp's portion of the evening had been serene, even reverent, Rainer's was rowdy. Tharp's performance unfolded in the magnificent isolation of all outdoors; Rainer's had the clangor and conviviality of a Horn & Hardart.

This casual good humor transferred easily to a postperformance party the festival was giving in a dormitory living room. That's where I found out that Twyla Tharp's dance was still going on, down the corridor. The mosquitoes outside had been voracious, and Tharp had decided to move the last few solos indoors. So there, in that dark room, with half a dozen people quietly watching, Sara Rudner concluded her adagio. There was something very beautiful and very right about this finale to an evening that had been so vivid and so full of ideas.

August 25, 1969

Two Museum Pieces

A museum is customarily thought of as a static place dedicated to preservation and the resisting of change, while dance by nature is almost completely ephemeral. Many young choreographers are disregarding this apparent clash of aesthetics because museums offer scale and flexibility not possible in the theater, as well as an opportunity to experiment with the performer-audience relationship. Meredith Monk, who gave one of the season's important museum pieces at the Solomon R. Guggenheim Museum, has previously performed at Chicago's Museum of Contemporary Art and the Smithsonian Institution. Twyla Tharp had choreographed for railroad stations and parade grounds before working in the Metropolitan Museum of Art.

Miss Monk's concert was the first of three evenings, under the collective title *Juice*, that explored what could be done with the same thematic material in three spaces of diminishing size: the Guggenheim, Barnard College's Minor Latham Playhouse, and a loft-studio on lower Broadway. Miss Tharp's piece was entitled *Dancing in the Streets of Paris and London, Continued in Stockholm and Sometimes Madrid*. This referred, the choreographer explained in a lecture-demonstration that followed the performance, to movie musicals like *An American in Paris* in which "people were always dancing when they could be walking, singing when they could be talking. There's no reason except that you want to do it." In other words, you don't have to be in a theater to do dancing, but the act of dancing in the street may possibly have some kind of effect upon the street.

Miss Monk's concept of dance is highly theatrical in a traditional sense. After years of chance events, improvisation, "found" movement, and choreographers who would like to refuse all responsibility for what the audience experiences, Miss Monk has reassumed the right of the artist to be in absolute control. It matters very much to her what the audience sees, and she consciously chooses costumes, makeup, lighting, sounds for their dramatic effect. Even the audience was choreographed in *Juice #1*. Ushers and diagrams in the program prescribed where and when to sit, stand, and walk during the performance.

Juice #1 was in three parts. During the first section, with the audience seated on the floor of Frank Lloyd Wright's beautiful spiral tower, various actions took place on the ascending ramp. A quartet of red-painted, red-booted peasants, huddled together and looking like refugees from a Brecht play, slogged its way to the top of the ramp. Big choirs of people dressed in white appeared, hung over the railings at different levels, hummed a single note, sank back out of sight. Spotlights picked out girls posing in period costume, a trio of ladies singing—then honking —a three-note tune, people twanging jew's-harps and violins.

After the peasants had reached the top and Miss Monk had chanted something between a child's going-to-bed song and a call to Mecca, the entire group surged down the ramp and it was the audience's turn to go up.

In the exhibit spaces and stairwells along the ramp Miss Monk had placed small groups of solemn dancers doing continuous, minutely changing activities. Forty-five minutes were allotted for viewing these specimens, which tended to be less interesting than the parade of friends and strangers strolling up and down. Finally we became aware that all the dancers had slipped away and gathered down below, in what had been our space, and were shuffling out the door playing their jew's-harps.

Everything Miss Monk does has a studiously childlike quality. The trappings may be very grand and grown-up, but the underlying movement, sounds, and structure tend to be disconnected, at times almost preverbal. Other artists have tried to recapture the innocence of childhood, but Miss Monk's work isn't so much simple as simplified. She deliberately cuts off the succession that makes events logical or harmonious. In movement she avoids the natural, sequential flow of energy through the body. A typical attitude finds her lying on her back and waving her feet and arms in the air. In this position she completely immobilizes the propulsive center of weight, the connection between the upper and lower halves of the body. Most people stop wanting to do this when they learn to walk.

Miss Tharp's evening began with a near-riot as a couple of hundred people more than had been expected clamored at the Met Museum entrance to be let in, and it continued in the same disorderly but nonviolent fashion. The dancing, some of it very simple, some complicated, took place on and around the museum's majestic staircase and an adjoining sculpture court. Printed instructions advised the audience that these would be the areas used and told how to reach them, but did not specify when or where any of the dance action would take place. The result was a strange game of mass hide-and-seek.

A large group of dancers would be zigzagging up and down the staircase, and just as you got into a good position to see them, the dancers would have darted away into the crowd. Looking for them in the next room, you might find only one dancer and a few spectators, or following a group, you would come out at the top of the stairs and look down their sweeping length to see a line of dancers come snaking out from the midst of the crowd at the bottom. The dancing space and the space occupied by the audience were constantly expanding, shrinking, flowing into one another—sometimes the dancers would be very close to us, like street orators pressed into the middle of a crowd; sometimes a big dancing area would mysteriously open out.

Some of my notes from that evening read as follows: piles of coats—noise in some rms, quiet others—pied piper—a lady falls down a few steps, bumps into a friend she hasn't seen in weeks —Aren't you following the dance? We're waiting here, it'll come by—unusual no. of children—Twyla (fading into the crowd): Yeah I know they can't see, so what?

None of this is to imply that the concert was disorganized or unplanned. Miss Tharp has a mind IBM would be proud to have manufactured, and her methods of devising movement, patterned after Merce Cunningham's chance operations, are complex and didactic. She explained some of them at her lecture-demonstration—one had to do with fragmenting movement by passing a phrase, count by count, from one dancer to another; one required the dancer to do a series of actions while reciting the exact words she had been speaking at, say, eight o'clock that morning. Cunningham started all this by maintaining that the choreographer's psychological biases should not be allowed to color the movement, and people have been throwing dice and consulting the *I Ching* ever since in search of objectivity. Curiously enough, despite all her cool machinations, Miss Tharp choreographs the most personal and interesting dance movement since Cunningham himself, and knowing or not knowing how she made it doesn't make a bit of difference to the viewer.

It is another happy inconsistency of Tharp's recent work that, although using a tightly structured plan, she allows the environment to work upon the dancers, and often creates—or happens on—events of astonishing beauty and spontaneity. Miss Monk used the Guggenheim in its most literal sense, as a theatrical setting for the exhibition of "objects" and as an architectural device for moving a great many people over the same ground in a short time. Miss Tharp did not allow the Met to impose its classical grandeur on her idea. What she did use was the building's generous and varied space, and as the dancers and audience moved helter-skelter through this space, a kind of transformation occurred. Dancers, people, and space began swirling together and a new organism was created, unique to that particular occasion.

Happenings went out of style here some time ago, which is odd when you think of New York's mania for the new and freaky. But perhaps these two concerts hint at the reason. Prevailing opinion has it that Miss Monk's approach—half schoolmarm, half kindergartner—is very creative and avant-garde, while many people at Miss Tharp's concert were disturbed and suspicious because no one told them what to do.

March 22, 1970

Trip in a Time Machine

The most useful thing to be said today about the dance avant-garde is probably that there isn't one. At least there isn't some doctrinaire and radical entity unanimously espoused by the intellectual young. Most choreographers since Merce Cunningham have been concerned with "pure" movement that doesn't depend on worn-out theatrical tricks, and with finding new ways to use sound and visual effects, objects, and events from everyday life. Otherwise they haven't much in common, and although many people will rush to see anything labeled avant-garde, it makes more sense to keep these young innovators separate and find out what special thing each one of them does.

Rudy Perez's choreography—seen last week on the NYU Dance 70 Series—would be the perfect entertainment for a rocket-load of emigrants going to Mars. It demands a certain removal

—your imagination needs to expand and contract in leisurely disregard of the ordinary configurations of time and space.

Scrapping the conventional, almost subconscious rules of dance phrasing and structure, and the urgent rhythms of everyday behavior, Perez takes his time. And having taken it, he doesn't always use it as we would expect, to build up an effect or press a point, for instance. Where Perez seems to be stopping, he may be listening; what seem to be repeats may be refinements. His contemplation of a movement or a visual idea is unusually stretched out. You don't look to Perez for the quick and blaring, for hasty conclusions and action-packed sequences.

In the opening section of *Off Print*, Perez, Barbara Roan, and Anthony La Giglia are seated on chairs facing the audience. They go through a series of small body adjustments and gestural changes, moving one at a time—blip-pause-blip-blip-pause—somewhat like stop-action photography. They wind up in their original positions, but facing upstage, away from the audience, where they do it all again. This time, though, their shadows are projected onto the backdrop. Now we can see, because their images are magnified, the tiny shifts and vibrations that occupy their bodies all the time; there really are no pauses.

Off Print began with the sound of barking dogs and then a relieved silence. In other performances of this work the "overture" was a long series of beautiful color slides of seashore, woods, and city instead. Perez puts irrelevant things together like that, or makes changes from one apparent irrelevancy to another. Not for the sake of surrealism, I suspect, but to isolate the action still further, to make us look harder.

Sometimes the sound, film, or light effects do trigger off a response in the dancers, but then it is likely to happen much later on, or to be quickly sidetracked. *Arcade* begins with the sound track of a prizefight. Though this event is nowhere in evidence when the curtain opens, toward the end of the dance three men have a brief jumping contest under the kind of tight, glaring lights that might overhang a boxing ring. At another point, a tinny piano hammers out the persuasive *oom* pa pa, *oom* pa pa of a ballet class; the dancers assume the appropriate lineup for a studio exercise—and then do a very unregimented, unballetic combination.

Like many of his contemporaries, Perez uses everyday movement and dance movement impartially, depending on what fits his context. Whatever its character, though, the movement is apt to be quite simple, often unfolding and then folding back onto itself—a series of repeated jumps, pointings, lunges, a flinging corkscrew turn that winds down to the floor and unwinds again. Perez appears not to be interested in making extended phrases, or pursuing the shape or direction of a movement impulse beyond the dancer's immediate reach and verticality. Each dancer seems to be moving serenely within his own personal envelope of space.

Perez puts his dances together like games with very complicated rules. Sometimes his group works look like track meets choreographed by Yvonne Rainer, with the dancers running or jumping athletically, embracing, smiling at each other. But even in these less formal sections there is apt to be a carefully calculated strategy of floor patterns, speed, and duration. It isn't necessary for the audience to figure out the rules, but, as with the movement itself, we have to curb our natural impatience for climaxes, recapitulations, and resolutions.

In the early moments of *Arcade*, for instance, a band plays Sousa, and the dancers advance solemnly on the audience in time to the music, looking very military and proper; except that their leg and arm movements are scarcely perceptible. It seems an eternity before they cross the stage. The irony of this device becomes even more pointed when it reappears about fifteen minutes later, at the very end of the dance. This time the dancers take up precise positions around an imaginary rectangle and step toward each other, narrowly missing collisions when they get to the center, and finally, when they have gathered into a close group, break cadence and embrace each other very slowly and lovingly.

Off Print has a similarly elongated "plot"; after the first sequence on the chairs, several other seemingly unrelated events, sounds, props, and images appear and vanish. The dancers do end up on the same chairs, and when we see them there we realize quite a lot has happened to them while we've been watching. We could give these parts a conventional emphasis and continuity if we replayed the dance mentally later, telescoping the parts into a more manageable time package. But, once we know we can do this, the choreography acquires its own immediate interest, like those nineteenth-century novels where the main character doesn't even appear till page 100.

I think Rudy Perez is the only contemporary choreographer who is experimenting with time in this way. Others, notably Martha Graham, have broken up and rearranged the order of things, but no one else has gone so far in trying to see what a drastically different time sense does to the *look* of movement. Without the connotations that dancers usually give to movement by speeding up, compressing, and rebounding with time, Perez's movement has a moment-to-moment importance that is in some ways even more suspenseful.

His solo, *Countdown*, is a perfect example of this idea. The music is two of those exceedingly romantic and familiar Songs of the Auvergne. The dance begins as Perez, dressed in brown sweat shirt and pants, stands in an atmospheric downlight. He sits on a stool, puffs a cigarette, puts it in an ashtray on the floor, stands, blows a kiss into the distance, reaches out to the other side, draws his fingers down his cheeks leaving streaks of green paint (ritual tears?), picks up his cigarette, and puffs as the light goes out. A lover's farewell, perhaps. Yet it is performed with such drawn-out, deliberate understatement that the piece looks utterly unsentimental despite its gooey trappings, and the simple series of actions takes on mystery, persuasiveness, and an entirely unforeseen emotionality.

February 25, 1970

Dancing in the Trees and over the Roofs

If Merce Cunningham gives two-week seasons at the Brooklyn Academy Opera House—and he does now—dance must indeed be booming. But then, where is the avant-garde? Well, dancing in trees, in swimming pools, on rooftops, and on the rocks in Long Island Sound for one thing. To watch dance in recent seasons, I sat on a marble floor, inched through a corridor with two hundred other panicky people in a blackout, and was caught in a motorcycle stampede. I witnessed two full-blown nudity scares and hours of polite pornography. People danced with statues, played with animals, played badminton, walked on a wall, and hurled themselves at a stepladder blindfolded.

Modern dance in its short history has gone through two great cycles of exploration; it may now be entering a third. If I had to pick out the one driving preoccupation of Martha Graham's that has had the most widespread and lasting influence on other choreographers, it would be her concern with emotionality. No modern dancer since Graham has been able to avoid dealing with the idea that dancing is always an expression—or a denial —of the dancer's feelings. Merce Cunningham's most crucial legacy has been the idea of chance—the basic uniqueness, and hence equality, of all things.

By rejecting traditional balletic form as the only acceptable Western dance image, Graham and the early moderns enlarged the expressive possibilities of all dance. Similarly, Cunningham broke open the compositional Pandora's box so that whole new notions about the nature of the dance process could begin to circulate. Although Cunningham personified the most revolutionary element in dance for twenty years, he remains tied to traditional theater dance in two important respects. He still uses highly trained dancers doing those stylizations of movement most people recognize as dance. And his works are customarily presented in proscenium stages within the conventional theater's notions of time, space, and a tolerably distant reciprocity between performer and audience. Virtually every young choreographer has freed himself of one or both of these preconditions.

The post-Cunningham dancers were quick to welcome "mixed media"—film and other technological devices—but they have long since relinquished its development to the more affluent popular arts, from rock to opera, where it is used mainly as an extension of ordinary theater techniques. Instead, choreographers are investigating film, video, and tape as elements that are in themselves interesting, and that can not only accompany and sometimes change the dance, but often transform it. Seamus Murphy's *Fabrication* (1971) televised the audience coming in and the dancers warming up, and screened them in a dark room where we waited for the piece to begin. At the end of the evening, video tapes that had been made of the audience during the performance were shown on four monitors. Thus the audience became performers as well as spectators.

Some choreographers have experimented with collage effects, requiring that the viewer suspend his need to perceive a whole thing at any given time. We must, instead, accept a more extended or pieced-together logic; we must agree that to see only a part of the dance is, in fact, to see the dance. In many of his works Rudy Perez intersperses movement with film or sound phrases. At the beginning of *Arcade* (1969), the audience successively hears the sound of a prizefight, sees a film of the dancers in the studio, printed in reverse in Day-Glo colors, then finds in the brightening stage lights a line of dancers marching very slowly toward the footlights. Sometimes the dance movement will refer back or ahead to images in the film or sound score; other times they overlap, as when the sound of a Ping-Pong game is heard and the dancers stand very still and whip their heads around to look in the direction where the ball was hit . . . and keep looking toward that side while the invisible ball is ralleyed back and forth several times.

The elements Perez puts together often seem incongruous, but his work is not surrealistic. In fact, none of the new generation is using found objects and irrelevant noises purely for the sake of Dada, chance, or shock. When Perez puts on roller skates in *Transit* (1969), they serve as a form of transportation and also become the object of an envious competition between himself and two other dancers. His use of white coveralls, a blue hard hat, a red headband, masking tape laid out in finicky lines on the floor, a Spanish conversation, and Kate Smith singing "God Bless America" in *Coverage* (1970) makes its own kind of nonlinear sense.

What Perez does with mixed media, Twyla Tharp did with

278

space and people in her piece at the Metropolitan Museum of Art, *Dancing in the Streets of Paris and London, Continued in Stockholm and Sometimes Madrid* (1970). Tharp herself explained the piece later as having been about a certain kind of duality that the dancer experiences, of plain ordinary living going on at the same time as dancing. For the spectator, the evening had a hectic, jumbled feeling from the start, so that one was often unable to tell who was dancing and who was watching. The piece was actually an assortment of short dance ideas, performed in various parts of the museum. Some things took place simultaneously in different rooms, some themes were repeated. No particular dancing space was delineated—some spaces were suggested by the museum's architecture, like a sculpture court or a staircase, but others just evolved as blue-jeaned dancers erupted out of the audience or led little processions of spectators from one place to another. The predictability of the event was further broken up by the fact that the audience numbered several hundred, so that even if you knew where a part of the dance was taking place, you couldn't always get in a good position to see it.

Taken as a series of incidents and settings, *Dancing in the Streets* was a collage, but the piece also made a flowing, constantly changing whole, like a carnival. It would have been impossible for any two members of the audience to perceive the dance alike. Many critics and spectators, in fact, were deeply disturbed by this. As soon as they realized that no one was going to tell them what "the dance" was—show it to them in one neat package of space and time—they became anxious and even hostile. They worried that they were missing "the dance" because some things were happening that they could not see. Or they concluded that the whole affair was a put-on.

There is another segment of the contemporary dance scene that is kinder to the audience's undeclared need for authority and its fear of anarchy. These choreographers, of whom the best known is probably Meredith Monk, also employ the loaded visual field, the abundance of simultaneous and apparently unrelated stimuli. But they help the viewer locate the most important part of any given scene by more traditional theater methods.

Technology suggests new ways to present the dance image. Choreography, like film and tape, has become for the artist less a method of recording than a process of selection, distortion, and juxtapositioning of images. In Monk's *Needle-Brain Lloyd and the Systems Kid* (1970), there was an extraordinary croquet game that, although it was always visible to the audience, had the effect of a series of still pictures or movie frames with long mysterious gaps between exposures. The game occupied a small corner of a vast space—the main campus of Connecticut College, in fact. Because there was a great deal of activity going on in the rest of the space, one noticed the croquet players only intermittently. The game was designed so that the players proceeded fairly conventionally for a few moments, then accelerated into drunkenness or violence or perhaps the irrationality born of a broken movie projector; then they froze as if they had been sprayed with a paralyzing liquid. All the time they were advancing toward the audience across the campus, but they never came within close range.

Like a tape loop, a dance idea can be cut at a certain point, joined to itself, and repeated almost indefinitely. Repetition is used by many people to create a kind of boredom as a cleansing antithesis to theatricality. Sometimes, however, the repeated act becomes something else simply because of its repetition. Yvonne Rainer's *Connecticut Composite* (1969) took place in the Connecticut College gym. If one looked down on the gym floor from the balcony one could see four or five clearly defined areas, with different activities going on in each. Down the center length of the room marched Rainer's People Wall, a line of people whose task was to walk, shoulder to shoulder, back and forth from one end of the gym to the other. The solid phalanx they formed, eight or more abreast, proved unstoppable; it slid over, under, and around anyone in its way, and eventually people from the audience began joining it. The People Wall, having established an impervious path, divided the room lengthwise, even though it was not always physically occupying that entire route.

The repetition of a pattern creates certain expectations in the viewer. When William Dunas, a brilliant soloist whose work often depends upon doing violence to himself, begins shaking his head very fast with a smile on his face, we think first of irony, hypocrisy, madness. Dunas keeps shaking his head, though, and shaking it, until we begin to experience kinesthetic discomfort of some kind—horror, distaste, tension, nausea—and the visual illusion that his face is wider, distorted, smiling and smirking and grotesquely stretched, like a Cubist painting.

Seamus Murphy's *Velvet* (1970) depended on the idea that the mind can retain images and superimpose one image on another. His dance consisted of four sections, of basically the same choreography, that took place in four parts of a single building. At no time was the audience able to "see" the entire dance. First the dancers were in a room with glass walls, the audience outside looking in at them. Though the dancers had music, the audience could not hear it. Drapes obscured parts of the room all the time. In the second section the audience peered over the edge of a balcony into a sculpture court, seeing only snatches of movement but hearing the music, Satie's first "Gymnopédie" in an orchestrated version. Then, in a theater, we could see everything, but there was no music. Finally, in another theater, the dance, with sound, was done in the dark. Not only could we tell what was happening by that time, but when some new thematic material was introduced, aurally, we had an idea what that was too.

The mechanical processes of film and tape make alterations in time a simple matter; the time context of movement can also be varied. Rudy Perez is a master at prolonging movement. His dances proceed with an unhurried care, as if each instant were precious. The viewer may be impatient with this decelerated pulse, but after his nervous sytem accommodates to it, he can look at the dance with unusual attention, and when the scene quickens for any reason, events assume an unusual urgency.

Many people have reconsidered the time span of a dance. Conventional theater practice demands that the progress and duration of a dance be ordered to build a climax, die down a little, build higher, and finally come to an end. Merce Cunningham dispensed with all that, proving that a dance could be accomplished within a given clock time as well as dramatic time. After that someone like Phoebe Neville could decide to let the dance flow on without much change in tension, to an ending that suddenly seems quite dramatic because it brings together all the previous unstressed images to make a very strong statement. In her *Untitled Duet* (1970) a woman with a cloth covering her head kneels beside a man stretched out on the floor. The man slowly moves his arms, one joint at a time, through a series of positions that suggest praying, embracing, pleading. Finally the man's arms go limp and the woman bends over his body.

Meredith Monk and the more cinematically inclined choreographers also play with time, often using a slow-motion approach that differs radically from Perez's stretched-out sense of time or Neville's delayed impact. Monk achieves a very slow speed by demanding that the dancer put his body under tight control, holding back his energy so that, like a movie, he could be stopped at any moment, in any position. This puts great restrictions on the type of movement; it will have to be relatively simple, earthbound, and planned. Meredith Monk has not been interested in complicated dance movement per se for some time, though, and her work depends as much on objects, symbols, colors, spaces, sounds, and fantasies as on the people who inhabit them.

I often have the feeling that Meredith Monk regards people as objects, and I get the same feeling from Robert Wilson, who, in *The Life and Times of Sigmund Freud* (1969) and *Deafman Glance* (1971), used a proscenium stage as a container for what seem to be the total ingredients of a mind he has invented. This subconscious space is crowded with images that shift gradually into and out of prominence, memories that articulate themselves and fade away, visions and conflicts and paradoxes that up to now have existed only in the incoherent recesses of the psyche. Poets have captured some of the mind's confusion, but probably no artist has given a better visual representation of its flow and intricacy.

There is in the approach of Meredith Monk, Robert Wilson, and others a return to the idea of the artist-creator, the single mind shaping and governing all elements of a stage work, that relates them to Martha Graham and perhaps to theatrical figures like Schlemmer, Meierhold, and Cocteau, instead of to their

nearer forebears. One possible link between the dance genera-
tions is Alwin Nikolais, who has always been his own designer,
artisan, and inventor, as well as choreographer, composer, and
conceptualizer.

But while Nikolais was working away in his Lower East Side
theater, Merce Cunningham and John Cage tended a caldron of
violent reaction against the controlling genius who imposed his
will on the event. They insisted on the right of the event to be
itself, and they devised innumerable schemes for keeping themselves out of its way. In many respects the current generation
of choreographers can be discussed in terms of whether they are
still pursuing the theories of Cunningham and Cage, or whether
they have returned to more traditional, authoritarian forms of
art.

Cunningham's dances are always concerned with immediacy,
with the realness of what the dancer is doing at that moment.
He refuses to assume a metaphorical or illusionary intent. In
other words, his dancing is not about anything else. He means
for whatever theatricality there is to arise out of the accidental
conjunction of events as they happen.

In different ways this kind of concreteness characterizes several people's work. Rainer's dancers, for instance, and those of
Perez and Cunningham, experience—rather than act out—fleet-
ing pleasure, occasional somberness or surprise, and most consistently a state of alert receptivity. William Dunas, whose aim
is to probe deeper into the emotions, laughs till he retches, runs
till he exhausts himself, swallows handfuls of real pills. Gus
Solomons, Jr., in *Cat. #CCS70-1013NSSR-GSJ9M** (1970), does a
long series of difficult Cunninghamesque movements—isola-
tions, contortions, counter-rhythms. Suddenly, coolly, as if his
head had nothing to do with what is on his body's mind, he
cancels out all those conflicting energies by slashing an ob-
scenity across a caricature he has drawn of himself. Kei Takei
invests one section of *Light* with real difficulty and even danger
by having the dancers blindfolded; but then, unexpectedly, the
dogged earnestness with which they accomplish a long series of
tasks under this restriction begins to evoke memories and ideas
of tremendous scope. These dances, in a sense, become their
own metaphors.

In Elizabeth Keen's *On Edge* (1970), four dancers perched, swung, leaned, balanced in a row of brick arches bordering a roof fifteen stories above the street. *On Edge* was given only once, to a small invited audience. Miss Keen told me later, sounding as if she had just rescued someone from drowning without knowing how to swim; "I'm sorry I tried it. It was foolish. Someone could have gotten hurt."

From the idea of the dance being what it is and nothing more comes the denial of character. Cunningham's dancers never impersonate anybody, neither literary personages, nor philosophical ideas, nor even dancers bristling with stage animation. Yvonne Rainer, proceeding from this assertion of the dancer's integrity, stripped away his other disguises—costume, the trappings of the stage, performing style, and even technique and choreography. She gave him very simple movements to do, games to play, tasks to accomplish. It is the energy of the event that she considers important. Trisha Brown focuses on very taxing physical exertion, such as working against gravity to create an illusion of uprightness while walking sideways on a wall, supported by a harness. Steve Paxton has been working on the phenomenon of performing itself, trying to find out if the performer can preserve anything of himself while several hundred people are looking on. This has led him to use the simplest kinds of activity—walking, turning, sitting—and to employ nudity in some circumstances as, I suppose, the ultimate form of exposure.

Conversely, Monk's and Wilson's work could be called the ultimate form of disguise. Whatever they are, the dancers must not be themselves. In a concert Monk gave at the Billy Rose Theatre (February, 1969), the audience was directed to "lobby exhibits" during intermissions. These turned out to be people huddled in boxes with peepholes. No matter how close the audience can get physically to these performers—and often it's close enough to touch—ordinary signs of communication are not allowed to flicker through their poses. Monk deliberately removes her work from its audience; instead of here and now, she wants us to be conscious of there and then, the image she so elaborately puts together. In *Needle-Brain Lloyd* there is, among other assorted characters and grotesques, a party of pioneers that makes its way across a field and sets up camp. When the audience comes back for the second half of the piece, it is night. The pioneers sit in front of their tents in the dark, light campfires, cook food, sing.

To sustain such intense, complex imagery requires an almost hermetic concentration. This kind of art is exclusive rather than inclusive. The work is what the artist says and nothing more. Cunningham, on the other hand, says the work is that and everything else, the skittish remarks of the audience, a plane flying overhead, accidental darkness, smoke, and all the other chance events we euphemistically ignore in the conventional theater. Meredith Monk does everything she can to see that they don't even occur. Her programs are filled with admonitions to "withhold applause until the end of the program," "stay seated until an usher assists you to the ramp or the elevator," and to go at certain times to certain places described or drawn very explicitly. During *Needle-Brain Lloyd*, technical director Beverly Emmons walked along pushing spectators off a minute strip of turf. "Things happen in this foot of grass," she told us.

Very large-scale works are being tried by nearly everyone, but not for the sake of achieving mass precision-drill effects or spectacles, as they were in pre–World War II Germany, for instance. Choreographers want to find out what very large numbers of people or enormous spaces will do to the performing process and to the audience's experience.

Meredith Monk used a college campus in *Needle-Brain Lloyd* because she wanted to dramatize ideas of panoramic proportions. Since the Renaissance, the theater has simulated deep space with painted scenery and numerous other illusions. Why not use real space? Aside from sports, the only planned events we ever see in large spaces are created for film. What happens when the artist has real distance to play with, instead of the flattened-out dimensionality of the screen? People rowing across a lake with a lantern in the bow of the boat. Horses galloping down a field. Motorcycles roaring like mad cyclopes through the darkness. Cryptic tableaux being enacted high in the windows of a blacked-out building. You could see those things on a screen too, but they never happen *to* you, so they are always to a much greater extent fictitious.

In the less representational imagery of Twyla Tharp's *Medley* (1969), given first at Connecticut College and later in Central Park, thirty-odd people fanned out across a large field and did one movement sequence as slowly as they could. This did not produce unison movement, of course, since every individual's slowest speed is different. The great distance forced the spectator's gaze to splay out, noting individuals briefly, glancing off, returning to see that they had changed position, like the dolls in *Coppélia* that come to life only when your back is turned.

The inherent fascination of people-as-themselves is assumed —and without artifice—by Yvonne Rainer and several others. Deborah Hay, who shared a program with Rainer at the Billy Rose Theatre (1969), showed a piece called *26 Variations on 8 Activities for 13 People plus Beginning and Ending.* The thirteen people were all girls, variously dressed, variously locomoting across the stage, ascending or bypassing some low ramps, jumping or stepping off the ramps, and turning to go back to their starting point. Rainer and Steve Paxton have noted that a dancer's training gives him a certain way of moving and of presenting himself as a performer. They like to use non-dancers to avoid this stereotype, and they assert that the less complex the movement, the more individual and personal will be the characteristics presented.

Another way of using the very large group is to create with it and for it a religious atmosphere. James Cunningham, in many ways the most irreverent of all the young choreographers —because he dares to be funny—is also the most successful at invoking a kind of unrehearsed spirituality. Cunningham, who begins classes, rehearsals, and often performances with Yoga exercises, seems to touch a nerve of communal expression. Whether it's twenty people quietly placing lighted candles on the floor (*The Sea of Tranquility Motel*, 1969) or nearly a hundred doing a mass rock improvisation which the audience joins (*The Junior Birdsmen*, 1970), Cunningham develops a mood that is theatrical without the theater's detachment.

Arriving at group experience through Central European theories of pure movement, the Philadelphia-based Group Motion can put itself into near-trance or work up an orgiastic rage. Following a New York performance of *The Great Theatre of Oklahoma Calls You* (1970), the group did exercises in transferring impulses and energies from one dancer to another. The performance ended with members of the audience participating in an experiment that involved touching, moving, and trusting others. This last looked like a gentle sort of group therapy session, but there were moments earlier in the performance of such compelling intensity that one could easily see the roots of mob violence and manipulation if some less supportive, permissive leaders were in control.

Nearly all experimental dance has a lot to do with the relationship of the performance to the audience. It's no longer a question of whether there should be "audience participation," but in what way the audience will contribute to the event. Meredith Monk and Seamus Murphy assume that the artist is a kind of instructor, who imparts his vision to an essentially passive audience; hence we are directed, herded, sometimes stampeded from one place to another during the performance. We are even made to get in each other's way if the plan calls for a crowd so dense that viewing will be difficult.

Rainer and Tharp, on the other hand, let us wander wherever we wish and see whatever we discover, as if we and the performers were all attending the same party. The use of non-dancers can help bring performers and audience closer together. But asserting that the audience has some responsibility for what takes place instead of merely witnessing it is not to say there is anything haphazard about the choreographer's view of the work. Even those works that are "improvisational" are not free-for-alls, but are based on previously established rules—a time structure, certain movement materials, a problem to be solved —and often the dancers have worked with these rules until they are honed to a fine degree of responsiveness to each other. Then, as in Tharp's *Dancing in the Streets*, the very presence of the audience transforms a fairly stable performance situation into an improvisational one.

In their different ways, most experimental people are choreographing for the audience as much as for the performers. They are all, it seems to me, trying to involve us more, to make us aware how special is the moment of our attendance, whether they include us in their games, like Rainer; make us part of the scenery, like Tharp; elicit our physical discomfort by brutalizing themselves, like Dunas; or pull us into the flow of their personal dynamic, like Perez. James Cunningham invites us up to dance; Seamus Murphy austerely points out how distant performers and audiences are from each other, then by degrees draws us in closer to the performed world, until we are all in the dark together. Even Meredith Monk, whose pieces seem the most dogmatic and predetermined, the most like movies, works with such enormous and complex production elements that we are aware as the thing is reeling off around us that there can be no rerun.

If I have not mentioned specific content, themes, ideas in describing these choreographers' works, it's not because there are none. These works are concerned with dancing, performing, living, and the processes by which those things are accomplished, much more than they are with any literary, dramatic, or philosophical themes. The choreographers want us above all to see what the work *is*, not what it means.

When James Cunningham puts on a mask or does a soft-shoe dance or sings a perfectly good homemade imitation of something we first heard in a Fred Astaire movie, he is, I think, focusing on James Cunningham the performer and on the way that that performer uses these traditional theater devices; of only secondary interest, if at all, is what the song says and how it fits in with all the other songs and events in that particular entertainment. If Rudy Perez's *Coverage* collects artifacts of the hard-hat psychology, what's important about the dance is the slow intensity and deliberate care with which Perez looks at the collection, not his moral attitude toward it. Meredith Monk alludes to all sorts of political, social, and cultural trends, but her works are really monuments to their own epic creation. Twyla Tharp, before she started allowing the environment to work its own process on her dance, used to insist that the audience concentrate on the spiderlike methodology by which she had devised the movement, until even the excitement of the dancing was segmented into ticks of a metronome and boxes marked out on the floor.

Someone going to see any of these choreographers for the first time might well ask the familiar question: But is it dance? No. And, most emphatically, yes. What makes these works dance when they have denied so many of our notions about what dance is, and when they employ so many techniques that have become identified with other theater forms, is their emphasis on the flow of events through time and space, and their belief that this flow creates its own validity independent of words or techniques. Experimental dance today is about dancing, in the broadest sense, and it will probably take at least another twenty years to explore the possibilities of that.

Autumn, 1971

Tasks and Games

Merce Cunningham's most important gift to choreography may turn out to be freedom of form. Just about every discussion of experimental work that starts out ". . . but is it dance?" can be traced back to Cunningham, who decided that dance doesn't have to be a pattern of virtuosic actions set in advance by a single choreographer/dictator. Without this reassurance, the Judson Dance Theater of the early sixties and most of the contemporary dance scene might never have occurred.

Two Judson alumni, Trisha Brown and Rudy Perez, gave concerts recently here, proving how far the artist's imagination could be extended once the compositional lid came off. Both Brown and Perez work with trained dancers and non-dancers, and both evenings de-emphasized theatrical qualities in order to concentrate on pure movement.

At the Whitney Museum of American Art Trisha Brown gave her dancers a series of physically exacting tasks related to upsetting the body's accustomed verticality. Most spectacular was *Walking on the Wall,* in which the performers stood and walked parallel to the floor, along two right-angled walls, while suspended in special harnesses rigged on cables from tracks along the ceiling. As many as six walkers could be in action at once, and, encountering each other, they would have to back up or scramble past the other person's harness. Some people developed a loping facility, while others lurched and tugged at the apparatus.

It's not nearly as easy as it sounds, maintaining an upright, natural-looking position while hanging on your side in the air. In fact the whole piece made me wonder about that comforting cylinder called up and down by which we orient ourselves to a vertical existence. From where I sat I seemed to be looking "down" at the dancers, as if they were in the street and I was in a building "above" them. Wiggy.

People worked in pairs in Brown's *Leaning Duets II* and *Falling Duet I and II.* The first of these pieces had the couples roped together and leaning against little wooden boards. The object was to gain as much movement as possible, including locomotion, by inclining outward from the other partner. In *Falling Duet I* Barbara Lloyd and Miss Brown took turns falling and catching each other; Brown and Steve Paxton got more vigorous in *Falling Duet II,* bumping hips and climbing on each other's shoulders, usually falling together. These activities all had to do with trusting, I thought. The most daring and active of the performers were those with the most faith in their partners, the most successful couples were those most keenly tuned in to each other's changes and intentions.

The evening ended with *Skymap,* a narrative in which Miss Brown traces an imaginary map of the United States on the ceiling and reminisces quietly about this and that. The audience views it by lying on the floor in the dark. It made me think of long-ago Vermont nights by a campfire.

Rudy Perez's new work, *Monumental Exchange,* was given in the spacious Merce Cunningham studio at the top of Westbeth, our new artists' housing project. Perez's choreography, like Brown's, evokes a nice, easy athleticism that lets each performer's distinctive habits of moving show through. Perez, however, seems less interested in the improvisatory possibilities of setting various people to a given task than in the mass effect of crowds doing structured movement in random time and space patterns.

Monumental Exchange begins with Perez rolling a white stick the length of the studio floor, in that deliberate way of his—he squats, mentally takes the measure of the pole, places his hands on it, considers, pushes, waits for it to stop, gets up and begins again. When he finishes, twenty-two people explode into the room, rolling fast down the same track he's laid out, then running back over the line of revolving bodies. The dance continues with a series of variations on simple activities like this: a shoulder-to-shoulder line of people jogging, breaking ranks one at a time and running at the audience and back into place; boys carrying girls on their shoulders; great big sideways steps versus tiny forward steps; a grinning, low-key chorus line to a Fred Astaire tune.

Monumental Exchange is a lovely event. It comes out looking miscellaneous in spite of its rather rigid design, because the participants are so individual, and Perez is so willing to have us notice their differences. His older works, *Arcade* and *Coverage*, shown the same evening, are more theatrical and lost a lot of their metaphorical strength in the studio's honest light and open space.

There is a proletarian quality about concerts like these: the audience is mostly young, mostly not from the dance community. Admission is free or very cheap. You probably sit on the floor. The performers are dressed a lot like the audience and behave as informally. Only a few years ago you attended this kind of event with a suspicion that somebody was going to make you "participate," or put a spotlight on you at an inconvenient moment, or somehow make you feel silly. Now it's a lot more relaxed. People like Perez and Brown don't play tricks on the audience, or make bargains—"I'll pretend you're special if you pretend I am." All they ask is the audience's attention, enjoyment, and maybe their love, and they usually get it.

April 18, 1971

Psyched Out

Watching *The Life and Times of Sigmund Freud* is like rummaging around in somebody else's attic. Everything up there is very interesting, but there's no use trying to figure out why it's there or what it all means, and when you come downstairs again you realize you haven't accomplished anything in the past three hours, but you've seen a lot of curious things.

The Life and Times of Sigmund Freud is about symbols and disguises and time, about the heaps of forgotten identities and dislocated scenery scattered around the interior of the subconscious, about the people, known and not known, who are endlessly plodding back and forth across the dim recesses of the mind, and about the imperceptible way this landscape shifts and changes before we can become quite familiar with it. The work, incidentally, is also about the life and times of Sigmund Freud, but this reviewer has only a parlor acquaintance with the good doctor, so I cannot discuss its biographical fidelity.

Robert Wilson, creator of *The Life and Times . . .* , calls his work a dance play, which is a misleading description however you look at it. There is scarcely any movement, let alone dance, and though a play usually contains dialogue, this one has none; in fact, long stretches of it take place in complete silence, and what few sounds there are tend to be nonverbal. It seems to have more to do with literature and painting than with theater, except that it makes use of the theater's time and dimensionality to carry out its essentially static conception.

As in the scenario of the mind, Wilson's people and animals and vistas are fixed in all their specificity. They must play out their appointed roles, always the same way; they can only change in perspective—as the light shifts around to another quarter, or other scenes and characters partially obscure them.

They cannot interact with each other, except as they were related in real life, but they can exist on the same mental plane. In the second act, a kind of party is taking place, attended by some characters who have appeared before and some who have not. They enter, fix themselves drinks, and go to their places in the room. There they remain frozen until it is time to make their move—three men ponder over a chessboard; a woman fussily puts plumes in her cuffs; people bring in a ladder and drape themselves over it; a camel looks in at the door and withdraws; a woman sits down at the piano, plays a few bars of Satie, is drowned out by gospel music, continues playing; a walrus with a fan waddles up to listen.

But Wilson is building something more than a surrealistic waxworks. His theatrical imagination is fantastic, and also remarkably controlled. Everything comes into view very slowly and without dynamic emphasis—a presence is not announced, a change is not dramatized—you just get around to noticing, eventually, that the shadows and shapes are different.

Act One takes place on a sort of beach, where people move continuously in never-meeting lines parallel to the horizon. Sometimes the air is filled with fine dust raised by someone's agitated shuffling in the sand. A pipe is lowered from the flies until it is just visible below the proscenium arch. A pair of bare feet walks across the pipe. For the first-act finale, Wilson invokes an army of black mammies, of all sizes and sexes, grotesquely padded front and rear, dressed in crimson dresses with white aprons and with their heads done up in kerchiefs, moving in suffocating parody of outspread mammy welcome. (This is a play about Freud, remember.) The last act is heavily symbolic, taking place in a Platonic cave or a manger, with outsized animals lying around, and a beautiful black lady with a crow perched on her hand, and Humanity filing past in the glare outside, and a lot of other things, including Sigmund Freud and a little boy whimpering at his feet.

I have never seen anything like *The Life and Times of Sigmund Freud*, although Meredith Monk seems to be on somewhat the same track as Wilson. It is theater—if it *is* theater—totally dictated by and dedicated to a central idea. It encompasses a vast range of specific elements, but they are all objects, manipulated by the director to produce an effect. What is important about an actor or a dancer in *The Life and Times* . . . is not what he does or how he changes, but the way he fits into the total scheme; he is a puppet, changing not from some power within himself, but because some higher force moves him around in juxtaposition to other actor-objects. For the audience, this is theater that is done to you, not theater that you have to do. You sit there as it unreels before your eyes, and you say either "Oh, wow," or "So what?"

The first thing the audience saw when entering the lobby of Brooklyn Academy, where the piece was presented last weekend, was two men dressed in hobo costumes, hawking TLA-TOSF posters at $5.00 each. Robert Wilson sometimes goes under the name of Byrd Hoffman, and he presides over a School of Byrds whose function it is difficult to ascertain. These facts are not unrelated to *The Life and Times*. . . . While one sector of our dance world is trying to bring the audience closer to the artist in his natural skin, another group is retreating behind ever more complex and fascinating masks.

May, 1970

Mind's-Eye Theater

Robert Wilson is creating a theater of the mind's eye. His work of last year, *The Life and Times of Sigmund Freud,* and his new piece, *Deafman Glance,* both given at Brooklyn Academy, are not like anything this observer has ever seen on a stage. By that I don't mean that they are bigger or more puzzling, that they use more stage effects or stranger-looking people or weirder ideas than other theater pieces, though they do.

I mean that Wilson's whole conception of what you put on a stage is unique. In many ways he's a theatrical primitive—his things are too long, they're fantastically boring, they seem immobile and cryptic—and only a naïve sensibility could imagine the theater as a place to show the sequence of changes and recognitions, the melting together of things and the imperceptible emergence of things, that rumbles around so much of the time in the back closets of the human mind.

Wilson is interested not merely in the fantasies and odd perceptions that the mind eventually produces, but in its process of arriving at them. What he does is less like a diary or a psychoanalytic interview than a film of the entire mental apparatus, with all its dross and irrelevancy, before the significant events have been selected out.

Deafman Glance, which Wilson says was suggested by a young black boy who is deaf, opens with a tableau of a boy sitting on a stool and a woman standing by a table, both of them facing a gray stucco wall. For the first half hour this is all that happens. Except that you begin to notice bizarre things: smoke drifts out of a pipe in the wall; the mother is dressed in a black Victorian dress, and is wearing one black glove; something, another child or an animal, squirms under a sheet on the floor; there is a pinkish cement lion, the kind that lives in formal gardens, at the feet of the boy.

The action begins slowly—all the action will be slow and unaccented—as the mother seems to be putting the little boy to bed. She pours him a glass of milk, which he drinks. Then she tenderly stabs him with a dagger before tucking him under a sheet. After dispatching the little girl under the other sheet on the floor the same way, she leaves with another boy who seems to be her real child because his clothes are of the same period as hers. This little boy, who has uttered some inarticulate sounds while waiting for his mother, turns out to be the hero, the Deafman. But he doesn't do anything, he just watches all the marvels and minutiae that parade past him for the next three hours.

Deafman Glance could be seen as the florid daydreams of the boy after he and his mother leave the gray, grainy scene of the prologue and enter a technicolor land where animals drink martinis and a boy can be appointed Messiah. Or it can be seen as an allegory of mankind—birth, death, religion, hell and damnation, and the resurrection of the apes, illuminated by mythic and mystical symbols. Or it could be just a pageant, a technical tour de force.

The program lists eighty-seven performers, including infants, pregnant women, and a monkey named Morris. A lady with a goat's beard lives in a cabin (Uncle Tom's?) that is also an altar, with a row of votive lights alongside and animal skulls adorning the roof. The cabin gives out smoke for an hour or two, and finally burns down at about the same time the Deafman is being blessed by a bishop, flagellated, and lifted in a throne high above the ground. Some people dressed in sophisticated black clothes have dinner with a frog, they send out fragmentary messages in strange languages, they amuse themselves with odd toys—dirt, a quill pen, a hand. Silver-painted naked people walk past in the distance. A boy on an ox and some beggars journey toward the east. A pyramid looms behind them. An old woman dressed in white with an arrow through her head lies down in a fishpond. And on and on.

Wilson jams every bit of the stage full of images all the time —not just the floor but the space above it. Yet he keeps things moving slowly into and out of focus, assisted by John Dodd's beautiful lighting. Like all figments of the mind, whatever happens is under control, it's not spectacular in any ordinary sense. The symbols are consistent and, though often violent, not emotionally disturbing. Wilson probes the brain clinically and allows us to examine his findings without getting blood spattered on us. This may turn out to be the most important factor in his work.

Deafman seemed to have rather more of a "plot" than *The Life and Times of Sigmund Freud,* which I found incomprehensible. Yet, perhaps for this very reason, it wasn't as extraordinary as *Freud.* Or maybe the first time you see Wilson is going to be extraordinary, whatever piece you see.

March 21, 1971

Virgin Vessel

You could think of Meredith Monk's *Vessel* as a ship of fools. Or, since its theme is the story of Joan of Arc, you could interpret the title in the biblical sense to mean a person who carries the word of God. Or you could find in the gigantic course of this three-part "opera epic" various water images or various cooking receptacles to support various senses of the title word.

But I'll leave the literary exegesis to the music critics or theater critics who probably saw the piece during its two-week run here. *Vessel*, like all of Monk's work, was enormously complex and dense in its layers of imagery, and—also like all of her work —some of it was inaccessible to me, some of it seemed overintellectualized, and some of it was unimaginably beautiful.

There's no easy way to describe *Vessel*. It begins in Monk's garret in a Great Jones Street loft building. Part Two takes place in the Performing Garage, erstwhile home of Richard Schechner's *Dionysus in '69*, and the last scene is a downtown parking lot and adjacent church. All of these locations are in the absolute bowels of New York City—the decaying industrial core that is worse than any slum, because it's been abandoned by everybody but the scavengers.

Vessel is so determinedly literary and symbolic that I was acutely aware of the distance between the real, raunchy world Meredith Monk inhabits and the make-believe one she wants to create. In fact, this distance may be one of the crucial things about Monk's theater.

The piece begins as the audience is led into the pitch-dark loft a few at a time by someone with a flashlight. You sit on a backless bench waiting for the process to be completed, and you hear a woman's voice somewhere in front of you, reciting a surrealistic story in a very peculiar, melodramatic *sprechstimme* style, like a bad actress doing the Duchess in *Alice in Wonderland*. As your eyes get used to the dark, you see a smoggy glow from some windows, and another from a barred skylight. You've entered inner space.

A match flares, and in a thin spill of light from a partly hidden candle you can just make out a woman in profile, seated at an organ console. She plays a series of syncopated, repeating chords, and after a long time she starts to crow—a single note pitched high, higher than a person can sing—in a complementary rhythm. Staring straight ahead, she sings and plays and rocks back and forth from the base of her spine.

Other lights come on and we see a group of people dressed in black seated casually around a living room. They begin doing tiny things with their hands—pantomimed games of catch, outlining shapes in the air, wiggling their fingers. Facing us with their backs to the living room group a pale, naked couple with long fuzzy hair sit side by side at a table.

The people in black disappear one by one and come back dressed in different costumes as if to announce a previous incarnation. A man in a suit and derby becomes a king who throws money on the floor and intones portentous French words. Later a girl comes out in a plaid wool shirt and a long cotton-batting beard and rakes up the money.

A procession of peasants comes up the stairs and makes its way across the loft, stopping as though on a long journey to rest and play snatches of music on a jew's-harp and flute. Another man follows after them scattering ashes along their trail.

The organist (Meredith Monk) stands at the far end of the loft and gives, very simply, a brave speech from Scene V of Shaw's *Saint Joan*. Then she whispers the same speech. The living-room characters line up formally, and, one by one, they each repeat a movement sequence, accelerating into near-frenzy, until they are stopped by a clap and a guttural "tee hee!" from a sort of stage manager identified in the program as Host.

Part One ends with a vision: a bushy-haired girl, white-robed and flooded with saintly light, gazes in at us from the fire escape while Monk shrieks her way through another primal solo.

Parts Two and Three contain these same elements, sometimes in different forms, always increasing in size and sweep. In the multilevel scaffolding of the Performing Garage, the living-room characters have one long vocal ensemble; later they do solo bits and low comedy in a blue spotlight. A girl juggles oversize money in Part Two; she becomes a whole troop of clowns who tumble out of a microbus at the parking lot. Two peasants wearing silver hood-masks duel with rakes in Part One; in the last act, two peasant armies charge at each other.

Each section culminates in a striking apotheosis, with Joan/ Monk finally immolating herself—dancing, twitchy and frenzied, into the blue-white-yellow blaze of a welding torch.

I always find Meredith Monk's pieces more interesting in the aftermath than in process. I think this has something to do with the restraint she imposes on her performing canvas. She only allows one thing to happen at a time, so as a spectator you know you must wait out each episode until the next one begins, while in thinking it over later you can make the events flow and intermingle in your mind.

The point is, the separate event as it happens is static. It's as if Monk were showing you a picture album of her trip in the Joan of Arc vessel—now here are the pioneers, she seems to say, and these are the children playing a-tisket a-tasket, and then the dragon comes in. Everything is done very slowly and deliberately and the phrasing—whether vocal, motional, or theatrical —seldom gets more complex than a repetitive, bare in-out sequence or a ring, swept clean of rhythmic emphasis. Although the images are sometimes startling, strange, even occult, they are always maintained at low intensity; the performers are composed, they're artificial.

Monk's raw materials are simple, even childlike, but so brilliantly controlled that they can become universal. A character who looked like a fifteenth-century monk to me reminded someone else of a rabbi. Little touches of costume—heavy boots or an apron—place the character, not specifically but according to type. The pioneers could be crossing the American plains or medieval Europe. The vividly dressed, well-behaved children might belong to a French court or an English country house. The vocal sounds, virtuosically produced, are at the same time unheard-of, unearthly, and evocative.

Meredith Monk's imagination is so clever, so far-reaching, yet so careful. With a sacrificial purity, an unaggressive assurance, she drags us down into the city's viscera, only to transport us out of the grit and the garbage in an elaborate, watertight fantasy. It's her detachment rather than her involvement, I think, that fascinates people. What a cool, permissive saint she makes, offering Nirvana to a decrepit city!

November 14, 1971

⚯

Sensitivity Performing

Ann Halprin's *West/East Stereo* defies analysis. I'm not even sure it should be reviewed. Except that Halprin spent so much time in New London explaining her methods and intentions to critics, dancers, and audiences that she must have wanted us to understand more about it than the bare performances showed.

The piece, given during the last weekend of the Connecticut College American Dance Festival, was a highly structured group improvisation on the theme of animal behavior. Not much problem with that, once I got past my prejudice against people imitating animals. The Halprin group, San Francisco Dancers' Workshop, has apparently done research at the zoo and gives as good a version of jungle life as I've seen on any stage. I especially liked the heavy, loping gait of their tigers; their flapping, gawky-necked big birds; and a howling gallery of monkeys perched in a circular staircase at the back of the stage.

By the second performance I was into the animal imagery and could appreciate the birth of a fawn, the killing of a deer by a lion and the arrival of other lions to eat the carcass, and similar events. I could enjoy the fantasy and discount most of the stuff I'd seen the first time, which had nothing to do with animals.

Halprin works with the techniques of sensitivity and group encounter—getting people to let go of their inhibitions and relate to each other more directly. She's also very verbal and explains a lot, which isn't always a useful technique if you're trying to break down the defenses built by words. Then, rather than let the improvisational process run its often disorderly course, she puts the whole event into a highly complex, intellectualized structure devised by her husband, the environmentalist-architect Lawrence Halprin. A drawing of the "score" on the back of the program looks like an elaborate road map, with obstacles labeled "growth," "courting," "burden," stuff like that, and a huge intersection at the edge of the page called "confrontation."

Experimental though it all sounds, there are persistent reminders of old-fashioned theater. A huskily sincere, benevolent Stage Manager from *Our Town*, theatricalized version of the T-group leader, brings individuals out of their animal states after deep encounters, confronting them by name, asking them how they feel about what just happened to them. ". . . Man, I feel good . . ." they answer, trying to sound convincing. Or they shuffle their feet and shrug, in postures of being overwhelmed. One girl did a dance of glee—the same dance at both performances.

What's really going on here, I kept wanting to know. I suspect the animal imitations were the *least* real thing about the piece, serving as a convenient disguise for the displays of power, hostility, and perhaps exhibitionism that almost all the participants were engaged in. Encounter people talk a lot about love and relating and community. These seemed to show up mostly in the context of sexual aggressiveness, although the group as a whole had the comradely good spirit of any effective team. Halprin herself plays permissive mama; the others are her big, boisterous kids.

Mostly, I guess, I missed the spontaneity that these methods are supposed to release. There was a lot of motion and vocalizing all right, and a stomp-chant at the end with audience participation—now as ritualized in this kind of dance as applause is at the ballet. But it was all under control, all calculated. One man did get stripped naked, which hadn't been rehearsed; a pretty tame game four years after Halprin's own mind-bending *Parades and Changes*, the first nude dance.

Among the mock fornications and real anger, the studied

verbalizings and the genuine physicality, the naïve theater and the dramatic innocence, it was impossible for me to find the truth of this dance. Neither the metaphor nor the reality took possession of the event.

Ann Halprin seems to be caught somewhere between art and therapy, and what she needs for herself is probably different from what she intends for the members of her company. *West/ East Stereo* made me wonder if the artist has the right to expose a real therapeutic situation to an audience, or if the therapist has the right to interfere with the therapeutic process in the interest of effective theater. Or indeed whether a therapeutic change can take place at all in the presence of spectators. If Ann Halprin gets a consistent answer to these questions she may really come up with something.

September 5, 1971

Jazzing

There is a certain strain in American dance that derives a lot of its character from the popular arts but doesn't especially try to be popular itself. James Waring has applied the mauve passions of musical comedy and operetta to ballet. Meredith Monk's episodic, masqueradelike spectacles owe a great deal to the adventure comic strips and radio serials of the 1940s. Twyla Tharp's *Eight Jelly Rolls* is the latest distinguished addition to this line. It digs into the kinetic fiber of jazz in a way that no choreography has done before.

Jazz is not only the property of black people in our culture, although most black choreographers have rightfully employed it as an expressive medium, and most whites have turned out something slick or self-conscious with it. Jazz—not the treacly, processed goo that flows out of supermarket ceilings, but the jazz of vaudeville, jam sessions, and hoofing—is an authentic part of our biracial heritage.

It's the energy, virtuosity, and smooth extroversion of old-time jazz that Twyla Tharp explores in her eight dances to music of Jelly Roll Morton. Like most of her earlier work they contain prodigious gobs of pure, driving motion carried off with the utmost nonchalance and unstressed humor.

But where her previous works, Merce Cunningham-like, usually spilled out multidirectionally into space or confined themselves to private performing enclaves, *Eight Jelly Rolls* is built for the audience; it projects out front all the time. This kind of confrontation makes a lot of difference in Tharp—this recognition that we are there, we ourselves, not some remote theoretical presence outside the walls of her concentration.

For the first time her dancers have character—not, certainly, anything big and unconvincingly show-biz, but something that grows almost involuntarily out of the movement. There's a sense of absurdity about the unmanageable shape and weight of the body—about being able to mobilize great feats of levity and quickness when one's natural condition is the slump. The dancers regard the audience with stony-faced bravura or belligerent surprise, as if to say, What did *I* do?

The work also has a very clean shape that one could see even in the open thrust stage of Central Park's Delacorte Theater, where it was shown here September 16. The solos happen downstage, the chorus prances in the background. Tharp creates a visual order here that's unusual for her, but the order looks rudimentary, perhaps intentionally sketchy, as if she were the first dancer to discover the uses of the conventional stage.

The movement is eccentric, surprising, impressionistic. Tharp does an incredible solo where she keeps threatening to fall, just grabs her balance in time, only to throw herself off center again, while Sara Rudner scrambles and wriggles but can't seem to find the right coordination of parts to lift herself from the floor. Another time Tharp reaches out so far with one leg that she seems about to split, then hitches the other leg up to it like a nervous caterpillar and starts out again.

A lot of this comes from the professional hoofers, and some of it recalls the tongue-in-cheek sexuality of burlesque—Sara

Rudner's understated bumps and grinds with one arm dangling high in the air, for instance, or Rose Marie Wright doing leggy glides and slow, shrugging turns while five girls in unison take suspended, fashion-model poses.

But the dance doesn't rely on its nostalgia; it's too forcefully a thing all its own. It's not pure clowning either, and it skirts the easy route of parody.

I suppose one could have seen *Eight Jelly Rolls* coming; it's a logical progression out of Tharp's earlier work. *The Fugue* (1970), seen at the same Central Park performance, is a trio consisting of short, complex contrapuntal sections done in silence punctuated by the amplified sounds of the dancers' boots stamping or pattering on the stage. It looks and sounds a little like tap dancing—it has the frontal orientation, the emphasis on changes of time, the thrust of weight going into the floor and springing out again, the loose disregard of all but the working body parts.

Last spring Tharp showed parts of a work that had three dancers accompanied by three simultaneous, different jazz piano selections—each dancer had to listen to her own loudspeaker. *Eight Jelly Rolls* seems to crystallize everything Tharp has been doing all this time, and put it into its proper form at last.

This, of course, is a dangerous thing to say about any experimental choreographer, and Twyla Tharp has already told me she doesn't want to do *Eight Jelly Rolls* again after she takes it to Paris in November. She's against repertory because she feels it stops her from growing; keeping old dances in good condition takes time away from making new dances.

I'm aware that a constant evolution of style seldom happens in a company that does repertory for a living, and that the creative artist can't keep going back and reproducing his old work. But *Eight Jelly Rolls* is one of those rare, infinitely satisfactory pieces that leave you unsatisfied. After it was over I left in mid-concert. I didn't want to see another thing, unless it was *Eight Jelly Rolls* all over again.

October 3, 1971

ACKNOWLEDGMENTS

Title	Source
11 Troubles, Trifles, and the Return of a Prodigal Son	*New York* Magazine
15 New York City Ballet Opens	*The Boston Herald Traveler*
17 *Suite No. 3*	"
19 *Kodaly Dances*	"
20 Home on the Back Burner	*Los Angeles Times*
24 *The Goldberg Variations*	*The Boston Herald Traveler*
25 *Square Dance*	"
27 *PAMTGG*	"
28 Another Opening	"
30 Dancers Upstage Repertory	*New York* Magazine
33 Makarova's Ballet Theatre Debut	*The Boston Herald Traveler*
35 *A Rose for Miss Emily*	"
37 ABT Ending Season	"
39 A Great Opening Night	"
40 *Paquita*	"
42 *La Sylphide*	"
43 *Romeo and Juliet*	"
45 *Romeo and Juliet* (II)	"
46 *The Miraculous Mandarin*	"
48 Every Inch a King	*New York* Magazine
50 Bread and Circuses	*Los Angeles Times*
53 More Geese than Swans	*New York* Magazine
57 *Petrouchka*: A Modern Fairy Tale	*Los Angeles Times*
61 *The Green Table*: Movement Masterpiece	*Arts in Society*

Acknowledgments

	TITLE	SOURCE
66	Maximiliano Zomosa (1937–1969)	*Dance Magazine*
67	Dancing on a Precipice	*New York* Magazine
73	Esprit de Joie	*The Wall Street Journal*
76	Eliot Feld and the Extinct Metaphor	Brooklyn Academy program
79	They're Alive. That Counts.	*The Boston Herald Traveler*
81	*Romance*	"
83	*The Gods Amused*	*The Boston Herald Traveler*
84	*Theatre*	"
86	Noblesse Oblige	*Arts in Society*
98	Ballet Patronage: How Not to Do It	*Los Angeles Times*
109	Creeping Orthodoxy	*New York* Magazine
111	Moon Worship, circa 1968	"
114	Spare the Confetti	*The Wall Street Journal*
117	*Trinity*	*The Boston Herald Traveler*
118	*Reflections*	"
120	*Valentine*	"
121	Real Rock Ballet: Why?	"
124	Louis Falco	"
125	Lar Lubovitch	"
127	Béjart Opens	"
129	Poster Art	"
131	I Can't Hear the Music	"
137	Dance Muzak	"
143	Starting with Dance	*Arts in Society*
148	New York Goes Tap-Happy	*New York* Magazine
150	Selling Soul	"
153	A-Changin'	*Ballet Today*
156	*Flowers*	*The Boston Herald Traveler*
158	*Choral Dances*	"
159	*Child of the Earth*	"
160	*Cry*	"
162	Modern Dance—with Pizzazz	*Los Angeles Times*
166	Dance Theatre of Harlem Debut	*The Boston Herald Traveler*
168	Home to Harlem	*Los Angeles Times*

Acknowledgments

	TITLE	SOURCE
171	The Pattern-Breakers	*The Boston Herald Traveler*
179	Are Graham's Gods Dead?	*New York* Magazine
183	Graham in Brooklyn	"
185	Martha, or Mother	*The Hartford Courant*
187	Mailing Her Letter to the World	*The Boston Herald Traveler*
190	Ex-Post-Graham	"
193	Early Floating and Twilight Turbulence	*New York* Magazine
195	Zone of Safety	*Ballet Today*
197	Something Beyond Steps	*Juilliard News Bulletin*
203	Spoils of Success	unpublished
209	Food for the Eye	*New York* Magazine
212	*Big Bertha*	*The Boston Herald Traveler*
213	The Theater of Vision	unpublished
218	Deus ex Machina	*New York* Magazine
220	Nikolais' Theater of Marvels	*The Wall Street Journal*
223	*Scenario*	*The Boston Herald Traveler*
224	The Reluctant Showoff	unpublished
227	The Real McCoy	unpublished
230	Reaction and Vanguard: Which Is Which?	*New York* Magazine
233	Cunningham's Here and There	"
236	Come in, Earth. Are You There?	*Arts in Society*
244	More than the Museum	*The Boston Herald Traveler*
253	*Televanilla:* Theater in Two Flavors	*New York* Magazine
256	Working Out	"
258	Marathon at Manhattan School	*Ballet Today*
261	Smut and Other Diversions	*New York* Magazine
264	Radicalizing the Dance Audience	unpublished
267	Progress in a New Environment	*New York* Magazine
269	Two Museum Pieces	*Los Angeles Times*
273	Trip in a Time Machine	*The Wall Street Journal*

Acknowledgments

	TITLE	SOURCE
276	Dancing in the Trees and over the Roofs	*The Hudson Review*
289	Tasks and Games	*The Boston Herald Traveler*
292	Psyched Out	unpublished
294	Mind's-Eye Theater	*The Boston Herald Traveler*
297	Virgin Vessel	"
300	Sensitivity Performing	"
302	Jazzing	"

Abyss (Hodes), 91, 92
Acme Dance Co., 249
Acrobats of God (Graham), 191
Actus Tragicus (Béjart), 130
Adams, Carolyn, 212
Adaptations (Litz), 226
Afro-American Dance Ensemble, 156
After Eden (Butler), 92, 96
Afternoon of a Faun (Robbins), 133
Agathe's Tale (Taylor), 204, 205–206, 208, 210, 211
AGMA (*see* American Guild of Musical Artists)
Agon (Balanchine), 12, 22, 167
Ailey, Alvin, 28, 118, 139–140, 141, 150–153, 154–155, 156–159, 160–166, 171, 178, 209: *The River*, 39–40, 41; *Feast of Ashes*, 90–91; *Blues Suite*, 152, 163; *Revelations*, 152, 161, 165–166, 170; *Quintet*, 152; *Reflections in D*, 152; *Streams*, 154; *Gymnopédies*, 154; *Flowers*, 156–158; *Choral Dances*, 158–159; *Cry*, 160–161, 163; *Hermit Songs*, 161; *Knoxville: Summer of 1915*, 161
Alcestis (Graham), 185, 189
Aleko (Massine), 30
Allegro Brillante (Balanchine), 119
American Ballet Center, 111
American Ballet Company, 10, 67–86
American Ballet Theatre, 3, 10, 14, 17, 30–47, 54, 57, 58, 59–60, 69, 70, 75, 84, 89, 105, 106, 131, 198
American Dance Festival, 182, 185, 186, 202, 203, 267, 280, 286, 300
American Dance Theatre, 1964–65, 3, 197
American Guild of Musical Artists, 100, 102
Ames, Jerry, 149
Antic Meet (M. Cunningham), 240
Antonio, Juan, 125
Appalachian Spring (Graham), 181, 188
Arcade (Perez), 259, 274, 275, 278, 290

Arpino, Gerald, 19, 88, 106, 228: *The Clowns*, 107, 110; *Fanfarita*, 109; *A Light Fantastic*, 109, 111; *Incubus*, 110; *Nightwings*, 110; *Elegy*, 110; *Cello Concerto*, 111; *Solarwind*, 116; *Confetti*, 116, 118; *Trinity*, 117–118, 121, 122, 123; *Reflections*, 118–20; *Valentine*, 120–121
Arthur, Charthel, 119
Asakawa, Takako, 181, 186
Ashton, Frederick, 22, 50–51, 55: *Monotones*, 49; *Symphonic Variations*, 49; *Jazz Calendar*, 49; *Enigma Variations*, 50; *The Dream*, 50; Birthday Offering, 51; *Daphnis and Chloë*, 51; *A Wedding Bouquet*, 51, 52; *Façade*, 51, 52
Astaire, Fred, 30, 149, 288, 291
Astarte (Joffrey), 54, 67, 90, 107, 110, 111–113, 122, 123, 198, 237
Atlas, Consuelo, 159, 160, 165
At Midnight (Feld), 32, 69, 70, 71, 73, 77, 85
Aurora's Wedding, 40
Australian Ballet, 127, 158
av Paul, Annette, 89

Bach, J. S., 24, 126, 128, 130, 131
Bach Sonata (Béjart), 131
Bailin, Gladys, 222
Balanchine, George, 11, 12, 13, 14, 15, 16, 17, 20, 21, 22, 23, 24, 25, 27, 28, 105, 111, 134, 166, 167, 169, 182, 204: *Serenade*, 7, 8, 22, 35; *PAMTGG*, 7, 27–28; *Suite No. 3*, 7, 17–18, 39, 119; *Ivesiana*, 7; *Swan Lake*, 12; *Firebird*, 12; *Raymonda Variations*, 12; *Four Temperaments*, 12, 23, 206; *Agon*, 12, 22, 167; *Bugaku*, 15–16, 23, 26; *Symphony in C*, 16; *Tschaikovsky Pas de Deux*, 16; *Theme and Variations*, 17, 18, 38, 39; *Scotch Symphony*, 20; *Concerto Barocco*, 20, 22, 54, 170; *Prodigal Son*, 22; *Stars and Stripes*, 23; *Western Symphony*, 23; *Divertimento No. 15*, 23; *Monumentum pro Gesualdo/Move-*

Index

Balanchine (continued)
ments for Piano and Orchestra, 23; *Square
Dance*, 25–26; *Who Cares?*, 26, 29–30; *La
Sonnambula*, 28–29; *Donizetti Variations*,
29; *Swan Lake*, 56; *Harlequinade*, 85; *Alle-
gro Brillante*, 119, *Pas de Dix*, 119, *Slaugh-
ter on Tenth Avenue*, 148, 167; *A Midsum-
mer Night's Dream*, 167, *Episodes*, 167;
Don Quixote, 262
Ballet of the 20th Century, 108, 127–134
Ballet Rambert, 103
Ballet Review, 105
Ballet Theatre (*see* American Ballet
Theatre)
Ballets Russes de Serge Di̤ghilev, 57, 114,
115, 132
Barnes, Clive, 9, 10, 69, 90, 95, 262, 263
Baroque Concerto (Walker), 191
Barrios, Maria, 199
Bartók, Béla, 13, 47
Bates, Ronald, 18
Batsheva Dance Company, 190–192
Bauman, Art: *Errands*, 257
Bayadère La, 49
Beatty, Talley, 139, 141, 151, 153, 164: *The
Black Belt*, 152; *The Road of the Phoebe
Snow*, 152
Beethoven, Ludwig van, 130, 203
Behrman, David, 245
Béjart, Maurice, 41, 108, 127–134, 157, 248:
Choreographic Offering, 127–128; *Bhakti*,
128; *Erotica*, 128; *Le Sacre du Printemps*,
130, 132, 133; *Actus Tragicus, Opus 5*, 130;
Bach Sonata, 131; *Firebird*, 131, 132; *Renard*,
132; *Les Fleurs du Mal*, 132–133; *Symphonie
pour un Homme Seul*, 133
Bellini, Vincenzo, 29
Ben-David, Ehud, 191, 192
Benois, Alexandre, 58, 114
Benois, Nicholas, 18
Berg, Henry, 119
Berg, Leslie, 259
Bergsma, Deanne, 52
Berio, Luciano, 126
Berman, Eugene, 44, 45
Bernstein, Leonard, 13
Bhakti (Béjart), 128
Big Bertha (Taylor), 212–213
Billy the Kid (Loring), 32
Birch, Patricia, 187, 190
Birthday Offering (Ashton), 51
Black Belt, The (Beatty), 152
Black Lake (Hawkins), 196
Blair, David, 54
Blues for the Jungle (Pomare), 152
Blues Suite (Ailey), 152, 163

Blum, Anthony, 16, 17, 20
Boris, Ruthanna: *Cakewalk*, 67, 110
Bortoluzzi, Paolo, 128
Boston Ballet, 108
Botka, Lola, 197
Bournonville, August, 42, 43: *Konser-
vatoriet*, 114
Bradley, Lisa, 197
Brahms, Johannes, 77, 82, 208
Brahms Quintet (Nahat), 41
Brahms Waltzes (Weidman), 229
Brehm, Alvin, 120
Britten, Benjamin, 110, 158
Brock, Karena, 38, 41
Brood, The (Kuch), 61
Brooklyn Academy of Music, 3, 154, 162
Brown, Carolyn, 234, 245
Brown, Trisha, 284, 289–290, 291: *Walking
on the Wall*, 290; *Leaning Duets II*, 290;
Falling Duet I and II, 290; *Skymap*, 290
Bruhn, Erik, 30–31, 34, 38, 40, 42, 47
Bugaku (Balanchine), 15–16, 23, 26
Buirge, Susan: *Televanilla*, 253–256
Burke, Dermot, 118
Butler, John, 91, 106: *Sebastian*, 89, 92; *Car-
mina Burana*, 92; *After Eden*; 92, 96; *A
Season in Hell*, 92; *Landscape for Lovers*,
93, 94

Cage, John, 234, 236, 239–242, 245, 283
Cain (Nebrada), 92
Cakewalk (Boris), 67, 110
Canfield (M. Cunningham), 236–243
Canticle for Innocent Comedians (Graham),
189
Cantilever (Hawkins), 194
Canto Indio (Macdonald), 93
Cantos from a Monastery (Pomare), 155
Caprichos (Ross), 70
Carlson, Carolyn, 222
Carmina Burana (Butler), 92
Carmines, Al, 226
Carnaval (Fokine), 70, 84–85
Carroll, Elisabeth, 89, 93
Carter, William, 40
Cartier, Diana, 116
Casey, Susan, 32
Castelli, Victor, 28
Cat. #CCS70–1013NSSR-GSJ9M* (Solo-
mons), 283
Cave of the Heart (Graham), 180, 181, 188
Caviar (Falco), 108, 125
Cello Concerto (Arpino), 111
Center Break (Perez), 257
Cernovitch, Nicola, 159
Chase, Lucia, 55, 69, 70

Index

Chavez, Carlos, 93

Child of the Earth (Rotardier), 159–160

Chilean National Ballet, 61, 197

Chopin, Frederic, 14, 39

Choral Dances (Ailey), 158–159

Choreographic Offering (Béjart), 127–128

Christensen, Lew, 111: *Con Amore,* 110

Christopher, Patricia, 164

Chryst, Gary, 116, 118

Circe (Graham), 181

City Center Joffrey Ballet (*see also* Joffrey Ballet), 3, 25, 26, 51, 57, 59–60, 61, 62, 84, 89, 105, 107, 109–121, 191, 198

Clear Lake (Lubovitch), 126

Clifford, John, 13–14, 18, 19, 20, 28: *Prelude, Fugue and Riffs,* 13; *Kodaly Dances,* 19–20

Clockwise (Marks), 81

The Clowns (Arpino), 107, 110

Cohan, Robert, 180, 181

Cohen, Frederic, 62

Cohen, Moss, 186

Cohen, Zeeva, 173

Cole, Jack: *Requiem for Jimmy Dean,* 95

Coleman, Michael, 50, 52

Coll, David, 38

Collage III (M. Cunningham) 234, 235

Coltrane, Alice, 161

Comedy (Limón), 262

Compton, Gardner, 112, 198

Con Amore (Christensen), 110

Concerto Barocco (Balanchine), 20, 22, 54, 170

Confetti (Arpino), 116, 118

Connecticut College American Dance Festival (see American Dance Festival)

Connecticut Composite (Rainer) 268–269, 280

Consort, The (Feld), 25, 80–81

Continuous Project—Altered Daily (Rainer), 268

Continuum (Litz), 227

Coppélia, 30, 31, 34, 37, 49, 50, 74, 286

Corelli, Arcangelo, 26

Corkle, Francesca, 25, 26, 116, 119

Corsair Pas de Deux, 38

Cortege Burlesque (Feld), 67, 70, 80

Cortege of Eagles (Graham), 185

Cortege Parisien (Feld), 80

Countdown (Perez), 276

Coverage (Perez), 278, 288, 290

Cranko, John, 105, 134–136: *Romeo and Juliet,* 44, 135; *Pineapple Poll,* 116; *Eugene Onegin,* 135; *The Taming of the Shrew,* 135

Crises (M. Cunningham), 244

Croce, Arlene, 105

Croll, Tina: *One Space, One Figure and Oc-*

Croll (continued)
   casional Sounds, 258; *Ground-Work,* 259; *Fields,* 259

Crome Syrcus, 112, 122

Cropley, Eileen, 212

Cry (Ailey), 160–161, 163

Cullberg, Birgit: *Miss Julie,* 32

Cultural Council Foundation, 228

Cunningham, James, 249, 250, 288: *Lauren's Dream,* 125; *Skating to Siam,* 258; *The Sea of Tranquility Motel,* 259–260, 286; *The Junior Birdsmen,* 286

Cunningham, Merce, 112, 124, 147, 182, 209, 228, 230, 231–246, 247–248, 250, 261, 262, 264, 272, 273, 276, 277, 281, 283, 284, 285, 289, 290, 303: *Summerspace,* 14, 90, 240, 244; *Winterbranch,* 232, 234, 235, 238; *Place,* 232, 234, 235, 238, 240, 244; *Field Dances,* 233, 236, 238; *Scramble,* 233, 234, 237, 238, 244; *Walkaround Time,* 233, 234, 238, 244; *How to Pass, Kick, Fall and Run,* 233, 234, 242, 244; *Suite for Five,* 234, *Variations V,* 234, 237, 241; *Nocturnes,* 234; *RainForest,* 234, 235, 237, 238, 239, 244; *Untitled Solo,* 234, 235; *Collage III,* 234, 235; *Canfield,* 236–243; *Antic Meet,* 240; *Story,* 240; *Crises,* 244; *Signals,* 245; *Objects,* 245–246

Curtains (Schenfeld), 191

Dali, Salvador, 104

d'Amboise, Jacques, 16, 30

Dance Mobile, 146, 147

Dance Theater Workshop, 256–261

Dance Theatre of Harlem, 166–171

Dances at a Gathering (Robbins), 7, 14, 16, 25

Dancing-Ground (Graham), 181

Dancing in the Streets of Paris and London, Continued in Stockholm and Sometimes Madrid (Tharp), 270, 271–273, 279, 287

Danias, Starr, 119

d'Antuono, Eleanor, 37, 39

Daphnis and Chloë (Ashton), 51

Dark Corner (Louis), 216

Dark Meadow (Graham), 183, 190

Davison, Robert, 92

Day of the Dead, The (Martin), 125

Deafman Glance (Wilson), 282, 294–296

Death and Entrances (Graham), 189

Debussy, Claude, 83, 132, 135, 229

de Jong, Bettie, 204, 205, 212

de Lavallade, Carmen, 152

Delius, Frederick, 44

Dello Joio, Norman, 180

de Mille, Agnes, 32, 213: *A Rose for Miss Emily,* 35–36; *Oklahoma!,* 36; *Fall River*

Index

de Mille (continued)
  Legend, 36, *Golden Age*, 92
Denard, Michael, 41
Denishawn, 162
de Udaeta, Jose, 103
Diaghilev, Serge, 57, 114, 115, 132
Diamond, Matthew, 124, 125
Dim Lustre (Tudor), 13
Diversion of Angels (Graham), 184, 186, 192
Divertimento No. 15 (Balanchine), 23
Dlugoszewski, Lucia, 194, 196
Dodd, John, 296
Dolin, Anton: *Variations for Four plus Four*, 92
Don Quixote (Balanchine), 262
Donizetti Variations (Balanchine), 29
Donn, Jorge, 131, 133
Dowell, Anthony, 48, 50
The Dream (Ashton), 50
Druckman, Jacob, 120
du Bois, Raoul Pene, 92
Dudley, Jane, 189
Dunas, William, 280, 283, 288: *X*, 257
Duncan, Isadora, 247
Duncan, Jeff: *Three Fictitious Games*, 258; *Resonances*, 261
Dunham, Katherine, 153, 156, 171
Dunn, Judith, 238
Dvořák, Antonin, 208

Early Floating (Hawkins), 194
Early Songs (Feld), 73–75, 78
Echo (Nikolais), 221, 223
Echoes (Sokolow), 200–201
Echoing of Trumpets (Tudor), 61
Efrati, Moshe, 191, 192: *Sin Lieth at the Door*, 191; *Ein-Dor*, 191
Eight Jelly Rolls (Tharp), 302–304
Ein-Dor (Efrati), 191
Eisenberg, Mary Jane, 124
Elegy (Arpino), 110
Elementary & Secondary Education Act, 1965, 2
Elgar, Edward, 50
Ellington, Duke, 39
Embattled Garden (Graham), 192
Emmons, Beverly, 285
Endo, Akira, 40
Enigma Variations (Ashton), 50
Episodes (Balanchine), 167
Erdman, Jean, 189
Erotica (Béjart), 128
Errand into the Maze (Graham), 184, 192
Errands (Bauman), 257
Eugene Onegin (Cranko), 135
Everett, Ellen, 41, 43

Every Soul is a Circus (Graham), 186–187, 190, 191
Exiles, The (Limón), 192

Fabrication (Murphy), 278
Façade (Ashton), 51, 52
Faison, George, 140–141
Falco, Louis, 108, 124–125, 264: *The Gamete Garden*, 108; *Caviar*, 108, 125; *Ibid*, 124; *The Sleepers*, 125
Fall of the Leaf (Litz), 226
Fall River Legend (de Mille), 36
Falling Duet I and II (Brown), 290
Fallis, Barbara, 70
Fancy Tree (Robbins), 32
Fandango (Litz), 225
Fanfarita (Arpino), 109
Farber, Viola, 250
Farm, The, 249
Farrell, Suzanne, 11, 12, 14, 128, 131, 133, 148
Feast of Ashes (Ailey), 90–91
Feet, The, 138
Feld, Eliot, 10, 25, 30, 67–86, 131, 134: *Harbinger*, 10, 69, 70, 76, 77, 78, 82, 228; *The Consort*, 25, 80–81; *At Midnight*, 32, 69, 70, 71, 73, 77, 85; *Cortege Burlesque*, 67, 70, 80; *Meadowlark*, 70, 77, 78; *Intermezzo*, 70, 73, 74, 77, 78, 82, 229; *Pagan Spring*, 70; *Early Songs*, 73–75, 78; *A Poem Forgotten*, 80; *Cortege Parisien*, 80; *Romance*, 82–83; *The Gods Amused*, 83–84; *Theatre*, 84–86
Fernandez, Royes, 40
Festival Ballet, London, 70
Fête Noire (Mitchell), 167
Field Dances (M. Cunningham), 233, 236, 238
Fields (Croll), 259
Fille Mal Gardée, La, 51
Firebird, 12, 89, 95, 131, 132
Fleurs du Mal, Les (Béjart), 132–133
Flindt, Flemming: *The Lesson*, 110
Flowers (Ailey), 156–158
Fokine, Michel: *Petrouchka*, 7, 57–60, 85, 114–116, 228; *Les Sylphides*, 38, 39, 228; *Carnaval*, 70, 84–85
Fonteyn, Margot, 48–49, 50, 52, 54, 55
Ford Foundation, 3, 11, 21, 102, 166, 169, 262, 263
Four Temperaments (Balanchine), 12, 23, 206
Fracci, Carla, 30–31, 34, 37, 39, 42, 43, 44, 46
Françaix, Jean, 81
Frank, Bill, 222
Freedman, Doris, 146–147

From Sea to Shining Sea (Taylor) 203, 208, 213
Frontier (Graham), 182
Fuchs, Harry, 82
Fugue, The (Tharp), 304
Function (Maxwell), 172

Gadd, Ulf: *The Miraculous Mandarin*, 46–47
Gaîté Parisienne (Massine), 38
Games (McKayle), 70, 71
Gamete Garden, The (Falco), 108
Geography of Noon (Hawkins), 194
Gershwin, George, 26, 29
Giselle, 30, 31, 33, 34, 35, 37, 38, 41, 49, 68, 69
Glyph, The (Litz), 226
Godreau, Miguel, 155
Gods Amused, The (Feld), 83–84
Goldberg Variations, The (Robbins), 24–25
Golden Age (de Mille), 92
Goodman, Erika, 115, 119
Gore, Walter, 103
Graham, Martha, 51, 62, 89, 92, 107, 132, 155, 160, 165, 177, 179–190, 191, 194, 195, 197, 204, 216, 226, 228, 247, 250, 256, 276, 277, 282: *Seraphic Dialogue*, 96, 184; *The Lady of the House of Sleep*, 179, 180–181; *A Time of Snow*, 179–180, 185; *Night Journey*, 180, 181; *Cave of the Heart*, 180, 181, 188; *Plain of Prayer*, 181, 184; *Dancing-Ground*, 181; *Secular Games*, 181; *Circe*, 181; *Appalachian Spring*, 181, 188; *Primitive Mysteries*, 182, 183, 184; *Frontier*, 182; *El Penitente*, 182, 186, 188; *Herodiade*, 182; *Dark Meadow*, 183, 190; *Diversion of Angels*, 184, 186, 192; *Part Real–Part Dream*, 184; *Errand into the Maze*, 184, 192; *Alcestis*, 185, 189; *Cortege of Eagles*, 185; *Every Soul is a Circus*, 186–187, 190, 191; *Phaedra*, 189, 262; *Canticle for Innocent Comedians*, 189; *Letter to the World*, 189, 190; *Deaths and Entrances*, 189; *Acrobats of God*, 191; *Embattled Garden*, 192
Grand Union, The, 249
Grands Ballets Canadiens, Les, 122
Gray-Cullert, Dyane, 132
Great Theatre of Oklahoma Calls You, The (Group Motion), 287
Green, Chuck, 149, 150
Green Table, The (Jooss), 54, 61–65, 66, 67, 110, 116
Greenspan, Joan, 101, 103
Gregory, Cynthia, 31, 37, 38, 40, 41
Ground-Work (Croll), 259
Group Motion, 287
Guggenheim Museum, 270–271, 272

Guidesong (Posin), 260
Gutelius, Phyllis, 189
Gymnopédies (Ailey), 154

Hall, Arthur, 156
Halprin, Ann, 254: *West/East Stereo*, 300–302; *Parades and Changes*, 301
Halprin, Lawrence, 301
Handel, George Frederick, 126, 198, 204
Harangue and Inner Thots with Big Sister (Litz), 225, 226, 227
Harbinger (Feld), 10, 69, 70, 76, 77, 78, 82, 228
Harkarvy, Benjamin, 98, 99, 101, 103
Harkness: Ballet, 16, 47, 86–104, 107, 147, 169; Ballet School, 97, 102; Foundation, 88, 97, 98, 99, 101; House for Ballet Arts, 88, 101, 102, 103; Youth Company, 102; Youth Dancers, 101, 102
Harkness, Rebekah, 86–88, 94, 95, 98, 100, 101, 102, 103, 104
Harlem Cultural Council, 143, 145–146
Harlequinade (Balanchine), 85
Haskell, Arnold, 150
Hawkins, Erick, 193, 194–196: *Tightrope*, 194; *Early Floating*, 194; *Cantilever*, 194; *Naked Leopard*, 194; *Lord of Persia*, 194; *Geography of Noon*, 194; *John Brown*, 194; *Black Lake*, 196
Hay, Deborah, 249: *26 Variations on 8 Activities for 13 People plus Beginning and Ending*, 286
Hayden, Melissa, 16
Haydn, Franz Joseph, 77, 204, 211
Head Start, 143–148
Helpmann, Robert, 51
Henry, Pierre, 133
Henry Street Playhouse, 218
Hermit Songs (Ailey), 161
Herodiade (Graham), 182
Hill, Thelma, 152
Hill, Martha, 199
Hinkson, Mary, 181, 186, 189
Hodes, Stuart: *Abyss*, 91, 92
Hoffman, Byrd, 294
Holden, Stanley, 51
Holder, Christian, 59, 115, 118, 120–121
Holder, Geoffrey, 156
Holm, Hanya, 216
Holmes, Georgiana, 124, 125
Horst, Louis, 186, 256
Horton, Lester, 151, 159, 162, 168
Horvath, Ian, 32, 40
House, The, 249
Hovhaness, Alan, 36
Hoving, Lucas: *Icarus*, 151, 164–165, 166

Index

How to Pass, Kick, Fall and Run (M. Cunningham) 233, 234, 242, 244
Humphrey, Doris, 177, 216, 228, 231, 247, 256
Humphrey-Weidman Company, 177
Hunter College, 3, 102
Hurok, Sol, 53, 70

Ibid (Falco), 124
Icarus (Hoving), 151, 164–165, 166
Idols (Nikolais), 217
Imago (Nikolais), 63, 218, 219, 220
Improvisations on a Dream (Maxwell), 172
Incubus (Aprino), 110
Intermezzo (Feld), 70, 73, 74, 77, 78, 82, 229
In the Night (Robbins), 16, 25
Intravenous Lecture (Paxton), 264, 265–66
Issac, Ronald, 158
Isaksen, Lone, 89, 91, 96, 103
Ivesiana (Balanchine), 7

Jackson, Denise, 119
Jamison, Judith, 161, 165
Jardin aux Lilas (see Lilac Garden)
Jay, Leticia, 148, 149
Jazz Calendar (Ashton), 49
Jenkins, David, 123
Jenner, Ann, 50
Jenney, Neil, 246
Jhung, Finis, 89
Joffrey, Robert, 87–88: *Astarte*, 54, 67, 90, 107, 110, 111–113, 122, 123, 198, 237; *Pas des Déesses*, 114
Robert Joffrey Ballet (see also City Center Joffrey Ballet), 87, 99, 109, 197
John Brown (Hawkins), 194
Johnson, Carole, 146
Jooss Ballet, 61
Jooss, Kurt, 197: *The Green Table*, 54, 61–65, 66, 67, 110, 116
Joplin, Janis, 157
Jorasmaa, Sirpa, 199
Jowitt, Deborah: *Zero to Nothing*, 260
Judson: Church, 125, 226, 248, 249, 263; Dance Theater, 258, 289
Juice (Monk), 270–271
Juilliard Dance Ensemble, 197
Juilliard School of Music, 13, 53, 182, 193, 197–202
Junior Birdsmen, The (Cunningham), 286

Kaalund, Raymond, 149
Karavan, Danny, 191
Karinska, 16
Kayle, Milton P., 98, 100
Keeler, Elisha, 26

Keen, Elizabeth: *That's That*, 257; *On Edge*, 283
Keene, Christopher, 80
Kellaway, Roger, 27
Kelly, Gene, 149
Kent, Allegra, 13, 15, 16, 23, 29, 56
Keogh, M., 93
Kerendi, Jaleh, 132
Khristiaann, Maathews Kheaann, 124
Kimura, Yuriko, 186
Kinetic Pantomime (Weidman), 229
Kirkland, Gelsey, 18
Kirkland, Johnna, 20
Kirstein, Lincoln, 11, 27, 130, 166, 169
Kivitt, Ted, 38, 39, 40, 43
Knoxville: Summer of 1915 (Ailey), 161
Kodaly Dances (Clifford), 19–20
Kódály, Zoltán, 19
Koner, Pauline, 164, 224
Konservatoriet (Bournonville), 114
Krenek, Ernest, 155
Krokover, Rosalyn, 44
Kuch, Richard, 189: *The Brood*, 61

Lady of the House of Sleep, The (Graham), 179, 180–181
Laerkesen, Anna, 82
La Giglia, Anthony, 274
Lamhut, Phyllis, 216, 221
Lander, Harald, 42
Lander, Toni, 32
Landscape for Lovers (Butler), 93, 94
Lang, Pearl, 32, 189, 191, 264
Lapsezon, Noemi, 180, 181
Larkin, Robert, 103
Lauren's Dream (J. Cunningham), 125
Lawrence Pauline, 202
Lazowski, Yurek, 115
Leaning Duets II (Brown), 290
Lee, Elizabeth, 75, 82, 83, 85
Lee, Keith, 154
Leland, Sara, 16, 25, 28, 30
Lento (Taylor), 203–204, 205, 208, 210, 211
Lesson, The (Flindt), 110
Letter to the World (Graham), 189, 190
Levins, Daniel, 80, 82, 83–84
Lewis, Nancy, 164
Lichtenstein, Harvey, 3
Life and Times of Sigmund Freud, The (Wilson), 282, 292–294, 296
Light (Takei), 283
Light Fantastic, A (Arpino), 109, 111
Lilac Garden (Tudor), 37, 38
Limón, José, 125, 171, 172, 197, 201–202, 228, 230–231: *The Moor's Pavane*, 38, 40, 41, 231; *There is a Time*, 158, 231; *The Exiles*, 192;

Index

Limón, José (continued)
  La Piñata, 201; *The Winged*, 231; *Missa Brevis*, 231; *Comedy*, 262
Litz, Katherine, 224–227, 229: *Harangue and Inner Thots with Big Sister*, 225, 226, 227; *Fandango*, 225; *Fall of the Leaf*, 226; *Recitativo: Aria (Duettino)*, 226, 227; *The Glyph*, 226; *Adaptations*, 226; *Continuum*, 227
Lloyd, Barbara, 290
Loading Zone (Perez), 257
Lommel, Daniel, 128
Lords of Persia (Hawkins), 194
Loring, Eugene: *Billy the Kid*, 32
Louis, Murray, 198, 216, 217, 221: *Dark Corner*, 216
Loyd, Sue, 119
Lubovitch, Lar, 107, 125–127: *Some of the Reactions of Some of the People Some of the Time Upon Hearing Reports of the Coming of the Messiah*, 126; *Whirligogs*, 126, *Social*, 126; *Clear Lake*, 126
Lucier, Alvin, 246
Ludlow, Conrad, 18

Macdonald, Brian, 95, 97, 99: *Zealous Variations*, 89, 93; *Tschaikovsky*, 92: *Canto Indio*, 93; *Time Out of Mind*, 94, 103; *Firebird*, 95
MacMillan, Kenneth: *Romeo and Juliet*, 44, 48, 49, 50
Magallanes, Nicholas, 29
Magno, Susan, 60, 115
Mahler, Gustav, 77
Mahler, Roni, 34
Maids, The (Ross), 70
Makarova Natalia, 33–34, 37, 38, 40, 46, 47
Marks, Bruce, 32, 38, 40, 44, 60: *Clockwise*, 81
Marshall, Minnie, 165
Martin, Ervin: *The Day of the Dead*, 125
Martin, John, 216
Martins, Peter, 11, 16, 25
Masekela, Hugh, 159
Mason, Kenneth, 50
Mason, Monica, 51
Massine, Leonide, 115: *Aleko*, 30; *Gaîté Parisienne*, 38; *Three-Cornered Hat*, 57
Massine, Lorca, 19
Match (Perez), 259
Mathis, Bonnie, 44
Maxwell, Carla, 171–173: *Function*, 172; *Improvisations on a Dream*, 172
Mazzo, Kay, 16, 18, 28, 29
McBride, Patricia, 23, 25, 30, 133
McDowell, John Herbert, 208, 212

McGehee, Helen, 181
McKayle, Donald, 139, 141, 153, 155, 171: *Games*, 70, 71
Meadowlark (Feld), 70, 77, 78
Medley (Tharp), 267–268, 286
Meekins, Strody, 155
Mejia, Paul, 11
Memories (Sokolow), 193
Mendelssohn, Felix, 126
Metallics (Sanasardo), 164
Metropolitan Museum of Art, 271–273, 279
Midsummer Night's Dream, A (Balanchine), 167
Mielziner, Jo, 27
Milhaud, Darius, 135
Miller, Joan, 156
Minkus, Leon, 40, 42
Miraculous Mandarin, The (Gadd), 46–47
Miss Julie (Cullberg), 32
Missa Brevis (Limón), 231
Mitchell, Arthur, 141, 166–171: *Tones*, 167; *Fête Noire*, 167; *Rhythmetron*, 167
Moncion, Francisco, 16
Monk Meredith, 249, 263, 279, 282, 284, 287, 288, 293, 302: *Juice*, 270–271, 272–273; *Needle-Brain Lloyd and the Systems Kid*, 280, 284, 285–286; *Vessel*, 297–300
Monotones (Ashton), 49
Montresor, Beni, 151, 165
Monument for a Dead Boy (van Dantzig), 92
Monumental Exchange (Perez), 290–291
Monumentum pro Gesualdo / Movements for Piano and Orchestra (Balanchine), 23
Moore, Jack: *Parsley All Over the World*, 258
Moor's Pavane, The (Limón), 38, 40, 41, 231
Morgan, Clyde, 141, 171–173: *The Traveler*, 173
Morrice, Norman: *Rehearsal! . . . (?)*, 191; *Percussion Concerto*, 191
Morris, Marnee, 18
Morton, Jelly Roll, 303
Moth and the Star, The (Weidman), 228
Movement for Two (Pomare), 155
Moves (Robbins), 110, 116, 119, 192
Mozart, Wolfgang Amadeus, 53
Muller, Jennifer, 125
Mumma, Gordon, 240, 242, 245
Murphy Seamus, 287, 288: *Fabrication*, 278; *Velvet*, 281
Mythical Hunters (Tetley), 192

Nagrin, Daniel, 172, 249
Nagy, Ivan, 34, 39, 43, 44, 46

Nahat, Dennis, 43, 60, 198: *Ontogeny*, 38, *Brahms Quintet*, 41
Naked Leopard (Hawkins), 194
National Ballet of Holland, 103
National Endowment for the Arts, 70
National Foundation on the Arts and the Humanities (*also see* National Endowment for the Arts), 2
Nault, Fernand; *Tommy*, 123
Neary, Colleen, 19
Nebrada, Vicente: *Cain*, 92
Needle-Brain Lloyd and the Systems Kid (Monk), 280, 284–286
Neels, Sandra, 245
Netherlands Dance Theater, 99
Neville, Phoebe, 281: Untitled Duet, 282
New York City Ballet, 3, 11–25, 27–30, 39, 52, 53, 89, 103, 105, 106, 109, 128, 131, 133, 166, 167, 169, 218
New York School of Ballet, 70
New York State Council on the Arts, 2, 61, 259
New York University, 264–266
Night Journey (Graham), 180, 181
Night Song (Walker), 90, 94
Nightwings (Arpino), 110
Nijinsky, Vaslav, 130
Nikolais, Alwin, 63, 112, 198, 209, 212–224, 226, 283: *Imago*, 63, 218, 219, 220; *Somniloquy*, 213, 214–217, 219, 220, 221; *Triptych*, 213, 217; *Scrolls*, 217; *Putti*, 217; *Idols*, 217; *Tower*, 219, 220, 223; *Vaudeville of the Elements*, 219; *Tent*, 219, 220, 221, 223; *Structures*, 221–222, 223; *Echo*, 221, 223; *Scenario*, 223–224
Noces, Les (Robbins), 14, 32
Nocturnes (M. Cunningham), 234
Noguchi, Isamu, 96, 184
Nureyev, Rudolf, 40, 48–49, 50, 51, 52, 54, 55, 127, 157, 158
Nurock, Kirk, 260
Nutcracker, 22, 123, 150
Nyro, Laura, 161

Objects (M. Cunningham), 245–246
O'Brien, Shaun, 29
Odes (Sokolow), 193
Off Print (Perez), 274, 275
Office of Cutural Affairs, New York City Parks Department, 143, 146
Ohman, Frank, 28
Oklahoma! (de Mille), 36
Oliveros, Pauline, 239
On Edge (Keen), 283
One Space, One Figure and Occasional Sounds (Croll), 258

Ontogeny (Nahat), 38
Opening Dance, Opus 51 (Weidman), 228
Opus 5 (Béjart), 130
Opus '65 (Sokolow), 110
Orbs (Taylor), 203, 206–207, 208, 210, 211
Orr, Terry, 32, 34, 43

Pagan Spring (Feld), 70
Palms (Weidman), 228
PAMTGG (Balanchine), 7, 27–28
Paquita, 40–42
Parades and Changes (Halprin), 301
Paris Opera Ballet, 41
Park, Merle, 50, 52
Parks, John, 155
Parsley All Over the World (Moore), 258
Part Real–Part Dream (Graham), 184
Party Mix (Taylor), 203, 206, 207, 208, 210
Pas de Dix (Balanchine), 119
Pas des Déesses (Joffrey), 114
Paul, Mimi, 38, 40
Paxton, Steve, 264–266, 284, 286, 290: *Intravenous Lecture*, 264, 265–266; *Satisfyin' Lover*, 265
Peck, Ande, 260
Peer Gynt (Stevenson), 103
Pelléas and Mélisande (Petit), 49
Penitente, El (Graham), 182, 186, 188
Percival, John, 52
Percussion Concerto (Morrice), 191
Perez, Rudy, 249, 264, 273–276, 279, 281, 282, 283, 288, 289: *Center Break*, 257; *Loading Zone*, 257; *Arcade*, 259, 274, 275, 278, 290; *Match*, 259; *Off Print*, 274, 275; *Countdown*, 276; *Transit*, 278; *Coverage*, 278, 288, 290; *Monumental Exchange*, 290–291
Petipa, Marius, 16, 199
Petit, Roland: *Pelléas and Mélisande*, 49
Petrouchka (Fokine), 7, 57–60, 85, 114–116, 228
Phaedra (Graham), 189, 262
Phillips, Burrill, 201
Picasso, Pablo, 57
Pillar of Fire (Tudor), 32, 54, 199
Piñata, La (Limón), 201
Pineapple Poll (Cranko), 116
Place (M. Cunningham), 232, 234, 235, 238, 240, 244
Plain of Prayer (Graham), 181, 184
Pleasures of Merely Circulating, The (Uthoff), 198
Poem Forgotten, A (Feld), 80
Pomare, Eleo, 155: *Radiance of the Dark*, 140; *Blues for the Jungle*, 152; *Movement for Two*, 155; *Cantos from a Monastery*, 155

Posin, Kathryn: *Guidesong*, 260
Post Meridian (Taylor), 203
Powell, Robert, 181, 187, 189, 192
Prelude, Fugue and Riffs (Clifford), 13
Primitive Mysteries (Graham), 182, 183, 184
Primus, Pearl, 153, 171
Prinz, John, 38, 46
Prodigal Son (Balanchine), 22
Prokofiev, Sergei, 44, 49, 77, 135
Public Domain (Taylor), 207–211
Puccini, Giacomo, 208
Putti (Nikolais), 217

Quartet (Uthoff), 198
Quintet (Ailey), 152

Radiance of the Dark (Pomare), 140
Rainer, Yvonne, 238, 248, 249, 261–263, 267, 275, 283, 284, 286, 287, 288: *Connecticut Composite*, 268–269, 280; *Trio A*, 268; *Continuous Project—Altered Daily*, 268
RainForest (M. Cunningham), 234, 235, 237, 238, 239, 244
Ramos, Diana, 155
Rauschenberg, Robert, 232
Raymonda, 12, 49, 119
Redlich, Don, 263
Recitativo: Aria (Duettino) (Litz), 226, 227
Reflections (Arpino), 118–120
Reflections in D (Ailey), 152
Rehearsal! . . . (?) (Morrice), 191
Reinhart, Charles, 262
Renard (Béjart), 132
Repertory Dance Theatre, 178
Requiem for Jimmy Dean (Cole), 95
Resonances (Duncan), 261
Revelations (Ailey), 152, 161, 165–166, 170
Rhodes, Lawrence, 89, 91, 92, 98, 99, 101, 103
Rhythm Red, 149
Rhythemtron (Mitchell), 167
Ricercare (Tetley), 96
Riegger, Wallingford, 80
Rieti, Vittorio, 29
Rigg, Jean, 243
Rite of Spring (see Sacre du Printemps, Le)
River, The (Ailey), 39–40, 41
Road of the Phoebe Snow, The (Beatty), 152
Roan, Barbara, 274: *Up Cover Under Off*, 257
Robbins, Jerome, 22, 24, 27, 30, 69, 76, 120, 134, 155, 213, 247: *Dances at a Gathering*, 7, 14, 16, 25; *Les Noces*, 14, 32; *In the Night*, 16, 25; *The Goldberg Variations*, 24–25; *Fancy Free*, 32; *West Side Story*, 69; *Moves*, 110, 116, 119, 192; *Afternoon of a*

Robbins (continued)
Faun, 133
Robinson, Alma, 152
Robinson, Bill "Bojangles," 149
Robinson, Chase, 164, 165
Rockefeller Foundation, 178, 259
Rodger, Rod, 143–148, 248: *Tangents*, 144
Rodriguez, Zhandra, 38, 41
Romance (Feld), 82–83
Romeo and Juliet (Cranko), 44, 135
Romeo and Juliet (MacMillan), 44, 48, 49, 50
Romeo and Juliet (Tudor), 7, 43–46
Ron, Rahamim, 192
Rooms (Sokolow), 90, 110
Ropes of Time, The (van Dantzig), 51
Rose for Miss Emily, A (de Mille), 35–36
Rose, Jurgen, 135
Billy Rose Theatre, 262, 263
Ross, Bertram, 180, 181, 186, 187
Ross, Herbert: *Caprichos*, 70; *The Maids*, 70
Rossini, Gioacchino, 116
Rotardier, Kelvin, 155, 159, 165: *Child of the Earth*, 159–160
Royal Ballet, 48–53, 55, 156, 199
Royal Danish Ballet, 82
Royal Winnipeg Ballet, 70
Rudner, Sara, 269, 304
Ruiz, Brunilda, 89, 92

Sacre du Printemps, Le (Béjart), 130, 132, 133
Sadler's Wells Ballet (*see* Royal Ballet)
Salatino, Anthony, 199
Sanasardo, Paul: *Metallics*, 164
San Francisco Dancers' Workshop, 300
Sapiro, Dana, 119
Sargeant, Winthrop, 89
Sarry, Christine, 32, 67–68, 74, 75, 78, 80, 82, 83, 85
Satie, Erik, 155, 234, 281, 293
Satisfyin' Lover (Paxton), 265
Scenario (Nikolais), 223–224
Schaeffer, Pierre, 133
Shadowplay (Tudor), 50
Sharaff, Irene, 27
Shostakovich, Dmitri, 167
Sibley, Antoinette, 48, 50, 52
Sichter, Hermann, 47
Skating to Siam (J. Cunningham), 258
Skelton, Tom, 36, 62, 112
Skibine, George, 99
Skymap (Brown), 290
Slaughter on Tenth Avenue (Balanchine), 148, 167
Sleepers, The (Falco), 125

Index

Sleeping Beauty, 41, 49, 50
Slyde, Jimmy, 149
Smith, Oliver, 69
Smuin, Michael, 31, 32, 38, 59
Soares, Janet, 201: *Z6508 Times*, 258
Social (Lubovitch), 126
Soederbaum, Ulla, 61
Sokolow, Anna, 25, 170, 172, 193–194, 195, 197, 200–201: *Time + 7*, 61; *Rooms*, 90, 110; *Opus '65*, 110; *Tribute*, 193; *Memories*, 193; *Odes*, 193; *Steps of Silence*, 193–194; *Echoes*, 200–201
Solarwind (Arpino), 116
Solomons, Jr., Gus, 141: *Cat. #CCS70-1013NSSR-GSJ9M**, 283
Some of the Reactions of Some of the People Some of the Time Upon Hearing Reports of the Coming of the Messiah (Lubovitch), 126
Somniloquy (Nikolais), 213, 214–217, 219,
Schenfeld, Rina, 191, 192: *Curtains*, 191
Schirren, Fernand, 128
School of American Ballet, 11, 12, 13, 167, 169, 197
Schumann, Robert, 84
Scotch Symphony (Balanchine), 20
Scramble (M. Cunningham), 233, 234, 237, 238, 244
Scrolls (Nikolais), 217
Scudorama (Taylor), 203, 204–205, 208
Sea of Tranquility Motel, The (J. Cunningham), 259–260, 286
Season in Hell, A (Butler), 92
Sebastian (Butler), 89, 92
Secular Games (Graham), 181
Segarra, Ramon, 157, 165
Seraphic Dialogue (Graham), 96, 184
Seravalli, Rosanna, 44
Serenade (Balanchine), 7, 8, 22, 35
Sergeyev, Nicholas, 199
Serrano, Lupe, 38, 39
Setterfield, Valda, 245
Seymour, Lynn, 156, 157–158
Signals (M. Cunningham), 245
Simon, Victoria, 26
Sims, Sandman, 149
Sin Lieth at the Door (Efrati), 191
Singleton, Trinette, 67, 111, 113
Sonnambula, La (Balanchine), 28–29
Sousa, John Philip, 275
Sowinski, John, 67–68, 74, 80, 86
Square Dance (Balanchine), 25–26
Stars and Stripes (Balanchine), 23
Stella, Frank 237
Steps of Silence (Sokolow), 193–194
Stern, Nurit, 192

Stevenson, Ben, 101, 102: *Peer Gynt*, 103
Story (M. Cunningham), 240
Strauss, Richard, 74, 85
Stravinsky, Igor, 58, 89, 115, 130, 131–2, 135
Streams (Ailey), 154
Structures (Nikolais), 221–222, 223
Stuttgart Ballet, 105, 134–136, 150
Submerged Cathedral (Weidman), 229
Suite for Five (M. Cunningham), 234
Suite No. 3 (Balanchine), 7, 17–18, 39, 119
Summerspace (M. Cunningham), 14, 90
Surinach, Carlos, 204
Sutherland, Alec, 212
Sutherland, Paul, 26
Swan Lake, 7, 8, 12, 18, 30, 31, 35, 47, 49, 53–57, 58, 69, 123, 168, 199, 208
Sylphide, La, 42–43
Sylphides, Les (Fokine), 38, 39, 228
Symphonic Variations (Ashton), 49
Symphonie pour un Homme Seul (Béjart), 133
Symphony in C (Balanchine), 16

Takei, Kei: *Light*, 283
Tallchief, Marjorie, 99
Tamiris, Helen, 177, 224
Taming of the Shrew, The, 135
Tangents (Rodgers), 144
Tanner, Richard, 19
Tap Happening, 148–150
Tarnay, Linda, 259
Taylor, Burton, 116
Taylor, Ed, 145–146
Taylor, Paul, 124, 203–213, 250, 260: *Scudorama*, 203, 204–205, 208; *Post Meridian*, 203; *Party Mix*, 203, 206, 207, 208, 210; *From Sea to Shining Sea*, 203, 208, 213; *Orbs*, 203, 206–207, 208, 210, 211, *Lento*, 203–204, 205, 208, 210, 211; *Agathe's Tale*, 204, 205–206, 208, 210, 211; *Aureole*, 204; *Public Domain*, 207–211; *Big Bertha*, 212–213
Televanilla (Buirge), 253–256
Tent (Nikolais), 219, 220, 221, 223
Ter-Arutunian, Rouben, 96, 180
Tetley, Glen, 107: *Ricercare*, 96, *Mythical Hunters*, 192
Tharp, Twyla, 238, 249, 250, 263, 268, 269, 287, 288: *Medley*, 267–268, 286; *Dancing in the Streets of Paris and London, Continued in Stockholm and Sometimes Madrid*, 270, 271–273, 279, 287; *Eight Jelly Rolls*, 302–304; *The Fugue*, 304
That's That (Keen), 257
Theatre (Feld), 84–86
Theme and Variations (Balanchine), 17, 18, 38, 39

There is a Time (Limón), 158, 231
Thomas, Richard, 70
Thompson, Clive, 165
Thompson, Frank, 85
Three-Cornered Hat (Massine), 57
Three Fictitious Games (Duncan), 258
Tice, David, 226
Tightrope (Hawkins), 194
Time of Snow A, (Graham, 179–180, 185
Tim + 7 (Sokolow), 61
Time Out of Mind (Macdonald), 94, 103
Tiny Tim, 257
Tipton, Jennifer, 85, 96
Tomasson, Helgi, 16, 25, 89, 92, 93, 103
Tommy (Nault), 123
Tones (Mitchell), 167
Tower (Nikolais), 219, 220, 223
Trammell, Sally, 126
Transit (Perez), 278
Traveler, The (Morgan), 173
Tribute (Sokolow), 193
Trinity (Arpino), 117–118, 121, 122, 123
Trio A (Rainer), 268
Triptych (Nikolais), 213, 217
Truitte, James, 152, 165, 168
Tschaikovsky (Macdonald), 92
Tschaikovsky Pas de Deux (Balanchine), 16
Tschaikovsky, Peter, 17, 119
Tudor, Antony, 22, 32, 35, 82, 134, 197, 198–200: *Romeo and Juliet,* 7, 43–46; *Dim Lustre,* 13; *Pillar of Fire,* 32, 54, 199; *Lilac Garden,* 37, 38; *Shadowplay,* 50; *Echoing of Trumpets,* 61; *Undertow,* 123
Tudor, David, 240, 242, 245
Turney, Matt, 189
26 Variations on 8 Activities for 13 People plus Beginning and Ending (Hay), 286

Ullate, Victor, 132
Undertow (Tudor), 123
Universal Dance Experience, The, 141
Untitled Duet (Neville), 282
Untitled Solo (M. Cunningham), 234, 235
Up Cover Under Off (Roan), 257
U.S. Institute for Theater Technology, 220
Uthoff, Ernst, 61, 197
Uthoff, Michael, 197–198, 202: *Quartet,* 198; *The Pleasures of Merely Circulating,* 198

Valentine (Arpino), 120–121
van Dantzig, Rudi: *The Ropes of Time,* 51; *Monument for a Dead Boy,* 92
Varèse, Edgard, 201

Variations for Four plus Four (Dolin), 92
Variations V (M. Cunningham), 234, 237, 241
Vaudeville of the Elements (Nikolais), 219
Vaughan, David, 242
Velvet (Murphy), 281
Verdi, Giuseppe, 93
Verdy, Violette, 16, 23, 33
Vere, Diana, 51
Verso, Edward, 84, 85, 115
Vessel (Monk), 297–300
Villella, Edward, 12, 15, 16, 18, 29, 133
Vivaldi, Antonio, 26, 191
Voices of East Harlem, 161
von Aroldingen, Karin, 17, 29, 30

Wagner, Richard: *Youth,* 93
Wagoner, Dan, 205, 250
Walkaround Time (M. Cunningham), 233, 234, 238, 244
Walker, Norman: *Night Song,* 90, 94; *Baroque Concerto,* 191
Walking on the Wall (Brown), 290
Walton, William, 51
Warhol, Andy, 237
Waring, James, 302
Watson, Gwendolyn, 121
Wayne, Dennis, 119
Weber, Diana, 34, 39, 41
Webern, Anton, 135
Wedding Bouquet, A (Ashton), 51, 52
Weidman, Charles, 177, 227–230: *Opening Dance, Opus 51,* 228; *The Moth and the Star,* 228; *Palms,* 228; *Kinetic Pantomime,* 229; *Submerged Cathedral,* 229; *Brahms Waltzes,* 229
Weinzweig, John, 200
West/East Stereo (Halprin), 300–302
West Side Story (Robbins), 69
Western Symphony (Balanchine), 23
Whirligogs (Lubovitch), 126
White, Glenn, 119
White, Tony, 149
Who, The, 123
Who Cares? (Balanchine), 26, 29–30
Wiener, Liz, 146
Wigman, Mary, 216
Wilde, Patricia, 26
Williams, Dudley, 152, 154
Wilson, Chuck, 228, 229
Wilson, Robert, 284: *Deafman Glance,* 282, 294–296; *The Life and Times of Sigmund Freud,* 282, 292–294, 296
Wilson, Sallie, 32, 35, 36, 40
Winged, The (Limón), 231

Index

Winter, Ethel, 181
Winterbranch (M. Cunningham), 232, 234, 235, 238, 240, 244
Wong, Mel, 245
Workgroup, The, 249
Wright, Rebecca, 116, 118, 120–121
Wright, Rose Marie, 304

X (Dunas), 257

Young, Gayle, 36
Young, La Monte, 232
Youth (Wagner), 93

Zealous Variations (Macdonald), 89, 93
Zero to Nothing (Jowitt), 260
Zide, Rochelle, 26
Zómosa, Maximiliano, 66–67, 111, 113
Z6508 Times (Soares), 258